NICK
AND NOEL'S
CHRISTMAS
PLAYLIST

CODI HALL

sourcebooks
casablanca

Published by Sourcebooks Casablanca, an imprint of Sourcebooks
P.O. Box 4410, Naperville, Illinois 60567-4410
(630) 961-3900
sourcebooks.com

Originally published in 2020 as an audiobook by Audible Originals.

Library of Congress Cataloging-in-Publication
Data is on file with the publisher.

Printed and bound in the United States of America.
KP 10 9 8 7 6 5

Chapter 1

NICK

THE CRISP NOVEMBER WIND HIT Nick Winters square in the face, causing his eyes to tear. There were already several inches of snow on the ground that crunched under his feet as he exited his friend Noel Carter's car. Acres of Douglas and noble fir trees spread out on both sides of his childhood home, their branches glittering with ivory snow. The short walkway curved toward a covered porch and red front door. After eight years away except for brief stints on leave, it was amazing how little the log cabin style five-bedroom, three-bath house had changed.

"I'll Be Home for Christmas" popped into his head and he sighed happily.

"Glad to be back home?"

Nick smiled at Noel over the top of her silver Subaru. "Absolutely. In fact, I may make a special playlist about what home means to me."

"I assume the first song won't be Nelly's 'Hot In Herre.'" She shivered for emphasis.

"As much as I love that song, I feel that 'Colder Weather' by the Zac Brown Band would be a better fit."

Since they were barely out of diapers, Nick and Noel had shared a passion for music. Their parents had dozens of video tapes of the two of them singing on an old karaoke machine. They'd swapped CDs and spent hours on the phone discussing artists from the Beatles to Kenny Chesney.

"Probably." Noel's dark eyes twinkled under the brim of her blue beanie. "I imagine freezing your balls off in Idaho is better than sweating them off in the desert."

"Hell yes. I can't wait to sleep in my own bed. Hug my mom. Fish with my dad. Start my dream job. Kiss my girl."

Noel wrinkled her slim nose. "Don't make me gag."

Nick huffed as he grabbed his army-green duffle from the back seat of Noel's car. "I don't understand why you're so down on her."

"You mean Amber?" She came up alongside him, her expression mockingly thoughtful. "Maybe because she's a self-absorbed brat who walks all over everyone she meets?"

Nick didn't want to argue with Noel. It was obvious there was no love lost between his best friend and long-time girlfriend, Amber Quint. Back in high school, Amber ran in a different crowd than them and hadn't always been the nicest to Noel, but that was years ago. They were all adults. Maybe since he was officially home, he could be the conduit that brought Amber and Noel together. At least create a reason for them to be civil.

"How about we go in and surprise my parents? We can argue about my taste in women later."

Noel laced her arm through his. "Oh, there is no need to argue. If your taste in women had a theme song, it would be 'Trashy Women' by Confederate Railroad."

"Your smart mouth is gonna get you in trouble one day," Nick whispered in her ear. He noticed she was wearing the blue topaz earrings he'd sent her for Christmas last year. They looked nice with her shoulder-length dark hair and olive skin.

"So I've been told. Maybe that's why some guy hasn't snatched me up yet. I'm too mouthy."

"Nah, it's because most men are morons. You're the best person I know." Nick kissed the top of her head.

"I guess the whole not wanting marriage and kids can throw them off too."

Nick shook his head. Ever since she lost her parents, Noel insisted she didn't want any attachments. He suspected if she didn't already have people in her life who loved her, she'd have kept her distance from his family and the rest of Mistletoe. Someone as awesome as Noel shouldn't close herself off, but it wasn't his business to tell her how to live her life.

"Not everyone needs those things to be happy. You do you."

Noel laughed. "God, you sound like a meme."

"That doesn't sound like a good thing."

"Eh, I still like you, though."

"I like you, too." He patted the hand looped through the crook of his elbow. "Thanks for grabbing me from the airport, by the way. I know you probably had better things to do on a Saturday morning."

Noel pinched him lightly. "Stop fishing. You know I'd do anything for you."

"I feel the same way about you, but still… It means a lot."

"Ugh, don't get sappy. It's not like I had anything better to do. Except sleep."

Nick chuckled. Noel didn't handle sentimental well, usually deflecting with humor and mild exasperation. Still, he thought it was important to let her know he cared. That she was important and appreciated as an adopted member of the Winters family.

"If it hadn't been for you, I would have had to ask one of my sisters and you know they can't keep a secret to save their lives. Mom has been counting down the days until my discharge and I wanted to surprise them."

"It's an amazing early Christmas present. Your mom is going to flip her shit when she sees you."

"Now, Noel," he said in a high-pitched voice. "You know how I feel about you swearing like a sailor."

She laughed. "Your poor mother tried her hardest to make a lady out of me. And it's soldier, not sailor."

"How could I forget." Like Nick, Noel had served in the army right out of high school. She'd gone in six months after him and discharged after four years. She'd finished her nursing degree at Boise State, bringing all of her experience with her, and took a job at Mistletoe Memorial in the labor and delivery ward as a nurse.

"Let me get the door, since you're packing that big-ass bag."

Noel unlocked the front door with her key and pushed the door open. Nick stepped over the threshold behind her and the familiar scent of pine and cinnamon enveloped him. The house was dimly lit in morning light, revealing the white walls of the living room splattered with framed family photos. The plaid green-and-white sofas his mother loved were set against the walls with decorative blankets tossed over the backs. His dad's brown leather recliner sat at an angle, looking just as beat up as he remembered. The long chestnut coffee table positioned in the middle of the furniture with a decorative centerpiece on top of rustic fall leaves, marking the changing of the seasons.

As they rounded the corner into the kitchen, a loud bay destroyed the peaceful quiet of his childhood home. The scuttle of nails on the wood floor echoed down the hall as Butch, his parents' nine-year-old bloodhound, emerged at a lope. His big black ears flapped up and down as he raced toward them. His jowls, dripping with jellified drool, went up at the same time, giving the illusion he was flying.

Nick dropped his bag and kneeled. "Butch, my man."

Butch launched all one hundred and sixty pounds of himself against Nick's chest, knocking him back against the wall. Wet doggy kisses rained down all over his face and he wrapped his arms around the dog's neck. Butch was barely a year when he'd left the first time, but he'd never forgotten Nick. Every leave, the big hound greeted him at the door with the same enthusiasm.

Laughing, Nick pushed Butch away and the dog turned his attention to Noel. Abruptly, the big hound buried his head in her crotch and she stumbled back with a gasp, cradling the dog's head in her hands as she tried to remove him from the awkward location. Nick burst out laughing as Noel wrestled with the dog.

"Dammit, Butch! I hate when you do that."

The dog pulled his head back and released another delighted bay. Then, he turned around and leaned his entire body against

Noel so hard she hit the counter. Her hat fell off and landed on the floor.

"Ouch, crap."

Nick chuckled. "Are you okay?"

"Yeah, sure, the big klutz just broke my hip, but I'm good."

The dog leaned his head back against her, exposing his neck and she obliged him by scratching his chest.

"You are a monster. Good thing you're cute."

"What in the blasted hell is going on out here?" a deep voice boomed.

The shape of a man stood in the hallway clad in a dark robe. He flipped on the kitchen light, blinking against the brightness.

Nick climbed to his feet with a smile. "Hey Pop."

Christopher Winters's craggy face broke out into a wide grin, his salt and pepper hair standing on end. "Nick! You said you'd be here after Thanksgiving!"

"I wanted to surprise you."

"Well, you sure as hell did." His dad held his arms wide. "Come here."

Nick crossed the tile floor and flung his arms around him. His dad returned the hard hug, pounding his back. Although he now stood several inches taller than his father, Chris had a wider frame than his son. And a rounder stomach.

His father pulled back, patting Nick's shoulders. "Well, take off your coat and sit a spell. You hungry? We've got bacon, eggs, hash browns—"

"I'm good, Dad." Nick shrugged out of his coat and took Noel's coat and hat when she handed them to him.

"Since you're hanging yours up, anyway," she said.

"Of course, princess. My mama always taught me to dote on my womenfolk."

"Okay, too far."

His dad ignored their conversation, his head buried in the fridge. "We also have ham! You still like meat, right?"

"Yeah, I do, Dad, but I don't need anything. We grabbed coffee when we left the airport."

Noel elbowed him. "That was an hour and a half ago. I'm starving."

Chris pointed his finger at his only son. "Coffee isn't sustenance, it's a stimulant. A man cannot live on Starbucks alone."

"Chris, what's going on?" a woman called from down the hallway.

Victoria Winters appeared at the edge of the kitchen in her furry pink bathrobe and messy blond hair, staring at them. Her hazel eyes widened behind her dark-framed glasses when her gaze landed on her son.

"Look who wanted to surprise us!" His father said.

With a squeal, she launched herself at Nick and he caught her with a grunt of amusement. Nick embraced his emotional mother as she bawled into his shirtfront.

"Gee, Mom, I thought you'd be glad to have me home."

She smacked his back. "Of course I am. These are happy tears."

His mom pulled away and squeezed his face between her hands. "You look gaunt. You haven't been eating enough."

The statement didn't require a response.

His dad crossed his arms over his chest, throwing him under the bus. "He was just telling me how coffee was a balanced breakfast."

"We will just see about that!" His mom kissed his dad as she passed him in the kitchen and his gaze followed her. After thirty years together, the love between his parents never dimmed. Nick wanted what his parents had: a relationship based on love, respect, and mutual life goals.

His mom grabbed a loaf of bread from the cupboard and Nick shook his head. "Really, Mom, you don't need to go to the trouble."

She waved away his protests as she went to the fridge and started pulling items out, lining them up across the counter.

"Noel, get in here. I have a bone to pick with you, young lady," his mother warned.

Noel laughed, coming up along beside her. "It wasn't my fault! He swore me to secrecy."

"You aren't supposed to keep secrets from me!" his mother responded, playfully smacking her with an oven mitt. "I don't care who is doing the asking. I trump my son every time!"

Noel hugged Nick's mother from behind and kissed her cheek. "Wasn't it a good surprise, though?"

His mother patted Noel's arms. "Yes, baby, it was. Thank you for picking him up."

"My pleasure."

"Now, get to cracking those eggs," his mother ordered. "You can do with a bit of fattening up too. I know that hospital runs you ragged, helping all those pregnant moms."

"Yes, ma'am."

It shouldn't surprise him that his mother treated Noel as if she were her own. Noel's mother, Heather, and his mom had been best friends all their lives. More like sisters.

Although they'd grown up together, he wouldn't exactly say that he held sisterly feelings for his best friend. Even when Noel teased him mercilessly, he never needed a break from her the way he did his siblings. In fact, not talking to Noel would drive him crazy. She'd been there for all of his ups and downs and vice versa.

Victoria wiped her hands on her robe. "I better go get my phone and call your sisters. They'll be so glad to have you home."

Nick pulled his own phone from his pants pocket. "You do that. I'm going to text Amber."

His mother and Noel made identical faces and he groaned. "Mom! Not you too!"

A sheepish grin split his mother's face. "I'm sorry, honey. I know you've been off and on since you were eighteen, but I don't think she is right for you. She's very..."

Noel opened her mouth, but Nick pointed his finger at her. "You hush it."

"You ought to watch the way you speak to the woman cooking your breakfast." Noel cracked an egg against the side of the counter without breaking eye contact and dropped the contents into a large mixing bowl. "Never know if she'll add a little something extra."

"Mom, you wouldn't let her hurt me, would ya?"

His mom snapped her fingers, the cell phone cradled in her other hand against her ear. "Self-centered. That's the word I'm looking for."

"Mom, she is threatening your only son."

His mom tilted the phone away from her mouth to respond. "Nick, I love you, but you better be nice to her. I'm not policing her cooking. Yes, good morning, sweetheart." She turned her back on them to talk to one of his sisters, missing the childish face Noel made at him. "You will never guess who is home. Nick!"

Nick curled his lip and crossed his eyes at Noel, earning a chuckle. When Noel went back to egg cracking, Nick typed out a text to Amber.

> Just got home. Would love to see you ASAP. I missed you.

He tucked his phone back into his pocket and leaned against the counter. Knowing Amber, it would be hours before she responded. She wasn't a morning person.

If he was being completely honest with himself, there could be other reasons why she wouldn't respond right away. Things were strained between them the last few months, but he figured it was just the distance getting to her. They'd started dating when he'd come back from boot camp and only had a few weeks before he left for his first tour. She'd wanted to stay with him despite the distance and the stress. Although they'd broken up and gotten back together several times over the years, he hoped once he got home for good that things would be better.

Lately their conversation always ended in a fight, usually with Amber hanging up on him. It drove him crazy. Most of the time, he'd call right back and they'd make up, but he'd been too exhausted to play the game last time. They hadn't spoken in five days, but Nick hoped when she saw him, all the tension would dissipate and it would just be the two of them, ready to be together all the time.

As a couple, they had a lot in common. They'd spent years talking about their futures. They'd buy a decent-sized house with property. Three kids. Maybe a dog. He would have proposed years ago, but he hadn't wanted their relationship to be a cliché. Now that he was home, if everything went the way he hoped, he'd ask Amber on one knee with his grandma's ring.

"Hey," Noel said.

He swirled around and met Noel's contrite brown eyes. "I'm sorry. I know I give you a lot of crap about Amber, but it's only because I love you and want what's best for you. You know that, right?"

Nick walked over and pinched her straight nose, returning her smile. "I do. And I love you, too."

"Good." She leaned against him, the sweet scent of strawberries and vanilla tickling his nose. "I may pass out if I have to wait much longer for your mom to get off the phone and resume her culinary arts."

"How about I hop in there and hurry things along?" he teased.

"Ew, no thank you. You have many fine qualities, my friend, but you did not inherit your mother's cooking skills."

"Man, I've been back for two hours and you haven't stopped giving me shit."

Noel laughed. "That's what friends are for."

Chapter 2

NOEL

THE WINTERS FAMILY REUNION WAS filled with warmth and laughter. Once Merry and Holly arrived, the noise level tripled and Noel almost wished it wasn't too cold to slip outside for some peace and quiet. Although she loved Merry and Holly like they were her blood sisters, they were as bad as her friend Gabby when it came to that high-pitched girly noise they made when they got excited. It was enough to have her swallow a bottle of Tylenol like a shot.

The three siblings were very close in age, although their coloring differed. Nick was the oldest at twenty-six, born the fourth of December. Two years later on December tenth, Merry made her appearance. Then on the sixteenth of December just a year later, Holly had come into the world.

Noel used to envy Merry's long wavy blond hair, hazel eyes, and lush bee-stung lips. More than one person in Mistletoe had compared Merry to the golden angels she resembled, and only those closest to her knew beneath the sweet exterior lay a terrible

NICK AND NOEL'S CHRISTMAS PLAYLIST 13

temper. Noel fingered her own coarse dark hair as she watched Holly toss back her fiery red locks, a gift passed down from her great-grandmother on her dad's side. Like her big brother, Holly's eyes were a deep chocolate brown, and her full figure had been the envy of her female classmates in junior high. All of the Winters children were kind, funny, and well respected throughout the town of Mistletoe, and there would no doubt be a parade in Nick's honor the minute people realized he was back for good.

Noel stood off to the side, drinking her coffee as she watched Nick's sisters take turns filling him in on all he'd missed.

Merry didn't have quite as much to share, because she'd only returned to the heart of her family's bosom before Halloween, a sudden and unexpected move. Victoria let it slip once that Merry went through a bad breakup, which didn't shock Noel. Merry's relationships never seemed to last. Holly griped often about Merry's atrocious taste in men.

Holly came back after college and opened A Shop for All Seasons a few years ago. What she lacked in age, she made up for in common sense and a head for business. The girl was a marketing whiz, and as for her extracurricular activities, well, they'd all sworn not to tell her mother about her YouTube channel, *Holly the Adventure Elf*. It sounded crazy, but it was actually really popular. Who didn't like watching an elf skydive?

"Are you all right?"

Noel hadn't heard Chris come up alongside her and jumped at his question.

"Yeah, I'm good. Just letting them catch up."

"You don't have to hang on the outskirts. Get right in the

thick of it! You're family." Chris pulled her in for a hug and a hefty pat on the back. "One of my girls."

Noel kissed his whiskered cheek, even as her stomach twisted in emotion. If her parents hadn't made a will years ago, she would have ended up in the system instead of moving in with the Winterses. They helped and held her through the bad spells in her adolescence and she would always be grateful to them. Times like this were still bittersweet though.

"I know that. Sometimes I just like to hang back and watch. I'm creepy like that."

Chris chuckled. "Okay, kiddo." He squeezed her face between his big warm hands. "I just don't want you feeling left out."

Noel didn't tell Chris it was unavoidable. Being around the warmth of the Winters family was a blessing and a curse. Especially this time of year, when the loss of her parents weighed heaviest on her.

Instead she covered his hand on her cheeks and pushed, making a squishy face at him and talked through her fish formed lips. "Is this the face of a lonely person?"

Chris opened his mouth to respond, but Victoria tapped her spoon on the counter, interrupting them. "Breakfast is ready. Everybody, grab a plate."

Chris released her face and gave her a gentle push toward the kitchen. "You better hurry and get yourself a plate."

"I think your son is going to beat me to it," Noel said with a smirk.

Nick was the first to jump up off the couch, his tall muscular frame graceful as he slid into the kitchen.

Chris huffed. "Wasn't hungry, eh?"

Noel burst out laughing and Nick glanced up from his heaping plate, watching them suspiciously. "What are you two going on about?"

"Nothing, son." Chris winked at her before heading to the kitchen sink to wash his hands, bumping his son gently with his shoulder as he passed.

Nick came around next to her, pausing with his brown eyes narrowed. His sandy hair was buzzed short, but Noel knew when it grew out it would have strands of gold and mahogany. In his red plaid flannel shirt and blue jeans, he looked good. Grown. Hot.

She stole a bacon strip from his plate and bit into it, ignoring his huff. "Whatchu looking at?"

"A bacon thief and co-conspirator. What were you and my dad discussing?"

"Nunya."

Nick rolled his eyes. "So mature." When she went for his plate again, he smacked her hand away. "Get your own, mooch!"

Noel laughed, watching Nick head into the living room, admiring the wide shoulders of his back. Yeah, all right she could admit it. Her best friend was a bona fide hottie, which unnerved her a bit. She still remembered the five-foot-seven string bean who'd left for boot camp. Two months later, she'd hardly recognized him. A late bloomer, Victoria had called him. He'd grown several inches and put on fifty pounds of muscle. He was even taller now and it didn't mean anything that she'd noticed. Just that she had two eyes and a brain.

Besides, even if she'd been genuinely attracted to Nick, she'd never make a move. No use destroying twenty-plus years of friendship when she already knew marriage and kids weren't in the cards for her. Two things Noel knew her best friend definitely wanted.

Probably why he'd held onto this pseudo relationship with Amber for so long. His parents were married young and still very much in love. She couldn't blame him for wanting the same thing.

While her parents also shared a deep and abiding love, the thought of marrying anyone left Noel sweaty with panic. It's why she kept things casual and easy. Like what she had with Trip Douglas. Hot, heavy, and no complications. All of her relationships were this way and she enjoyed the simplicity. If you didn't get attached, you couldn't get hurt.

Noel checked the clock on her phone. She'd wanted to stay and eat with them, but she had a mandatory staff meeting at the hospital in an hour. Afterwards, she'd be free. Most weeks she worked 6:00 a.m. until 6:00 p.m. Monday through Thursday, but after Thanksgiving she'd be on nights. At least she had the next two days off. Noel was supposed to hang with Nick and the guys tonight and she couldn't wait to get the gang back together.

Unless Nick wants to hang with his girl instead. Or invite her to tag along.

Noel wrinkled her nose at the thought. Since the end of high school, Noel and Amber kept their distance unless unavoidable. The fact that she had to share her two favorite people, Nick and her closest girlfriend, Gabby Montoya, with the bane of her teenaged years, burned her potatoes.

"Noel, come get a plate!" Victoria called.

Noel headed around the big kitchen island and snagged a piece of sausage. When Victoria tried to shove a plate in her hands, Noel set it back down and kissed Victoria's cheek. "Thanks, but I should go. I hate to eat and run, but I've got a work thing."

Victoria huffed. "Really? You can't stay and eat more than a link?"

"Wish I could, but it's mandatory. I didn't realize how late it was and my boss will come for me if I try to sneak in."

"Well, let me at least make you a Tupperware to take with you." She poked Noel in the collarbone. "You've lost so much weight I could snap you in half."

Victoria told her the same thing every time she shared a meal with the Winterses. She'd stopped arguing with her long ago and simply smiled.

"That would be great, thanks." Noel watched Nick reach into his back pocket and pull out his phone. From the frown on his face, Noel assumed Amber hadn't responded.

It didn't surprise Noel in the slightest. She hadn't wanted to stir things up, but she'd seen Amber hanging around a few guys over the years. She couldn't say for sure if something was going on, but she had a feeling they weren't quilting buddies. Nick seemed blind when it came to Amber. Guess it had to do with her big blue eyes and impressive rack. Amazing as Nick was, he wasn't above being a total guy.

Noel didn't need to be the messenger that brought about her bestie's broken heart.

Victoria held out the large tub of food, frowning. "I really wish you could stay. We don't see enough of you."

Guilt niggled at Noel. She needed to make more of an effort

to see them. Maybe after the holidays, when her emotions weren't running so high. "I'm sorry, duty calls. I'll see you all later."

"I'll hold you to it," Victoria responded sternly.

Noel embraced her. "I will."

"Fine, go, be free."

Noel made her way around the counter and crossed into the living room where everyone else sat eating. She bent over the back of Chris's chair and hugged him. Though a mouthful of food, he mumbled, "You leavin'?"

"Yeah, I have a work meeting."

"Well, have a good day. We love you."

The words stirred to life memories of different faces, smiling and echoing the same words. Raw emotions clogged her throat. "I love you all too."

Merry and Holly gave her double fist bumps over the back of the couch, but Nick climbed to his feet and caught her at the door. "I'll walk you out."

Noel waved one more time before she stepped out the door. She watched Nick bend over, rummaging through his duffle through the open doorway.

"Hey! You're letting all the cold air out! Were you born in a barn?" Victoria hollered from inside.

"Geez, I'm going!" He pulled it shut with a boom, one hand held behind his back. The space between his eyes was knit with concern as he asked, "You okay?"

Noel released a shaky breath. "Yeah, just been a while since we've all been together. A little overwhelming."

Nick placed a hand on her shoulder. "I know it isn't easy for you during the holidays, but maybe this will help." He brought his arm around and held out a CD. "I made you a holiday survival playlist."

Noel took the CD, grinning down at the face of it. He'd doodled a Christmas tree, holly berries, and a snowman in colored sharpie. *Noel's Christmas Playlist* was scrawled around the middle circle.

"You are so old-school with your mixed CDs. Get with the times, man."

"Hey, I bought stacks of them for ninety percent off and I'm going to use every single one!" He squeezed her upper arm. "I just wanted to make you smile."

Noel appreciated Nick's concern. Their shared love of music remained a constant bright spot, even after her world crumbled ten years ago.

"Thanks. I'll pop it in on my way to work."

"I'd suggest starting with number seven. Really get yourself grooving." He tried to dance, but his moves were awkward and spastic.

"You are a goober."

"An adorable goober." Nick leaned over and brushed his lips across her cheek. Unexpected tingles laced along her skin and she stilled.

"Have a good day at work. I'm going to get back in there before my sisters eat all the food."

She cleared her throat. "Have fun. I'll see you tonight."

"Definitely. Looking forward to having the gang back together," Nick said before heading back inside.

Noel stared at that cherry-red door for several beats. What

was that? There'd been years of sleepovers, joint family vacations, and even shared holidays with Nick and never had she noted the softness of his lips.

She spun away from the front of the house and made her way down the snow-covered sidewalk. Even as she climbed into her car, her thoughts dwelled on her reaction to Nick's casual kiss goodbye.

It wasn't the first time Nick kissed her, of course. He'd pressed his mouth to the top of her head earlier and countless times before that, but against the skin of her cheek it left a warm impression, as though branding her with his touch. It was the oddest sensation, especially because it was *Nick*!

Nick, who used to love playing Barbies with her, although he denied it as an adult. Who'd cleaned up her skinned knee and blown on the wound to ease the sting.

She rubbed her cheek with a laugh. The Winterses were a very affectionate group. They were always hugging, kissing, and enjoying the closeness. The kiss meant nothing to Nick. Or to her.

So why had a simple peck on the cheek made her react so unexpectedly?

Because Nick is the only man in your life who shows you affection?

The thought was true. She hadn't had a real boyfriend in years and the casual encounters with Trip were basically wham-bam-boom. Not a lot of snuggle time in between.

That was on her though. She'd been telling herself for years that she was too busy for a real relationship, but in truth, she just didn't like getting close to others. Letting people into her heart led to the pain of losing them. The Winterses were already hers before she shut herself off from the world, but it just seemed like a hard leap to open up her emotions to anyone new.

If she were being honest though, it was strange picking Nick up from the airport after years without him, knowing he was home for good. They'd shared Facetime calls, Snapchat, and texts, but without thousands of miles between them, what would Nick say when he realized she'd become a holiday hermit?

Noel climbed into the car and turned the heater on full blast, rubbing her hands together. Even the short walk from the house had turned her fingers to icicles. Before she put her car into drive, she slipped the CD into her player and tapped through to number seven.

Britney Spears's "My Only Wish" blasted through the speakers and Noel laughed. Her favorite Christmas song. When they were eleven, Noel choreographed a dance to it and Nick laughed so hard he'd curled up on his side, holding his stomach until she pounced on him.

Singing the lyrics loudly on the way to her apartment, it startled her when Lizzo's "Truth Hurts" interrupted her personal serenade. She tapped the answer button on her steering wheel without looking at the number, because she'd only assigned one person that ringtone.

"Hey babes, what's happening?"

"I'm engaged!" Gabby Montoya screamed through the speakers.

Noel's jaw dropped. In any other universe, tomboy Noel and girly Gabby should have never been friends. When Gabby moved from Texas to Idaho their freshman year, she'd immediately been scooped up by the popular kids. Noel, an honor student who'd enjoyed tutoring, was paired with Gabby, who needed help catching up. Their instant connection was cosmic and they'd been inseparable ever since.

"Whoa, what?! That's amazing. Congrats."

"I know, right? We were just hanging out in Drew's kitchen after his little brother's birthday and suddenly, both our families are standing against the wall and he's down on one knee telling me I'm the one. That he can't live without me and then he whips out this gorgeous ring. I couldn't stop crying, I was so happy. I still can't believe it!"

"I can! Drew knew he needed to lock someone as fantastic as you down before you got snatched up and after the lengthy chase you gave, he wasn't taking any chances."

"Well, now I need a maid of honor. I want to get together tomorrow for lunch if you're free? I promise to make it all official, but I can't wait until then to ask." Gabby released a dramatic sigh. "Noel Carter, will you be my MOH?"

"That depends," Noel teased. "Can I have input in the bridesmaids' dresses?"

"Nope."

"Do my own makeup?"

"Uh-uh."

"How about my hair?"

"Maybe."

Noel laughed. "Eh, screw it, I'm in. You two settle on a date yet?"

"Christmas Eve."

Noel didn't remind Gabby that Christmas Eve also happened to be Noel's birthday. It wasn't like Noel enjoyed celebrating, anyway.

Something else clicked though. "Wait...this Christmas Eve?"

"Yep!"

Her voice reached screech level. "Are you crazy?! That's five weeks away!"

"I know, but I really want a Christmas-themed wedding and there is no way I'm waiting a year! I'm too impatient. Besides, we're going to keep it small. Just family and close friends."

Noel shook her head, pushing down the panic bubbling in her stomach. Gabby loved the holidays and it made sense she'd want a wedding that reflected her joy. It seemed no matter how hard she tried, Noel wouldn't be able to completely block out Christmas this year.

"I don't know how you're going to swing it, but I'm here to help with whatever you need."

"Thanks, sis. Okay, I love you but I have dozens of other calls to make, so I'll talk to you later."

"I love you. Bye."

Noel clicked off the call and released a wet chuckle, completely unaware she'd teared up. Gabby was getting married. Crazy. It seemed like they were just graduating high school, trying to sneak into bars and worrying about their futures. Now Gabby had a great career, a tight-knit family, a handsome adoring fiancé, and Noel...

Well, she had her work. Which she loved. She had the Winterses, Gabby, Anthony and Pike, her closest male friends besides Nick...

And Trip.

Maybe she'd ask Trip to go with her to Gabby's wedding. Not because she wanted anything more, but because she didn't want to attend a Christmas wedding on her own. She could ask Pike or Anthony to go, but at least with Trip she'd get consolation sex after the festive nuptials.

She just hoped this wasn't the start of a domino effect. First Gabby and then one after another her friends would get married, and pretty soon Noel would be the last single person in Mistletoe.

The thought wouldn't have been so troubling, if it didn't mean Nick would be married to Amber. He could do so much better, but if Amber made him happy, Noel would put forth the effort to be nicer to her.

As rough as it would be, Noel would do anything for Nick.

CHAPTER 3

NICK

"NO?" NICK STOOD ON AMBER'S front porch, staring into his girlfriend's heart-shaped face. The day turned out to be sunny and beautiful, a direct contrast to the chilly reunion he was experiencing. "What do you mean, no?"

Amber leaned against the doorframe with a rather large box in her hands. She set it down on a side table next to snow-covered patio furniture before crossing her arms over her generous chest. Her blue eyes popped under the rainbow of color adorning her eyelids, something new and different from the last time he'd seen her. "I mean that no, I'm not interested in continuing a relationship I know isn't going anywhere."

Nick stared at the woman in front of him, processing how very wrong he'd been about this moment. He'd imagined walking up to her place and stopping on the top step as the front door flew open. Amber would cry out happily and he'd catch her in midair as she flung herself into his arms.

Instead, while she had thrown open the door, she'd done

so with a less-than-joyful expression on her face. The look was downright grim.

Now he knew why.

"When did you decide that?" he asked.

"When I met someone a few months ago. Someone who doesn't disappear to play hero halfway across the world."

Nick's jaw clenched. While Amber made it clear she wasn't a fan of the military, he'd thought she at least understood why he signed up and supported him. He'd wanted to make a difference for not just America but other countries that needed help.

"You've been cheating on me?"

Her mocking laughter raced through him like being doused with cold water.

"Cheating on you? Are you serious?"

How could he have been so wrong about her? Where was the warm and loving woman he'd dreamed about every night for eight years?

"What's funny about that?"

"Grow up, Nick. We weren't engaged or married. I've seen you, what? Maybe a half a dozen times over the course of eight years? Facetiming once in a while and emailing does not a relationship make."

Her casual argument hit him like a stack of bricks. He'd been committed to her. Thought they were in this together, and she was just biding time.

"You knew what you signed up for when we started this. Why didn't you tell me months ago instead of acting like everything was fine?"

She tossed back her blond hair, a gesture he'd once found sexy. Now, it grated on him, especially accompanied by her snide tone. "Because I'm not a jerk. I wanted to do this in person. After being together so long, I felt you deserved at least that."

It made absolutely no sense. Why the hell would she care about dumping him in person if she didn't think what they had was real?

"I thought we had something good here. That I'd come home and we'd finally be together."

"We aren't kids anymore, Nick. When we first started dating, you were hot. A good guy. I thought we could be end game, but distance didn't make the heart grow fonder for me." With the first spark of real emotion, she put a hand on his arm. "I'm sorry. I like you, Nick. But life didn't just stop for the rest of us. I've grown and changed and I want something different. I've moved on. You should too."

Before he could even respond, she pointed to the box. "That's your stuff. If I find anything else, I'll give you a call. Whatever you find of mine, you can toss. If I haven't missed it in eight years, I don't need it now."

The door closed with a snap once she'd disappeared inside. Numbness rushed through every body part, his legs heavy as he crossed the porch to examine the mementos of the only meaningful relationship he'd ever had.

Nick stood there for a moment, staring into the contents of the box. A few stuffed animals he'd given her. A T-shirt she'd borrowed and never returned. An Army ball cap he'd let her keep after the first time they made love. All piled haphazardly on one side of the box. On the other side she'd stacked dozens of CDs and thumb drives he'd sent her. Playlists he'd made to convey his feelings for her.

Nick rummaged through the rest and realized that she'd kept the diamond earrings he'd bought her last Christmas. Anything of value he'd ever given her was also missing, but he didn't really care. Was there something more he could have done? He wracked his brain for any kind of sign this was coming, but nothing stuck. They'd fought, but he'd assumed the strain of the distance was the cause of it.

With one last glance at her door, he carried his box down the stairs to his dad's old Tacoma and set it down hard on the front seat. The truck had been his before he went to basic and his dad bought it for the farm when Nick wanted to sell it. Now, the beat-up blue truck became his temporary ride again, a bitter reminder of his first night with Amber. They'd made love on the front seat and as he set the box down on the passenger side, a fog rolled over him.

The drive through town and back to his parents' farm was a blur. Normally he'd check out the little shops on Main or the pines that lined the road as it twisted and turned, but his mind raced with the reality of his homecoming.

How could he have missed this? The last few weeks, everything had been coming up Nick. He'd landed an amazing job at Battlefield Gaming, creator of some of the best strategy apps out there. He'd been coding since he was nine and with his military background, they'd been eager to offer him a job. The best part? Besides a few times a year when he'd have to go to headquarters in Colorado, he could work from home. He could live near his family and friends in Mistletoe.

Although, at the moment, he wished he could escape his small town. Gossip spread faster than the high school kids drove and the last thing he wanted to see was a bunch of people whispering about *poor Nick*.

When he arrived home, he parked in front of the house and retrieved his box from the seat next to him. His parents hadn't mentioned him helping out at the Christmas tree farm today, which was good. Nick wasn't feeling particularly social, but he wouldn't want to disappoint his mom and dad.

Nick stumbled inside the house with his box as though in a trance. Butch came skittering out from the back, but stopped in his tracks, sensing Nick's mood. The hound trotted behind him down the hall, watching him from the doorway as Nick set his breakup box in the corner of his bedroom. The dog disappeared and Nick shut his door with a click.

He flopped across his bed and sent a snap to Noel and his childhood friends, Pike and Anthony. They were supposed to go out for drinks tonight. He took a picture of the breakup box and typed, Amber dumped me. Not feeling the bar. I'll text you tomorrow.

The level doorknob flicked several times, as though someone was trying to open it. Finally, it popped open a crack and Nick lifted his head. His door swung wide and Butch stood in his doorway, whining with a stuffed Christmas tree in his mouth.

"Hey Buddy. I'm having a rough day."

The large hound leaped up on the bed and snuggled against Nick's side, chewing the squeaky tree with gusto.

"Suit yourself."

He opened up Spotify on his phone and made a new playlist.

Holiday Breakup Songs. He added three hours' worth of music and he lay back against his pillow, closing his eyes with a heavy sigh.

When "Last Christmas" played the first time, he knew it was the end of the playlist. Instead of starting over or putting on another list, he just hit repeat on the song.

It blasted out of the speakers for the twelfth time before the front door crashed open and closed.

"Where the hell are you, Nick?" Anthony Russo hollered.

Butch lifted his head with a high-pitched howl and jumped down to greet the intruders.

Anthony and Pike Sutton stood just inside the room, their faces twisted in identical expressions of disgust.

"Who the hell is this sad sack and where have you taken our broski?" Pike asked.

Nick sat up with a wince. "It's good to see you too. Guess you didn't get my snap."

"Oh we got it. We just chose to ignore it." Anthony leaned over him until they were nose to nose. His bushy black brows wiggled. "Are you 'pressed'?"

"No."

Pike came over too, pushing his face next to Anthony's. "Sad? Upset? Mad?"

"You assholes need to stay off TikTok."

Anthony stood up. "Whew, we should back off before he Hulks out."

Pike punched Nick's shoulder lightly, ignoring Anthony's warning. "Seriously, bro, what's up?"

"Again. I. Got. Dumped."

"We know, but so what?" Pike rolled his eyes. "She did you a favor. Now you can go forth and meet other hotties. You're too young to tie yourself down."

Nick glared at Pike. They'd been friends since third grade, but their goals in life were polar opposites. Pike liked being single and planned on staying that way for the foreseeable future, while Nick always imagined settling down early and starting a family. And the differences spilled over into their outward appearances.

Pike was short and stocky, with a round face covered by a perfectly formed dark red beard. He kept his auburn hair shaved close on the sides and two inches of just-got-out-of-bed styled awesomeness stood on top of his head. Nick was a jeans and T-shirt kind of guy, while Pike had been known to sport funky bow ties when the mood stuck.

Pike threw up his hands as though to ward off Nick's hostility. "Hey, I'm just being honest, pal. You're twenty-six. No man should lock a woman down until he is well over thirty."

Nick sat up and shot Anthony a hard look. "Can't you control him?"

Anthony's full lips pursed, as though he was fighting a smile. "I've tried, but he always slips his leash." He scruffed Butch behind the ears, shooting Nick a pitying glance. "Besides, he's not wrong. You shouldn't be thinking of anything but what the hell you're going to do now that you're a civvy."

"I already know what I'm doing. I have a job that I start on Monday and I need to buy a truck. I'm looking for an apartment. I had everything I wanted, but now..."

Pike jumped in, finishing his thought for him. Poorly. "Now you can take your time and have fun. You've spent eight years fighting the good fight. You deserve to come home and reap the benefits of being a hero."

"I'm not a hero and I don't want to date a bunch of random girls. I'm into a solid, in it until the end, monogamous relationship."

"Why would you want that with Amber?" Pike asked.

Nick flopped back on the bed with a groan. "Not you too. My mom, Noel…did everyone hate Amber and just fail to mention it?"

Anthony grabbed his hand and hefted him back into a sitting position, his expression sheepish. "We figured you'd realize she wasn't right for you once you got home."

"Well, she beat me to the punch on that."

The echo of the front door opening and closing and the tap of footsteps down the hall preceded Noel standing in his doorway. She had on a pair of painted-on jeans tucked into knee-high brown boots and a puffy white parka zipped halfway up her chest. Her dark brown hair perched atop her head in a high ponytail, swinging saucily as she glanced between each of them.

"What's happening?"

Butch launched himself at her, burying his face between her legs and she slammed back into the door, gripping the dog's head between her hands.

"Goddamn you, dog."

Pike and Anthony burst out laughing while even Nick cracked a smile.

"Nice. Room full of so-called gentlemen and you all stand

NICK AND NOEL'S CHRISTMAS PLAYLIST   33

around, yucking it up while I'm assaulted by this fool." Noel pushed Butch away gently and the hound sat back, staring up at her with his tongue lolling out but she ignored him. She wiped her hands off on her jeans and they finally settled on her hips as she studied him. "You don't look as bad as I thought you would."

"Thanks. That's the nicest thing any of my friends have said to me."

"You're welcome."

"How bad did you think he'd look?" Pike asked.

"Dawson-ugly-crying-on-the-dock bad."

Pike chuckled. "You should have been here when we arrived. Listening to 'Last Christmas,' laying on his side with snot dripping from his nose."

Nick glared at Pike.

"Glad I missed it." She walked into the room and over to his closet. She pulled out a blue collared shirt and held it up in front of her. "Go put this on. We're taking you out."

Anthony tipped his Denver Broncos hat back, revealing his olive skin and sympathetic green eyes. "I don't think he wants to go, sugar."

"*We* do not care what he wants. Only what he needs."

Nick smirked. "I need some alone time and a bottle of Crown."

Noel threw the shirt at him. "I'll buy you the Crown for later, but you are leaving this house. I'm not letting you spend your first night home moping. We are gonna show Amber that you don't give a flying frickety frack about her."

Pike came over next to her and put his head on her shoulder, gazing up at her adoringly. "Have I told you I find your made-up words adorable?"

Noel rolled her eyes. "Never gonna happen, Fish."

Nick stood up, clutching the garment in his fist. "If I put this shirt on, will you all stay silent for ten minutes?"

"Maybe," Noel said.

"I'll take it."

CHAPTER 4

NOEL

NOEL LEANED AGAINST HER CAR in the Brews and Chews parking lot, frowning down at her phone. She'd texted Trip after her meeting earlier this afternoon, asking him if they could talk, but he'd said he was busy today. So, they'd set up dinner for tomorrow and she'd gone about her day of cleaning her apartment.

But when she'd taken a breather after her meeting and decided to scroll through Instagram, she'd noticed something interesting. Trip's last post was a selfie of Jillian Groves sucking his neck on the lift chair. Struck dumb, Noel stared at his boyish grin and twinkling blue eyes under his brimmed black beanie, her heart constricting. Jillian's perfectly contoured cheek, heavy fake lashes, and glossy lips didn't need a filter. She was always camera-ready beautiful, while Noel's Insta boasted pics of the things she loved like sunsets, BBQ pork sandwiches, and her friends instead of her usually makeup-free face.

They looked perfect together, a wonderfully romantic moment captured and memorialized forever.

God, she was an idiot. At least she hadn't voiced her idea about taking him to the wedding. He probably would have squeezed her arm like they really were old pals and given her some gentle letdown so he could still come off smelling like a rose.

Technically, he didn't do anything wrong. You weren't even together; just hooking up.

However, they had agreed to talk if something changed and the fact that he hadn't mentioned Jillian spoke volumes.

"Hey! This was your idea. You coming or what?" Nick called from the entrance.

Noel slipped her phone into her clutch, swallowing past the lump in her throat. "Yeah, yeah, don't get your boxers in a twist."

She traipsed across the gravel parking lot where Nick waited at the door for her. She couldn't quite meet his eyes; afraid he'd notice the slight sheen to hers. She wasn't crying, not really, but they burned something awful. She'd put her feelings aside because Noel knew Nick needed to get out of the house, but honestly, she wished now they'd just stayed in watching a movie.

"Everything all right?" Nick asked.

"It's great. Never better." She squeezed his arm and discreetly dabbed at her eyes. "I can't wait to get you drunk and watch you lose at pool."

Nick looped an arm around her shoulders, sounding like the cheerful Nick she knew and loved. "It doesn't matter how much I drink; I don't lose."

"First time for everything."

They flashed their IDs at Paulie, the bouncer, even though they were the same age. Paulie's stern features gave way to a grin when he spotted Nick.

"Nick, I heard you were getting back soon!" Paulie grabbed Nick and pulled him in for a one-armed hug. "Glad you're in one piece, buddy."

"Thanks, man."

"It's good to see you too, Paulie," Noel said loudly.

Paulie snorted. "I see you almost every weekend, gorgeous. I would have said hi."

Noel huffed. "Uh-uh, you had your chance."

She breezed past the laughing bouncer and waited inside the entryway for Nick.

"Let me know if she is too much for you and I'll boot her," Paulie teased.

"I heard that!"

"You were meant to. I love it when you're all fiery."

Noel grinned at the bouncer's flirting, feeling slightly better about Trip's rejection.

Nick patted Paulie on the shoulder. "Great to see you."

"Have fun, you two."

Noel rolled her eyes. Even as kids, Nick was affable and fun to be around and people flocked to him. Now that he was back, she knew everyone would want to say hi, and hopefully it made him feel better about his breakup and not worse. Nick didn't need hundreds of people asking him about his ex.

Pike and Anthony were already seated near the dance floor. While she'd stayed behind and waited for Nick to get ready, Anthony and Pike took off to pretty themselves up. Anthony's dark hair parted on the side and lay flat against his head, shiny with whatever product he'd used to slick the strands down. The black button-up showed off broad shoulders, something more than one girl had pointed out to Noel over the years. Noel noticed with amusement that several women were slyly scoping out her two friends, even though Pike looked like a lumberjack dandy in a green-striped dress shirt and yellow bow tie. With his cheesy lines, it shocked her how much action he got.

"Oh my God, how does Fish not get thrown out of here looking like that?" she asked.

Nick chuckled. "I think Paulie is a second cousin or something. Only reason I can come up with."

"Mercy me, I'm going to burn all his bow ties."

He looped his arm around her neck, kissing the side of her head. "Don't even bother, he'll just buy more. I don't think his look is going down without a fight."

Had he always been so affectionate with her? Nick was a hugger. He treated everyone like a dear old friend, but the weight of his arm on her shoulder left Noel with the urge to snuggle closer. To soak it up. She realized that despite her desire to stay single, Trip and Jillian's picture bothered her because she craved that kind of closeness. Cuddling. She told herself that she didn't want all the baggage a relationship carried, but a part of her still desired that special intimacy.

When Nick dropped his arm so they could weave single file through the tables to get to the boys, Noel balked at how bereft she felt.

The dinner crowd was winding down, making way for the

rowdy citizens of Mistletoe who liked to party. There wasn't much to do on a small-town Saturday night but drink, dance, and do the deed.

"Finally! What took you so long?" Anthony asked.

"What can I say? Nick loves to primp."

Before she could sit, Pike pointed to her. "First round's on you."

"How do you figure that, Peewee?" she asked, dropping her jacket on the back of the chair next to him. The humidity of the bar hit the exposed back her blue halter top didn't cover.

Pike's gaze narrowed at the dig. "'Cause you are the last person to sit down who is currently not nursing a broken heart."

Anthony nodded thoughtfully, stroking his chin. "Sound logic."

"I thought so."

"Whatever." She turned to leave, but Anthony stopped her.

"Don't you want to know our drink orders?"

Noel spun around with her left hand on her hip. "I'm not your waitress. If I'm buying, you'll drink what I get you."

"I want Jack and Coke!" Pike hollered.

Noel rolled her eyes. "You get what you get, and you don't pitch a fit."

Nick sat down with his back to the dance floor and gave her a salute. "Yes, ma'am."

"Suck up," Pike snorted.

Noel flipped Pike off and swirled away. She pushed a path to the bar counter and waved Ricki Takini down. The taller woman flipped her long black hair over her shoulder as she leaned over in front of Noel.

"What can I do you for, Noel?" The light caught the glitter of her diamond nose ring, and the black tank top showed off her generous cleavage and intricate tribal tattoo sleeves along the golden skin of her arms.

"Can I get three screaming orgasms and one pink flamingo?"

Ricki glanced over Noel's shoulder at the table of men and quirked a brow. "Really?"

Noel flashed a devious grin. "Oh yeah. They said surprise them."

Ricki chuckled. "Coming right up."

Noel leaned on the wooden counter top, waiting for Ricki, when she noticed Trip come through the door with a group of his friends. His brown hair flopped over his forehead as he leaned over to whisper something to Jillian, who looked awfully cozy pressed against his side, his arm wrapped around her petite shoulders.

She turned away. Noel didn't want to deal with Trip tonight. As casual as their relationship may have been, not once in the months they'd been sleeping together had he ever posted a selfie with her. Maybe it was petty and prideful, but what the hell? It's not like they'd never left the bedroom. They'd gone places. Done things. She might not look like an Insta-star, but she could have squeezed in and smiled for the camera.

Geez, she was confusing her damn self. She was mad at Trip because he didn't show her off? Did she wanted a cuddle buddy now and not just someone in her bed?

That's a boyfriend, honey. Boyfriends lead to monogamy and till death do us part. And we don't want any of that, remember?

Luckily, Ricki came back with the shots and a pretty martini glass of pink liquid with a flamingo straw, pulling her out of her head. "Here you go, Noel. That will be twenty dollars."

"Thanks, Ricki. You're awesome." Noel handed her thirty from her clutch and picked up her drinks.

"Do you need change?" Ricki asked.

"Nah, that's for you."

"Thanks, babe." Ricki shot her a wink and took off for the other end of the bar.

Noel headed back to the table, doing her best not to spill. She set the shots in front of Nick and Anthony, and placed the Pink Flamingo before Pike. He sent her an exasperated look.

"You are a pain in my ass."

He reached for her shot, but she picked it up, sliding into the chair with ease. "Hey, get your own screaming orgasm."

Anthony and Nick burst out laughing.

"What the hell?" Nick asked.

Noel dropped her clutch on the table and gave him a smirk. "The shot is called a screaming orgasm. It's tasty and something Fish has never given a woman."

"I always leave my partners satisfied," Pike growled.

"Satisfied like, 'It was all right'? 'Okay'? 'Adequate'?" She tipped the shot back and swallowed. The creamy liquor slid down smoothly and she tapped the glass against the table. "Anthony, you got next round?"

"That I do." Anthony downed his shot and winked. "You're a savage, N."

"This I know," she said, smacking his butt as he headed for the bar. "Hurry up!"

Pike pushed away the martini glass with a grunt. "You can question my sexual skills all you want, but I'm not drinking this glass of sugar-sweet crap."

"How do you know it's sugary?" Nick asked.

Pike held up the glass. "There is pink sugar around the rim! Nasty."

Noel tweaked his bow tie with her finger. "Maybe next time don't boss me around like I'm your bar wench."

Nick reached across and took the flamingo, sliding the shot to Pike. "I'll swap you."

"Hey! If he doesn't give one, then he doesn't get one!"

"Give me a chance, beautiful, and you'll be shaking the walls."

"Gross."

"Says you." Pike gulped down the shot and licked his lips. "Mmmm, it's good but a letdown from the name."

Noel watched Nick suck on the pink straw, his neck muscles working as he swallowed. Nearly a fourth of the drink disappeared before he came up for air.

"Now that is tasty."

Noel pointed at Nick with a smirk. "See? This is what a real man looks like."

"Whatever," Pike said.

Anthony came back to the table with four glasses of amber brew and four shots. "Hey, Noel, I thought you and Trip were getting it on?"

Noel winced. "Not anymore."

Pike reached for the drinks Anthony set down. "Thank God. He's a douche."

Noel leveled him with a glare. "You know when you call him a douche, you're calling me dumb, right?"

"Huh? I am not! You just deserve better than him. You deserve a guy who will open doors, pay the dinner tab..." He stroked his facial hair. "Can grow a real beard."

Noel smothered a grin. "I appreciate the sentiment behind it. Really."

"I didn't know you were dating Trip," Nick said.

Noel's face flamed. She'd been hoping to avoid talking about relationships with Nick. Not because he cared what she did, but their views on dating were so different, it was awkward to discuss.

"It was only a few months."

Anthony piped in. "Plus, they were just fucking."

Noel snatched one of the glasses and dropped the shot in. "Thanks for making me sound like a class act."

"There's nothing wrong with hooking up," Pike said.

"Oh my God, can we please stop talking about this?" Noel chugged the Jägerbomb, her face scrunching as the licorice aftertaste hit her. She shook her head, coughing a few times and finally sighed.

"We're just saying..." Anthony stammered.

"I know you are trying to make me feel better, but sometimes hanging with you is worse than spending the day with Gabby. Always telling me how I can do better. That I should look for something real. Why can't a woman just get a little D when she wants it without putting up with a guy's BS?"

Several tables swiveled her way and she wanted to sink into the floor. Anthony and Pike started talking at once, but Nick stood up and held his hand out to Noel. "Come on, Noel. You love this song."

Noel listened to the old Mindy McCreedy melody for a half a second before she took his hand. The guys were still jabbering on, now arguing with each other on double standards and relationships. The rescue was timely and appreciated. As much as she loved Anthony and Pike, they still treated her like a little sister instead of one of the guys.

Well, Anthony treated her like a sister. Pike was protective, but loved to flirt with her. Maybe a third cousin for him.

Noel giggled at her silent joke and Nick quirked a brow. "Something on my face?"

"No, you're good. Just funny thoughts."

"Hmmm, I get the feeling our boys were the butt of whatever joke you had rolling through that head of yours."

"I'll never tell."

Nick chuckled, pulling her against him. "About Trip…"

"I don't want to talk about it."

Really, talking about it with Nick, sweet, perfect Nick who'd stayed with the same girl for eight years? They'd never really talked about their sexual conquests, but Noel had a feeling Amber was Nick's one and only. It was hard to discuss her sexual exploits with such a paragon of virtue.

She hadn't danced with Nick since high school and the press of his body to hers felt brand new. He was definitely harder all over than as a teenager. Noel still remembered the shock when he'd come back from boot camp and he'd stood in formation, his shoulders broader, his arms defined. No longer the skinny kid that left but a man. She hadn't known what to do until after he finished hugging his parents and yanked her into his arms.

The awkwardness passed and they were Nick and Noel again.

She slid her arms around his waist and her hands stilled as the muscles in his back bunched. His fingers laced together behind her, resting at the top of her jeans. She could feel the warmth of his skin through the fabric at her back, a pleasant sensation.

When Nick shuffled his feet, she swayed with him happily. Nick wasn't the best dancer, but his slow dance shuffle worked.

"Thanks for dragging me out here. That was embarrassing."

"Why? It's just us and no one's judging you. We've all had friends with benefits."

"Really?" Noel quirked an eyebrow. "All of us?"

Nick chuckled. "All right, so maybe not me, but I understand why it's nice to sometimes have someone you can call any time you need the *D*."

Noel groaned. "I can't believe I said that in front of you."

"Why in front of me?"

"You know...we haven't hung out in person for a while. Even though you're still my Nick, being away, we've missed a lot of each other's day-to-day." She cleared her throat. "I'm a little worried about you learning something about me you won't like."

Nick's arms tightened around her. "I've seen you covered from head to toe in Beef-a-roni. Nothing could be worse than that."

She dropped her forehead to his chest with a groan. "You were supposed to burn that picture."

Nick grinned sheepishly. "Sorry, my mom hid the negatives." He ran his hand gently over the top of her head and she pressed her cheek into his shoulder. "I don't ever want you to be embarrassed with me, Noel. I'll always have your back."

Noel breathed him in shakily. She opened her eyes just in time to catch Trip staring at them. His tight T-shirt showed off the hours of work he put in at the gym his parents owned, but all that bulk had never been good for cuddling. Nick, on the other hand, was muscular without being uncomfortable to snuggle with.

Noel closed her eyes again, the familiar scent of Nick's woodsy cologne surrounding her. The smell reminded her of his parents' farm in December, Christmas trees and falling snow. Home. Nick smelled like home to her.

Noel felt Nick stiffen against her and glanced up at him. He was staring towards the entrance of the bar, his lips pinched. She looked over her shoulder and saw Amber wrapped around a guy who bore a striking resemblance to Chris Hemsworth. Nick's ex glanced their way briefly before doing a double take, her mouth rounded in surprise. With a flip of her hair, Amber straddled the guy's lap as he sat on the barstool, her profile clearly visible. A smug smile curved her pink shiny lips and Noel turned away to assess Nick's reaction.

Nick's crestfallen expression yanked at her heart strings painfully and before she realized what she was doing, she held the back of his neck in the palm of her hand. His brown eyes settled on hers and she pulled him down. He could have fought her if he wanted, but he let her guide him down. Noel's lips brushed against his, noting the way they opened slightly, Nick's sweet breath whooshing out quietly. Her tongue traced across his bottom lip, hoping that Amber and Trip liked the view.

Suddenly, Nick's hands came up to cradle her cheeks and his mouth slanted across hers. His tongue delving in, playing with hers, and flames licked their way across her skin. The sensation shocked her at first and she stumbled against Nick, pressing her breasts into his front. Her nipples peaked to attention, and a slight moan escaped as Noel forgot they were standing in a crowded bar and pulled him into her, deepening the kiss.

Nick was the one to break the contact, his lips pressing against hers in a sweet, soft peck before putting several inches of distance between them.

"Thank you," he whispered.

CHAPTER 5

NICK

NICK'S HEART CRASHED AGAINST HIS chest bone as he stared down into Noel's dazed gaze. What the hell was that? Not the kiss. Nick knew she'd done that to get his focus off Amber and the man who'd replaced him, but that zing of energy still shooting through his nerve endings? Unexpected and new, especially in conjunction with Noel. His best friend. The sweet taste of her still clung to his lips and without thinking, his tongue licked along the surface. Her eyes narrowed, focused on his face and he had the bizarre urge to kiss her again.

Noel blinked several times and whatever spell that rendered him temporarily insane dissipated.

"Are they still watching?"

They? It took Nick a moment to sift through the fog and realize she was talking about Trip and Amber.

Nick cupped her cheek and leaned over, pressing his face into the side of her neck so it would look like he was nuzzling her. Her hair smelled sweet and he stopped himself from breathing her in.

His gaze shifted behind her from Amber to Trip. Amber's face scrunched up in either annoyance or disgust, he really couldn't tell. While Trip seemed utterly befuddled. Probably couldn't believe Noel hadn't stayed home and cried herself to sleep over him.

Nick glared at the idiot. He couldn't imagine Noel moping over any man, let alone Trip. Pike hadn't been wrong when he'd called him a douche, but Nick understood why Noel didn't like the term. Nick felt the same way about his friends and family bad mouthing Amber. If she was such a horrible person and he'd stayed with her anyway, hadn't seen any of her character flaws, then that made him an idiot too, right?

His lips grazed her ear as he whispered, "They were watching."

"Good." Her warm breath rushed across the skin of his neck and he involuntarily breathed her in. God, she smelled a-fucking-mazing. He wanted to press his lips down and run his tongue over—

"Nick?"

His eyes popped open and he jerked back. The air in the bar hung hot and heavy around them as he stared down into her confused brown eyes. This was wrong. He shouldn't be reacting this way to Noel.

This was the result of sexual frustration and heartbreak. He hadn't had sex in fifteen months and considering Amber was the only person he'd ever been with, the times they'd made love were few and far between. Now here he was single for the first time in eight years and pressed against his best friend who curved in all the right places...

Air. He needed air.

Nick took her hand. After the show they just put on, he wasn't about to leave her on the dance floor. She was coming with.

"Let's go for a walk."

"All right."

He ignored Anthony and Pike's wide-eyed stares as they passed, lancing through the crowd of drinkers until they exited through the front door. The chilly weather engulfed him, freezing the exposed skin of his neck and face, bringing him back to himself. This is good. Exactly what he needed.

"Damn, it's colder than a well digger's ass in January," Nick said.

Noel dropped his hand and laughed, taking a few steps ahead of him. The halter shirt left her upper back and arms exposed and he noted the expanse of gooseflesh across her skin in the dim outside lights. When she turned back around, Nick almost swallowed his tongue when he saw her nipples hard and pushing against the cotton of her shirt. Either she wasn't wearing a bra or the thin material of one didn't hide much.

Stop staring at her chest, you fucking pervert!

"You sound like your dad," Noel said, closing her eyes. "It feels good though."

"Yeah, it was hot in there," he said. "Sorry I dragged you out like that."

"It's all right." I get it. Probably just drank too fast. Alcohol gets you all hot and bothered."

Nick blinked at her choice of words and cleared his throat. "That's probably it. I really do appreciate you...well, what you did in there. I probably looked like an ass when they walked in."

"Don't mention it. It was mutually beneficial." She released a shaky laugh. "The last thing I wanted was Trip thinking I cared he'd dropped me without actually doing the deed."

"I'll go back in there and punch him, if you want."

Noel shook her head. "Like Anthony said, we were just fucking. Nothing to be upset about. Even if I was, he's not worth it."

"He's not, but if it would make you feel better…"

"Nah." Noel cracked her knuckles with a smirk. "Want me to rip out Amber's bleached blond hair? I'm pretty sure it's all extensions, but I may get lucky."

"Thoughtful, but I think her brother is with the police department now."

Noel scoffed. "Darin? Ha! He likes me better than her. He'd applaud."

"You're probably right." Nick smiled, already feeling more like himself. "Did you see that guy Amber was with?"

"I did."

"And?" He felt like a tool asking, but Nick's pride still stung that Amber had walked in with a Norse god on her arm.

Noel wrinkled her nose, which made her look younger. Adorable. "Too much hair for my tastes. I'm not interested in men who have you hocking up hairballs after one kiss."

Nick laughed, tension easing out of his shoulders. "Not into beards and long hair, huh?"

"Not particularly. I like my guys clean-cut. If they do have a little scruff on occasion, that's fine. Just need to keep it trimmed."

The air seemed less charged outside and he wondered if

the cumulation of loneliness and alcohol had been the catalyst behind his abrupt break with sanity. This was Noel. They'd been in each other's lives since infancy. Was she amazing and beautiful? Absolutely, but he'd always known that. Never acted on the knowledge to see how things went.

The only time it crossed his mind was when he got home from bootcamp. They'd gone to a bonfire out at the lake and they'd been sitting at the fire together. The flames danced across her skin and when her brown hair fell forward, he'd brushed it back. Silky soft, it slipped through his fingertips slowly. He remembered staring at her lips right before she jumped up and left to get them another beer.

Amber sat down in her place and the thought hadn't crossed his mind again. Until now.

"Is that why Pike never had a chance? Too fuzzy?" he teased.

She shook her head. "Pike is my buddy. I don't go there with people I actually care about. It's hard enough saying adios when it's casual, but add in feelings?"

"What do you mean?" he asked.

Noel's voice softened. "I don't want to lose anyone important to me. Not again."

Her meaning washed over Nick and he pulled her against him, wrapping her up in his arms. He rested his chin on top of Noel's head and her body melted into his. "I understand how you feel, but you can't close yourself off from love because of your parents. They wouldn't want that for you."

"I know they wouldn't, but I just can't. I like to compartmentalize my life. If something grows with someone I'm dating, fine.

NICK AND NOEL'S CHRISTMAS PLAYLIST   53

I'll accept that. I don't want to take a friendship that is amazing the way it is and ruin it with sex."

Nick chuckled. "I don't know how sex can ruin anything, unless it's bad sex."

Noel hit him in the arm. "Such a guy thing to say!"

"Well, last time I checked..."

"Oh my God, enough. I don't need to hear about you jerkin' your gherkin."

Nick bent over with loud guffaws. "Ah, man. I missed you."

"Missed you too."

When Nick's mirth finally subsided, he caught her watching him closely.

"What's that look for?"

"Just happy you got your smile back."

"Yeah, well, it's hard to fight when I'm with you."

"So you're glad you came out tonight?"

"Glad? No." He nudged her shoulder. "But it wasn't as bad as I thought it would be. Seeing Amber with someone else was shocking but not really painful. I'm actually more concerned about people pitying me once they see my replacement. The dude is hot, and I'm man enough to admit it."

Noel took his hand, and he noted her cooled skin. "*You* are hotter. You are also funny, kind, smart, and only the tiniest bit irritating." She flashed him a teasing grin as their fingers interlaced. "No one is going to pity you, Nick. They'll feel bad for her. Only a loser dumps a guy like you for Cousin Itt."

The sincere tone brought on the strangest urge to kiss her again, but that would be weird, out here for no one's benefit.

"You're freezing. Let's go inside."

"Sure." Noel placed his arm around her shoulder and wrapped hers around his waist. "Feel like putting on a show?"

Damn, she fit perfectly against him. How had he never noticed before?

Stop it, Nick. This isn't real. Get ahold of yourself.

"What did you have in mind?"

"Follow my lead."

Nick nodded.

As they walked back into the bar, Noel slipped her hand into the back pocket of his jeans and it took everything in him not to jump.

"You copping a feel?" he asked.

"Maybe. Do you mind?"

"Not at all." The minute he'd felt her fingers against his ass through the denim, his cock stirred to life. After this, he was going to need a cold shower. He was sick and tired of Rosy Palm, but he was used to her.

Pike and Anthony stared at them in horror as they sat back down, their hands connected on the tabletop.

"Ummm…" Anthony started.

"What the hell is going on?" Pike finished.

"How about you act normal and stop asking questions?" Noel ground out between her teeth.

"But everything started out normal. We all got here, had a few laughs. Then you guys made out, disappeared, and came back in holding hands! Excuse me for having a couple questions."

Anthony caught on quicker and elbowed the other man.

NICK AND NOEL'S CHRISTMAS PLAYLIST   55

"They'll explain later, wide mouth. Just button your lip until we get out of here. Or go get us some more drinks, since it's your turn."

"All right, all right." Pike stood up and smoothed down the front of his shirt. "I'll grab some beers to slow this party down."

Nick glanced at Noel with a grin. "Good idea."

A shadow passed over their table and Nick noticed Noel tense. He looked over his shoulder to find Trip and Jillian standing behind him.

"Hey there, Nick. Welcome back!" Jillian batted her thick black lashes at him, glued to Trip's side. The girl was a world-class flirt, but Nick didn't hold it against her.

"Thanks, Jillian. It's good to be back." Noting the way Noel gripped his hand, Nick brought it to his mouth and kissed her knuckles. She immediately relaxed, giving him a small smile.

"When did you two become a thang?" Trip asked, drawing out *thang* sarcastically.

"What do you think, babe?" Noel's eyes twinkled as they met his. "A little after lunch."

"Honestly, I knew the minute I got out of the terminal and saw you that we belonged together. That it was you. It's always been you."

Noel snorted softly at his speech, her lips pressed together like she was about to explode with laughter.

"Isn't that sweet?" Jillian pulled on Trip's arm. "Don't you think so? And you were all worried to tell her about us." Jillian addressed Noel as she continued, "Trip told me about your arrangement." Jillian winked at Nick. "Guess you just needed the right man to come along and swoop you into a real relationship."

Nick asked because he knew Noel needed to know. "And how long have you been seeing each other?"

"Three weeks or so. We wanted to be sure before he told you. Hope there are no hard feelings."

"Of course not." Noel's sweet tone covered the trace of anger only Nick noticed. "Congrats. I wish you both all the happiness in the world."

Nick grabbed the back of her chair and slid it over next to him. He nuzzled her neck before leaving a kiss on her cheek. "Isn't she the best? Beauty. Brains. Drive. Damn, I sure am lucky."

"Come on, Jill. I need a beer," Trip muttered, pulling Jillian towards the bar.

"Have a good night," Noel called after them, barely containing a giggle.

Anthony shook his head. "Is that what all this is about?" He waved his hand between them for emphasis.

Nick kept his arm on the back of Noel's chair as he lowered his voice. "Noel was trying to help me out after Amber walked in with her Thor Wannabe and we figured putting on a show would stick it to all of them."

"Good idea, except one thing…"

"What's that?" Nick asked.

"Amber looks like she's about ready to break her six-inch heel in someone's ass."

Noel and Nick turned around and caught the venomous expression on his ex's face. Her new man tried to kiss her and she pushed him away with a glare, before her focus returned to them.

NICK AND NOEL'S CHRISTMAS PLAYLIST 57

"Damn, she looks pissed," Noel laughed. "Good thing plastic blonds don't scare me."

Pike returned and set three beers and a creamy shot down. "Beers for the gentlemen and fuzzy balls for the lady."

Noel glared at Pike. "Really? Thought we all needed to slow down?"

"This one is straight revenge. Hopefully you enjoy it."

Noel tipped back the shot and smirked. "Delicious."

A loud cow bell rang from the bar and Ricki shouted, "How did the hairy balls taste, Noel?"

The room quieted and Nick was ready to hold Noel back if she decided to choke Pike.

To everyone's amusement, Noel yelled back, "Sweet and salty, just the way I like 'em."

The whole bar burst out laughing, including Pike. After a minute or so, Noel whispered to Nick, "You can let me go now. They all left."

Nick completely forgot that they were only acting and reluctantly removed his arm. Holding Noel had felt good. Right.

Maybe they shouldn't pretend to be together for anyone's sake. For something that was supposed to be fake, it had felt too real.

CHAPTER 6

NOEL

NOEL WALKED INTO PAULETTE'S CAFÉ just before noon on Sunday, not at all surprised that she was the first to arrive. Gabs was always running fifteen minutes behind. Noel had no idea who else was in the bridal party but had a sneaky suspicion one of the coveted spots would be taken by Amber.

Noel had never seen the appeal, but Gabby and Amber clicked in high school. While Noel had been the steadfast, low-key friend, Amber was the fun one. She liked to party and shop for hours. Talk girly things like hair, makeup, and boys. Even though they didn't hang like they used to, Gabby still considered Amber a close friend.

Which meant for the next month, Noel would be spending a lot of time with the narcissistic witch who'd hurt Nick. Noel didn't understand what she'd done to deserve that karma, but nothing she could recall warranted being stuck planning Gabby's wedding with the she-devil. The girl tortured Noel in high school and moved in on Nick at a bonfire when Noel walked off to grab beers.

She still thought about that night, although looking back, it was for the best. Since the minute they'd picked him up from basic in his parents' car, Noel sensed something different between them. More touching. Laughing. Watching the way the fire danced across his face. For a moment, she thought he might kiss her. She'd panicked and run off to get them another couple of beers and when she'd come back, Amber sat next to him, running her hand over the newly developed muscles of his arm.

Noel never wanted to punch someone as hard as she did Amber in that moment, but instead she'd walked away. Caught a ride home with Anthony and Pike and the next day, Nick and Amber were official. They'd never talked about that night again.

Perhaps it was time to let bygones be. With the exception of this month, Noel didn't have to see Amber at all anymore except in passing. She could be cordial.

The cute little café bustled with people and usually stayed jam-packed until they closed at two. The pretty hostess, Kalynn, stood behind the podium and smiled as Noel approached. "Hi, Noel. How many in your party?"

"Hey. I'm not sure. It's under Gabriella Montoya."

Kalynn ran her finger over something on the podium and tapped it. "Ah, gotcha. Right this way."

"Thanks."

Noel trailed behind Kalynn to the table and sat down, pulling off her knit cap and gloves and slipping them into her simple black tote purse.

"I'll have your waitress get you some water for the table. Have a good meal."

"Thanks." Noel was still smoothing her hair when Amber walked in, wearing ridiculously high heels and a barely-covering-her-ass dress. The song "Witchy Woman" by the Eagles popped into her head as Amber approached, her hips seeming to sway in slow motion. Her blond hair fell over the collar of her short, puffy jacket, which lay open, revealing the low cut of the dress. God had definitely given Amber a double dose of blessings up top.

Noel fiddled with the zipper of her jacket. She wasn't as well-endowed as her nemesis, but she sported more than a handful.

Why am I even comparing myself to her? Get it together, Carter.

Finally, she slipped it off, draping it over the back of her chair. Amber sat down with a smirk, giving Noel's simple sweater and jeans outfit a once-over.

"Hello, Noel." Amber's tone was sickly sweet. "You are looking rumpled. Did you have a good night or just forget to do something with yourself?"

I hope you slip on a piece of ice and bruise your butt.

Noel picked up her napkin and draped it over her lap with a smile. "I had a great night, Amber. How about yourself?"

"Yes, I'm very happy. You saw the guy I was with at Brews. Isn't he gorgeous?"

Noel shrugged. "He's okay if you like men who use more hair product than you."

Amber scooped her menu up with a huff. "Like you'd know anything about men. You can't even keep them satisfied. Everyone knows about Trip dropping you for Jillian. You sure do like to jump from guy to guy." Amber didn't even glance at her as she

NICK AND NOEL'S CHRISTMAS PLAYLIST   61

delivered the dig. She simply continued to study the menu while Noel glared daggers at her.

"Maybe in the past, but I think I landed on the right one this time."

Amber finally met her gaze, her pouty lips pressed in a thin line. "I'm assuming the development between Nick and yourself is recent?"

The waitress came by and set the pitcher on the table. "Hi, do you need another moment?"

"Yes, we're still waiting," Noel said.

"Sure, I'll check back in a bit."

Noel snatched up the water pitcher in the middle of the table, letting Amber stew.

"I asked you a question," Amber ground out.

Just a slip of the wrist and the cold liquid would wipe away the blue glitter on Amber's eyelids. It would be hysterical to watch Amber jump up screaming, swiping at her face and fishing ice cubes out of her bra.

But today was about Gabs, and no matter what the heinous witch pulled, Noel would not rise to the bait.

Noel filled her glass and set the pitcher gently on the table. "Are you worried he was cheating on you, Amber? Because that's your move, not his."

Amber snatched up the water pitcher, watching Noel with a coy smile. "So, you two happened after I broke up with him *yesterday*? Talk about fast. You are a very brave woman."

"What does that mean?" Noel snapped.

"I'm just saying I wouldn't want to get involved with a guy

coming out of something long term, that's all. You should probably take things slow. For your sake. It's so hard to go from fab to... well..." Amber took a sip of her water, drawing out the tension. "Drab."

Noel leaned across the table, lowering her voice to a hiss. "I know you're trying to push me into losing my cool, but it won't work. I am here for Gabby."

"Ahh, so noble."

Noel took a deep, calming breath before picking up her water glass and holding it up in salute. "Besides, everyone in town knows you weren't the perfect military girlfriend sitting home knitting Nick socks. Seems behaving like a decent human being already makes me better than you. I mean, I care for babies and you... what? Give men happy endings?"

All right, so not exactly cordial, but the woman pushed all the buttons.

"I am a licensed massage therapist," Amber snarled.

Noel sipped her water before holding a hand over her heart in feigned concern. "Damn, did I strike a nerve? So sorry, but you know, you start something and us *drabs* will finish it."

"You think you're so funny. Is that how you two got together? He was hurting and you swooped in with your jokes? Seduced him with your *charming* personality."

"How about you concentrate on your own man and leave my relationship alone."

"Relationship?" Amber scoffed. "You've been hooking up for a minute, while he and I were together for years. You could barely call what you two have a *relationship*."

I should just keep my mouth shut until Gabby gets here.

Sound advice, but she was too riled up to listen. "Admit it, Amber. Nick was always a backup plan. You could have your cake and still flit around town gobbling up all the snacks you wanted behind his back, but once he came home, you had to break up with him or the truth about you would come out."

Amber's hand covered her décolletage like a turn of the century heroine who'd been unjustly insulted. "I never cheated on Nick. I had friends, but eight years is a long time. People grow apart. That doesn't mean I don't want the best for him."

Noel snorted. "Girl, who are you kidding? I've been his friend since we were in diapers and you dumped him the minute he got back from defending our country."

"You don't know what you're talking about, bitch."

"I'm simply calling it like I see it."

Amber seemed to regain her composure and her glossy lips spread in a wicked smile. "And I'm just looking out for *you*, hon. Wouldn't want you to think this was something serious."

Noel's jaw clenched and she ground out. "What makes you think it isn't?"

"'Cause any man who jumps into something that quick is looking for rebound sex. Plain and simple. Although, come to think of it, I'm pretty sure I heard you were really good at that kind of thing. Bed buddies is what you like best, right, *sweetie*?"

Noel picked up her fork, debating on which psych defense she could use if she stabbed Amber with it. If she described the condescending sweetness in Amber's tone to a jury, would they really blame her?

Gabby saved Amber's life when she burst into the restaurant with a pink folder in one arm and a Coach purse hanging off the other. Her curly brown hair flowed around the top of her blue jacket as she waved excitedly, coming dangerously close to clobbering several patrons with her bag.

"Maybe for Gabby's sake we only speak when absolutely necessary."

Amber looked down at her glittery talons. "Fine by me."

Gabby came tapping across the wood floor and flopped into the chair next to Noel.

"Hey, sorry I'm late!" She slid her sunglasses up her forehead and into her hair. Her golden-brown eyes sparkled with excitement and Noel couldn't help returning her joy. Gabby's enthusiasm was infectious. "I have a new student I'm working with and the adjustment's been hard for him. What were you two yakking about?"

"Just celebrating new relationships," Amber said, cheerfully.

"Is the kid okay?" Noel asked.

"He will be. I'm awesome at what I do."

Gabby wasn't exaggerating. Gabby's older brother had autism and after watching the struggles and frustrations her parents and Edward went through with the education system, Gabby decided to get her teaching degree. As the IEP teacher for Mistletoe Elementary, Gabby worked hard on her enrichment lesson plans and was beloved by her students and their parents. Just another thing that made her an amazing person who deserved a fantastic, drama-free wedding.

Amber waved her hand in the center of the table. "Before we do anything else, I want to see that ring."

Gabby held out her hand with a giggle, Amber oohing and ahhhing over the princess-cut diamond. Noel really wasn't into big, sparkly jewels and what she did wear was small and sentimental. Noel inspected the ring with the proper amount of awe, before grabbing a honey scone from the basket their waitress set down.

"So, who is in a new relationship?" Gabby asked, stealing Noel's scone.

Noel grabbed another with a glare, but Amber jumped in before Noel could open her mouth. "Oh, well, you already know since Nick and I broke up, I'm officially with Guy."

Guy? Noel coughed to cover her laugh, but Amber's gaze narrowed in her direction.

"The exciting relationship news is Noel."

"You made things official with Trip?" Noel heard the disapproval in her friend's voice. She'd never liked Trip, even in school and hadn't been shy about letting Noel know.

"No, but—"

"Trip who?" Amber laughed, scooting over and putting her arm around Noel like they were dear friends. "No, Noel is with Nick."

Gabby swung Noel's way, scone crumbs flying out of her mouth as she squealed, "What?! How could you not tell me this?!"

Noel shot Gabby a weak smile, hating the hurt in her eyes. Since the minute they'd clicked, there had been no secrets between Noel and Gabby, at least, none on her end. She didn't want Gabby thinking Noel wasn't being honest.

She shook off Amber's arm, fighting the urge to accidentally knock the meddlesome woman out of her chair. "It just happened so fast, I haven't had time to fully process it."

"It's been twenty-four hours, Noelie. Surely you could have made time to share your good news."

Amber fluttered her falsies innocently, but Noel wasn't fooled. The evil wench thrived on stirring the pot.

"Nick and I wanted to enjoy some alone time before we told people."

Amber grinned like a cat toying with its prey. "Alone time, huh? Is that why you made out on the dance floor at Brews and Chews?"

Gabby stared at Noel, blinking rapidly. "Who are you?"

Noel grimaced. Gabby knew she'd never been one for PDA and there was no way Noel could tell Gabby the truth with Amber sitting there watching gleefully as Noel squirmed.

"Can we get back to the reason we're here, which is planning Gabby's wedding?" Noel was done being Amber's cat toy. "Who else are we waiting for?"

"My cousins, Emilia and Sarah." Gabby raised an eyebrow and gave her an obvious, *we are not done with this conversation* look. "But we can get started without them." Gabby flipped open her pink binder, the pages inside bursting with magazine cutouts and notes in sparkling gel pen. "Our colors are going to be red, silver, and green. We'll have the reception at Lynwood Barn and every table will have a poinsettia in the center. Now, because we have such a short time frame, my mother is planning my bridal shower the week before the wedding and I want my bachelor-ette party that night." Gabby looked up from the binder and met Noel's gaze. "What do you think, Maid of Honor?"

"Sure. We could go to Boise for an overnight and hit

downtown and continue on Sunday with a spa day before we come home."

Amber rolled her eyes. "Why do we need to go all the way to Boise when Mistletoe has an all-male review debuting next month at Brews and Chews?"

"What?" Noel spluttered.

Gabby bit her lip. "I don't know about strippers. Drew might flip his lid."

Noel jumped in. "Plus strippers are gross."

"Oh come on! Do you really think Drew's boys aren't going to hire half naked girls to entertain them? There are movies based on the seedy stuff that happens at bachelor parties. We'll keep it PG-13." Amber laced her fingers together and leaned on the table, like a super villain revealing her evil scheme. "Here is what I propose! We go to the all-male review and get so fired up that we go back to our men and have wild, crazy sex! We can save the spa for the wedding day when we need to relax. It's a bachelorette par-tay...you want to go out with a bang!"

Noel shook her head. "I don't think Gabby wants a bunch of dudes rubbing their crotches in her face."

"Well..." Noel's jaw dropped when she caught Gabby's sheepish grin. "She does have a point about men's bachelor parties. Why can't we get a little down and dirty?"

Amber met her gaze and grinned triumphantly. She'd won, yet again. Even in high school, Gabby would convince Noel to tag along with her to something Amber planned. Only Noel would end up rescuing her when Amber bailed. Parties in high school when Gabby got drunk and Amber was too busy hooking up to care. All the nights Gabby called from whatever club they were at because Amber ditched her to head to an after-party. With all the times Amber let her down, Noel couldn't believe Gabby stayed friends with her, let alone listened to her advice now.

Still, whatever Gabby wanted, Noel was determined to make it happen.

She kept her expression in check and smiled. "It's your party, babe."

Gabby giggled and Noel's gaze met Amber's smug blue eyes. "This is going to be great. Maybe you could get Nick to make us a playlist for the party. He's good at that."

Just another subtle reminder of the connection Amber and Nick had.

Yep, the next five weeks were definitely going to be painful.

CHAPTER 7

NICK

"DIDN'T I JUST PICK YOU up from the airport?" Noel grumbled from the passenger seat, her head flopped back against the headrest.

Nick grinned, keeping his eyes on the traffic in front of him. He'd insisted on driving Noel's car to the airport so she wouldn't have to drive the entire five-hour round trip from Mistletoe to Boise and back. "You did and I appreciate that. Merry can get me Wednesday when I get back from Colorado. We are going to do some car shopping for me."

Nick did a little dance in his seat and Noel laughed.

"I don't mind dropping you off and getting you. That's the whole reason I took a vacation day. But I hate Boise traffic. Freaking Californians."

Nick chuckled. Over the last ten years, Boise's population had boomed with an influx of people from other states, but it was a rite of passage as a native Idahoan to blame California for...well, just about everything.

"I won't need to go to Denver for many moons after this trip, so rest easy."

"Many moons? Seriously? I think you need more coffee," Noel said.

"If you want more coffee, Noel, just say so. There is a Human Bean up the way from the airport."

Nick caught Noel's grimace out of the corner of his eye. "Ew, the Human Bean is a terrible name for a coffee company. It makes me think they poop out the coffee beans and feed them to people."

"Where the hell do you get these ideas?" Nick shook his head and took a right. "Dutch Bros it is then."

"See, that's not a weird name! Plus their coffee doesn't taste like butt crack."

"How old are you?" Nick asked.

"Oh come on! I've heard you and Pike and Anthony all say, *'this tastes like shit!'* It is such a double standard that guys can talk nasty but girls are supposed to be magical rainbow creatures who never fart or curse."

"So you're saying you're not a unicorn?" he teased.

She popped him in the arm and he laughed, "Hey! I'm driving here!"

Noel flopped back in her seat. "Don't be a baby."

"You pack a hard punch."

"For a girl?" she sniped.

"Whoa, I did not say that. What's wrong with you?"

"Ugh, so much." Nick didn't come back with a smart-ass reply, just let her keep talking. "You know how Gabby's getting married?"

"Yeah?"

"Amber is in the wedding too."

Nick made a face. It was surprising how being home, around the people he loved made him see Amber in a whole new light. Yesterday he'd found himself on Facebook and a relationship quiz had popped up in his feed. He'd never tell Pike or Anthony, but he took it in regards to Amber and himself. Depressing. The only word he could come up with to describe the dismal nineteen percent he'd gotten on it. Amber really had a point that they barely knew each other, even after staying together for eight years.

"Amber helping out with the wedding plans, huh? That must be fun," he quipped.

"Tons. The first thing she did after making fun of my appearance? Grill me about you for a solid five minutes until Gabby saved me. Then she threw me under the bus by telling her we were together. I explained later to Gabby what was up, but it's like Amber is trying to cause trouble for me."

Nick waggled his eyebrows. "Well, you did kiss her ex. Hussy."

Noel groaned. "Ex being the key term and she broke up with you! There is no reason she should be giving me grief. She. Broke. up. With you. In fact, we should play that Walker Hayes song for her, since it isn't sinking in."

"Seems her reaction is understandable. Didn't you tell me I'm a great guy and she was crazy to dump me?"

"I don't remember saying that exactly."

"I was paraphrasing."

"Regardless of what I may or may not have inferred, she should be taking her regret for dumping you out on you, not me.

Mean girls were supposed to vanish when I graduated high school. *I ain't no hollaback girl.*"

"Oh boy. Breaking out the old school Gwen, huh?" Even though he knew she was already prickly, Nick added, "I know you don't like her, but Amber prodding you for information doesn't really sound like bullying, Noel."

Noel turned in her seat, scowling at him. "She also implied that the only reason you would be with someone like me is so you could get laid. Because according to her, I wouldn't know a real relationship if it bit me in the bahookie."

The image of Noel in bed flashed through his mind and he gulped. "I don't think I've ever seen you in a relationship."

Noel's scowl darkened, her eyebrows nearly touching in the middle. "I haven't had many, but that is beside the point. She tried to shame me for embracing my sexuality. It is the modern era! If I want to get down with no strings attached, I am allowed to do so."

Nick raised his fist in the air. "Amen! Hallelujah!"

"Shut up," Noel laughed.

"You want me to find us an angry rock song to scream sing? Would that make you feel better?" Nick picked up his phone and handed it to here. "Scroll through and pick anything you want."

Noel groaned, taking the phone from him. "I am sorry I'm such a grump this morning."

"Eh, you've been worse."

"Thanks, pumpkin." Her thumb stopped on the screen and an Imagine Dragons song burst through the speakers.

When it finished, Nick cleared his throat. "Out of curiosity, what did Amber say about me?"

"'Bout you directly? Not much. She wanted to know how long we'd been together. Called me a rebound."

"I can't believe she'd say that to you." Nick heard the fleck of hurt in her voice, even if she'd never admit it and took her hand. "Forget her, okay? I'd be lucky to have a girl like you."

"But I'm not a unicorn."

Her soft hand fit into his like God fashioned it for him and he got caught up in the warmth of her whiskey brown eyes.

Where do these crazy notions keep coming from?

Someone honked loudly and Nick jerked his attention back to the road.

"Whoa, Nick. I'd like to make it out of this city in one piece."

"Sorry, I was just thinking…"

"About?"

"That unicorns are overrated. You're a hippogriff."

Noel burst out laughing. "That may be the nerdiest thing a guy has ever said to me."

"I wouldn't doubt it, but it's still true. Hippogriffs are strong, loyal, and rare." He squeezed her hand. "Just like you."

Noel grew quiet and when he stopped in the Dutch Bros line, Nick looked her way again. He caught the shimmer in her eyes and sputtered.

"Are you about to cry?" he asked.

"No." She sniffled, rubbing at her eyes. "Maybe."

Nick stared at Noel in astonishment. In her oversized hoodie and sweats, her hair pulled up in a messy ponytail, she looked younger. Vulnerable. He'd only seen his tough, no-nonsense best friend cry a few times in her life and it was over heavier subjects than being compared to a mythical bird beast.

"Why?"

"Because it's early, I've had one weak-ass cup of coffee, and you're being sweet to me, damn it!"

"I'm always nice to you!" he yelled back.

She pushed him in the shoulder playfully. "Well, stop it!"

The kid taking coffee orders knocked on Nick's window. He rolled it down.

"How you doing today, sir?" The kid glanced between the two of them and Nick groaned, knowing the kid had heard them shouting.

"Doing all right, how about yourself?"

"Not bad. What can I get started for you?"

"Large coffee for me and a large double dirty Christmas morning extra hot with the works for the lady."

"You got it."

Nick paid for their coffees and once the window rolled back up, he asked, "What's up with you?"

"Nothing," she sulked.

"Don't give me that bull. You've been weird since Saturday night." Nick cleared his throat. "Did I do something to make things awkward?"

"No. It's nothing you did. I've just been getting a lot of unwanted attention."

"What do you mean? From who? Guys?" It wouldn't surprise him if there were dozens of men waiting in the wings for Noel to

NICK AND NOEL'S CHRISTMAS PLAYLIST   75

take notice, but the idea irked him. Especially since according to the gossip of Mistletoe, she and Nick were going hot and heavy.

"No, not from guys. People in town. Everyone wants to know about us. I had three expectant mothers come in wanting me to distract them with details about you and me."

"You and me..."

Noel threw up her hands. "Sex, Nick! Our little display at Brews and Chews has the whole town buzzing about us. Not just Amber and Trip but everyone wants to know what's going on!"

"Whoa, women in labor were asking you what I was like in bed?"

"Yes!"

Nick pulled forward again, a sly smile on his face. "What did you say?"

She glared. "I told them you were amazing, that you're hung like a donkey and I came four times in ten minutes."

"No you didn't. Although..."

"Do not tell me anything, you boob! I explained to them we'd just started dating and hadn't gone that far yet. Then they asked how far we had gone."

"Tell anyone that asks it's none of their business."

"Believe me, I have, but repeating the same thing over and over is frustrating. I'm about ready to start throwing out ridiculous stories about your prowess just to shut them up."

Nick rolled down the window to get their coffees and handed one to Noel, sliding the other into his cupholder. "I'm sorry. I didn't mean to put you in an uncomfortable position."

"I started it. It's just...I didn't really think this through." She cupped the coffee between her hands, seeming to search for the right words. "Where do we go from here? Do we pretend we are dating in public every time we're together?"

Nick's heartbeat kicked up a notch. One night of crossing the line with Noel had him thinking all kinds of insane thoughts, but continuing the ruse for weeks? Months?

The idea of being able to kiss Noel whenever he wanted held appeal, and he didn't know what to make of it. "Do you want to do that?"

"I don't want things to get complicated, but...I also can't stand Amber thinking she was right about me being just a rebound." Noel grinned. "I really like her nose bent out of joint about us."

"Is that the only reason?" he asked.

Noel blinked. "What do you mean?"

"I'm saying kissing you isn't a hardship on my part. The truth is, I enjoyed it. And as I'm not sure I'm ready to actually jump back into the dating pool..."

"You want me to be your beard...with benefits?"

Nick couldn't pinpoint the tone in her voice, but the last thing he wanted was to weird her out or worse, insult her. So he played it off.

"Ah, no! Not like that. If you think about it, we hang out most of the time anyway." Nick waggled his brows before turning out onto the street. "A little canoodling in front of the locals once in a while shouldn't be a hardship."

"Canoodling?" she laughed. "What century are you from?"

"I'm the reincarnated soul of Theodore Drizzle, salesman of fine snake oil," Nick said, mimicking the craggy voice of an old miner. "Wanna sample my wares, pretty lady?"

"You are such a goob."

Nick knew she wanted a serious answer from him, but he wasn't sure about admitting to Noel how much he'd enjoyed their kiss on Saturday. He didn't want to spook her, especially with her open disdain for relationships. Putting himself out there and asking her about what she was feeling might send her hightailing it for the hills.

The best part about their friendship? They knew what to expect from the other, could nearly finish each other's thoughts and sentences. Admitting the sexual chemistry from Saturday aloud terrified him, so he kept his tone light. Nonchalant.

"All joking aside, I mean it. If you care what Amber and other people are thinking about us, then why not keep 'em talking until they find something else to gossip about." *And give me a chance to sort through all these new thoughts and sensations.*

"Won't that get confusing? Pretending to be into each other"

"Not for me." *I hope not.* If anything, he prayed this would clear things up.

"All right." Noel held her coffee up to him in a toast. "Here's to fake dating."

Nick picked up his cup and tapped it to hers. "Cheers."

"Now, stop talking. I love this song," she said, turning up the volume on the mixed CD he'd been playing in the background. NSYNC sang in tandem about romancing the object of their affections under their tree and Noel sang along with them.

The thought of kissing Noel in front of a brightly lit tree popped into his head. Lowering her down to the tree skirt. Kissing his way down her neck.

"Hey, genius, you're about to get back on the freeway. You need to get over."

Nick swerved over swiftly and Noel gasped. A series of angry honks erupted behind him.

"What the hell was that?"

"Maybe I need more caffeine too," he muttered.

"Let's concentrate on getting both of us to the airport in once piece, all right?"

He nodded, pushing all thoughts of tree kissing out of his head. Maybe he'd take Pike's advice and download Tinder while he was in Colorado. If he just cleared the pipes, he should stop having sexual fantasies about Noel.

"Hey." Noel placed her hand on Nick's leg. "You sure you're all right?"

"Yep, yep. Just nervous about work."

"You're going to kick butt."

Her hand hadn't moved from his thigh. In fact, she'd given his knee a little squeeze. It warmed the skin beneath his jeans and suddenly, he wished she'd move it just a little higher...

When she removed her hand, the breath he'd been holding rushed out.

"You good?" she asked.

"Yeah. Great."

Nick definitely needed to get laid.

CHAPTER 8

NOEL

TUESDAY EVENING, NOEL DROVE OUT to the Winters home, parking behind Victoria's SUV in the driveway. Normally she would be home by now, but Victoria left her a message yesterday asking her to stop by. That it was important.

The stress of said importance bubbled in Noel's stomach all night and Victoria wouldn't give her a hint about what this impromptu visit was about, much to Noel's frustration. As she climbed the stairs to the front porch, she opened the unlocked door and stepped over the threshold.

"Good evening," she called.

"Hi Noel!" Victoria came into the entryway with her arms out. "Long night, sweetheart?"

She hung up her jacket on the coat rack before giving Victoria a hug. "Yes, but a good one. All my mamas safely delivered healthy babies. Definitely something to celebrate."

"I'm glad to hear it. You want something to eat or drink? Chris is at a fire board meeting, so it's just us."

Noel followed her into the large kitchen, splaying her hands across the tile countertop of the island. Off-white cupboards and a gray-and-white backsplash covered the walls, leaving little space for décor except the space above the sink. Above the gauzy curtains was a long, rectangular sign that read *Good Moms Let You Lick the Beater... Great Moms Turn Them Off First.* A Mother's Day present to Victoria from all of them several years ago that was too fitting to pass up.

"I'd love some tea, if you have it. I plan on going to bed after this and if I have any more caffeine, I'll never close my eyes."

Victoria bustled to the cupboard and held up a box. "Pick your poison while I heat up the water."

Noel smirked as she thumbed through the flavors. "Don't you just set the cup under the spout and push a button?"

"Hush now. You are downplaying the importance of my role."

"Please forgive my impertinence." Noel pulled out a lemon pack. "I have found the chosen one."

Victoria held the pouch in the air with her eyes closed. "Oh honorable chosen one, we sacrifice you to the stomach gods."

Noel snickered. "You're in a good mood. Being the week of Thanksgiving, I thought you'd be exhausted getting ready for this weekend."

"I am tired, but in the best way. Life is good. My baby boy is home, all of my girls are happy...I feel like it needs to be documented."

"Documented...how?"

"Family pictures! I had the appointment booked for after the New Year, but she had a cancellation for Tuesday, the first, so

I took it. She'll be here at four forty-five and I know you are switching to nights, but can you swing by? It's only a half an hour."

"I promised Gabby I'd do some shopping with her that day." Noel couldn't take Victoria's crestfallen expression and added, "But I am sure I'll have plenty of time to get here."

"Oh, I am so excited. It has been so long since I've had you all here at the same time. I haven't updated our family picture since your and Nick's senior year."

She looked at the framed canvas on the wall. Nick stood between his dad and Noel, with his arm around both of them while Victoria and the girls were on the left. It was taken before Nick's growth spurt, so he was only an inch taller than Noel. Nick sported a cheesy grin for the camera, while Noel's lips barely tilted up. She hadn't wanted to take the picture with them, but Victoria insisted.

"I guess it's about time. Nick looks like a completely different person now."

Victoria beamed. "Yes, he's grown into a fine man."

Fine is definitely the word I'd use.

Noel choked with surprise at her own lecherous thoughts. In his mother's house.

She was going to hell for sure. Straight. To. Hell.

"Are you all right?"

"Yeah, I'm good." Desperately needing to get off the subject of Nick, she noted the pile of dishes in the sink with a nod. "Doing some baking?"

"Actually, I was." Victoria stretched to grab a Christmas tin off the fridge. She popped off the metal lid and held out the contents for Noel's perusal. "Take one and tell me what you think."

Noel's heart thundered in her ears as she stared down at the lightly powdered squares inside. "They look like my mother's lemon shortbread cookies."

"That's because they are. I pulled out her recipe and followed it to the letter, but I need you to be my official taste tester."

Her mouth dry and chalky, she took a cookie from the tin. The Carter Lemon Shortbread Cookies were a coveted recipe. No one outside the family had ever seen it before.

"Did...you never told me my mother gave you the recipe."

"She left a copy in her will for me. You don't mind, do you?"

"No, I don't mind." Noel hadn't used the recipe since before her parents' death, hadn't wanted the reminder, but with Victoria eagerly watching her, Noel had no choice but to take a bite.

The powdered sugar dissolved on her tongue even as the tart lemon and buttery base of the cookie swirled together, triggering a flood of memories projecting through her mind like a video reel. She could hear her mother humming "O Christmas Tree." Her father's laugh when he stole a cookie before she could catch him. Noel's small hands covered by her mother's as they pressed down on the square cookie cutter into the cold dough. The warmth of her mother's skin as she spun Noel around the kitchen, their hands clasped together. Flour swirling through the air like fairy dust.

"Noel?" Victoria's voice, flooded with concern, brought Noel back to the present. "Honey, are you all right?"

"Yeah. I mean...yes. I'm fine." Noel blinked rapidly against the blurriness in her vision, refusing to let tears fall. "These are perfect. Can I ask what prompted you to make them?"

Victoria opened the tea packet and dropped the bag into Noel's cup of hot water before answering. "Have a seat and I'll explain." Noel sat in one of the stools at the counter, setting the cookie next to her cup. If she finished it now, there would be no stopping the onslaught of emotions and she was barely hanging on.

Victoria picked up a stack of photos and held them out to Noel. "I know this time of year is rough for you. It's hard for me as well. Your mother and I were friends since we were in diapers, just like you and Nick. We were sisters in every way but blood."

Noel looked through the photos of her parents, most taken as they performed together at the annual Mistletoe Christmas Concert. Both were musically gifted and they'd met during choir practice in high school. Her father came from a long line of Carter musicians who took their careers on the road. Her parents both went to college but spent their summers performing in local venues, spreading their love of music. Neither of them had the fame and fortune bone, though, and they came back to Mistletoe to settle down and start a family. Her mother took over the choir at the high school and her dad put his business degree to good use. He opened a music store and filled it with instruments, CDs, and vintage vinyl records. Weeknights and weekends, adults and children alike attended classes at Carter's Symphony, learning how to play guitar and piano. She'd spent most of her own childhood standing in the doorways, listening as skills improved.

Her mom and dad loved that store, but even before their death, it had taken a downward turn with the rise of online shopping.

After they were gone, Noel couldn't bear to go back inside and the Winterses had sold everything at her behest with the exception of a few items locked away in storage.

Noel stopped on a photo of Victoria and her mother, Heather. Each held a chubby baby in their arms, smiling for the camera. By the blue and pink outfits, Noel knew it was her and Nick.

Her mother's joyful face staring back at her stirred the memories she kept buried. A painful lump nearly choked her and she couldn't look anymore.

"I know how close you were," Noel whispered, setting the stack of photos down.

"I need to talk to you about something very important. Your parents loved the Christmas concert. It was their event…"

Oh God. Noel knew what was coming and she was already formulating her polite refusal.

"We've honored them every year since their passing, never deviating from their playlist. This year we wanted to do something really special for them and I was hoping that you would be a part of it."

"What…what do you want me to do?"

"I would like you to sing, baby. This event was created by the Carter family not soon after the town of Mistletoe was founded. A Carter should continue the tradition. Don't you think?"

"Honestly, no. Every Carter except my great-great-great-grandfather left this town and my dad was an only child. I think the tradition should be expanded to include other people, if you want to keep the concert going." Noel cleared her throat, fighting past the lump of panic. "Plus, I don't sing. Not in public, anyway."

"It would mean a lot to everyone, especially me. As much as we've all tried to do right by your family and the concert, it would really brighten spirits to see you. To hear you sing the songs your parents loved." Victoria ran her hand over Noel's cheek, tears glittering in her eyes. "I know the Christmas Concert holds painful memories for you, but the good ones should outweigh the bad. I'm sure it would do your parents proud."

A shaky breath escaped her. "Maybe, if they were here. But they're dead. They died on the way to their beloved concert. Instead of staying in Boise overnight and waiting out the storm, they tried to make it on time. Only they didn't make it at all."

"I hope you aren't blaming them for the accident."

"Of course not," Noel snapped.

Victoria's eyes widened with hurt, but she didn't reprimand her. Instead, she patted her hand and urged her. "Just think about it, all right? I know it probably feels as though I am springing this on you, but it's been ten years. With Nick being home, we have so much to celebrate, and I feel like it's time we remind the town why this concert is so special. Your family is a huge part of that, but if you really don't want to participate, I will let the matter drop."

Noel cradled her tea cup in her hands, searching for something to say. Ten years of avoiding the Christmas concert and all reminders of the night her parents died. Ten years and it was still as fresh as if it were yesterday. The pain hadn't eased. She'd just pushed it to the back of her mind.

Even the counselor Victoria and Chris sent her to hadn't been able to open her up. In all honesty, she probably would have shut down completely if it hadn't been for Nick, Gabby, and the rest of them.

The Winters family had done so much for her. She could do this for Victoria. Noel didn't believe for a second anyone else in town cared if she sang or not, but if she didn't attend, Victoria would be disappointed.

But an evening of constant reminders of her parents? Could she get through it without falling apart?

She took a sip of her tea and spoke before she changed her mind.

"I'll do the concert."

Victoria turned away from the dishes she'd started and the pure joy on her face hit Noel like a punch in the gut. "Oh, I am so glad! You don't need to worry about being alone up there. Merry and Holly will be covering the bass and drums and I've got a fantastic guitarist. It will be a beautiful tribute concert, I promise you."

"I'm sure it will be," Noel said with little conviction.

"There is one more thing. For the tribute, I was hoping to display some of their mementos in the town hall. Would it be possible for us to get into the storage unit?"

Noel nodded. "I can drop the key off tomorrow on my way to work."

"Oh, well, I thought we could do it together."

"To be honest, I haven't been in there since it happened and I don't think I want to tackle it right now. But you're welcome to go through and pull out what you need."

"I appreciate it, sweetheart."

Noel finished her tea and stood with the empty cup and discarded cookie in her hands. "I hope you don't mind if I take off, but I am beat."

"Of course not. Get some rest."

Noel returned Victoria's hug. "I am sorry for snapping at you."

The older woman patted her shoulder. "Apology accepted." Victoria pulled back and cupped her face. "You know I love you, right? And you are as much a part of this family as the children I gave birth to?"

Noel nodded, because what else could she do? As much as she loved Victoria, she missed her mother. Victoria and Chris welcomed her into their home with open arms, but they couldn't replace the parents she'd lost. She didn't want them to.

Victoria released her, taking the cup from her. "I'll see you later then."

"See you." When Victoria turned back to her dishes, Noel discreetly threw the remainder of the cookie in the trash.

CHAPTER 9

NICK

NICK DIDN'T LIKE HITTING ROCKING Rochelle's on a regular night, but Anthony and Pike dragged him out for Singles Hump Day on Wednesday night after he'd returned from Colorado. As much as he'd wanted to head to bed early, he couldn't blow off his guys when they seemed bound and determined to help him through his breakup.

Plus, it gave him an excuse to show off his new truck.

Still, the amount of meat being marketed around the two-story club should be criminal. It was eleven degrees outside and some women were in scraps of material just big enough to cover their bits. He could enjoy the view like any other red-blooded male, but they had to be freezing.

Pike nudged him as a girl in leather pants and a cropped tube top walked by. "Whoooeee, what about her?"

As pretty as she was, Nick shrugged.

"You're killing me," Pike muttered, downing the rest of his brew.

Nick had never been the club type and hooking up with a stranger didn't appeal to him. He'd given Tinder a shot while he was in Colorado, but nobody stood out as he swiped through profiles. After his meeting, he'd stopped at the hotel bar and met a woman who'd been more than interested. They'd talked for a while, had a few laughs, but right as he'd made the decision to invite her up, his phone dinged with a Spotify notification. Noel sent him a song and suddenly, all he'd wanted to do was go up to his hotel room alone and listen to it.

As much as he longed for a little touch, hooking up with a bunch of random partners with names he couldn't remember didn't appeal to him. He wanted something real with someone special.

Someone who could be my best friend.

It wasn't the first time the thought crossed his mind over the last week. Being home for good flipped a switch in him that Nick hadn't been prepared for. Noticing the flecks of black in Noel's dark eyes. The freckles that dotted the bridge of her nose and cheeks. How good her curves felt being pressed against his body.

He'd known how amazing she was for years, but he'd never thought of her as anything more than Noel. Well, besides the night he'd returned from boot camp. Sitting by the bonfire while other couples milled around them, he'd nearly kissed her. If she hadn't disappeared and Amber never sat down next to him, would things have turned out differently? There was no way to know for sure.

Now, after the recent moments they'd shared and that kiss? He realized the attraction he felt for her was the strongest he'd ever experienced.

Even stronger than with Amber.

But they'd both convinced themselves that they were better off friends. How did he break the news to her he'd changed his mind and wanted to take a chance? Even if it was a small step, like dinner, just the two of them.

Them putting on an act for Mistletoe gave him a chance to explore everything he was feeling without worrying about scaring her off. But what would he do when the ruse ended and he realized he had real feelings for her?

Nick rubbed a hand over his face. She'd never go for it, not the way she felt about relationships and romance.

Anthony came back to the table with another round of beers and Pike growled. "Would you do something about him? He is killing the vibe!"

While Anthony and Nick were in casual shirts and slacks, Pike looked like he was ready to do a cover shoot for some cheesy romance novel. Blue silky shirt. Gray slacks. Black leather jacket. The one thing to throw it off was the black and gray polka dot tie.

"Pretty sure nobody is interested in your *vibe*," Anthony razzed.

Nick laughed.

"Hate all you want, but the ladies love my swagger."

Pike danced in place and winked at a couple of women walking by. They giggled, but kept going.

"See?"

Anthony snorted in disgust.

"Guess they weren't that impressed," Nick said.

Anthony flipped Pike's tie over his shoulder. "You look like the guy on the Bounty paper towels...sissified."

Pike shook him off and straightened his clothes. "Shit, I look good."

"You'd be all right if you lost the tie."

"I will...later. Let some girl tie me up with it." Pike raised his hand, expecting a high five. "Come on, don't leave me hanging."

Anthony rolled his eyes. "Why are we friends with you?"

"No, the question is, why are we friends with this eunuch?" Pike did the robot, ending with his fingers pointing at Nick.

Nick glared at Pike. "I just don't feel like chasing after women tonight."

Pike chugged his beer and set the glass down with a smack. "Why not? You're single as a Pringle and if I know you, you probably haven't been with anyone but Amber. Am I wrong?"

Pike wasn't wrong and Nick hated it.

"No. I haven't been with anyone but Amber."

"Pringles come packed on top of each other and you should eat them in bunches, so your turn of phrase makes no sense." Anthony placed his hand on Nick's shoulder. "You know I don't often agree with Pike, but despite his idiotic colloquialisms, I think it would be good for you to get back out there. Even if it's only a conversation."

Pike ran his fingers through his beard, watching something over Anthony's shoulder. "It should be more than talking. Our boy needs some action. And not the fake action like with Noel."

Nick stiffened, Pike's words triggering irritation. Nothing about the way he'd felt kissing Noel was fake but she'd made it clear for years that even if she met someone she could love, she never wanted to get married or have kids. Nick dreamed of those things. It didn't make sense to push for a relationship that would end in heartache and potentially lose him one of the few people he truly loved.

He still couldn't seem to get her out of his head and no random girl in his bed would change that.

Opting for a change of subject, he said, "Before I forget, would you two help me move, not this coming Saturday but the next? I swung by those apartments on Palmer and they had a unit available."

Anthony cocked a dark brow. "Are those the same apartments Noel lives in?"

"Yeah, why?"

Anthony and Pike shared a heavy glance. "Just curious."

"What?"

"I'm just wondering if you might be setting yourself up to finally take the plunge," Anthony said.

"Plunge?"

"With Noel," Pike interjected. "I figured you were blinded by the fact you'd known her forever, but she is stupid hot, bro. The type of girl that could make even the baddest player settle down."

Nick narrowed his eyes. He'd always assumed Pike flirted with Noel to mess with her, but perhaps his friend's feelings ran a bit deeper. He didn't like the notion.

"It's an apartment and there aren't a lot in town. It has nothing to do with Noel. I've been living with a bunch of guys for eight years and as much as I love my parents, I can't wait to have my own place."

Pike grinned. "So you don't mind if I keep swinging, then?"

Nick considered punching his friend in the nuts to get his point across, but Anthony saved them both. "And striking out."

"It's all part of the game, my man."

Anthony snickered. "Your game is weak. Back to the subject at hand, moving you next weekend. I'll help if you're buying lunch."

Nick nodded. "Sure. I'll even throw in breakfast if you'll be at my parents by eight."

"Damn, man. Eight o'clock on a Saturday morning?" Pike made a clicking noise. "You better throw in coffee, too."

"Deal." Nick caught a glimpse of shimmery blond hair and grimaced. "Shit."

Anthony followed his gaze. "Uh-oh. Isn't that Amber?"

"Yes."

Amber danced at the edge of the club floor with Kelly Davis and Yancy Edwards. She'd been friends with them since high school and they'd never been Nick's biggest fans. The feeling remained mutual. All three of them wore sequined halters and black pants, looking like a trio of twinkling disco balls.

"Are they all wearing the same shirt?" Anthony asked.

"Yeah."

"Why?"

Pike shook his head. "Girls do that kind of shit all the time. They think it's cute or something."

"It's fucking weird," Anthony said.

"I agree. I'm going to get us another round."

"None for me. I'm done." Nick took a long pull of his beer, finishing it off.

Pike scowled. "What? Why?"

"If I don't stop now, I'll end up crashing at your place and it smells like ball funk."

Anthony chuckled. "Probably all the products he uses on his face pubes. I swear, he gets high from the mixed fumes. Only excuse for his wardrobe."

"Fuck you both." Pike backed away with both his middle fingers up, saluting them.

Anthony shook his head. After a few seconds he sobered, catching Nick's gaze. "I know he can be ridiculous, but he's worried about you."

"Why? I'm fine. Honestly, after that first day, I realized you all were right. I didn't know the real Amber. I had this fantasy built up in my head and now that I know the truth, I feel good. Happy. Ready to take on the world." Nick glanced toward the bar where Pike leaned close to a curvy brunette. "Not screw my way through it."

"Go easy on the guy. He doesn't talk about it much, but some girl last year messed him up bad. He got really depressed. Gained weight. Didn't want to do anything. Took him a while to snap out of it. When he did, he started working out and turned into the fashion diva you see before you. I think the way you are right now takes him back to that place and he wants to fix you so he doesn't think about it."

"That's pretty insightful."

"I have my moments," Anthony said.

"I had no idea Pike met someone. Who was she?"

"I don't know, she was from Emmett or something. All I know is she hurt my boy and that, I cannot abide."

A hand landed on his arm and Nick turned to find Amber fluttering black false lashes at him. "Hi, Nick. I thought that was you."

Kelly and Yancy flanked her, watching him with distaste.

"Hey."

Amber tossed back her hair, her gaze never wavering from his. He'd like to think that she'd changed so much over the last eight years, but if he was being completely honest, it seemed more likely he'd never really known her to begin with. They'd only been dating a few weeks before he'd left for his placement and although they'd talked about their futures, he couldn't remember them ever having deep conversations about themselves. The night she'd sat down next to him, he'd been flattered. Gorgeous and built, she could have chosen any guy at the campfire and she'd picked him. If he'd stayed in town, perhaps they wouldn't have lasted as long as they did, but there was no way to know for sure.

"What are you doing here on singles night? Shouldn't you be at home bingeing something with your new girlfriend?"

"Noel doesn't care if I have a couple drinks with my friends. She isn't insecure."

Amber's catty grin dimmed at the dig. She'd thrown bitch fits anytime he'd come home from leave and planned a guys' night. It should have been a red flag, but he'd stupidly thought it was about missing him and wanting to spend as much time as possible together. Anymore, Nick realized it was just her way of controlling him.

"It's awfully early for her to be so comfortable." Amber leaned over the table, pressing her breasts against the wood. Her cleavage went all the way to her neck and Nick looked at Anthony for an assist. His buddy's focus was on his ex's rack. Traitor.

"She has nothing to worry about. I take commitment seriously."

"Oh, so this is serious then?"

"Very." Nick sensed Anthony's gaze swing his way and he silently prayed his friend would back him up. "Where is your new man tonight?"

"Oh, Guy and I are casual. Since I haven't been back on the market long, I like to keep my options open. Wouldn't want someone to get hurt when I realized I wasn't really ready for something long term so soon."

"Well, you know yourself best. Sounds like we're both very happy with how things turned out."

Amber moved closer to his side, lowering her voice so he had to bend to hear her over the music. "I do miss you. I was thinking, since Noel and you are so in sync, maybe we could still be friends? We have a lot of history together and I know I can trust you in times of crisis."

Nick knew from experience that saying the wrong thing to Amber could result in a scene, so he kept his response ambiguous. "We'll see."

Before he could move away, she kissed his cheek. "Think about it. Have fun tonight, boys."

The trio of women walked away and Nick stared at Anthony. "What the hell was that?"

"Women, man. Can't figure 'em out."

Pike came back to the table with three beers, ignoring Nick's directive that he'd had enough. "What did I miss?"

"I think Amber still wants a piece of our Nick."

Pike's expression hardened. "Fuck her and the broomstick up her ass. Nick deserves better."

"Thanks, buddy."

"Like her." Pike pointed to a brunette in a jean skirt and waggled his brows. "I'll bet you a hundred she's got no panties on underneath that scrap of denim."

"You're a sick man, Pike," Anthony said.

Nick's phone vibrated and he opened Snapchat. Noel sent him a snap of her holding a baby, "Silent Night" playing in the background. A text came through next.

> They named him Reagan, which means king, so I
> thought the song fit.

Nick smiled at the combination of exhaustion and elation on her face.

"Earth to Nick! You gonna take the bet?"

Nick opened Spotify and shook his head. "Nah, you go for it, buddy. I'm good."

He ignored Pike's groans and added "I Just Can't Wait to Be King" to their playlist and shot her a link. His notifications dinged a moment later.

> I LOVE it! 😍

Nick couldn't keep the shit-eating grin off his face.

CHAPTER 10

NOEL

PREGNANT WOMEN AND BABIES DIDN'T seem to realize that it was Thanksgiving and Noel hardly had a chance to breathe her entire shift, let alone eat. The hospital staff laid out a potluck in the breakroom and with it being well after six in the evening, most of the good stuff was picked over.

Noel glanced over the nearly empty trays of food and loaded a plate with a few pie slices. She could always whip up some ramen and veggies for a quick meal before diving into dessert.

Or not. There would be no one around to lecture her if she had dessert for dinner.

She headed out of the parking lot, the foil-covered plate sitting on the seat next to her. If she stopped by the Winterses, she knew that Victoria would fix her up a plate of food, but she didn't have the energy to be social.

When she got home, she'd curl up on the couch watching *A Charlie Brown Thanksgiving* while eating the various slices of dessert and then pass out. That sounded like a solid plan.

It's Thanksgiving, baby. We can do whatever we want today.

Noel smiled, remembering the Thanksgiving her dad was stuck in Chicago and they'd locked down the airport. Her mom still prepared the massive feast, but they started the day with pie for breakfast. She'd been nine, snuggled up against her mom on the couch while they watched a slew of Christmas movies with more whipped cream than pie on their plates. They'd given each other mani-pedis and facials, even had a dance party in their living room. Both her parents worked, so she'd always treasured any and all the alone time they spent together.

While she loved her dad, it was her favorite Thanksgiving memory.

Noel parked in the spot closest to the iron stairs, noting the nearly empty lot. The community center put on a big dinner every year that a lot of the town attended. Most of the folks in her apartment building were single people of various ages, all living alone, so it made sense they wouldn't be here.

She walked up the stairs and noticed Trip sat on the top step waiting for her, dressed in a blue collared shirt and khaki slacks. His normally mushed hair was styled conservatively, probably because he went to his parents' today. He stood up as she approached, a boyish grin on his handsome face.

"Hey, Noel."

"Trip. What can I do you for?"

He shoved his hands into the pockets of his pants, lowering his eyes coyly. Noel found his antics charming once upon a time, but the rose-colored glasses were off. "I wanted to wish you a happy Thanksgiving."

Noel passed him on the stairs, her shoulder brushing his chest as he turned to let her by. "You could have texted to tell me that."

"I know, I just...I wanted to deliver it in person," he said, trailing behind her on the fenced pathway to her second story apartment.

Like you told me in person you were hooking up with Jillian too?

Over the last few days, she'd done a lot of soul searching on why she was so angry at Trip and decided it was more to do with honesty. If she'd been hooking up with someone else, she would have said something for the safety factor alone. Yes, Trip and she had always used condoms, but accidents happened. Before they slept together, they'd been tested, but introducing another sexual partner without the other's knowledge? Bad form.

Plus, Jillian was prettier. She could admit that stung. Shallow as it may be.

"Happy Thanksgiving," she said, politely. "Now, if you'll excuse me, it's been a long day and I want to eat my pie in peace."

She juggled her pie in one hand as she unlocked her door.

"Noel..." he whined like a child.

Her annoyance got the best of her and she sniped, "Hey, didn't you get a girlfriend? Shouldn't you be spending your first Thanksgiving together? Feeding each other dessert and sitting around the table talking about how thankful you are to have found each other?"

"No. She left yesterday to visit her dad." He squared his shoulders, all the vulnerability erased from his expression. "You can't be mad at me about Jillian. We weren't even really together."

Noel left her keys in the doorknob and turned all the way

around to face him. "I am not mad at you. I was irritated when I found out you'd been seeing her for three weeks and still sleeping with me, but I'm over it. Bygones."

"Because you're dating Nick Winters?" His tone dropped to a growl.

Oh my God, is this a male pride thing? He didn't want me, but no one else can either?

"No, because like you said, we weren't really together." Then, because she couldn't help needling him, she added, "Having Nick home is a bonus."

"A lot of people are talking about you two. Saying that you've been waiting for him and that's why you never get serious with anyone. Were you just using me because he was gone?"

"Why do you care?"

"Nobody likes to be used."

"People also don't like to find out their fuck buddy replaced them via Instagram, but here we are."

"I didn't replace you. Jillian and I shared a connection, but I was going to tell you."

"Were you? Or were you going to date her, screw me, and hope neither one of us said anything?"

His expression actually brightened. "See, you sound jealous."

"I'm not. At all. I never tried to lock you down and now we're both with other people. Happy. So, no harm no foul. You can go on with your life knowing I am not secretly constructing a voodoo doll in your image and planning to extract bloody revenge."

"But about Nick...were you planning on dropping me all along as soon as he got back?"

Noel didn't bother to answer, too tired and frustrated to deal with Trip's bruised ego tonight. Or any other time. "Good night, Trip."

Trip touched her shoulder, staring at her earnestly. "I miss you, Noel. We had fun together, right? Couldn't we still be friends?"

"Sure, we had fun. But we were never friends. You're with Jillian and I'm with Nick. Let's leave things where they belong."

Noel closed the door on his crestfallen face. The nerve of him showing up here, looking for attention when his girlfriend was out of town.

Noel snorted. As if this behavior really surprised her. She hadn't started hooking up with Trip because he was a good guy. She'd picked him because he wasn't the type you got attached to.

Unlike Nick.

Over the last few days, this whole situation between the two of them weighed heavy on her mind. It was one thing to play couple for the Brews and Chews crowd, but what did they tell his sisters? His parents? That it was all make-believe to save both their pride?

Once word made its way around, Noel had a sneaky suspicion it wouldn't be that simple.

She went into the kitchen of her one-bedroom apartment and grabbed a fork from the drawer. The place was so quiet at night, giving her too much time to think. It had been the same at her childhood home after her parents passed. The Winterses offered to keep the house up for her until she was ready to live on her own since it was paid off, but she didn't want to live in a place with so many memories of her family. After living in the Winters home, which was boisterous and fun, then the barracks, it had

NICK AND NOEL'S CHRISTMAS PLAYLIST   103

been hard being all alone. But she couldn't move back in with the Winterses after she was discharged, and while she was in school she'd hardly been home anyways. Work was consuming, but she still found herself struggling to keep busy so she wouldn't get lost in her thoughts.

Maybe she should get a pet. She could afford the deposit and then at least she'd have someone to come home to. Something that was hers.

Noel slipped a bite of store-bought pumpkin pie past her lips just as someone knocked on the door.

"Geez, Trip, I swear." She dropped her fork onto her plate and stomped into the other room. What in the hell did he think would happen? That if he waited long enough he'd wear her down and she'd let him in?

She threw open the door with a scowl. "What?"

Nick quirked a brow at her, holding up two brown paper sacks. "Ummm....food?"

Noel froze. She hadn't seen him since she'd waved goodbye at the airport and they'd decided to keep this whole pretend relationship going. Standing there in a simple blue T-shirt and jeans, he made her heart beat faster. She didn't want to admit she'd been thinking about Nick, their kiss, and their arrangement all too often. She'd even had a rather erotic dream about him last night that ended in her helping herself along this morning.

She could feel her cheeks warm remembering. "Hi."

"Hey. Mom wanted me to bring this by for you since you couldn't come over for Thanksgiving. And return your storage key. She sends her thanks, by the way, and will get the items back to you after the concert." Nick held out the key to her, which she took. "But I seem to have caught you at a bad time and feel like I should just leave this and back away slowly."

Noel shook her head. "No, sorry, I thought you were someone else."

"Whoever you thought I was, I'm scared for them."

Noel rolled her eyes. "Get in here."

Nick passed by into the apartment, his Christmassy scent trailing behind him. Noel smiled as she closed the door, leaning back against it to find Nick looking around her place. She hadn't done much to the apartment since she moved in after college and Nick had never been there before. They'd always hung out at his parents' place while he was on leave or went out with the guys. To his eye, it probably looked barren. No pictures on the walls. A simple gray couch and loveseat set. TV and black entertainment center. Black coffee table.

It wasn't that she didn't enjoy art and she had boxes of pictures in storage tubs. All of her parents' framed photos. She could always go through, sort and display those, but she didn't want walls full of reminders of her childhood. Besides, she only came home to sleep and eat. The rest of the time, she went out with friends, hiking, doing anything else. Spending money on a bunch of pictures and throw pillows made very little sense to her.

"Love what you've done with the place."

"What?" she scoffed.

"It's like a bachelor pad, minus the half-naked girl posters and neon beer sign."

Noel tried to take one of the bags from him but he held it away.

"Shut up and feed me."

"Whoa, now. You should show some respect to the man with the bags."

"The man with the bags better recognize the danger he is in, keeping food from a hungry nurse."

"Fair point," Nick said, flashing that adorable grin. "Show me to the kitchen, wench."

Noel laughed, leading the way. There wasn't much to the small kitchen with oak cabinets and white walls, but it served its purpose. Her mouth watered when he pulled one tub after another out of the first bag. He started working on the second bag and Noel held her hands up. "That is a lot of food! Did your mom seriously pack all of that for me?"

"Yep." He held up two tubs, one in each hand. "She even packed you extra potatoes because she knows how much you love them."

"She's trying to fatten me up."

"I'm not saying she is, but there might have been some discussion about you working too hard. Not eating enough. Gonna blow away with a strong wind."

"Oh geez, she did not."

"No, she said, 'Take these to Noel. And give her our love.'"

Noel's heart soared. "I'll have to give her a big hug next time I see her."

"I'm sure she'd appreciate that."

Noel grabbed a plate from the cupboard and held it up. "Are you still hungry? There is enough to share."

"No, this is all for you. I ate so much I created a food baby."

Noel glanced down at his flat stomach and scoffed. "Wow, you're hardly showing. What is your secret?"

He cupped the side of his mouth and whispered, "I skipped breakfast to make more room."

She shook her head, setting her plate down on the counter. "Such a dork."

"You might say I'm a-dork-able."

"No, I wouldn't."

"Ouch. I was going to ask if I could keep you company, but you're kinda mean tonight."

"No, that's just my personality. You should be used to it by now." Noel opened the container with rolls and helped herself to one. The soft, buttery bread practically melted on her tongue. "God, that is good."

"I'll pass along your enjoyment to the chef. Seriously, though... do you mind if I hang out?"

Noel snagged a stray flake of role on her thumb with her teeth. "Why would I mind?"

"I didn't know if my idea freaked you out? When I suggested we keep pretending we're dating?"

Noel paused her chewing, considering whether freaked out was the right phrase. "No, I'm not freaked out. Are *you* freaked out?"

"Far from it." His words were warm and soothing. "I just don't want to make things awkward between us."

"No, I'm good. I have been kind of thinking..."

"Yeah?"

"Should we tell your family what we're doing? So they don't hear it from someone else?"

"I can do that. They'll be disappointed."

"What do you mean? In me?"

"No. That it isn't real."

"Oh." Noel coughed, hoping he hadn't heard the slight tremble in her voice. She pulled out a spoon and dished portions from every container. Turkey, ham, yams, potatoes, green beans, and macaroni were soon piled up high. She popped it into the microwave for a few minutes.

He came around the counter and stood only a few inches away. "Noel?"

"Yeah?"

"You're not looking at me."

Noel turned, tilted her head up and met his gaze. "I am."

"Not really. You were looking at the floor. The food. Even now, your gaze keeps shifting toward the microwave."

"I told you I'm hungry."

"Uh-huh." He sounded unconvinced.

"What?"

"Nothing. Just distracting you so I can do this."

The minute his fingers touched her rib cage, she squealed. "No! No, stop! Damn it!"

Nick held her against him, his fingers moving up and down her sides until she couldn't breathe. She squirmed to get away, turning in his arms. When his hand grazed her breast, they both froze.

"Sorry, didn't mean to do that."

Noel was acutely aware of his arm locked around her waist, her back plastered against his front. His warm breath puffed against her neck, close enough that she could imagine his mouth dipping lower to brush against her skin.

"It's okay." Her words hushed, fully aware he hadn't let her go and a tiny voice inside didn't want him to let go.

Being held by Nick felt too damn good.

His hands flattened against her stomach, as if reading her mind. "Things just seemed so tense and I wanted to snap us out of it."

Honesty won out and she blurted, "I'm not tense I just...I didn't expect to like kissing you."

"You thought kissing me would be bad?" He sounded offended and she smiled.

Noel's heart galloped in her chest as she admitted, "I've only ever thought about it one time."

"When?"

"The night you came home from basic."

This time, she didn't have to imagine his lips on her neck. He pressed a light kiss there and whispered, "Me too."

Noel closed her eyes for the briefest of seconds, memorizing the warmth. The texture. The sensation of electro shocks racing down her spine. "You did?"

"Yes. I almost *did* kiss you. But then you ran off and..."

He didn't need to finish the sentence. She'd taken off, scared of her feelings, and left the space open for Amber to step in. His words broke the spell and her eyes flew open. She was in her kitchen with Nick, letting him trail kisses along her skin. Enjoying it. Craving it.

But Amber managed to worm her way back in, ruining everything.

She jumped away before she fell further down the rabbit hole, his arms falling away easily, leaving her bereft of his warmth. Several seconds of silence ticked by with their breathing the only sound in the room. Finally, Nick reached out and laid a hand on her arm.

"Noel… Look at me."

Noel turned, facing him.

She couldn't keep her hands still and settled finally on smoothing them over her pink scrubs. "What are we doing?"

Nick shook his head, as if trying to get a grip on himself. "I don't know. I thought we were being honest."

"Yeah, but we don't want to do this. We only kissed the first time to save face in front of Amber and Trip. Not actually jump into something that could potentially ruin twenty-plus years of friendship!"

"We also admitted we've had these feelings before."

"Just because we have these feelings, doesn't mean we should actually act on them. Does it?"

Nick nodded. "No, of course not. I think we're both lonely and comfortable with each other and mistaking that for something more."

The conviction in his tone didn't match the emotion she saw in his eyes, but Noel ignored it. Getting caught up with feelings of attraction for Nick was a bad idea, for both their sakes.

"I completely agree."

Liar.

Nick pushed off the counter, keeping his distance. He ran a hand through his hair as he said, "So, from now on, we'll just tell people we are better off as friends."

"Absolutely. Just friends."

"Good." He cleared his throat. "I guess I should let you eat."

Noel didn't remind him that he'd wanted to stay and keep her company. Her resolve not to kiss him could snap at any moment. "Thanks for bringing the food. Tell your mom I will be by soon."

"Will do." He took a step toward her and seemed to think better of it because he stopped. "Happy Thanksgiving, Noel."

"Happy Thanksgiving."

He ducked around the corner and Noel slumped back against the counter. The microwave dinged, announcing her dinner was warm and ready, but she'd suddenly lost her appetite.

She'd turned to Jell-O at the mere touch of Nick's lips on her neck. How the hell were they going to ignore that?

CHAPTER 11

NICK

"NICK! I NEED YOU!"

Nick shifted his attention from sliding Mr. Cutter's noble fir through the yellow netting to his mother hollering at him from across the tent. He'd agreed to come over Saturday and Sunday to help his parents out, as the weekend after Thanksgiving was the busiest for the tree farm. Hearing his mother call out that she needed him was just par for the course.

"Be right there!" He secured Mr. Cutter's net and hauled it out to his truck for him. Mr. Cutter had been coming out to the farm since Nick could remember and he'd always liked the former shop teacher. They'd chatted a bit while he'd helped Mr. Cutter with his tree and learned that he'd retired, his wife passed last year, and he had six grandchildren all coming with their parents to help him decorate his tree. The conversation was a fantastic distraction from everything lurking at the back of his mind.

Between work and the farm, he'd kept busy, which stopped all thoughts of Noel from creeping in. This whole week had been one roller coaster of emotions and he just wanted life to get back to normal.

Mr. Cutter dropped the tailgate and Nick set his tree in gently. The older man closed the truck up and pulled a ten from his pocket.

"Thanks for the help, Nick."

"I appreciate the offer sir, but keep your money. I am happy to do it."

Mr. Cutter held the money out insistently. "Just take it, son. It's been a long time since you loaded my tree for me and I know ten bucks ain't much, but we're all glad you're back home safe."

"Thank you." Nick took the ten and shook the older man's hand.

When he came back into the tent, he shook the freshly fallen snow from his head and shoulders. It had been snowing steadily all morning, dropping another four inches of fresh powder on the ground, but that didn't stop the crowds from selecting the perfect tree. Even though the uncut trees at the Winters' Christmas Tree Farm were twenty bucks more than the ones precut at the grocery store, people were willing to pay the difference for not just beautiful trees, but the family experience and memories of cutting their own.

Nick came up alongside his mom behind the checkout table. She had her hair up in a ponytail, a gray headband covering her ears. Even though there were several space heaters inside the tent, wind still whipped arctic blasts inside, swirling with snow.

"You needed me for something?"

She handed Mrs. Olsen her change, ignoring him. "You take care now. Thanks for coming."

"Absolutely. I'll see you at church." Mrs. Olsen smiled brightly at Nick. "Welcome home, Nicholas. Everyone here appreciates your service, but we're happy to have you back safe."

Although it made him uncomfortable accepting gratitude from strangers, hearing it from his third-grade teacher with so much pride in her voice made him smile. "Thanks, Mrs. Olsen."

Once she was gone, his mother took him aside, letting the other cashier, Linda, handle transactions.

"I have a favor."

"Ominous, but go on."

"Frank Halifax broke his arm snowboarding and can't play guitar for the Christmas concert."

Nick grimaced, already knowing where she was headed. "Oh, mom…"

"Please! I need you to do this for your sisters and besides, even Frank didn't hold a candle to your playing and he used to front a band!"

The Mistletoe Christmas Concert was the biggest event during the holiday season, besides the Festival of Trees. When he was a kid, his parents would drag him every year and it had been a blast when the Carters ran it. After they passed, he'd chosen to stay home with Noel instead of attending and that's exactly what he wanted to do now. Skip it and keep a low profile with the breakup and new job, not stand on stage in front of the whole town playing Christmas songs. Watching people dance, eat, and make merry.

But with his mother making big puppy dog eyes at him, how could he possibly tell her no?

"All right, but you owe me."

His mother scoffed. "Please, I gave you life, changed your diapers, did your laundry, fed you, and kept you alive for eighteen years. When I ask for a favor, it's all for show."

Nick chuckled. "When do they rehearse?"

"They haven't started yet. Their first one is this afternoon. I just talked to Noel on Tuesday—"

His heart beat quickened. "Whoa, Noel's doing it too?"

Nick hadn't seen her since Thursday, although they'd texted and snapped quite a bit. The usual silly GIFs and faces when they were bored, being too careful with each other. The thought of being near her so soon made him as nervous as the first time he took a girl out, which was crazy. He'd been there for Noel when she got her first period and had to get her mom for her. She'd dabbed a washcloth on his neck and forehead when Nick drank for the first time and puked his guts out. They'd seen each other at their worst, yet crossing the line with Noel made him jitterier than a jackrabbit in a den of foxes.

His mother arched an eyebrow. "Yes, she's singing lead. Is that a problem?"

"No, of course not." Nick wasn't about to tell his mom how he'd almost made out with Noel in her kitchen and since then, he'd given her a wide berth. She was right that they shouldn't complicate such a great friendship. Even though Nick discovered he wasn't the casual hook-up guy, that didn't mean he needed to jump his best friend.

Although he still couldn't stop thinking about kissing Noel, no matter how hard he tried.

"Good," his mother said. "When you finish up here at four, you can meet them in the house."

"I guess it works out I didn't have plans tonight."

"I suppose it does," she said, patting his cheek. "Thank you. I appreciate you and your sister helping out this weekend."

His mother turned, took one step and slowly swung back around. "Just so we're clear...there isn't anything you'd like to tell me about, is there?"

"Um, I don't think so. Is there something you want to ask me about?"

"I heard through the grapevine that you and Noel might be more than friends."

Her tone remained neutral, giving him nothing. "Only a rumor."

"I see. If something changes, please be careful."

"Of what?"

"With Noel. She's got a lot of hurt built up inside she still needs to work through."

"I know that better than anyone."

"Which means if something is going on, you need to take it slow. Life doesn't happen on some imaginary timeline."

Nick's mouth dropped open. "You think I'm going to push her into something she doesn't want?"

"No. I think you have had your life planned since you were in middle school and Noel had hers blown to smithereens. She's got some ideas that might not line up with yours and you need to be sure you can be patient with her."

"So you don't want me to date Noel?"

"Land sakes! I guess I need to be plain with you. That girl is as much my child as you are and if you push her away, further than she's already run herself, I will be mighty sore. Proceed with caution."

"All right..."

"However...if you two do end up taking things to the next level, I'd be happy as a clam."

Nick shook his head as his mom went back to the checkout table, thrown for a loop. He had her approval, as long as Noel and he worked out, but if they didn't, it wasn't just his and Noel's hearts they had to think about.

His family. Their friends.

Still, Nick couldn't help feeling annoyed. Everyone liked to poke their nose in other people's business, even his own mother. As if he couldn't navigate his own love life without her input.

His sister Merry waved as he passed her. She handled the wreath section, making festive circles of evergreen and bows to sell through the holidays. Holly ran her own store in town that was open six days a week, so she only got over on Sundays to help out at the farm. As a way to contribute, she'd buy their parents' overstocked wreaths to sell in her store. She'd add her own flair to them, of course, but it still made a difference.

The afternoon flew by and they headed back to the house just after four. The snow finally slowed to a mere flurry and Nick couldn't wait to get inside and change into dry clothes. The in and out of the tent today had left his jeans damp and his skin chilled.

Nick saw Noel parking in front of the house as they rounded the corner. When she climbed out of the driver's side, bundled up in her puffy jacket and beanie with her jeans tucked into a pair of white snow boots, she looked like she should be modeling on an L.L.Bean catalog.

Nick held his hand up awkwardly to wave and she did the same. He noted that Noel's already rosy cheeks darkened when she smiled at him and Nick wondered if she was as out of her depth as he was.

Merry jogged up to his side and elbowed him. "Feels like you never left, huh?"

"I wouldn't say that. Some things are definitely different." Nick's gaze shifted to Noel and Merry followed it, smiling.

"Can I tell you something?"

"Sure, what's up?"

"I love Noel."

Nick's brow furrowed. "Um, I kinda figured, since you've been tagging along after us trying to steal her from me since we were kids."

Merry pinched his arm and he jerked it away with a yelp. "Hey!"

"What I mean is, I heard about you two at Brews and Chews. I thought you should know I wholeheartedly approve. Noel is perfect for you and we all love her, so we wouldn't talk shit about her behind your back like we did with your ex."

He huffed with exasperation. "Why did no one except Noel ever tell me how they really felt about Amber?"

"If we actually thought you'd marry the succubus, we would have."

Nick burst out laughing. "Succubus? Really?"

"Absolutely. I know you can't see it, but she is a soul sucker. Had you married her..." Merry gave an exaggerated shiver and squeezed his arm. "You got out just in time."

Noel caught up to them on the walkway, snow clinging to her beanie and lashes. "Got out of what?"

"I was just telling my dear brother that Amber dumping him was a good thing. She would have drained his life force and bank account if he'd stayed with her, before leaving him for a gym rat with roid rages and a low sperm count. Let's just hope she sticks with such a man so she doesn't reproduce."

Noel bit her lip, but Nick could tell she was fighting a smile.

"I appreciate everyone using my love life as a punch line."

Noel threw her gloved hands up. "I didn't say a word."

"Today," Nick said.

Noel stuck her tongue out at him and his gaze locked on her mouth when it receded, her pink lips glossy.

"Actually, all my punches have been aimed at Amber, not you," Merry clarified.

"Oh, for the love of God!" Nick roared.

"Maybe we shouldn't bring up the *A* word anymore," Noel teased. "It tends to make him testy."

"He's just like that with me." Before he could agree, Merry clapped her hands. "Okay, I'm going inside to make some hot chocolate and a snack before we get this show on the road. You two coming or what?"

"Be right in. I need to talk to Noel."

"Ooooh!" Merry drew out the letter before racing into the house.

"What was that about?"

Nick cleared his throat. "Word got back to my family about us."

"Oh crap." The way she worried her bottom lip drew his gaze back to her mouth. "What did you say?"

What did I say about what? Shit. I was thinking about kissing her again and forgot what I was saying.

"Nick? What did you tell to your family about us?"

I need to get it together.

"I told my mom it was just a rumor. Didn't get the chance to set Merry straight."

"Oh, thank God. I worry about your parents more than your sisters." Noel brushed a snowflake from her cheek, her gaze locked on his. "How are you otherwise?"

"I'm awesome. I actually got an apartment."

"Really? That's amazing! Where at?"

"A few doors down from you, actually."

"Wow that's...that's fantastic." She chuckled weakly. "I'll have to borrow a cup of sugar when you get settled."

Crap, was Noel upset he'd rented a place near her? He didn't think she'd have a problem with it, but maybe with everything going on, she needed space.

"I'm sorry I didn't tell you on Thursday, but I was a bit distracted."

"You don't have to be sorry. Having you close by will be nice."

Relief rushed though him and he grinned. "In that case, would you want to come over next Saturday and help me move? The guys will be there."

"I would, but I'm going with Gabby to do some shopping."

"Ah, no problem. You can help me unpack."

Noel gave him a gentle shove. "Excuse you? No asking, just assuming?"

"Please help me unpack my stuff."

"Maybe."

He pretended to wipe a tear from his eyes. "That hurts."

Noel wrapped her arms around his waist with a laugh. "Oh, don't cry. I'll help you...for a Klondike bar."

"Damn, you're easy. I would have easily thrown in Chinese food." Nick found himself counting the dark flecks in Noel's eyes, tracing the lines of her face until his hand came up to cup her cheek.

Her eyes widened, dropping down to the area of his mouth. Then, just as suddenly, she patted his lower back and released him. "We better get inside. Lots of rehearsing to do."

Nick shook himself out of his trance when Noel passed him, following her into the house. He closed the door behind him, trying not to look at Noel's ass as she hung up her puffy coat, exposing another pair of butt-hugging jeans. He'd always thought Noel was beautiful, but this obsession with her various body parts was distracting.

He couldn't seem to take his eyes off her. Her dark hair fell in a messy braid, a stark contrast with the white off-the-shoulder sweater she wore. Casually feminine without being obvious. Noel had always been no frills, which was why hanging with her had always been so easy and enjoyable.

"Ahhh, there you are. Took you long enough."

"Your brother tried to rope me into manual labor, but I evaded his attempts. For the most part."

"Hmm, he is quite nefarious when he wants something."

"Hey, now, no ganging up on me!"

"Speaking of my brother's attributes, Noel..." Merry batted her eyelashes innocently. "What do you think?"

Noel's eyes widened. "Think about his...attributes?"

Nick glared at his sister. "Mer, what are you doing?"

"I'm asking her a simple question. What does she think of you?"

Noel glanced between the two of them, her gaze lingering on him briefly before she answered, "I think he is a really good friend."

"Boring," Merry scoffed. "I mean, do you ever think of him as a man? Like the two of you could ride off into the sunset together?"

Noel's face turned cherry red and Nick growled, "For the love of God, Merry, shut up."

"No, it's okay." Noel went to the fridge and grabbed a water inside, obviously over her initial embarrassment. "I think your brother is handsome, intelligent, fun, stubborn, annoying, and my best friend."

Merry's face fell. "So, no attraction then?"

Nick caught her nervous glance. "We're just friends."

Friends don't kiss like we do, he thought.

Thankfully, his sister didn't pick up on the tension between them and huffed. "Fine. I figured if you two could make a love connection, then all your problems would be solved. Nick could find a great girl to settle down with and we could officially call you a Winters."

Noel's eyes glistened for a minute and Nick knew his sister's words hit a sore spot, no matter how unintentional. "That is really sweet." She cleared her throat. "I need to use the bathroom."

Nick glared at Merry, who stared back, eyes wide. "What did I say?"

"You don't talk about family with Noel."

Merry's eyes lowered, abashed. "Oh. I didn't think. It's been so long…"

"Not for her." Nick squeezed Merry's shoulder as he passed. "I know you meant well, Mer."

He made his way down the hall to the bathroom and leaned against the opposite wall, waiting for Noel to come out. When she finally did, he wasn't surprised to find her eyes red and teary.

"It's a compliment, you know. She loves you."

"I know," she said, wiping at her tear stained cheeks. "I love everyone in your family. I just don't like feeling as though I'm replacing my parents."

Nick pulled her into his arms and held her close. "You're not and no one would ever think that."

Noel returned his embrace, sniffling against his chest. "*I* feel that way."

He squeezed a little tighter. "I understand, but please know, my parents and sisters aren't trying to make you forget your parents."

"No, I do that all on my own because it hurts too much to think of them."

"If you feel that way, then why are you doing the Christmas concert?"

"I didn't want to disappoint your mom. Plus, it's been ten years…a concert shouldn't render me catatonic, right?"

Nick hesitated, putting himself in Noel's shoes. Would he be over losing his parents at sixteen? Just imagining it hurt, but the reality of it would be devastating.

"I don't know. I'm not you, so I can't tell you how to feel."

"I feel...so lost sometimes, you know?" Her teary eyes lifted to meet his. "I threw myself into the army, then college, and work... kept busy so I wouldn't have to think about them. Miss them. I don't fall in love, because every new person I invite into my life reminds me of the empty places they left behind in my heart." Noel hugged him harder, burying her face in his shirt again so her voice came out muffled. "God, I don't know what is wrong with me. This is the second time I've gotten weepy in the last week."

"Noel, I don't want to upset you, but I'm worried."

"About me? Why?"

"Your barren apartment, for one thing. There isn't a trace of your parents anywhere. I know you went through grief your own way when they died, but maybe you should talk to someone."

Noel pushed back a bit, frowning at him. "Your mom made me go to a therapist, Nick. Remember? Standing appointment every Wednesday until I left for basic."

"I'm saying maybe it would help to go as an adult. You shouldn't cut yourself off from your past or limit your future."

"I keep you around, don't I? You're a part of my past. Your family is my past. Pike and Anthony. Gabby. Just because I don't want reminders of my parents around my apartment doesn't mean I didn't grieve them or move on. I just did it my own way."

"All right, I'm sorry. I won't bring it up again."

Noel relaxed against him and he breathed a sigh of relief.

Talking about her parents tended to be tricky and the last thing he wanted to do was upset her when they were on such unstable ground.

"It's okay. I appreciate you care. I worry about you too. I'm really glad you aren't going back overseas. You have no idea how scared I was every time your mom called or I didn't hear from you."

He held her a little tighter. "I'm sorry you were worried about me."

Noel shrugged. "We both had our reasons for going in. I know it was your job. That you needed to stay in longer. I wanted to be supportive, but I am not gonna lie. I'm happy you're staying put."

Nick brushed his lips against her temple. "Thank you. I know my mom didn't want me reenlisting, but like you said, I needed to do it. Plus, it paid for my education and now I have a great job where I can stay here most of the time and be with my family. I'm lucky." Nick made a face. "Even though my mother roped me into playing guitar for the Christmas concert."

Noel pulled away, wide-eyed. "But you hate performing in public."

"Yeah, but when my mom asks for a favor...let's just say the mom guilt was heavy with this one."

Noel laughed. "Oh yeah, Victoria can lay it on thick without you even realizing what's happening. Then she's got you hooked."

"So, no issues with me being in the band then?"

"Not at all. I'll feel better having you up there with me."

Her words sent a jolt through him and he took a deep breath, burying his face in the crook of her neck. Her breath rushed out, rustling along his skin.

"Nick…"

"Yeah?"

"Hey! What are you two doing down there?" Merry's voice carried down the hall from the kitchen.

Noel pulled away slowly, seeming reluctant to let him go and in that moment, he could have throttled his sister.

"Talking! Be right there." She cleared her throat. "Holly will be here soon, so we should get set up."

"Sure. I'm going to get changed first."

Nick took the sharp right into his room and shut the door. His dick pushed so hard against the front of his jeans it seemed like it would snap in two. God, what was she doing to him? How could something so little as touching her cause him to nearly explode?

He stripped down, thinking about unpleasant things, anything to make the hard-on dissipate. It took remembering the time Anthony hit a line drive into his nut sack before it disappeared. Once he had on dry clothes, he padded down the hallway to find Noel leaning against the counter, watching Merry make a sandwich.

"Well, you clean up nice," Merry joked.

Nick grinned. "I know."

Noel snagged a slice of turkey and popped it into her mouth. "That looks good."

"I'll make you one. Nick? You hungry?"

"Nah, thanks." Nick stood back, watching his sister and Noel ease back into a comfortable relationship, laughing and talking, and he couldn't help thinking about what Merry said about Noel being perfect for him. His parents loved her. She shared the same friends with him. She was fun to be around and called him on his bullshit. She was beautiful. Independent. Funny. Sexy.

Nick went to the sink and splashed some cold water on his face. Was he actually still thinking about this? What happened to them going back to the way things were?

All because of a couple of stupid kisses.

"Ummm, are you okay?"

Nick realized his sister and Noel were staring at him as though he'd lost his damn mind. He grabbed a dish towel out of the drawer and dried his face. "Yeah, I just got hot all of a sudden."

"Like a fever?" Merry asked.

Noel put the back of her hand to his forehead, frowning. "Are you getting sick?"

"No, I...not like that..."

Noel watched him with confusion, while Merry held up her fingers like a cross. "If you're getting something, then stay back, foul demon. I do not want any creepy crud!"

The front door opened, saving him from any more awkward explanations. Holly came in loaded down with bags and breathing hard.

"Whew, I made it a little early! I asked Reese to close down the store so you didn't have to hold rehearsal for me. Is Frank here yet?"

"Actually, Frank got hurt." Merry pointed her knife toward him. "Nick agreed to take his place after Mom threatened him. But I think he's coming down with something."

"Ew, what's he got? Nothing snotty, right?" Holly backed up a step and Nick threw up his hands in exasperation. He was a grown man, not a ten-year-old still scared of his mama or a diseased creature.

"She did not threaten me and I am not sick! I just got a little overheated is all."

"Uh-huh. Is it a stage fright thing?" Holly quirked a brow. "Not going to freak out and puke on us, are you, big brother?"

Nick glared at his sister's reminder of the fifth-grade talent show. "I'll be fine."

"Great," Merry said, taking a large bite of her sandwich. "We'll finish these in the basement."

Noel held half her sandwich out to him. "Here. I know you said you didn't want one, but I won't finish this."

Nick took the sandwich, their fingers grazing. The simple touch sent a shock wave down his arm and to cover up his reaction, he tapped the end of his sandwich to hers. "Cheers. Thanks."

They filed down to the basement while Nick grabbed his guitar and amp from his room. All reminders of Amber had been purged and placed into a box to be returned to her. All that was left were snapshots of family and friends. He hadn't dated much in high school, so there were no other girlfriends. In nearly every photo, Noel smiled back at the camera by his side.

Studying the collage of photos, Nick agreed with Merry. They did look good together.

Damn, he was driving himself nuts. He shoved the last two bites of his sandwich into his mouth and grabbed his instrument and equipment. When he cleared the stairs, Merry sat behind her drum set, tapping the skins. Holly strummed her bass and threw her hand up in a *rock on* symbol.

Noel stood in front of the mic, making weird noises in her throat.

"What are you doing?" he laughed.

"Vocal warm-ups."

"You sound like an angry turtle."

She flipped him off.

Nick chuckled as he got his stuff set up. When he finally stood up, guitar in hand, Noel glanced his way. "You ready?"

"Sure. What's the set list?"

"The same one my parents performed every year," Noel said softly.

Nick watched her expression, searching for any sheen of tears, but she looked away from him, down at the mic.

Holly handed him sheet music for "Holly Jolly Christmas".

"I'll get you a copy of the set list and a flash drive of the music so you can practice."

"Thanks, sis."

Merry counted them off and launched into a steady drumbeat. When Noel missed her cue, they stopped playing.

"Noel?" Merry called. "You ready, sweets?"

Noel's knuckles were white, she gripped the mic so hard. Nick took a step toward her, but she shook her head. "I'm ready. Really. Let's go again."

Merry flashed him a concerned look but counted off once more.

Noel's smooth soprano sang "Have a holly, jolly Christmas," all while tapping the side of her leg. Nick almost missed a chord, surprised at how amazing she sounded. He'd heard her sing during caroling when they were younger and the occasional humming after her parents passed, but now she sang with confidence. Slowly a bright smile spread across her face. Her cheeks deepened to a rosy hue and he couldn't take his eyes off her.

When she got to the bridge, Nick added his vocals with hers and she turned his way, her eyes sparkling. They finished directly facing each other, both breathing hard, and Holly whooped.

"That was great!"

Noel laughed breathlessly. "Yeah it was."

"You two sound awesome together," Merry piped in, a sheepish grin on her face.

Nick ignored her, his attention on Noel. "What's next?"

"'Baby, It's Cold Outside.'"

It was his mother's favorite song and Nick knew the chords without sheet music. "Let's do it."

Merry led them in again and to Nick's surprise, Noel took the mic off the stand and sashayed over to him. Only a few inches separated them as they sang the duet, eyes locked. When Nick sang about her lips, he took a step toward her.

Noel leaned into him, swaying close enough he could feel her body heat. Their voices trailed off on the last line and a heavy silence fell around them, their breathing the only sound in the room. Nick's body hummed with adrenaline and tingles spread across his skin as Noel's hand pressed against his arm.

"You two look like you're about to jump each other," Holly said, breaking the spell.

Noel fled back to her podium like she had wings on her feet.

By the expression on her face, he could tell she was just as caught up as he was.

"Should we move onto the next song or do that one again?" Merry asked.

Nick shot her a glare, wondering if his mother would actually miss her middle child. "I think we got it."

CHAPTER 12

NOEL

A SUDDEN WEIGHT DROPPED DOWN on Noel's bed, startling her out of sound sleep. She sat up with a gasp, blinking against the bright light surrounding her.

"Wake up, woman, we have a date!" Gabby crowed.

Noel groaned, rolling away from her bestie. "Ten more minutes. I spent all night calming pregnant women and helping deliver beautiful babies."

Gabby shook her shoulder. "Which is commendable, but still doesn't change the fact that we made plans for Tuesday, December First. I even let you sleep in an extra hour!"

Noel glanced at the clock. "One p.m. Thanks for that."

"You're welcome." Gabby gave her a smack on her rear. "Now stow the sarcasm and get up! It's time to shit, shower, and shove off."

Noel laughed hoarsely, despite every nerve ending in her body dying to go back to bed. They'd made plans to do some Christmas and wedding shopping, but six hours of sleep didn't feel like enough. This overnight schedule was kicking her rear. Thank God it would only be a few weeks, until her coworker, Laura, returned from vacation.

"That sounds like something your dad would say," Noel remarked.

"Daddy taught me how to curse and change a tire and Mama taught me everything else. Now scoot!"

Slowly Noel crawled out of her bed and did as Gabby commanded. As she absently washed her hair, she hummed softly to herself. Before she realized it, she was singing "Baby, It's Cold Outside." Noel knew it was Victoria's favorite song, but Noel had never really cared for it until recently. Hearing Nick's voice in her head, crooning to her. His baritone washing over her body like the warm water sliding down her frame.

Her nipples peaked and she leaned her head back against the tile, sighing. Nick had become a constant turn-on for her and she didn't know what to do about it. She hadn't had sex in three weeks. If this kept up, Noel would need to order a new vibrator at the rate she'd been entertaining herself and her fantasies about Nick. Although she agreed with him that keeping things between them platonic was for the best, it didn't stop her from longing for him.

Longing, bah. When had she turned into a sex-starved heroine in a historical romance novel?

By the time she climbed into the passenger seat of Gabby's Subaru, she felt less like a zombie, although she hadn't bothered with makeup or drying her hair. Besides, if they hurried, maybe she could take another nap before work.

"Don't you wanna blow dry your hair?"

Noel shot her a disgruntled look. "I don't have the energy."

"I thought you have pictures with the Winterses this afternoon..."

Crap. She'd completely forgotten about the family photo session.

"I'll let it air dry and curl it before I head over. Now, caffeinate me."

"Aye, aye." Gabby put the car into gear and headed into town. Noel stared out the window drowsily, homes and trees zooming past.

"Sooo?" Gabby drawled.

Noel turned to look at her. "So what?"

"How is Nick?"

She shifted in the seat, avoiding Gabby's gaze. After their chemistry overload on Saturday, Noel feigned a sore throat on Sunday and Monday. She wasn't scared of Nick. It was the incredible draw to him that had her freaking out. The last thing she wanted was Gabby getting involved in their already complicated situation. She'd scheme her little heart out until she had them hooked, lined, and married. But Noel couldn't do that to him. Even if they tried being more than friends and enjoyed each other, they wanted completely different futures.

"Nick is fine."

"Ugh, every girl in Mistletoe knows he is fine. Only you have been immune, until now." Gabby elbowed her playfully. "You two still pretending you're knocking boots? Fooling the whole town?"

"No, we decided it would be better if we went back to just friends."

"Why is that?"

Things were getting too intense and I panicked? Noel thought.

"Because next to you, Pike, Anthony, and the rest of the Winterses, Nick is the most important person in the world to me. I would hate for any of this to blow up our friendship."

Gabby pursed her full glossy lips. "Sounds to me like you're scared to take a real leap with Nick."

"I'm not scared. I don't *want* to. I love Nick, but he's just so…"

"Hot. Funny. Sweet." Gabby laughed. "Yeah, you're right. Those are terrible qualities in a lover."

Noel made a face. "Ugh, don't use that word."

"Hey, if it was good enough for the Spice Girls, it's good enough for me." Gabby burst out in an off-key rendition of "Wannabe."

"You are so crazy." Gabby always made her laugh, even in the darkest of times. She'd been a rainbow after her parents passed and Noel didn't know what she'd do without her.

"Part of my charm."

"Save your charm for Drew."

"I got enough to go around." Gabby shot her a sidelong look. "For real though. What's up with you two?"

Noel leaned her head back against the seat with a sigh. "I wish I knew. Everything has been weird since the kiss at the bar."

"Weird how?"

She bit her lip, afraid to say the words out loud. "Like I can't stop thinking about doing it again. And not stopping with just a kiss."

Gabby squealed, dancing in the driver's seat. "Girl, you've got it bad! Just give in already. I think you two would be great together."

"Except that he is a kind, handsome, patient, amazing guy and I'm a snarky, antisocial, impatient commitment-phobe."

"Come on, Nick has flaws, same as you, and you forgot to mention that you're caring, loyal, fierce, strong—"

"Gabs, you know how I feel about happily ever after. I have no plans to get married or have kids. Nick is the long-haul guy, which makes me want to run for the hills. And if I do that, it won't just hurt him, but destroy what we have."

"We can always attach some weights to your feet." She winked. "Should slow you down long enough for him to catch you."

Noel scowled at her. "I'm being serious. Nick and I have been in each other's lives since birth. Losing him would be like losing a kidney. Getting involved romantically is out of the question. Besides, he just got out of an eight-year relationship with your buddy Amber. Shouldn't you be telling me to stay away?"

"No, because Amber made the decision to dump Nick. I told her not to. Guys like Nick and my Drew come around so seldom that we need to snatch them up. If Nick had done the dumping, I may suggest you wait until after my wedding to make a move just to save me the drama, but eh."

Noel tapped her fingers against the dashboard nervously. "Can I ask you something?"

"Always."

"Why are you still friends with her? I never understood what it was about her in high school. I know she couldn't stand me, but…"

Noel trailed off, not wanting to make this about her. "She's left you hanging so many times. You're about to be married and she is talking you into wild bachelorette parties with strippers and—"

"Hey now, why are you bagging on strippers so much? Don't act like we didn't watch Magic Mike on repeat for years."

"Whoa, wait a second. First of all, we are talking about a movie with Channing Tatum. Real-life strippers are sweaty, probably stinky, all up in your personal space putting their head in your crotch, their G-string-covered dick in your face, and throwing you around like a rag doll."

"You say the last part like it's a bad thing." Gabby giggled, poking Noel in the side. "Seriously, you're not usually a judgmental sour puss. Is it just because it was Amber's idea? To be honest, I would have loved to head to Vegas for the weekend and seen the *Thunder Down Under* show, but we are in a bit of a time crunch."

Noel cracked a smile at Gabby's terrible Australian accent. "Okay, I may be a little harsher about the idea because it came from her. But, ugh, she bugs me. Before you showed up at brunch, she was giving me a bad time about Nick. Insinuating that I wasn't good enough for him."

"What?" Gabby put her hand on Noel's knee and squeezed, keeping the other on the wheel. "I'll talk to her. No one makes my Noelie feel less than amazing."

"I didn't tell you because I wanted you to talk to her. I appreciated you stepping in while we were in school, but I am a grown woman. I can fight my battles. I would just like to understand how someone so…" *Heinous? Spoiled? Bitchy?* "Difficult could win over awesome people like you and Nick."

Gabby shrugged. "I mean…Amber has her flaws and we don't hang like we used to, but she'd also had a lot going on in her personal life. If you'd seen some of the knock-down drag-outs her parents get into, you'd feel bad for her. Her dad is a total douche and tears her self-esteem to shreds, then turns around and buys her everything she wants to make up for it. I'm not excusing her being a shit to you and you can bet I *will* talk to her, but besides you, she's my oldest friend. Has our relationship always been perfect, hell no. But I still want her standing up with me on my wedding day. Could you try to get along with her?"

Noel leaned across the middle and laid her head on Gabby's shoulder, sighing loudly. "Yes, I can be nice. For you."

"And the strippers?"

"Sounds like fun."

Gabby kissed the top of her head with gusto. "There's my girlie! Now, back to your love life."

"No. No to Nick. Not going there." *At least, I'm going to do my best not to.*

Gabby grunted. "All right, no Nick. Still, you should open yourself up to the possibility of love and commitment." Using one hand to frame her own face, Gabby beamed and fluttered her eyelashes. "It's done wonders for me."

Sadness rushed through Noel as she thought about joyful times from her childhood. Dreams of happily ever after, like the love her parents shared, had died with them. Now, the thought of caring that much sent her into a blind panic.

There was a time when she'd dreamed about marriage and kids. The man she loved would ask her father's permission and after a bit of teasing, he'd give it. They'd spend months planning it and the day of, her dad would walk her down the aisle. Her mother would stand up at the ceremony and read the poem that Noel's grandmother read when her parents got married. She'd dance with her dad to some cheesy song and he'd pretend he wasn't crying even as he wiped his eyes...

Even if she found someone to love, she couldn't imagine getting married without them. Of having children. Finding happiness only to lose it?

Life gave out no guarantees. She knew that better than anyone.

"Maybe I'm just not the girl with the white picket fence and the happily ever after."

"You really don't want to have a family one day?"

Noel wished she could tell Gabby to drop it without hurting her friend's feelings, but maybe if she was clear, Gabby wouldn't bring it up again.

"I had a family and they died. I spend half my time delivering babies and being there for the good and the bad. When people lose spouses and children, it's like watching a part of their soul die. I think...if I let myself fall like that...it would destroy what was left of me."

Gabby reached across the seat and squeezed her hand. "I know how hard it was losing your parents, but love and loss are a part of life. You already love me. Nick. The Winterses. If we die, you'll still get hurt, but that doesn't stop you from being there for us."

"I don't know how to explain it. Losing my parents, I'm prepared for loss but I don't want to take on anyone else. I don't want my feelings for anyone to grow. And then when they're gone,

I have another hole in my heart." Trying to lighten the mood, she added, "Besides, many people go through life without love. Jane Austen wrote amazing books about love and remained unmarried."

"Are you comparing yourself to one of the most celebrated writers of all time?"

"No, I am simply saying that a woman can find fulfillment without walking down the aisle."

Gabby parked the car. "Well, I personally, cannot wait to see Drew standing at the altar. He is going to look so hot in his tux. I'll be counting down the minutes, but once I get him into the honeymoon suite, roar!"

"TMI, babe." Noel kissed Gabby's cheek. "I am so happy for you. You are going to be the most beautiful bride."

"Heck yeah I am. Now, let's get you coffee and shop till we drop!"

Noel climbed out and followed Gabby into the coffee shop. The lunch rush was winding down and only a few people were inside sipping their drinks. Scrolling through their phone or tapping away at a laptop. Gabby picked out two cute travel mugs, one in a camo design and the other blue with pink flowers. Both had the shape of Idaho on them. She set them on the counter next to the register, smiling at the barista, Jenny Guthrie.

"Boom. Sup, Jenny."

Jenny laughed, tucking a strand of dark hair behind her ear. "Not much. What are you guys up to?"

"Just a little Christmas shopping. These plus a bag of your breakfast blend, a skinny vanilla latte, and whatever she wants," Gabby said, pointing at Noel.

While Jenny tapped into the computer, Noel pulled out a ten and shoved it into Gabby's purse, ignoring her protests. "I'll take an everything bagel with cream cheese and a black coffee with cream."

Gabby shot her a disgusted look. "An everything bagel and no sugar in your coffee? Girl, you're gonna have some nasty stank breath."

Noel breathed in Gabby's face and she pretended to faint. Jenny giggled.

"You two act like my sister and me. That will be thirty-eight dollars and sixty-five cents."

Gabby handed Jenny her card and then looped one arm through Noel's. "Close enough. She is my sister from another mister."

Noel laughed, shaking her head. Jenny handed Gabby her card and bagged up the cups and coffee before walking away to help fill their order.

"So, I'm kind of glad you dragged me out today," said Noel.

"I knew you would be." Gabby held up her purchases proudly. "This takes care of my soon-to-be sister-in-law and her husband. Who is on your list?"

"You. Nick. I need two for him, since his birthday is Friday. I usually buy Pike and Anthony a little something. Victoria, Chris, Merry, and Holly. We do a Secret Santa at work, but other than that, I am good."

Jenny called out their names for their coffee and bagel. Once they had their sustenance in hand, Noel held the door for Gabby as they passed through.

"Let's go to A Store for All Seasons. I want to get a few ornaments for our tree. Maybe a cute wedding one."

NICK AND NOEL'S CHRISTMAS PLAYLIST 141

Noel's cheeks flamed at the mention of Holly Winters's store. Neither Winters sister had been shy about commenting on the chemistry between their elder brother and Noel during their duet on Saturday. Merry texted Noel after she left Saturday and ordered her to take the plunge with Nick. Holly wasn't quite as forward, but she could only imagine what would come up in front of Gabby and then she'd get it from all directions.

"Maybe we could do that another day?" Noel suggested.

Gabby stopped and turned to her, one perfectly painted brow arched. "But you love A Store for All Seasons."

"I do, but there are a bunch of stores we never hit. I was thinking it might be nice to dispense our money evenly among the local businesses."

"Uh-huh," Gabby said.

By the look on Gabby's face, Noel knew she wasn't getting out of this one. "Fine, fine. We will play favorites."

"I feel like you're avoiding Holly for some unknown reason."

"No, that's not it. I was just trying to be a good neighbor. Not put our chickens in one basket." Gabby kept staring at her without blinking and Noel finally groaned, "Can't you just accept that going to her shop is going to make things awkward for me without knowing all the details?"

"Nope. You're hiding secrets from me. Wild horses couldn't keep me from finding out what they are."

Gabby skipped ahead of her gleefully and Noel ground her teeth in irritation. She caught up to Gabby around the corner, standing in front of the large window of A Shop for All Seasons. The store title painted across the glass window in classic gold lettering, with snow-covered trees ate up the space around the script. A beautiful green wreath adorned the front door, with silver, gold, and white baubles decorating the evergreen circle. It was a welcoming store front, but Noel's stomach knotted nervously.

Gabby grabbed the door and held it for her. "After you, my dear."

Noel stepped over the threshold, the smell of cinnamon tickling her nostrils. Holiday music played merrily. Shelves of knickknacks and décor lined the walls and center of the shop, with two brightly lit Christmas trees set up in the far corners. Ornaments hung from every branch. In a separate room off the back, two long tables sat parallel. Once a week, sometimes more, Holly hosted how-to classes people could pay to attend. She taught them how to make various holiday décor, which were quite popular among the women of Mistletoe because tasting local wines was usually included. Noel took a few over the years and loved them, although her creations ended up in a Christmas tote she never opened.

Holly leaned against the counter by the computer, speaking to Declan Gallagher. Declan's family owned Mistletoe Hardware, located next door to Holly's shop, and from the expressions on their faces, Noel figured they were having quite the disagreement.

Declan's face flushed red above his brown beard, his burly arms crossed over his flannel-clad chest. "I only asked you to turn down that annoying crap. The walls are thin and I can hear every holly fucking jolly ring-a-ding-ding!"

"Like I told you, Mr. Grinch," Holly snapped, tossing her long red hair over her shoulder, "plug your ears if it bothers you, but the music is at a perfectly acceptable volume. So take your bah humbug attitude, and shove it up your bahookie!"

Gabby burst out laughing. "Yeah! You tell em, Holly!"

Holly and Declan swung their way, as though completely oblivious to their presence before she spoke.

"Hi ladies," Holly greeted them cheerfully.

"Hey, everything okay here?" Noel asked.

Declan nodded gruffly. "I was just leaving."

He turned his back on Holly and headed toward Noel and Gabby. Holly called out louder than necessary, "You have a wonderful day, Scrooge!"

Noel thought she caught a smile on Declan's face, but the way he slammed out the door, she must have been mistaken.

"That visit seemed friendly," Gabby said.

Holly came around the corner, waving her hand casually. "Just a little neighborly spat. Nothing I can't handle." Holly grinned at Noel. "So, given any thought to being our official sister yet?"

Gabby glanced at Noel, confusion written all over her face. "What's this now?"

"Nothing."

Gabby's eyes widened. "Wait, did Nick ask you to..." Gabby hummed the wedding march and Noel groaned.

"Of course not. Does Nick seem crazy to you?"

Gabby poked her in the arm. "Whoa, hold up, it is not crazy to want to get married."

"Not when you have been together for years, but Nick asking me now? Lunacy."

"Not really," Holly interjected. "You've been friends since you were babies. It actually makes a lot of sense."

"Friendship is different than being in a romantic partnership, and you are not helping!"

"Actually, it's beneficial that the two of you were friends first. Makes for a solid foundation for romance." Gabby winked at Holly, who nodded enthusiastically.

"Absolutely!"

"There is nothing going on with Nick and me."

"I beg to differ!" Holly ignored her warning look and continued, "Nick and Noel are singing together for the Christmas concert and when I say the heat between them is scorching, I do not exaggerate."

"Oooohhhh," Gabby drawled. "You thinking what I'm thinking?"

"Lock 'em in a cabin together for the weekend with no way to escape?" Holly teased.

"Why are all of you so obsessed with getting Nick and me together? The thought never struck you before, so why are you pushing me now?"

Holly raised her hand. "Hi, yeah, actually, Merry and I have been shipping this for years. We just had to wait until Amber was out of the picture to bring the matter to light."

Gabby held her fist up for Holly to punch. "#TeamNock all the way."

"You people need to get a life," Noel grumbled, taking a turn toward the baking aisle. She picked up a cute cake pan, fully intent on ignoring the two busybodies for the rest of the day if need be.

Gabby trailed after her. "We're just trying to help you out!"

"Let me be perfectly clear." Noel stopped and faced both of them, sternly meeting first Gabby's, then Holly's gaze. "Nick and I are friends. That is all we want to be. So, no cabins, no plots, twists, hints, or hashtagging terrible name mashups. We are perfect the way we are. Capiche?"

Gabby mumbled affirmative but Holly held her hands up. "I make no promises. All's fair in love and family. And there is nobody else more suited for my brother than *you*."

Her traitorous friend stroked her chin thoughtfully. "The girl does have a point."

Noel groaned, realizing that the only way to keep her friendship with Nick safe would be to avoid his sisters at all costs.

A little hard to do that when they'd be rehearsing three days a week until the concert.

I'm doomed.

CHAPTER 13

NICK

"I CAN SEE ALL THE way up your nostrils from this angle, man."

Nick laughed, holding his hands out to spot Anthony as he pushed through one more bench press. "Last one and then you can stop examining my nose hairs."

"Thank...*God*!" Anthony's breath whooshed out as he set the bar back on the rack. Nick grabbed the spray bottle and a handful of paper towels to wipe down the equipment.

"Ah come on. You don't like my sweat."

"Sorry, laying on a bench covered in another dude's juice is nasty."

Anthony punched him in the shoulder good-naturedly. "You'd be lucky to roll around in my juice. Might help you get your mojo back."

Nick scoffed as he slid onto the bench and gripped the bar in his hands. "There is nothing wrong with my mojo."

Taking a deep breath, he lifted and pumped.

"That's the way. Getting swole."

He laughed, a breathless wheeze between his teeth as his muscles strained under the weight. After being the scrawny kid most of his adolescence, he loved the sensation of working out. It's why he hadn't wasted any time signing up for a membership at Toe the Line Fitness. Anthony enjoyed working out as much as he did and would keep him honest.

When he finished his last rep, he grunted as he set the bar back in place.

"Isn't Pike meeting us?"

"Nah, he had to skip it. He's been pulling a lot of late nights and dragging ass at work. Called him out on it a few times, but he won't tell me what he's up to."

Pike worked on the road crew with Anthony during the week, but while Pike hadn't been interested in going to college, Anthony took several online classes every semester. It took him a little longer, but he would have his bachelor's degree after this semester.

"Maybe he's got a new girl?"

Anthony sneered. "Please, if he was getting laid, he'd be giving us a play-by-play."

"That's disturbing, but accurate," Nick said.

"You know he's into Noel, right?"

Nick stilled at his friend's bluntness. "I didn't know for sure."

"He's been carrying a torch for years, but she keeps him strictly in the friend zone. Just thought you should know."

"While I appreciate the heads up, nothing is going on with Noel. Not officially, anyway."

"Officially or not, I saw the way you two reacted to each other at Brews and Chews. Even if y'all aren't ready to admit it, there is something there. I'm only telling you about Pike so you'll have a care with how you handle it."

"I will." Nick hesitated, feeling a little vulnerable asking, but he needed to talk to someone and of his two male friends, Anthony was less likely to razz him too hard. "You really think she's into me?"

Anthony took a drink, studying Nick over his water bottle. He snapped the lid closed before answering. "You don't see the way she looks at you?"

"No."

"I know you and Noel have been close since the cradle, but you've been gone a while. We hang with her several times a week and I can say with confidence that Noel has always held you in a separate league than Pike or myself. She talks about you and her whole face lights up. She may not want to admit it, but her feelings go deeper than friendship." Anthony grinned. "Probably why she dogs on Amber so hard."

"I think that has more to do with their history than with me."

"Maybe so. Still, pretty sure it burned her bad that you fell for her nemesis. I know I'd have a hard time admitting my feelings for a woman who dated Tim Bateman before me." Anthony's face twisted into a harsh grimace. "That douche left a permanent indent in my ass crack from all the seventh-grade wedgies he gave me, before my brothers kicked his ass."

Anthony's insight left Nick defensive. He never meant to hurt Noel, but his friend's point of view made him feel like he should be apologizing. "It's not like I never thought about taking that next step with Noel. She didn't give me any indication she wanted me, even before Amber."

"Or she did and you couldn't see it because you're too close to the situation. The view is always better with a little distance."

Nick thought about all the times he'd given his sisters advice, simply because he was an outsider looking in and groaned, "You're right."

"Damn right I'm right."

Nick picked up his phone next to his water bottle and cursed. "I gotta go."

"Where are you running off to?"

"My mom booked a photographer to take family pictures this afternoon. I have just enough time to get home and shower before they get started."

"All right, I'll see you Thursday then. Same time." Anthony held out his hand and Nick took it, bringing him in for a hard hug.

"Thanks for the talk, bud."

"First one's free. After that, we'll need to discuss my hourly rate."

"Yeah, right."

Nick followed Anthony into the men's locker room and wasn't surprised to find Trip inside. He stood shirtless by his open locker and when he spotted Nick, he puffed out his massive, bald chest.

"Winters." Did his pecs just bounce?

"Sup, Trip."

"Nothing, just getting ready to hit the weights. Gotta keep these guns up." Trip flexed his arm and kissed the bicep.

Nick caught Anthony's *WTF* expression and barely caught a laugh.

"Something funny?" Trip asked.

"Nah, man. Have a good time."

"You know I will." Trip pulled on a sleeveless tee and slammed his locker closed. "You seen Noel lately?"

Warily, Nick answered, "Yeah, why?"

"Just curious. I stopped by her place last week." Trip didn't add more, obviously baiting Nick to ask what happened, but he already knew. Nothing.

"Good for you." Nick made an attempt to step around Trip, but the other man blocked his path.

"Are you actually a thing? Or you just hooking up?"

"Why do you care?"

"Just curious what makes you so special." Trip's cold gaze trailed over Nick, conveying with one look he thought Nick wasn't shit.

Nick bristled. "Come again?"

Anthony stepped in front of him, facing Trip. "Maybe you should step off and work out whatever's got you twisted up."

Trip threw his hands up. "I'm just asking. For years guys in this town have been chasing Noel, trying to crack through all her damage and here you come walking back into town, and suddenly she's relationship material?"

Nick stepped around Anthony, putting a reassuring hand on his arm. "Noel's always been relationship material. She was just waiting for the right man."

"And that's you?"

"You think it should have been you instead? Why? You didn't even have the balls to tell her when you started hooking up with someone else so I'll ask again…why do you care?" Nick punctuated every word, keeping his cool when what he really wanted to do was put the puffed-up asshole in his place.

Trip's face flushed purple. "Fuck it. I don't. You can have her. She—"

"You wanna think long and hard about what you're going to say next because that is my friend you're talking 'bout," Anthony growled.

Nick would have felt sorry for Trip if he wasn't resisting the urge to kick his ass. Nick was six-foot-two in his bare feet and Anthony topped him by an inch, plus another thirty pounds of muscle. It made Tony a beast on the football field and growing up as the youngest with four older brothers, he learned how to fight dirty early.

"All I was going to say is that she deserves to be happy," Trip gritted out.

"Don't worry about Noel's happiness. I got it covered."

Trip glared when Nick winked at him. Anthony trailed behind him out of the locker room, catching up when they reached the exit. Even with the sun shining above, there was still a sharp nip in the air and Nick pulled the sweatshirt he'd grabbed from the locker on over his head.

"What a douche."

"Couldn't agree more," Nick said, unlocking his truck. "Thanks for having my back in there."

"Always. Get home before your mom roasts you. See you Thursday!"

"Yep." Nick climbed up into his truck and took the long road through town, honking as he passed A Shop for All Seasons.

Holly's car was still parked down the street, so at least he wasn't running too late.

Nick walked through the door eleven minutes later and found his mom in the living room, folding clothes.

"Hey, Mom."

She shot him an arch look. "The photographer is going to be here in fifteen minutes."

"I know, that's why I'm here. Gonna hop in the shower and get pretty for the camera. It won't take me long." He took off toward the hallway.

"Your shirt is hanging up on the ceiling fan in your room."

He stopped midstride and spun around. "You bought me a shirt?"

His mom didn't even look up at his outraged tone. "Yes. I bought one for you and your father that match."

"Mom, I'm not seven. Being *twinsies*," he raised his voice an octave, "with my dad is just bananas."

She actually pretended to scratch under her armpits and jumped from foot to foot. "Well, then call me Cocoa the Gorilla 'cause this is happening." She picked up the laundry basket and passed by him. "Now go get cleaned up. You stink to high heaven. Are you wearing deodorant?"

"Of course I am!" He sniffed his pits to be sure, an evil grin spreading across his mouth. "Maybe you need to get closer."

Nick raised his arm as he chased after his mother, trying to put his armpit in her face. She screamed with laughter and threw a rolled-up pair of socks at him right before slamming her bedroom door. He heard the click of the lock.

"Get out of here! And bring me any laundry you want washed."

"I can do my own laundry!" Nick shouted, amusement and irritation swirling inside him.

He stomped down to his room and discovered the blue collared shirt hanging exactly where she said it would be. He felt like a kindergartner on his first day of school. His mother hadn't quite discovered that he wasn't eighteen anymore and he'd been out on his own for years. Nick knew she wouldn't stop mothering him when he had his own place, but at least it would curb some of this behavior.

Nick hopped in the shower, scrubbing his hair and body, tracing a hand over the stubble on his jaw. It would be ornery of him to walk out with a five o'clock shadow, so he opted to shave to appease his mother. After he made sure to apply deodorant, he wrapped the towel around his waist and headed back to his room. There was no way his mother could say he stunk now.

The sound of rummaging came from his room and he rolled his eyes. "Mom, I said I could get my own laundry— Noel?"

Noel spun around, dropping his gray laundry basket to the floor. "Oh! Hi!"

"Hey, um...what are you doing in here?"

"Your mom asked me to grab your laundry basket so she could start a full load."

"Son of a...I told her I could do my own laundry."

Noel's eyes darted around the room, her brown hair curled into loose waves. She wore a blue crop T-shirt and jeans.

"Yeah, I was outside the front door when I heard you yelling. I'm just doing what she asked."

Nick groaned. "We all do. Is that what you're wearing?"

"What? No. Your mom said she has a shirt she wants me to wear." Noel pulled on the bottom of her shirt. "Why? You saying I don't look nice?"

"No! I just..." he stammered, running a hand across his wet hair. "You look beautiful. I figured she'd have a shirt picked out for you too."

"She does. I'd say you look nice too, but it might come off a little inappropriate considering you're only sporting a towel."

Her gentle teasing eased the tension in his shoulders and he wiggled his brows. "You can still tell me. It's nothing I haven't heard before."

Noel rolled her eyes.

"Oh boy, when did your head swell so big?" She shook her head as she knelt down, collecting the items that had fallen out of his basket.

He dropped to his knees with her, keeping one hand on the knotted towel at his waist. "Here, I'll get these. You shouldn't be collecting my dirty drawers."

"It's not like I've never done your laundry before, Nick. Even your boxer briefs."

Their hands collided over a pair of his jeans and Nick smoothed his thumb over her knuckle. "Noel, I've been thinking about things with us—"

"Nick! Noel! I have your shirt! I hope you both are decent because Mom says if we aren't outside in two minutes, she's going to disown us all."

Merry's voice carrying down the hallway set Nick's teeth on

edge and he stood up the same time as Noel. Losing his grip on his towel, he scrambled to keep it in place, but his sister's scream gave him a clue he hadn't been entirely successful.

"Oh dear lord, I just saw my brother's butt crack!"

"Go away!" He strode over to the door and slammed it in her face.

"Rude! I'm the one scarred for life!" Something scraped against the other side of his door. "Noel, I'm hanging your shirt on the outside of the door. Hurry up!"

Nick turned his back on the door and leaned his head against it. "Fucking sisters."

Noel held her hands over her face, her shoulders shaking. When she peeked through her fingers, he heard her hysterical laugher echo through the room.

Reluctantly, Nick smirked. "I guess I'd be laughing too if the roles were reversed and you flashed your ass to a sibling."

"I'm sorry," she gasped, bent over with laughter. As if she couldn't hold herself up anymore, she collapsed back on his bed.

"Really making me feel good here, Noel."

She giggled harder. "I...can't...stop..."

Nick grinned devilishly and loosened his hold on the towel. "Well, if you don't actually want to get a show, I suggest you close your eyes. The last thing I need is my mother barging in here and getting the wrong idea."

Noel covered her face again.

"No peeking, now."

"I'm not."

Nick dropped the towel, his heart hammering in his chest.

Even as teens, Nick hadn't kicked Noel out when he changed, because he'd never thought for a second she would look. Why was it this time, he actually wanted her to?

He'd pulled his slacks into place when he caught her gaze in the mirror above his dresser. She sat up on his bed, leaning back on her hands as she watched him. Her dark eyes trailing over him hungrily.

Nick turned around, his body humming. "Thought you weren't going to peek."

"I'm not. I'm brazenly checking you out."

"See, now that isn't fair," he said, crossing the room to stand in front of her. "You can't say things like that to me if you want to be just friends."

"I was just being honest, Nick. We're adults and you're a lot of fun to look at."

"Oh yeah?" Nick leaned over her, waiting for her to pull back. To escape. "How's this for honesty?"

Nick's hand cradled the back of her head, bringing her up just enough to meet his kiss. After a week of thinking about nothing else but her mouth under his, he deepened it, wrapping his other arm around her waist. He lifted her up until she pressed against him and he slipped his tongue into her open mouth. She tasted of mint and smelled of fresh fruit and honey, sweet and delicious.

"Nicholas Christopher Winters! Get out here now!"

His mother banged heavily on the door and he pulled away, reluctantly releasing a dazed Noel from his embrace. Grabbing his shirt from the hanger, he unbuttoned it with shaking hands.

"I'm just putting on my shirt, Mom. Be out in a second."

"You better be!"

Once he had his shirt right, he faced Noel sheepishly. "Guess I'll see you out there."

"Yeah. I guess so."

Nick opened the door and grabbed Noel's shirt off the knob. He waved it in front of him wickedly. "Or, I could stick around."

Noel took the shirt from him with a yank. "And have your mother come back here screaming again? No thank you! I don't know how I'm going to look her in the eye as is."

"I promise, she doesn't suspect a thing." Nick snaked his arm around her and kissed her one more time, his lips barely grazing hers.

He released her with a whispered, "I'll see you out there."

Noel's eyelashes fluttered, her dark eyes heavy.

"NICHOLAS!"

Nick turned away from Noel, a smug smile tugging at his lips. Noel could deny their attraction, but the way she returned his kiss told him all he needed to know.

CHAPTER 14

NOEL

NOEL STOOD OFF TO THE side, watching Nick and his dad pose for a father-son shot, standing back to back with their arms crossed over their chest. They'd already done an all-girls pose with Victoria in the center surrounded by Merry, Holly, and Noel. She'd tried to stay out of it, but Victoria insisted.

The photographer positioned them in front of rows of snow-covered Douglas firs as a backdrop and Noel imagined it would make a beautiful contrast with the light blue of their outfits.

Nick grinned into the camera as his dad wrapped an arm around his shoulders and Noel's heart fluttered when his eyes darted toward her. Her lips still throbbed, remembering his passionate onslaught. From the minute she'd turned around and discovered him naked save for that butter yellow towel around his waist, her skin ran hot with awareness. She'd trailed her eyes along the muscles of his shoulders and back down to the firm globes of his ass. When he'd turned with his pants on and she'd gotten a good look at his rippling abs, she'd nearly drooled. She'd never understood what the term "heated gaze" meant until she met his and it radiated through her like a laser beam.

Then that kiss, whew. Their first kiss left her warm and dreamy but when Nick dropped his mouth to hers, shirtless, in the middle of his bedroom, she'd nearly combusted. A small part of her brain screamed to pull away, to stop and think about what they were doing, but then he'd pressed harder, urgently, and all rational thought went out the window.

Even now, she should be planning on what she would say to him. How they needed to stop this, whatever they were doing. It was getting out of hand.

But as he crossed over the dirt, his long legs eating up the space between them, she had to hold onto the closest tree when her knees buckled.

Weak in the knees?! What was happening to her?

"Enjoying the show?"

"Sure, except when I have to be a part of it."

"Come on," Nick said, putting his hand above hers on the tree trunk and leaning in. "You really hate being involved in all this fun?"

No, she didn't. She'd been happy to smile with Holly and Merry to please Victoria.

"I'm not really someone who poses on cue. With the exception of now and our senior year, I've only ever taken family pictures with my parents."

Nick bent his head, his forehead touching hers and she closed her eyes. He didn't say anything, but that simple touch radiated a unique understanding she'd only ever shared with him.

"Come on you two! We wanna do a group shot and then you're free!" Chris hollered.

Noel opened her eyes, smiling ruefully. "I think your dad is enjoying this more than your mom."

"Probably. He won't admit it, but he's a sentimental guy."

"I've known that for years."

Nick's hand rested against the small of her back, a firm but gentle guide across the uneven ground.

The photographer, Bonnie Rickets, looked up from behind her camera and waved her hand. "All right, Chris and Victoria, you'll be in the middle facing each other but turned out enough to look at the camera. Noel, you'll come in beside Victoria and then Nick beside you. Chris, Holly, and Merry, same thing on the other side. Let's see it."

They lined up as she instructed. Noel looped an arm through Victoria's crooked elbow, squeezing it gently when the older woman smiled back at her and patted her hand. Nick's left hand rested on her hip, stepping close behind her. Bonnie arranged them into the most flattering position, then counted down from three and they all smiled. The camera flashed several times.

"You know, I should have switched places with Merry. Pretty sure this is my bad side," Nick whispered in her ear.

Noel laughed, looking at him over her shoulder. "You don't have a bad side."

"One last time! Three. Two. One." Flash. "Perfect."

Victoria clapped her hands. "Oh, I'm so excited. Chris, would you settle up with her."

"On it, honey." Chris kissed her cheek as he passed by, a

completely natural gesture that left Noel wistful for a moment. Their love was so effortless, the same way her parents were with each other and she couldn't help thinking how nice it would be to have someone to touch. To share little moments with.

Until the moments ended and she was alone again.

Ignoring the heaviness in her belly, she forced a smile.

"Thank you for including me," Noel said.

"Baby, stop that! Get in here and give me a hug." Victoria wrapped her arms around her and squeezed hard. "Have a great day at work and don't forget about Friday."

"I won't."

How could she forget Nick's birthday? It was the first one he'd actually been home for in years.

"I'll walk you to your car," Nick said.

Noel nodded, nervously twisting her hands together as their feet crunched beneath them.

"How would you feel if we met for breakfast tomorrow? My treat."

"Sure, I'd like that. I get off work at six, but it usually takes me a little longer to get out of there. Would seven-thirty be okay?"

"Good for me." He leaned over and kissed her cheek. "Text me when you get to the hospital, okay?"

"I will." Noel climbed into her car, releasing a heady sigh. As she put her car into drive and pulled out onto the street, she contemplated the events of the last two weeks.

When Nick came home, she expected them to pick up where they left off as friends. She'd hoped that Amber wouldn't be a part of the scenario for long, but she'd never dreamed she'd find herself here. Kissing Nick. Having breakfast with Nick. Was this a date? Did she want it to be a date? God, she was like a yo-yo, bouncing back in forth between yes and no.

It wasn't just her own issues that gave her pause. Nick was the total package. He didn't have emotional issues, not the way she did. He saw the best in people and was the first soul to jump in his car to help out a stranger. The wrong person could take advantage of his good nature.

Noel, on the other hand, had enough hang-ups to be a coat rack. Self-esteem issues, emotional issues, attachment issues, commitment issues. The only issue she didn't have was with her sex drive and even someone like her, who wouldn't know a healthy relationship if it bit her on the ass, knew there was more to love than good sex.

God, she didn't want to think about this anymore tonight. She was driving herself crazy.

Noel flipped on the radio and "Complicated" by Carolyn Dawn Johnson blared through the stereo. She turned down the volume slightly, listening to the on-the-nose lyrics with frustration. She pressed the number two button. Colbie Caillat singing sweetly about falling for her best friend. "Lucky" button number three. Weezer's 2005 hit "My Best Friend" was the last straw and she gave up. It seemed the universe was hell-bent on her dealing with her conflicted emotions.

Noel parked two rows back in the employee parking at the hospital. She tossed her small duffle with her uniform, lunch, and snacks over her shoulder, her feet crunching across the freshly strewn salt layer on the asphalt parking lot. She pulled out her phone to text Nick she'd arrived and slipped it into her back pocket. Maybe if they took it really slow, they could see where things go.

Say we are going great and start talking about kids. Do I want to go there?

Noel couldn't imagine Nick not being a father. He was built for it. Like his dad, he was a sentimental softie. Denying him that wouldn't just hurt him. It would eat her up too.

Noel passed by the nursery on the way to the employee lounge, stopping outside the glass. Inside were seven bays with tiny swaddled cherubs, three with pink knit caps and four with blue. She loved babies, which was a big reason she'd gone into labor and delivery in the first place. Once upon a time, she'd imagined having her own.

The hospital faded away and she sat on the end of her bed while her mother ran a brush through her long hair. She'd been twelve, her nose wrinkled in disgust.

"No *way! I'm not doing that!*"

Her mother's *rich laughter washed over her. "You might think it's gross now, but when you are older and you meet someone wonderful, you'll change your mind." She tugged Noel's hair playfully. "Much, much older than you are now."*

"*Why would anyone want to do that?*"

"*Because it can be amazing with the right person.*"

"*I'll pass.*"

Her mother tickled her until she fell to the ground, squealing.

When her laughter subsided, she stared up at her mother's smiling face as she peered over the side of the bed.

"Like I said, sex is something you experience when you are much older, so you can pass for now. Someday, though, I want to be a grandmother."

"Ew, Mom!"

"Noel! Hey!"

Noel jumped when she heard her name called and spun around to find Hannah Draper striding toward her, all business. Hannah was her favorite co-worker, a hard-working whirlwind who remembered everything.

"You about to come on?"

She checked her smart watch with a nod. "Yeah, another ten minutes. Everything okay?"

Hannah shook her head. "We have a mother of triplets with some bleeding and I have a feeling her hubby is gonna be a fainter. Two women who are overdue and begging to be induced now. One of them has tried every old wives' tale in the book, including trying to sex the baby out." Hannah shrugged at Noel's raised eyebrows. "Her words, not mine. I have a feeling with the full moon, it's going to get even crazier so hold onto your scrub bottoms." Hannah snapped her fingers. "Also, Rayleen Givens was admitted about fifteen minutes ago and she's asking for you."

"Crap! Is she okay?"

"Get changed and I'll fill you in. It's not looking good."

A lump lodged in her throat as Noel took off for the lounge at a near run. Rayleen and her husband, Tate, both worked in the hospital cafeteria. They'd been married ten years and while Tate moved up until he was managing the kitchen, Rayleen preferred creating the meals patients and their families enjoyed. When people talked about bad hospital food, that wasn't the case in Mistletoe. Noel told Rayleen often that she could be a chef in a five-star restaurant, but Rayleen waved her off.

Noel caught up to Hannah. "What's the sitch?"

"They think she's got preeclampsia. They are still waiting for the results to come back on her urinalysis."

Noel grimaced. Rayleen turned thirty-five in October and suffered a string of miscarriages before that. "This sucks. She's only twenty-eight weeks."

"Hopefully, if it is that, they can keep her comfortable for a few more weeks. She wants you in there with her."

"I'll go in after I do my rounds." Noel patted Hannah on the shoulder. "Thanks for the heads-up."

"Any time."

It took her about an hour to do rounds and when she finally made it to Rayleen's room, the sheer joy on the woman's round, freckled face tugged at her heart.

"Hey Ray."

"Thank God you're here tonight, Noel." Rayleen pushed back a strand of flyaway red hair and took a deep breath, her voice breaking as she spoke. "Tate went to pick his parents up in Boise but their flight was delayed. I had this blazing headache and thought it was probably just me not drinking enough water, but then the swelling in my ankles kept getting worse. I called the after-hours nurse and she told me to come straight here."

"It's a good thing you did. You should always listen when your body is trying to tell you something, but don't worry. We're going to get you sorted." Noel washed her hands and went about checking Rayleen's vitals, noting the worn paperback on the side table. "Good book?"

"It's an old favorite of mine. I read it when I'm feeling low and anxious."

"Hmmm, I'll have to write it down." Noel checked out Rayleen's ankles and feet. There was no indentation where the ankles should be. She cleared her throat, covering the worry eating away at her. "I liked the last one you recommended. I got it in audio book and it took me about a month to get through it, but it was funny. And hot."

"I'll write down the name of this one for you before I go home tonight." Rayleen took another shaky breath and Noel noted the tears in her eyes. "I can't lose this one, Noel."

Noel squeezed her hand. "We're going to do our best to make sure you don't."

"Hi Rayleen," Dr. Copeland said, breezing in through the door with heavy, sympathetic eyes. Noel's heart sank as she broke contact with Rayleen and turned away to wash her hands again. She didn't know if she could bear to see Rayleen's expression crumble if the news wasn't good, but it was her job. Rayleen needed her to be strong.

Noel came up along the other side of the bed, across from the doctor.

Dr. Copeland sat down on the stool next to Rayleen, smiling kindly. His silver hair and craggy face would never land him a dreamboat role on *Grey's Anatomy*, but he was an amazing doctor.

"How are you feeling?"

Rayleen wiped at her eyes with a wet chuckle. "A little better. Helps to see some friendly faces." Rayleen winked at Noel, her sunny spirits shining through her worry.

"Well, the good news is, your sugars are normal. However, with your blood pressure being elevated and the swelling in your legs and feet, I want to continue to monitor you tonight. Right now, the shedding is low, but after I discharge you, I want to see you in two days. Until then, I need you to take it easy. Bed rest unless you need to use the bathroom and no salty or fried foods. Lots of fruits and vegetables. Can you do that for me?"

"Of course I can." Rayleen rubbed her protruding belly over the hospital gown. "I'd do anything for little bean."

"Good. I want to run a few more tests and then you'll be good to go. Is Tate coming?"

Noel smiled at Dr. Copeland. He made it a point to get to know his patients and their spouses, so they always felt comfortable.

"He's in Boise picking up his parents. I drove myself here."

Noel squeezed her friend's hand, noting the definite tremble in her voice.

Dr. Copeland didn't miss a beat. "In that case, I'd like to keep you overnight. Keep an eye on you and the bean. Sound good?"

Rayleen sighed with obvious relief. "Thank you, Dr. C."

"Now, don't you run my nurses ragged, you hear? Get some rest."

"I'll be right back," Noel said to Rayleen, who reached for her book. Noel caught up with Dr. Copeland in the hall, speaking softly.

"Are you going to pull the baby early?"

He spoke in a hushed, grave tone as they walked further away from the open door. "Most likely. I'm hoping with bed rest and low sodium diet we can get her to thirty-six weeks at least. Anything less than that and we'll have to send her to Boise."

Noel nodded. Boise would take good care of Rayleen and her baby if it came to that, but with Rayleen's anxiety, she'd do better in a familiar place.

She walked back into Rayleen's hospital room. "I'm going to pop around and check on a few other patients, but you need anything, just press the button."

"I will. I just hate sleeping in new places, you know?"

"If you can't get comfortable and Tate isn't back by the time I get off, I'll drive you home to rest." Noel held out a hand to the other woman. "Deal?"

Rayleen took her hand and brought it to her cheek. "Thanks, Noel. You're a wonderful friend."

The praise warmed Noel all the way to her toes. "I try."

Luckily, Tate showed up just before midnight to take Rayleen home, but by that time, Noel barely had a chance to wave. She ended up with two high-maintenance mamas pressing the button every few minutes and a mother who presented with placenta previa. They'd managed to get the bleeding stopped on the mother but the baby was stillborn. The woman's cries echoed through Noel's mind all the way to the car the next morning.

Noel sat in the front seat, waiting for her car to defrost and fat tears rolled over her cheeks. She hated nights like this. All Noel wanted to do was crawl into bed and sleep, but she'd have to take something. She definitely wouldn't be good company.

She pulled out her phone and texted Nick.

> I'm sorry I can't do breakfast. Had a rough night. Will text you later.

Noel set her phone on the seat, leaned back and closed her eyes. As much as she wanted to see Nick, her emotions were running too high. Talking could wait until tomorrow.

CHAPTER 15

NICK

NICK STARED DOWN AT NOEL'S text debating his next move. She could have cold feet about meeting him. Experiencing second thoughts about the road they were on had been rolling through his mind all night.

But if she actually had a bad night...

Nick sat down at his desk and put a CD into his portable CD writer. He knew it was old school, but it was a nostalgic practice he couldn't let go of.

Besides, he knew this would make her smile.

While the songs processed onto the CD he got up and went to his parents' cupboard, but they didn't have what he was looking for. He'd have to go by the store on his way to Noel's.

Nick went through his mom's gift closet, a stash of hoarded items she kept hidden from his dad so she didn't have to go shopping for last minute birthday and white elephant gifts. His dad pretended he didn't know about it, but if his dad or the rest of them ever needed something to gift, they all raided the closet.

He found a white wicker basket and some blue tissue paper. Nick went through a shelf of candles, sniffing each one until he found a sweet, fruity scent that reminded him of Noel.

By the time he left the house, the basket was half full with several awesome finds. Now he just needed the main event.

The grocery store parking lot only had a few cars in it and one he recognized. He debated hanging out and waiting for Amber to leave, but it would be worse if she caught him sitting in his car. Then he'd really be trapped.

It was wrong to avoid her because he didn't want any more socially awkward interactions, but he had no desire to hurt her feelings if she asked again if they could still be friends. They were never friends to begin with, so how could they be friends now? Especially since he hadn't missed her cattiness toward Noel. When he'd started dating Amber, she'd been sweet and funny, so different from the heinous bitch Noel described. He'd made it clear to Amber that Noel was family and she needed to treat her with respect. As far as he knew, Amber had never dogged Noel in the eight years they'd been together. It was only in the last two weeks he'd really observed the animosity between the two of them.

Nick passed through the electric doors and snagged a grocery cart on his way to the cereal aisle. While grabbing a gallon of milk, he heard Amber calling his name. He turned around to find her clicking towards him on four-inch heels and a tight black sweater dress.

"What are you doing here so early?"

"Grabbing some things. How did you make it across the slick parking lot in those shoes?"

"Years of practice, darling." She eyeballed the contents of his cart with a tsk. "Not a lot of healthy choices in there."

"Noel had a bad day so I'm surprising her with some comfort food."

"How sweet." Her dry tone contradicted her statement. "Are you excited for Friday, birthday boy? What are you doing?"

"Just another year older. My mom's making me dinner. Nothing big."

Amber set a hand on one hip, her expression benign. "Is your girlfriend going?"

Nick knew she was fishing, but he didn't mind taking the bait. If he made it clear Noel wasn't going anywhere, maybe Amber would back off.

"Yeah, Noel will be there."

"Oh, won't that be fun." The sarcasm hit a high note that ripped down Nick's spine like chalk on a blackboard.

"Hey, what's your problem with Noel?" Nick snapped.

She blinked big blue cow eyes at him, but he wasn't fooled. "What do you mean?"

"Come on, Amber, I'm not an idiot. You keep bringing her up and being snarky about us. I know you two had beef in high school, but can't you grow up and get over it?"

Her red lips curled into a snarl. "What about her? I know she talks shit on me every chance she gets, but I'm sure you aren't jumping all over her case to defend me."

"Amber, this may surprise you, but a lot of people talk shit about you." Amber gasped. "I am not trying to be a dick. I am saying that it isn't just Noel who has a problem with the way you treat people. I defended you for years, but I'm starting to see where they have a point."

She looked apoplectic for a moment and he waited for the explosion, but instead she closed her eyes, pulling in a long, deep breath. When she opened them, there was a definite sheen to their blue depths and he felt like a tool.

"You're right. I know I can be nasty and difficult. Certain people rub me the wrong way and I lash out. It's a reflex."

"I understand not liking everyone, but what's wrong with Noel? She's kind, funny, smart—"

Amber held up her hand. "To *you*. She is all those things to you, but she isn't all sunshine and rainbows either."

"I know that. In no way do I think Noel is perfect, but even if we weren't together, she would still be my best friend. We've been through too much and we know each other, better than anyone else."

"Oh really? I feel like we got to know each other pretty well over the last eight years. Intimately."

Nick glanced around, but there was no one else near enough to hear them. "I'm not just talking about sex. I'm talking about knowing someone, inside and out because you care about what makes that person who they are. You're right. Noel isn't always sunshine and rainbows. If she doesn't like you, she can be quite difficult. But when she loves you, she will do anything to ensure your happiness. Tell me, what do you know about me? What have you learned after eight years in my life?"

She seemed genuinely taken aback. "I know you're a good guy. That you love your family. You like music—"

"What's my favorite song?"

"Ummm..." Her eyes darted for several moments and she finally sighed, "I have no idea."

"All right, how about this." He pointed just above his eyebrow. "Do you know how I got this scar?"

"Nick, come on," she whined.

"I told you this one, because you noticed it."

"Some kind of accident."

Nick chuckled bitterly. "I crashed into a tree when I was twelve trying out my new snowboard behind my house. Noel fireman carried me across the farm, screaming for help. I had to have twelve stitches."

"I...I remember now." She sounded almost apologetic.

"Last one...how do I like my burgers?"

Amber threw her hands up. "Are you kidding me? We've had half a dozen burgers and the last one was over a year ago. How am I going to remember that?"

Nick shook his head. "I'm not trying to be mean, just trying to wake you up."

"To what? That I could never compete with your precious Noel?"

"There is no comparison. We got together when we were still kids, but didn't grow together, we grew apart. That's okay, it happens. But stop bagging on Noel or making snide comments about our relationship, because it's frankly none of your business. You and I aren't really friends. I will treat you with the same respect and dignity I give everyone else in this town, but that's all. You understand?"

"Yes," she ground out.

"Good. Have a nice day."

NOEL

Noel lay in bed, staring up at her ceiling, frustrated that she couldn't shut her brain completely off.

Her phone dinged on her nightstand and she rolled over to check the message.

> *Hey, girl. It's Amber. I wanted to help with planning Gabby's bachelorette party and she said you were on board with the strippers.*

Noel stared at her phone suspiciously. Anything involving Amber felt like a trap, but she did have the connections for the male dancers.

Amber attached a Magic Mike GIF and Noel snorted. Despite everything between them, Noel owed it to Gabby to try to get along.

> Yeah, I'm down for whatever Gabby wants. Since it's their first night performing, do we need to get tickets or something?

> *I already put us on the VIP list. Show starts at eight. I was thinking we could combine our ideas and maybe*

hire a mobile spa to come to us the next day. Do you
still have your parents' cabin?

Noel grimaced. The cabin was the one thing she hadn't been able to part with and she usually spent her vacations there in the summer, reading and getting away from everything. It wasn't a party pad and she didn't want Amber's toxicity permeating the wood.

Remember, be nice.

I do, but it's my private place. I don't want to use it for
a party pad. Sorry.

No offense, but that's a little selfish. It's Gabby's
bachelorette party and we are all adults. We aren't
going to trash the place.

Noel took a deep breath, her thumbs itching to bitch Amber out, but she refrained.

I will find the venue. No worries. It will be great.

Several moments ticked by before Amber responded.

Fine, but I've already been looking. Anything avail-
able right now is several grand. No one else can
afford that, but cool. Let me know what you come up
with.

Noel glared at the screen, before throwing her phone onto the bed and leaving the room. God, Amber acted as though Noel was some stuck-up rich girl. She really wanted to get along with Amber for Gabby's sake, but Noel wasn't being selfish. The cabin was the one place where none of the bad memories creeped into. Only the good ones.

Gabby would understand, even if Amber didn't.

Noel came out of the bathroom to rapid knocking on her front door. Who the hell would be here at this hour? Crossing one arm over her chest, trying to conceal the fact that she wasn't wearing a bra, she opened the door.

Nick stood on the other side, holding a white basket in one hand and two grocery sacks on the other.

"Hi. What are you doing here?"

"You said you had a bad night so I brought you some foul mood supplies."

Noel took the grocery sacks he handed her and peeked inside, grinning. "Lucky Charms and marshmallows?"

"Feel up to making some nummy treats?" He said the last with a salacious eyebrow waggle and Noel giggled.

"I can't sleep anyway. Whatchu got in the basket?"

"I raided Mom's hoarder closet." He stepped inside, closing the door behind him. He pulled a square case from the basket and sang, "Plus a crappy day plaaaaylissst."

"God, how much coffee have you had?"

They took off for the kitchen and set the supplies on the counter. "Would you believe none?"

"No." She pulled out the cereal and marshmallow fluff,

shaking one in each hand. "I'm having lucky treats, I'm having lucky treats, I'm having lucky treats today…hey…hey!" she sing-songed.

"Unless you burn them."

"That only happened once!" Noel took the rest of the items out of the bag, sneering at a box of Cocoa Pebbles. "Ew."

"Hey, stop dogging my pebbles. They make milk chocolatey delicious."

Noel laughed, coming up alongside him to peer into his basket. "You know you didn't have to do this, right? I'm a big girl."

"I know, but I wanted to. It's what we do, right? Figure out ways to make the other person feel better." He bumped her hip with his. "It's kinda our thang. Remember when I broke my leg riding Darren Wilson's dirt bike in eighth grade? It was the first day of summer. Your mom dropped you off every morning and you took care of me for two months until I got my cast off."

"Ugh, that was terrible. You were such a baby."

"I was a tough kid! My mom said so."

Noel snickered. "Well, she lied because I almost smothered you with a pillow several times when your whining got to be too much."

Nick wrapped his arms around her, squeezing her tight and lifting her off the ground. Their faces mere inches away.

"Take it back or I start tickling."

"Fine, fine! I take it back." He set her back on her feet and she stuck her tongue out. "Bully."

"Oh yeah, I'm so mean to you."

"No, you're amazing." She hugged him hard. "Thank you."

"You're welcome." Nick hesitated, finally clearing his throat. "Do you want to talk about it?"

The words echoed through her mind, remembering the night her parents died. She'd stayed in the Winterses' spare bedroom, but she couldn't sleep. Finally, she crossed the hallway to Nick's room. He'd sat up when she opened the door, shirtless and bleary eyed. In the dim hall light, she'd watched as he held his arms out and she'd closed the door. Crawling into his bed, they'd laid there, arms wrapped around each other.

"Wanna talk about it?"

She'd burst into tears, wracking sobs that lasted hours. Nick didn't ask her again, just rubbed her back and let her grieve.

"I just hate losing people."

"I know." Nick held her closer and her head dropped to his chest. Noel breathed in the scent of pine, smiling through silent tears.

"Has anyone ever told you that you smell like Christmas?"

"I was named after Ol' Saint Nick, so that makes sense."

She released a wet laugh against his sweatshirt, wiping it down with her palm. "Sorry for falling apart on you."

"Never apologize for your emotions, Noel. The way you care for other people is what makes you an amazing nurse."

"How do you know I'm amazing?" she whispered.

"Well, I've had my own experiences with your awesomeness, but it's not just me. I've bumped into a few fine citizens who sing your praises."

Noel shook her head in disbelief. Nick was the nice one. Unless they worked at the hospital, most people gave her a wide berth.

"What do you mean? Who?"

"People think we're together, remember? Apparently, you're pretty popular around here."

"No I'm not. You're the one everyone likes. I'm a snarky asshole."

"Not to everyone. Sarah Wilcox and her husband said you kept them calm while they worked on their daughter. Gretchen Meyers threatened my sack if I wasn't good to you! Mckensie Wilkson called you a godsend when she was in labor. That's a direct quote." Nick cupped her face in his hands and kissed her forehead. "So anytime you want to talk about something at work, good or bad, I'm here to listen."

Noel's eyes filled up with tears again and she sniffled. "Fuck, now I'm crying again."

Nick chuckled. "Ah, what an undercover softy you are."

"Don't tell anyone, okay?"

"Your secret's safe with me."

She covered his hands and squeezed. "Can we make the lucky treats now?"

"Yeah." He let her go and she grabbed a bowl from the cupboard, turning her back on him.

"Hey Noel?"

"Yeah?"

"What's my favorite song?"

She faced him again, setting the bowl on the counter. "Is this a trick question?"

"No, why?"

"Unless it's changed in the last year, your favorite song is AC/DC's 'You Shook Me All Night Long.'"

Nick smiled broadly. "You got it."

Noel cocked her head. "Why?"

"Just wondering if you remembered."

"Pshaw. How could I forget? You sang it every time my dad brought out the karaoke machine..." her voice trailed off. "Anyway, treats."

"Where can I pop your CD in?"

Noel pointed to the black boombox collecting dust. "There's a player on top of the fridge."

Nick's eyes widened. "Really?"

"Yup, I keep it around just for your mixed CDs."

"I feel special." Nick put the player on the kitchen table and plugged it in. The chords to "Bad Day" by Daniel Powter poured through and Noel groaned when Nick sang at the top of his lungs. He took Noel's hand, spinning her and she laughed, grabbing onto his shoulder as he danced her around her apartment, chasing away the last of her dark mood.

He's the only person who can.

The thought both comforted and scared her and Noel held him a little tighter, realizing how true that statement was. No one knew her like Nick. She couldn't lose him, no matter what.

CHAPTER 16

NOEL

NOEL STEPPED OUT OF THE dressing room in the dark-green bridesmaid dress and struck a pose.

"How does it look?"

Gabby's mother, Eleanor Montoya, clapped from the sitting area. Her dark hair secured back from her youthful face and hung down over one shoulder. Shorter and plumper than Gabby, Eleanor's eyes were a mossy shade of green.

"Gabriella! Come out here!"

Gabby's cousins were working until later this evening, so only Gabby, her mother, and Noel were in Vale at Heel Bridal Boutique. Amber was supposed to join them when she could duck out of the spa where she worked as a massage therapist but Noel enjoyed it being just the Montoyas and herself. It took her back to dress shopping their senior year, when Gabby insisted she needed to go to at least one high school dance. They'd gone together and Mrs. Montoya had taken them to get their dresses in Boise. It was still one of the best experiences of Noel's life.

Gabby came around the corner in a white corset and lacy white boy shorts. Her face split into a wide smile when she saw Noel. "Oh, that is your color! I was going to put you in red and the others in green, but Amber said green washes her out. But you look freaking gorgeous!"

"Gabriella, you do not run around a store in your underwear!" Eleanor gasped.

Gabby rolled her eyes so only Noel could see and backed around the corner. "I'm completely covered, Mom, and the windows are frosted. No one can see us."

"I don't care," Eleanor growled.

Gabby heaved a sigh. "Noel, will you tell my mother it's fine."

Noel glanced between Eleanor's arch expression and Gabby's exasperation. "Yeah, I'm not telling her jack. You're on your own."

"You're weak!" Gabby laughed before ducking back into the dressing room.

Eleanor shook her head, before shooting Noel a wink. "You're a smart girl, Noel. Respecting your elders."

"Yes, ma'am." Noel closed the curtain on the dressing room and changed back into her clothes. She'd had a little rest before meeting Gabby and her mother at noon for lunch, but luckily, she had the next two nights off. She'd probably take another short nap before Nick's birthday tonight, but tomorrow, she could sleep in.

Noel came out of the changing room and handed the dress off to the attendant behind the counter.

"Do you need any alterations?"

"No, I think I'm good."

"Great, that will be one hundred eighty-three dollars and thirty-seven cents."

"Noel!" Gabby cried behind her. "I told you I'd buy your dress!"

Noel handed the attendant her debit card and turned around, pausing as she stared in awe of Gabby. The strapless mermaid gown in ivory lace hugged her curves and the color set off the radiance in her golden skin.

"Gabs, that dress…"

"It's perfect," her mother finished, climbing to her feet.

Tears filled Gabby's eyes. "Really?"

Eleanor crossed the room, taking Gabby's face in her hands. "Drew won't be able to take his eyes off of you. I swear to you."

Gabby threw her arms around her mother, who returned the embrace. Noel watched them, mesmerized, bile crawling up her throat as memories overtook her.

It was a Saturday morning in the spring. They'd been cleaning out the spare bedroom and under the bed, Noel found a white bridal box. She'd been nine at the time and pushed it towards her mother across the carpet.

"What's this?"

Her mother's smile lit up her whole face, like sunshine breaking through storm clouds. "You've found my wedding dress." She lifted the lid and pulled out a pair of shoes with pearls covering the heel. Her mother waved them in front of her. "I danced the whole night in these, even though my feet felt like they were going to fall off. Here, try them on."

Noel remembered the excitement of kicking off her rainbow tennis shoes and slipping her sock-covered feet into the pumps. They were too big, of course, and she'd giggled.

Then her mom took her lacy wedding dress from the box and slipped it over Noel's T-shirt and jeans.

"Stuart! Bring the camera!"

Her dad walked through the doorway with the camera in hand just as her mom secured the veil on her head.

"You look beautiful, princess."

"Doesn't she?" Her mother beamed. "She'll make such a beautiful bride one day."

"Miss? Miss?"

Noel realized the attendant stood next to her, holding her card and receipt.

"Sorry. Thank you."

"You're welcome." She handed her a silver garment bag.

Gabby stomped down to confront her, hands on her hips. "I told you I was buying your dress."

Noel gave her a bear hug, fighting back a rush of emotions, still shaken by the memory of her parents.

"You have enough expenses without buying my dress." Noel pulled away, avoiding Gabby's gaze so she wouldn't see her tears. "So, do we have a winner?"

"Honestly, yeah. I don't need to try on anymore. They say when you know, you know, right?"

"And my veil will go perfect with it." Eleanor set her purse on the counter, rummaging through the black leather bag. "I want to pay for this dress."

"Mom! I can buy my own dress!"

"Shush. I already discussed it with your father, so I win."

Noel laughed. "You can't argue with that logic."

Gabby smiled, shaking her head. "I guess not." She hugged her mom from behind. "Thanks, Mom."

"You're welcome, baby. Now, go change out of that dress before you get something on it. I'll go down the street and get us some lattes to celebrate."

"I can come with you," Noel offered.

"Nonsense, you keep Gabby company. I won't be long."

"Thank you," Gabby and Noel said in unison.

The second attendant came up the two steps to take Gabby's hand, helping her down. The bell above the door dinged as Eleanor opened it.

"Hi Mrs. Montoya!" Amber said, coming through the doorway. She wore a black smock over black dress pants and simple black shoes. Her name was monogrammed on the top and her blond hair twisted on top of her head in a messy bun. The false lashes she wore gave her a doe-eyed look.

"Hello, Amber. The girls are inside. Wait until you see Gabby's dress! She looks beautiful."

"Nice! Where are you off to?"

"I'm going to grab lattes. Would you like one?"

"Please, nonfat?"

"Of course, dear. Be right back."

The door shut behind Eleanor, and Amber squealed when she saw Gabby. "You look gorgeous!"

"Thank you," Gabby beamed.

"Spin, spin."

Gabby did a little twirl, holding up the skirt of the dress. Noel grinned at the pure joy in Gabby's eyes.

Suddenly, Gabby stopped, frowning. "What's wrong?"

Noel's attention shifted to Amber, who covered her mouth in dismay. Noel's eyes narrowed suspiciously.

"Well, the way it clings to your butt…it makes it look a little… big."

"It does not!" Noel growled.

Amber rolled her eyes. "Noel, you don't have any cake, so stay out of it."

Noel's hand flew to her rear and Gabby stepped down between them. "Hey, now, stop this. Noel has a great ass, Amber. Apologize."

Amber pursed her lips. "Sorry, Noel."

Gabby shook her head, her mouth set in a grim line. "This is my wedding and I want you both to be a part of it. Get along or I'll cut you."

"Sorry, Gabs." Noel shot Amber a dark look. "But I disagree with Amber. You have amazing curves and that dress only accents them. Beautifully. Your mom and I wouldn't lie to you."

"But I would?" Amber snapped.

Noel grit her teeth. "I didn't say that."

"It was implied."

"Cheese and crackers, enough! I am going to get changed and as much as I appreciate your input, Amber, it's a done deal. My mom already bought the dress."

Amber shrugged. "Then it's settled. It *is* a beautiful dress. You know I didn't mean anything by what I said. I was just trying to be a good friend."

Amber gave Gabby a hug, which Noel noticed Gabby returned weakly. If Noel hadn't promised to behave, she'd have kicked Amber right in her big old booty for making Gabby feel insecure about her wedding dress.

When Gabby disappeared into the dressing room, Amber turned her attention to the bag in Noel's hand. "What did you get?"

"My dress. I'm wearing green. You're wearing red."

"Oh good. Green makes me look yellow. Red is fire. Totally sexy."

Of course Amber's main concern would be how she looked.

"Well there is a whole rack over there. Gabby said we can pick whatever style we want, so go nuts."

"Perfect." Amber sashayed over to the rack of red dresses that had been pulled for their perusal. She picked a red chiffon strapless and checked the tag. "Oh, this is the one."

"Great, do you want to try it on?" The sales associate behind the counter asked.

"No need. It's my size." Amber laid the dress over the cashier's counter and faced off with Noel, a wicked gleam in her eyes. "So, did you find a location for the bachelorette after-party?"

"Actually, I'm still looking. You were right. There isn't a lot out there for that date."

"I told you."

Gabby walked out of the changing room, with the associate right behind her, holding a silver garment bag.

"Told her what?" Gabby asked.

"I told Noel she should just let us use her parents' cabin for your bachelorette party and hire one of those mobile spas for the next morning." Amber sighed dramatically. "But she won't go for it."

Gabby shrugged. "I'm fine with just going to the bar to see the…" She glanced over at the attendants and lowered her voice, "entertainers and then going home."

Amber scoffed. "Really? You don't want to hang out with us girls and talk about the…*entertainers* over a couple cocktails?" Amber clucked her tongue, slipping her arm through Gabby's. "And wouldn't it be relaxing to sleep in the day after? Have a delicious brunch and then be pampered for hours?"

"Well, I mean…" Gabby glanced between Amber and Noel. "That does sound nice."

"Then that's what we'll do," Noel said, praying like hell she could come through for Gabby. "I will find us a kick-ass place to go after the bar. I will get you that mobile spa and everything will be exactly how you want it."

"Don't forget brunch," Amber sang.

Noel smiled, baring her teeth at Amber. "Of course not, complete with mimosas."

Gabby jumped up and down like a kid. "Eeeek, I am so excited!

Drew and his friends are going to Sun Valley to 'snowboard.' He won't be back until Sunday night, so this will be perfect!"

"He's okay with our stripper plan?" Noel asked.

"Oh, absolutely. That's why I used the air quotes. His best man already told me they're getting some in-room entertainment, but I trust Drew and he trusts me."

Amber piped in with a huff. "Besides, Noel, he isn't her daddy. He's her fiancé until he puts a ring on it and even then, he will not *own* her."

"It's not about owning," Gabby jumped in. "It's about mutual respect, which we have and Noel knows that. She's been Drew's champion before I even knew I was interested."

"That's sweet." Turning her attention away from Noel, Amber held up the red dress with a little dance. "Gabs, I found the one! Are you getting this or do you want me to—"

"Oh, no, I offered." Gabby took the dress from Amber and pulled her card out of her purse, passing it to the cashier. "This will be stunning on you."

"I know, right?"

Noel bit her lip. She had no idea how much money Amber brought in working at the spa, but Noel had a hard time believing she couldn't at least chip in for her own dress. Amber still lived at home and Gabby let slip once that her parents didn't make her pay rent. Noel promised to try to get along with Amber, but it rankled Noel that Amber took Gabby up on the offer to pay for her bridesmaid's dress. However, Gabby was a grown woman. If she wanted to buy Amber's dress, then Noel would mind her business. Reluctantly.

"Just give me a few more minutes. I want to look at the tiaras and shoes."

"Hurry up, sweets. I am starving." Once Gabby retreated to the other side of the room, Amber's blue eyes took on an evil gleam. "Oh, Noel, I heard there might be an open apartment in your complex. Maybe you could put in a good word for me?"

When hell freezes over.

"I think Nick already put down his deposit."

"Oh, really? You weren't ready to let him move in with you?"

What the hell happened? Amber's text made her think they were going to let bygones be, but here she was, poking Noel about Nick once more.

"Nick's been living with a bunch of men for eight years, Amber. Pretty sure he wanted his own space."

Amber tossed her hair over her shoulder. "Really? Because he talked about a future with me after our third date."

"And look how that turned out."

"Maybe he's just not that into you."

They were practically nose to nose now. "I guess we'll see, won't we?"

Amber's expression sucked in like she'd just swallowed a lemon. "Maybe you should concentrate on getting Gabby's bachelorette party set up and less on my ex?"

"I thought you were all too eager to help with that?"

"You're the MOH. I'm sure you can handle it."

Noel didn't have much experience dealing with jealous ex-girlfriends, since most of her past consisted of short-term casual encounters. Still, Amber's animosity for her, all over a guy

Amber had been quick to drop two weeks ago, seemed out of control.

"What happened to working together on this wedding for Gabby's sake?"

"What can I say, Noel? I guess you don't always get what you want."

What in the heck did that even mean?

Eleanor came through the door with a tray of lattes, cutting off their tense exchange. "I got the goods."

Gabby darted towards her mother. "Oh, a pick-me-up."

Gabby and Amber took theirs first, while Noel hung back. When Eleanor held the last cup out to her, Noel accepted it and the cardboard tray. "I'll toss this for you."

"Thank you, dear. So, what did we find?"

Gabby and Amber started talking at once, showing Eleanor the red dress, while Noel hung back with her latte and bag. Despite Amber clearly hurting Gabby's feelings earlier, she'd easily forgiven Amber. Noel knew it was just Gabby's nature to let things roll off her back, but Noel couldn't understand Amber. She seemed to genuinely care for Gabby one minute and then chipping away at her confidence the next. It was like Amber Jekyll and Bitch Hyde.

Once they hit the sidewalk, Amber started talking excitedly. "Oh, I forgot to tell you! I got Vienna to close the salon on Christmas Eve and all of the stylists are going to come do hair and make-up for you and your wedding party. Isn't that great?"

"Oh my," Eleanor said.

Gabby grabbed her arm. "Shut up! How did you swing that?"

"It's no big deal, Vienna was going to have short hours

anyway. You said you were looking for someone who could come to your house and do it, and I came through."

"You sure did."

Noel watched the two of them hug, hopping up and down together, and a knot of jealousy formed in her stomach. She didn't begrudge Gabby having other friends. She had Nick and the guys. The difference was Gabby, well, being the only girlfriend she hung with, who knew her almost as well as Nick, was special and it felt like she was slowly slipping away.

"Noel?" Eleanor prodded.

"Yes, sorry."

Gabby slipped her arm around her waist. "You seem out of it today. Everything all right?"

"I think I'm tired, is all. This night shift is really messing with my sleep regimen."

"You should go nap. You've got Nick's birthday dinner, right?" Gabby bumped her hip against her. "Did you get him something nice?"

"I think he'll appreciate it."

"What's this?" Eleanor's brow furrowed. "Are you seeing Nicholas Winters?"

"She is," Amber said dryly. "They are absolutely *adorable* together."

Amber's obvious sarcasm was hard to miss and a tense silence stretched across the group. Noel broke it by clearing her throat. "I think I'll take Gabby's advice and go get a few hours' sleep." Noel gave first Gabby and then Eleanor a hug. "Thank you so much for the latte and lunch, Mrs. Montoya."

"Good night, dear. Have fun at the party."

"I will. See you, Amber."

"I'll see you later, Noel!" Amber called sweetly.

Noel walked away, wishing she could get over her dislike of Amber. She'd settle for indifferent. It wasn't just her connection to Nick, although that hadn't endeared her to Noel. Or Amber's relationship with Gabby.

The animosity between Amber and Noel started long before her parents' deaths and only worsened after they were gone. While most of the other students were somewhat sympathetic, Amber never let up. When Noel quit the choir, Amber got every solo and continued to throw it in her face. When Noel dropped out of the spring musical, Amber, her understudy at the time, took over the role. Mocking her clothes. Her hair. Tearing her down bit by bit for years. As an adult, she should be over it, but when she looked at Amber, there was no goodness that she could see. Nothing redeeming.

But as long as she made Gabby happy, she could keep a smile on her face.

CHAPTER 17

NOEL

NOEL CLUTCHED THE FESTIVELY WRAPPED birthday present in her hands, waiting for someone to answer the door. She'd already rung the bell, but the distinct sound of loud music probably muffled the noise. Normally, she'd walk right in, but for some reason, everything involving Nick felt off, even barging into the Winterses' family home.

She unlocked her phone screen to shoot Nick a text and noticed he'd sent her a snap of him rocking his shoulders to the Beatles Birthday song. Noel grinned down at the goofy smile on his face, the way his brown eyes lit up on screen. God, he was cute.

"Noel?"

She turned to find Merry standing at the bottom of the porch steps, wearing a dark puffy coat and knit cap.

"Hi."

"What are you doing out here?" Merry came up alongside her and turned the knob.

"I tried knocking but no one answered," Noel said.

"What's this knocking bullshit? Family doesn't knock. Let's get inside. It's freezing."

"Right behind you." Noel followed her inside, where they found the rest of the Winters crew playing a karaoke video game. Holly shook her hips while singing "Proud Mary." Victoria and Chris sat on the couch, clapping along to the beat while Nick hung out in the corner, talking to Pike and Anthony. The moment he saw her, his face lit up and Noel's heart leaped with awareness.

"Look who finally decided to show up," Nick called as he made his way over.

Merry accepted his hug first, slapping him on the back. "Pardon me, big brother." She shrugged out of her jacket and whipped off her hat. She shook out her hair and handed both off to Nick. "It takes time to look this good."

"Yeah okay." He passed her outerwear right back to her. "You can hang up your own crap, unless you got a gift hidden somewhere for yours truly."

"Geez, rude. It's already here." Merry fluttered her lashes at her big brother. "I just need to sign the card."

"Ah so, Mom bought it and you are paying her to slap your name on it?"

"Absolutely. Be grateful. It's the thought that counts."

Nick shook his head. "Classy."

"Hell yeah I am. I'll let you say hi to Noel while I find the beer."

"Hey." Noel awkwardly held out the package she'd been clutching for five minutes. "I'm a little more original than your sister."

"Thanks." He took the present and wrapped her up in a hug. His breath rushed across her cheek as his body pressed closer to hers. "I'm glad you could make it."

"I wouldn't miss your birthday." She held on a little tighter, adding, "It's the first one I've actually been able to spend with you in years. It's been Skype and e-gift cards since we were eighteen."

Nick's hand slipped under her coat, splaying against her lower back. The heat of his skin burning through the fibers of her sweater. His lips swept across the skin of her jaw and she trembled.

"Ahem." Pike's throat clearing ended the intimate embrace. Tonight he sported a denim collared shirt and black bow tie, his hair gelled into a stiff, perfect wave. "Break it up. It's your turn on the mic with me, birthday boy. We are gonna rock and roll all night."

Nick shook his head as he released her, taking her present with him. He set it on the side table in the entryway, where several other festively wrapped gifts adorned the cherry wood surface. Nick rolled up his sleeves as he passed her by, shooting her a wink and her heart fluttered.

Nick took the second mic from Pike, rolling his shoulders and bouncing from foot to foot.

"You ready for this?" Nick made an air guitar motion with the mic in his hand and Pike laughed.

As they belted out the lyrics to "Rock and Roll All Nite," Noel couldn't keep her eyes off of Nick. His light blue T-shirt hugged his broad shoulders and back, loosening around his waist. The shirt was just short enough to show off the curve of his butt in his relaxed jeans and her mouth went dry.

"Noel?" Nick's mom called out.

Noel jumped. "Hm?"

"Maybe you want to hang up your coat and sit a spell?"

She did just that, squeezing in next to Holly. Merry sat on the other side of Holly and looked around her sister to speak to Noel. "Why were you standing on the porch staring at the door?"

"I wasn't."

"Yeah, you were. I pulled up and saw you there. It was several minutes before I walked up behind you and you seemed completely clueless."

Everyone except Pike and Nick watched her intently, waiting for her answer. She shifted uncomfortably on the couch, hoping for something to come to her that wouldn't make her feel even more of an idiot than she already did.

"I got lost in thought, I guess. It's been a busy week for me, especially at work. Even though it's the holidays, people don't stop having babies. I should have had an extra cup of coffee today."

Nick's mother laughed. "We know that firsthand. March was always a good month for us."

Holly blanched. "Please, do not explain to us how we were conceived. I'd rather listen to Pike hit the high notes for the rest of my life."

Nick and Pike finished their song, tongues hanging out of their mouths and hands in the air.

"You're just jealous of my wicked pipes," he said, proving Pike heard her insult.

"If you're comparing your voice to bagpipes, I'll agree. Like nails on a chalkboard."

"Nick, your sister's picking on me. Again."

Noel laughed. "You think you'd be used to it, Fish. She's been doing it since she was six."

"I *am* used to Holly being a punk to me. What I want to know is, why? And it's not just her. *You.*" He pointed from Noel to Merry. "And *you.* Actually, all women in my sphere seem to terrorize me. What's up with that?"

"Maybe you bring out the worst in them," Anthony suggested, leaning against the wall.

"Please, I'm charming and adorable." Pike straightened his bow tie and struck a pose. "Not to mention a snazzy dresser."

Merry scoffed. "If you say so."

Nick's dad got up from his chair. "Now, now. Let's ease up on Pike. You can't help feeling sorry for him. Unfortunate fashion sense and all that."

Pike covered his heart with a hand and pretended to stumble backwards. "Et tu, Chris? We men need to have each other's backs."

"When you start dressing like a man, son, I'll get right on that."

Noel fell back against the couch, wheezing with laughter. Even Pike smiled as Chris passed by, patting him on the shoulder. "I'm just playing, kid."

"I know, sir. No worries." Pike winked. "I got a mirror, so I *know* I look good."

"I'm going to check on the burgers," Chris said, shaking his head.

Nick's mom stood up and followed his dad out of the room "I'll help you."

"Who's next for karaoke?" Anthony asked.

"I think Nick and Noel should do one," Merry said, shooting to her feet. "And I have just the song."

Noel knew Nick's sister was up to something, but she didn't protest when Merry handed her the mic. Noel stood next to Nick, shoulder to shoulder as the melody kicked on. She muffled a groan when Toby Keith's "Kiss Me Again" showed up on the screen. Of course Merry would pick a love song about two friends discovering they have feelings for each other.

Would Nick forgive her is she murdered his sister on his birthday?

"I'm going to kill her," Nick mumbled.

Noel grinned. "I'll help you hide the body."

"Deal."

When the words popped up on the screen, Nick started in, with Noel just a second behind. Their voices blended perfectly, and before long, they stood facing each other. Caught up in the music, Noel didn't pull away when Nick took her hand in his, lacing their fingers together. Their voices trailed off on the last word and Noel realized she was pressed against his front, their hands still entwined, lips so close their breaths mingled.

Nick's head dipped slightly and Noel's eyes fluttered closed. Time slowed down and a thought flashed through her mind. *This is it.*

The room burst into thunderous applause and cheers. Although they froze in place, they didn't break apart.

Chris came into the entryway and stood at the edge of the room. "Soup's on!"

Everyone jumped off the couches and headed for the kitchen

except the two of them. Noel finally tried to break their contact but Nick held fast.

"We need to talk about this."

"This?" she whispered.

"Yeah." He waved his free hand between the two of them. "Us."

"Ooookay," she dragged out.

"Eat your burger and rendezvous in my bedroom in ten minutes." He said it in hushed tones, watching the kitchen entryway warily. "If you get caught up, make a noise like an owl."

Noel giggled. "You're so stupid."

"I know, but meet me anyway. Ready...break."

She followed him into the kitchen for burgers and tots. A fresh green salad with plenty of color, hardly touched, was the first item in the assembly line for food. Nick walked right past it for the buns and Noel scoffed.

"Excuse me. You need something green."

"Not today, I don't. It's my birthday." He topped his bun with four pieces of crispy bacon and popped a fifth in his mouth, crunching the meat between his teeth with a grin. "I do whatever I want."

The heat in his gaze created a hormonal reaction in Noel that made her whole body crank up the temperature. Her cheeks, arms. Stomach...everywhere seemed to light up like someone started a fire inside her.

"Fine, I'll back off. For today."

They joined the rest of the family at the dining table. Noel took her usual spot across the table from Nick, who had this insanely happy expression on his face. She couldn't help smiling back at the pure joy on his face.

"So, what's on deck for the rest of the birthday party, Mom?" Nick asked.

"Food. Games. Drinks. Dessert."

Anthony raised his beer bottle. "I like the drinks part."

"Me too." Pike tapped the neck of his to Anthony's.

Someone knocked on the front door and everyone looked around.

"Are we expecting anyone else?" Chris asked.

"Not that I'm aware of. Nick?"

"This was your idea, Mom. I didn't tell anyone."

Merry got up from the table with a huff. "Relax, I'll get it."

She disappeared around the corner. Noel was in the middle of chewing her second bite when Merry came back, looking grim.

"An unwanted guest for Nick," Merry hissed.

Suddenly, Amber popped up behind Merry, looking abashed. "Oh, I am so sorry to interrupt."

"Yeah, right," Holly muttered.

Nick stood up. "Hi, Amber. What are you doing here?"

Amber held up a black and silver wrapped package. "Surprise. I bought it before and...well, I know you said you were doing dinner tonight for your birthday, so I thought I'd bring it to you."

Noel's lips thinned. He'd told Amber about his birthday dinner and she'd thought it was okay to just show up?

"Amber, would you like to join us," Nick's mom asked politely.

"Oh, thank you Mrs. Winters, but I already ate. Although it looks tasty."

Amber's expression completely belied her sweet words, her nose turned up as she eyed Noel's burger. In response to her obvious disgust, Noel took a huge bite, the wet sensation of condiments on her mouth and chin. She smiled with meat most likely wedged between her teeth.

Amber looked away. Noel heard several male chuckles and caught Pike and Anthony watching her, amused.

"I should let you all get back to it. Nick...would you see me out?" Amber asked.

"Uh, sure."

Noel watched Nick come up alongside Amber, taking the present she offered him. When the two of them disappeared around the corner, Noel wiped her mouth delicately. They continued eating quietly and Noel noticed Merry hadn't sat back down. Instead she hovered just inside the dining room, her head turned intently.

"Stop spying on your brother," Victoria hissed.

"I'm not spying. I am protecting him in case Amber tries to suck his soul from his body."

Anthony and Pike smothered their laughter with a cough, but Noel couldn't find the humor in the situation. Amber shows up and Nick follows her around like a faithful dog, after the way she'd dropped him.

Why were men so stupid sometimes?

No one else said a word as Noel climbed her feet.

"Is anyone else finished? I'm full."

Victoria's expression warmed with motherly concern. "Are you sure, honey?"

"Yeah, I'm good. Don't worry about me."

Noel headed for the kitchen, refusing to look towards the entryway. She dumped her paper plate with half-eaten food into the trash.

After the way Amber broke up with Nick, why was he still nice to her? Nick was a good guy, but Amber didn't deserve his consideration or kindness.

Noel continued to silently berate her best friend inside her head until something struck her.

She was jealous. Green-eyed monster, wanting to punch Amber in the nose, jealous.

See, this is what happens when you kiss your best friends. Chaos. Mayhem. Anarchy.

Noel finished washing her hands and was still drying them when her phone vibrated in her back pocket. She pulled it out to find a text from Trip.

> *Please talk to me, Noel. We had fun together.*
> *Meet me tomorrow at Los Lobos, 7 pm.*
> *I'll buy.*

Noel's first instinct was to leave him on read. She'd said everything she needed to say to him the other night and he couldn't take the hint.

The she glanced out the kitchen window to find Amber and Nick standing by Amber's car. They seemed to be deep in conversation and something Amber said made Nick laugh. Noel twisted the dish towel in her hand as she watched like it was a train wreck. She couldn't stop.

Suddenly, Amber wrapped Nick up in a tight hug and although he didn't return it, merely gave Amber a half-hearted pat on her back, he didn't try to pull away and it bugged Noel.

Bad.

Her jaw clenched and before she could consider the implications, she messaged Trip back.

Fine. 7.

Noel wasn't leading Trip on. She agreed to the meeting for curiosity's sake. If hearing Trip out meant he'd finally leave her alone, she was all for it.

Plus, he was buying. Free food was hard to pass up.

Chapter 18

NICK

NICK STEPPED INSIDE KISS MY Donut, and the noise level in the bustling café made his head pound with the aftereffects of too many shots with his little sisters last night. He had no idea when Merry and Holly developed the skill to drink him under the table, but even after a shower and what seemed like a gallon of water, his pores still oozed Crown.

He shouldn't have drunk so much, but as far as birthdays went, last night took a turn he hadn't been prepared for. Nick, floating on air, ready to tell Noel he wanted to dive into something real with her, had the wind knocked out of him when Amber walked in. His whole family staring at him, waiting to see what he'd do. He wasn't going to humiliate her in front of a room full of people, so he'd casually followed outside, feeling the eyes of everyone he loved on his back.

When they reached her car, Amber spun around, staring at him earnestly.

"I wanted to come by tonight and apologize. Everything you

said to me the other day was true. When we got together, we were both kids and we didn't have time to really get to know each other before you left. I should have been a better girlfriend, a better person, and I'm sorry I couldn't be that for you. I hope you can forgive me."

He'd been so thrown by her sincerity, he'd simply nodded.

"I didn't mean to cause a scene. I actually hoped you'd be the one to answer the door and we could avoid anyone else knowing I'd come by."

He'd laughed. "Yeah, no chance of that. They're going to have questions."

"I just hated us leaving things on such a sour note. You're the kind of guy a woman needs to be ready for, and I just wasn't."

"I get it, Amber. No hard feelings. We're both happy with how things worked out."

"Yeah. Happy. On that note, I suppose I'll go." Before he could react, she hugged him hard. "Have a great birthday."

As soon as he'd come back inside, he'd been bombarded with questions. So many voices speaking at once that he didn't have a chance to catch Noel before she snuck out.

Nick couldn't blame her for ducking him last night, considering her feelings for Amber, but he was still disappointed. He'd wanted to speak to her about how stupid keeping their distance was. That they had feelings for each other they should embrace. Jump all in and see where things went. Considering the tension caused just as many problems between them, why not give being together a go?

The fact that she'd taken off without giving him a chance to speak his piece irritated him though.

No one understood her gift but him. She'd given him a box of bulk flash drives with *Nick's Playlist* printed on them. Inside was a card with a music gift card.

Now, throw away those CDs!

It was hard to stay mad at her when her gift was absurdly adorable.

He'd opened Amber's gift afterwards. A cologne gift set that smelled like spices. It was different than his usual and he didn't like it. It wasn't him.

The couple in front of him paid for their order and stepped out of the way, allowing him to check out what was left in the pastry case. He rattled off a dozen different donuts and three large coffees.

"Anything else?" she asked.

"No, that's it." He handed her his card and stepped to the side. He bumped into someone and spun around to apologize.

Noel gazed up at him, absently wiping at a wet spot on her down jacket.

"You got me good," she muttered.

"Sorry, I didn't see you."

"Well, yeah, you were walking backwards. You got eyes in the back of your head I don't know about?"

Nick caught the humor in her expression and took her sarcasm for what it was. Forgiveness.

"Can you hang for a bit until my order is up? I'd like to talk to you."

"Sure. I thought I was going to get to sleep in, but I'm going to meet Gabby again in a little bit to help her shop for wedding supplies. I have a minute or two, though."

"Thanks." The bakery employee called out his name and he grabbed his pink box and drink carrier from the counter. At seven-thirty in the morning, it was light outside but still frigidly cold. As he followed Noel out the door, neither of them spoke at first. He noticed her hands shoved into her pockets and cleared his throat.

"You forgot your gloves today."

"No, they're in the car. I didn't think I'd need them. Where are you parked?"

Nick pointed to his truck three cars down. "Just over there. How about you?"

"Around back."

"Ah, no wonder I didn't see you when I pulled in," Nick teased. "You weren't hiding in case I showed up here, were you?"

Her sheepish expression said it all. "Anthony may have mentioned he'd be helping you move today and you'd promised him donuts. This is the best place in town."

"Man. And you were that angry with me?"

"I'm not angry with you, Nick." At his arched brow, she sighed. "Okay, I was somewhat irritated you let Amber work you over, but I know you two have history. I've never gotten between you and I'm not going to start now."

Nick shook his head. He understood her hesitation. Only a few weeks ago he'd thought he had a future with Amber, but his eyes were wide open now. They'd been together a long time, but spent hardly anytime actually being together as a couple. Now that he'd been back and seen the real Amber, there was no way in hell he'd ever go there again. Especially when all he could think about was Noel.

"There's nothing to get between. She is an ex. I've seen her a few times this week, once at Rockin' Rochelle's and then at the grocery store before I surprised you. I may have mentioned we were staying in for dinner, but I swear, I didn't invite her to drop by."

Noel's eyebrow arched. "Rockin' Rochelle's huh? For Singles Hump Day?"

He groaned at the tone in her voice. "Pike and Anthony dragged me, kicking and screaming. Hog-tied. They threatened my dick if I didn't go with them."

Noel laughed. "Sounds brutal."

"It was, I'm telling you. The point is, I want nothing to do with Amber. You should have stayed to hear me out."

Noel took his admonishment in stride. "I saw the two of you laughing when she walked you out and I just didn't feel like being there anymore. I'd already had one nasty run-in with her yesterday, and watching you look so chummy just rubbed me wrong."

"She apologized to me."

"Why?"

"She asked if we could be friends. I said no. She reacted badly and wanted to let me know there were no hard feelings."

"Amber...wanted to be...friends?" She spoke the words slowly, as if they didn't make any sense to her.

"Yeah. I told her that we didn't start out as friends and we weren't going to be friends now. I wasn't mean about it, just honest."

"So, as long as you start off as friends with someone you date, it's okay to keep them in your life?"

Nick didn't know why but it sounded like a trick question. "I mean, I guess it would depend why we broke up."

"If the two of us dated and we had a bad breakup, you'd just say *see ya?*" Her voice went up an octave on the *see ya.*

"No, what we have is on a whole other level than just mere friendship, Noel, and you know it," he snapped.

"Do I?"

Nick took a deep, steadying breath, reining in his temper. "I'm sorry. I'm hungover and tired and explaining this so badly. You and I are more than friends and you aren't getting rid of me." Nick reached into her pocket and took her hand. "No matter what."

Noel extracted her hand. "You say that now, but there are no guarantees. You can't reason with emotions. They make people crazy. Amber wants to be friends and even though I don't care, Trip won't stop trying to make amends. It's so bizarre to me!"

"Wait, what? Trip wants to be friends?" Nick butted in. He didn't like being lumped into the category as that dick.

"Kind of. I think he just doesn't like being rejected and instead of letting things go, he has to try to fix us. Even though there isn't and was never an us. He kept messaging me last night, begging me to meet him for dinner. I finally said yes for my sanity, but lord, we weren't together. Was it crappy of him to be sleeping with Jillian and me and not tell both of us? Yeah, but I don't hate him for it. Just like I don't care two figs about what you and Amber are to each other. I just want people to make up their minds and stick to their guns."

Flames licked against the back of Nick's neck as his temper flared. "Wait, you're going out with Trip again?"

Noel huffed. "No, I am meeting him for dinner to talk."

"That sounds like a date."

"It's not."

"Does he want to work things out? Is that why you're meeting him?"

"Did you listen to a word I said? There is nothing to work out. I only agreed so we could meet up, bury the hatchet, and both move on. I have no interest in starting anything back up with Trip."

Nick searched her face, relief rushing through him as he realized he'd let his jealousy get the better of him. "I'm glad you aren't considering it. You deserve better."

Noel arched a brow. "You think I don't know that? I only hook up with guys like Trip because it's not complicated."

Not what he wanted to hear, especially because he still wanted to take a chance on them.

"Yeah, but don't you ever think about dating someone you care for?"

"Not until recently." Nick's spirits lifted at her words, until she added, "But honestly, I'm not sure I'm built for it. And I'd hate to figure that out while simultaneously ruining the best thing in my life. Hooking up with no strings attached works for me."

Nick knew she didn't want him to tell her how he felt. The

talk he'd wanted to have last night? She'd ducked out on him to avoid it so she wouldn't hurt his feelings.

"Well, that's a kick in the nuts."

"Seriously, you could spin in a chair and randomly pick any girl in town and she would jump at the chance to be with you. I am messed up, Nick. Worse than when I was sixteen. You are amazing and I would hate to drag you down with my fuckedupness."

"What if I like your fuckedupness? I like everything about you, Noel, even the shit that drives me crazy."

Noel laughed bitterly. "How do you know that? You've been home for a minute. You haven't really seen me at my absolute worst, not recently anyway. What if we get into this and I'm too much for you?"

This whole conversation had sent him on a roller coaster of emotions, but now, he was back to anger with frustration mixed in. "Was it Amber showing up? Or Trip? Which catalyst sent you ten steps back? Because when we kissed on Tuesday, I thought that was a turning point."

"Neither. Well, a little Amber, but I'm not trying to crush your nuts. I want to keep things good between us and if we take a leap, I'll crash us both into a hillside. Blood splurting from our arteries. Fires burning off all the flesh until our hearts disintegrate. Trust me, a kiss and a few charged moments aren't enough reason to explore this. Attraction comes and goes, but you and me? We'll still be annoying each other when we're hobbling around with walkers and fake teeth. Let's leave things the way they are."

Nick nodded. There was nothing else he could do. Arguing with her would only make her dig her heels in and besides, he'd spent the last eight years with someone who ended up not wanting him.

If Noel couldn't see how good they could be, then he'd let it go. For now.

She said he didn't know her? That he couldn't handle her at her worst?

Bring it on.

"All right, then. I won't bring it up again."

"Are we okay?" she asked, hesitantly.

"Yeah, but so we're clear, just because you want to ignore what's between us, won't make it go away." He held up the grub in his hands, looking for any excuse to end this torturous moment. "I better get these over to the house before they start calling me, wondering where I'm at."

Noel shuffled her feet, her hands back in her pocket. "I'll text you later."

"Sure. Have fun on your date."

She sighed. "Not a date."

Nick didn't argue anymore or look back as he set the pastries and drinks on his front seat. What an idiot he'd been, thinking that Noel was feeling it too. Maybe she did but she didn't want to do anything about it. He could admit it wounded his pride. He was a great guy, a catch. Noel told him so herself. Yet she didn't want to snatch him up?

Nick's head was still pounding by the time he pulled in front of his parents' house. He barely released a grunt in greeting as he walked up the porch steps to where Pike and Anthony waited for him. He handed the box to Pike and the coffees to Anthony.

NICK AND NOEL'S CHRISTMAS PLAYLIST   215

"Let's hoover this and get to it. I don't want to take all day." Nick pushed open the front door and stepped inside.

Pike followed him, muttering behind him. "Damn, Grinch, who pissed in your Who pudding?"

"Not in the mood."

"Danger. Danger Will Robinson," Anthony said.

Pike laughed, but Nick didn't even turn around. His parents were out on the farm, so the house was quiet except for the scuttering of nails on hardwood. Butch greeted Nick first and he scruffed the hound one-handed before grabbing his coffee from the carrier Anthony set on the counter.

"You's a good boy, huh, Butch? You think I'm great, right? I'm awesome."

Pike set the pastries down next to the coffees and opened the box. He took out a cinnamon roll and pointed it at Nick. "Ah, now I get it."

"Get what?"

"Why you're acting like a surly prick." Pike took a huge bite and with a mouthful, elaborated, "You got rejected."

"I did not."

"Who rejected him?" Anthony asked. "Amber?"

"Nah, too obvious and besides, he locked himself in a room with sad music when she dumped him. Nothing special about that. For Nice Guy Nick to turn into such a raging asshole, it has to be someone special." Pike took another bite and looked thoughtfully up at the ceiling, as though he really needed to think about it. "I'm gonna go with a certain brunette we all know and love."

Nick crushed his Styrofoam coffee cup in his hand before he

thought better of it. Piping hot coffee erupted all over his hand, sizzling across his palm and fingers. He dropped it and the rest of the contents onto his parents' tile flooring.

"Shit. Butch, get back."

The dog moved away from the dark liquid, sniffing Nick's hand with a whimper.

Anthony grabbed his wrist, checking out his hand. "Damn, are you okay?"

"Yeah, just burns," he gritted out.

"I rest my case." Pike took two more bites, swallowed, and smiled.

Nick glared at his grinning buffoon of a friend. "She didn't reject me. Didn't even give me the chance to do something to warrant a rejection. A simple *no thanks* before we even got started. You happy?"

"No, I'm not happy." Pike grabbed a paper towel and finally set his food down. "I'm actually surprised."

"Why?"

"Because I can tell she is into you."

"It's true, man," Anthony said. "I love Noel, but she doesn't get attached. Men are just convenient until they aren't. She keeps us around because she doesn't have to worry we'll step over the line, but since you've been back, she's twitchy. Every time the two of you are together either she is watching you when you aren't looking or you're eyeballing her. Not exactly the thing you do if you don't want something to happen."

Nick grabbed a dishrag from the drawer and cleaned up his mess. "Well, I got it straight from the horse's mouth. She doesn't want me."

"I think the horse be spitting some horseshit," Pike said.

"It doesn't matter if she's lying or not. I'm not chasing her if she doesn't want to be caught." Nick washed his hands and wiped them on his jeans, wincing as the rough fabric rubbed the burn on his palm. "I'm going to get started on the room. I'll see you in there."

"Want me to make some more coffee?" Anthony asked.

"Not right now."

Nick walked into his former bedroom and stood there staring at the boxes stacked along the left side of the room. He'd spent the week going through, getting rid of crap and deciding what he'd need once he got into his new home. He'd thrown out the box of Amber's stuff, since she'd told him to go ahead and do it. It was amazing how much of someone's life could be narrowed down and compacted.

He picked up the photo on his nightstand of him and Noel, dressed in their graduation caps and gowns, hugging each other. He grabbed his throw off the bed and wrapped the frame inside to keep it from getting broken. He slipped it into a half-filled box and closed it up.

Was he frustrated with the way things had gone today? Absolutely. But no matter what the future held, Nick couldn't be himself without Noel in his life.

CHAPTER 19

NOEL

LIPS. NICK'S LIPS ON HERS. His arms around her. Holding her. Her heart pounding. God, it felt so good. His mouth moving...

Trip's mouth was moving.

Noel jerked out of her fantasy when she realized that Trip was asking her a question, waving his hand in front of her face.

"Sorry, what?"

Trip sighed. "I asked if you wanted a margarita. I know how much you love them here."

"Oh, um, no thanks. I'm driving." And she was afraid alcohol on an empty stomach might make her do something crazy. Like stop by Nick's place. He moved in today and having him so close could be dangerous for her resolve.

"Come on, you can get a small one," Trip cajoled.

"I said no thanks." God, had Trip always been this pushy? Or was she only just noticing because she was already in a foul mood?

With only myself to blame.

The last thing she'd wanted to do this morning was hurt Nick.

When she'd bailed on his birthday, she'd just needed time to sort through her feelings. Amber showing up was like a sock in the gut and Noel could admit it. She'd wanted to lunge across the table and tackle her to the ground. Noel would never show up at her ex-boyfriend's birthday at his parents' house, unannounced and think that was okay.

But the entire Winters clan sat in silence, letting Nick handle it, and so had Noel, but she'd been seething. Even if Nick really was done with Amber, it seemed Amber couldn't let go of Nick. Noel could handle Amber's little digs while planning Gabby's wedding, but having her popping up during her personal time with Nick?

Noel knew better than to get involved with a guy getting out of a long-term relationship, but with Nick, it seemed impossible to be near him and not want to touch him. When she did need someone to talk to or make her feel better, he was the first one she wanted to call. That had to mean something and maybe if they waited a bit, gave Amber a little time to really get out of their lives, they could be something more.

God, who was she kidding? Anytime they were around each other, she ended up in his arms. There was too much between them. History. Chemistry. All the subjects she'd hated in high school were coming back to haunt her now.

If Amber hadn't shown up last night, if Nick had dragged her into a back bedroom and kissed her, she'd have given in. Thrown herself at the train wreck getting involved with him would become. Amber had done her a favor, arriving right before Nick met her in his bedroom. And today…

Well, having him bump into her hadn't given Noel a lot of

time to prepare. Winging it may not have been the best solution, but it got her point across. He'd backed off and she'd gone back inside for two eclairs, which she'd devoured before Gabby showed up.

The waiter, Matthew Larkin, came by for their drink order and Noel didn't argue when Trip ordered two margaritas. He could drink them both himself.

"How are you doing, Noel?"

Noel smiled broadly at Matt. His wife, Josie, had come into the labor and delivery ward in August with their first child. They were five years younger than Noel and Josie was terrified. Noel kept them calm by asking them about their life, how they met. High school sweethearts, married at eighteen. Josie had her cosmetology license and worked in a posh spa in Sun Valley, while Matt was in a technical program for welding.

"I'm great, Matt. How are Josie and Liam? When do you finish your program?"

"They are great. Liam's getting chonky. And the way he smiles, man…it's something."

"Aw, do you have pictures?"

"Yeah, yeah." Matt whipped out his phone and tapped a few times before handing it to her. "I finish my program next month and then I go for my test. My teacher actually put me in touch with a company out of Boise and once I pass my certification, he said he'd set up an interview."

Noel studied the baby, who'd been eight pounds at birth, and now looked as though he'd tripled in size. "His leg rolls are adorable."

NICK AND NOEL'S CHRISTMAS PLAYLIST 221

Noel handed him back his phone and Matt slipped it into his pocket. "I know, right? Listen, I don't know if I ever said thank you for keeping me calm. I know I wasn't chill when it was all going on."

"Matt, grown men in their thirties panic when their wife is in pain. You did great."

"That's good to hear, 'cause Josie keeps saying she wants a half a dozen kids and she told me if we move to Boise, I have to drive her all the way up here just so she can have you and Dr. Copeland." Matt chuckled. "You really made an impression on her."

"You tell her I'm not going anywhere and she can see me as often as she wants," Noel said with a wink.

"With all due respect, I will not tell her that! We'll end up with three sets of Irish twins."

Trip cleared his throat loudly, and Matt tapped the end of the table sheepishly. "I'll go put your order in. It was really good to see you."

"You too. Tell Josie I said hi and kiss Liam for me."

"I will."

Matt walked away and Noel caught Trip's glare.

"What?"

"That was rude."

"How? I was saying hi to someone I hadn't seen in a while and catching up. It only took a few minutes."

"Not just a few minutes, but you've also been out of it tonight. Not really listening, just nodding your head and smiling."

Rather than tell him what a child he was being, Noel opted to placate him. "Sorry, Nick's birthday was last night and I didn't get home until late. Then I got up with Gabby and did some shopping for her wedding and I guess I didn't get enough sleep."

"Giving him a happy birthday, huh?" Trip sneered.

"Not that it's your business, but no. We've decided we're better off as friends."

"Well, I'm sorry to hear that." Funny, he didn't look sorry. He preened like a self-satisfied peacock and Noel suddenly wondered what the hell she was even doing there.

"Trip, I want to get home early, so why don't we cut to the chase about why you wanted to meet up tonight."

He pretended offense. "I told you, I want no hard feelings between us."

"We're good. Don't know what else I can do to prove that."

"You're sure?"

"Yes. I'm fine. We're fine. All good."

"There is one thing…"

Here it comes. "Go on."

"Right, well, I know when we were hanging out, I mentioned my microbrewery idea to you a few times."

Noel had no idea what he was talking about, but she nodded. "I vaguely remember."

"In this economy, it is really hard to qualify for a business loan. But, if I get enough investors, I don't need to jump through the bank's hoops."

"Ooookay…"

"I know your parents left you some money and I was hoping, maybe you'd want to invest. Like a silent partner?"

Noel sat in disbelief, warring between *are you fucking crazy* or *are you just an idiot*? "You want me to give you money my *dead* parents left me...for beer?"

"No, not for beer. I am presenting you with a golden opportunity."

Idiot. Idiot. Idiot. The voice in her head chanted it to the beat of "We Will Rock You" by Queen.

"A golden opportunity to throw my inheritance at a harebrained scheme? Where is your business plan? Financials? I can't imagine you'd approach other investors without them."

Trip cleared his throat, his expression wary. "I have one at home. I'm coming to you as someone I care for." He took her hand. "We could help each other out."

Noel played with the straw in her water with her free hand, deciding that he was really just a stupid, arrogant prick. "How is that?"

"You invest, and I return with interest. Once it takes off, everyone wins."

"That does sound like a killer plan." No reaction to her peppy sarcasm. "You do realize if it doesn't succeed, I'm out of money."

"You gotta come at this with a positive attitude or it won't work."

"That's all it takes to launch a successful business? I had no idea." Mathew dropped off the margarita she didn't want, shooting her a baffled look. "What do you even know about beer, besides the fact it tastes good?"

Matt backed away from the table, so obviously she wasn't being subtle with her aggravation.

"I bought a bunch of books and did some local tours around some of the brewing companies in Idaho. You can trust me. I got this."

Noel extracted her hand. "Yeah, it sounds like you got this." She set her napkin on the table and grabbed her purse. "Excuse me, I'm going to the bathroom."

Trip stood with her, touching her arm. "Just think about it, okay? We can talk more when you get back."

Noel nodded, although she stewed the whole way across the crowded restaurant. How dare he ask her out under the pretense of making amends only to turn around and try to squeeze money from her. No shit a bank didn't want to loan him any money. He was up to his eyeballs in debt from the protein drink business his parents sponsored and he'd bailed on that in less than six months! His degree was in language arts or something. Not business. He didn't know the first thing about breweries, except it's where he could drink. What was he thinking?

Noel got Matt's attention as she passed by.

"Can I get the fajitas to go? With an order of cheesecake?"

"Sure. Should I pack up your date's as well?"

"Nope, not a date, and just mine." *He agreed to buy me dinner if I heard him out. Doesn't mean I have to stay and eat it with him,* she thought.

Matt's lips twitched. "Understood. I will get that bagged up in just a few minutes."

"Thanks."

Noel popped into the bathroom to pee before she drove home. As she was finishing up in the stall, the bathroom door opened and Amber's high-pitched laugh echoed off the tile walls.

"I still can't believe she is here with Trip. I should have known she couldn't be with just Nick. The girl gets around and a tiger doesn't change her spots."

Noel grit her teeth. *It's stripes, bonehead.*

"I don't think Noel is a slut." The voice belonged to Amber's longtime friend, Yancy. Noel would never forget Yancy's voice as she pantsed Noel at a high school football game when they were sophomores. Yancy mocked Noel's granny panties for years.

"What do you call it when a woman sleeps around?"

"I think she's embracing her sexuality. It's the twenty-first century. Slut shaming is a little outdated, don't you think?"

Noel cocked her head to the side, surprised. Maybe Yancy grew up.

"Please, after telling me how much better she is than me and then I see her getting cozy with Trip? She can kiss my ass." Noel peeked through the slit in the stall door and watched Amber blot her lips with a pop. "I still can't believe Gabby is friends with her. Although, if I'm being honest, Gabby hasn't ever been the brightest bulb. I love her, but it's true."

Noel opened the stall and stepped out, scowling at Amber. "You want to say that again?"

Amber turned, a sly smile on her lips. "Look who's creeping around in the bathroom. Just like in high school. Doesn't surprise me though. You've always been a piece of shit. You should feel very comfortable here."

"If you're talking about when I used to hide in the bathroom to avoid you, then who's the real shit? By the way, the correct answer is you."

"You always play the victim, but when you act like you're better than everyone else, you're going to get taken down a peg or two."

Noel's jaw dropped. "Are you for real? I've never thought I was better than anyone. In all honesty, I don't give two fucks what you think or say about me. But you don't get to sit around talking shit about Gabby. She's defended you way too many times and deserves better."

"Maybe we should go," Yancy said, trying to pull Amber toward the door.

She shook off her friend with a sneer. "No way. I'm not scared of her. I don't care if she is former military. She bitched out, anyway."

"I didn't bitch out. I just didn't reenlist. Stop talking shit about things you don't understand. Like Gabby. She isn't stupid. She is an amazing and loyal friend."

"It's not talking shit if it's the truth. Only an idiot would hang with you."

Noel's voice dropped to a hoarse whisper. "Interesting. Guess that includes Nick, too?"

"I didn't say it, but he went from me to you." The disgusted look Amber trailed from Noel's toes ended with her staring Noel in the face. "Definitely a downgrade."

Noel stepped into Amber. "Keep talking about the people I love and you're going to need another nose job."

Fear flashed in Amber's eyes before she laughed it off. "Please, I won my first pageant when I was a year old. I can take you anytime."

Noel picked up the lipstick Amber left on the counter and opened it. Twirling it all the way open, she glared at Amber.

"Oh, no!" Amber cried, mockingly. "Are you going to ruin my lipstick? Stupid bitch, I always have a back—"

Amber screamed as Noel dragged the cherry-red cosmetic from Amber's temple to her chin. Amber's hands flailed at her sides as Noel destroyed the rest of it against the front of Amber's white halter top.

"Is this silk? That's gonna be a bitch to clean." Noel dropped the tube on the floor and gave the wide eyed Yancy a little wave. "Have a good night."

Noel popped out to find a startled waiter standing outside the bathroom, glancing from the closed bathroom door to Noel.

"Is everything okay? I heard screaming."

"Oh yeah," Noel said, all smiles. "Just a little makeup malfunction. She'll live."

The waiter nodded, continuing into the men's room. Noel stopped by the kitchen and grabbed her food, enjoying the pep in her step. Taking the long way around the restaurant, she popped outside into the freezing cold. In her hurry, she'd forgotten her coat, but there was no way she'd go back for it now. She'd rather freeze to death than listen to Trip's narcissistic drivel or have another run-in with Amber. She could kick herself for agreeing to meet Trip tonight. Such a mistake.

Maybe she shouldn't be so hard on Nick about Amber. Sometimes you try to give people the benefit of the doubt and it bites you in the ass.

Noel was pulling out of the parking lot when she saw the

glass door of the restaurant swing open and Trip standing on the walkway. His head swiveled back and forth, searching for her, and she took off like a shot, headed for home. Her phone blew up next to her, blasting an old Justin Timberlake song repeatedly until Noel finally turned it on silent.

What the heck was happening in her life? Drama didn't normally factor in it, yet for the last two weeks, it had been nothing but. Her life had become a rating-seeking reality show and she half expected Nick Lachey to jump out from the shadows like, "Gotcha! You're on my new reality show, *Crazy in a Small Town!*"

Over it. That's how she felt. She'd lock herself in her apartment and refuse to come out if one more thing happened.

She climbed the stairs to her apartment and found a box sitting on the front porch. She opened it up and used her phone flashlight to study the contents. Pictures of Amber and Nick, a bottle of cologne, a T-shirt, and a tiny cactus with a bow. There was a white envelope with Nick's name on it. Didn't take a genius to know who'd left it and Noel doubted she'd mistakenly set it on Noel's doorstep. She should have broken Amber's nose instead of ruining her shirt.

Noel picked up the box and stomped three doors down to Nick's new apartment. After this morning, she'd planned on giving him space. Not now though. There was no way this box was going inside her apartment.

Balancing the box on her hip, she banged on his door with her food bag in her hand.

When he opened it, Nick stood in the doorway wearing a pair

of sweats, a T-shirt in his hands. His chest and abs were just as she remembered; chiseled from the granite of the gods. Pure perfection. Lickable.

When the heck had she become poetic about men's torsos?

"Hey," he said, gruffly, rubbing his eyes.

"Hi, did I catch you sleeping?"

"Yeah, took half the day to move in. The guys ditched me once the furniture got inside, so I carried up all the boxes on my own."

At the mention of boxes, Noel tore her eyes away from his pecs and held the one in her hands out to him. "Well, here is one more left on my doorstep by mistake."

Nick took it, using one hand to rummage through it. Noel's gaze trailed over his sculpted forearm as the sinew twisted under the tan skin.

Get it together, girl. They are just arms. You have seen half-naked men before.

The familiar sound of a turbo engine broke through the fog of lust and she didn't even look over the railing to check the parking lot. She pushed Nick back into his apartment and slammed the door, her back pressed against the white wood.

"What the— Noel! What's wrong with you?"

"Shhhh! Turn the light off." She ran over to his window, setting her food on one of the boxes strewn about the floor. She dropped the blinds and squatted down, peeking through discreetly.

"What is going on?"

Trip came up the stairs two at a time and disappeared to the right, no doubt heading for her apartment.

Nick hunkered down next to her. "What are you looking at—"

Even three doors down, an eruption of wall-shaking knocks shut him up.

"Noel! I can't believe you'd fucking dine and ditch me! I come to you with my heart open, offering you the chance of a lifetime, and you run out on me? Take advantage of my generosity?"

Nick nudged her shoulder. "His heart open?"

"Not the way you are thinking," she hissed. "He offered to buy me dinner because he wanted me to invest the money from my parents' estate into his microbrewery."

"Microbrewery," Nick snorted. "Douche."

"Exactly. So, after I listened to his pitch, I grabbed my dinner to go and bounced. On his tab."

Nick grinned. "Clever girl."

"I thought so."

Trip kept knocking and cursing. "I know you're here! I saw your car in the parking lot. You could have just said no, instead of being a fucking cowardly bitch."

"Fuck this," Nick said, standing straight. "I'm gonna knock his teeth in."

Nick took a step toward the door, but Noel tackled him before he could get further. They landed on the floor with an *oof,* Noel plastered across Nick's chest. She pushed herself up onto her arms, shaking her head.

"Just stay here, okay? He'll go away."

"I'm not going to sit in here listening to him call you names."

Noel rolled her eyes. "I don't care what he calls me. Besides, he's not wrong. What I did was a bitch move, no matter how bad he deserved it."

"Still, if he says one more thing…"

"Believe me, I've been called worse tonight and I don't need you to defend my honor."

"What are you talking about? By who?"

Noel didn't know if Nick noticed his hands drifted over her hips, but she couldn't ignore the heat of his palms through her jeans. She swallowed, resisting the urge to press her hips against him.

"Noel? Who called you names?"

"Amber. She was talking about Gabby behind her back and we got into it in the lady's bathroom."

Nick leaned his head back against the floor, closing his eyes with a groan. "Why does so much drama always occur in women's restrooms? It's a theme in every chick flick I've ever seen."

"Because art imitates life?"

"So how did it escalate from there?"

Noel didn't answer right away, listening to Trip's diatribe of her transgressions against him. When he started shouting about her giving him blue balls she cursed.

"Please tell me about the altercation with Amber so I don't have to listen to him bitch about your sexcapades. I don't know how much more I can take."

Funny how Nick sounded almost jealous, making Noel's body warm. He still hadn't seemed to notice she was practically straddling him. Or maybe he had and was trying to behave.

"She called me a slut, which is a little hard to defend right now with my ex-fuck buddy screaming about me leaving him hanging. Then she said I wasn't good enough for you."

"Wait how did it go from shit talking Gabby to me?"

"Because she isn't over you and I'm into you. Pretty much a guarantee every fight we have is going to end up coming back to you."

Nick's face broke out in a wide grin.

"So, on a scale of one to ten, how into me are you?"

Noel shook her head, fighting a smile. "If I answer this question, will you shut up?"

"Yep."

"One hundred thousand billion trillion infinity can't keep my hands to myself or even think about you without wanting to kiss you. Does that answer your question?"

He frowned up at her, but she caught the sparkle of amusement in his brown eyes. "Honestly, no. I asked for a number between one and ten. You need to follow directions."

Noel burst out laughing, snapping her mouth closed when she realized how loud it was.

"I'm pretty sure he didn't hear that," Nick said.

"Will you shut up?"

"Rude and not the way you should talk to someone you like a hundred bil—"

Noel slanted her lips across his to keep him quiet, but the minute his hand came up to cradle the back of her head, she forgot why she was kissing him. Only how much she'd missed doing it. The heat of his skin burned through her long-sleeved shirt, arousing her nipples until they poked against the cups of her bra.

Nick flipped them over, coming out on top. Taking control. Incredibly hot and not something she usually let guys get away with, but she trusted Nick with every part of herself.

Her eyes nearly rolled up in her head when he kissed her neck, nibbling his way to the soft spot beneath her ear. Noel's hands gripped his shoulders, moaning when he rolled her earlobe between his lips. For a guy with limited experience, he sure knew how to make a girl melt.

In the distance, she could vaguely hear the banging and angry shouts, another door opening and someone yelling about calling the police. But then Nick's hand cradled her breast, squeezing it, chasing away the background noise. Kneading her until she panted, wrapping her legs around his waist. For weeks she'd fantasized about Nick touching her like this and she wanted to get closer, with nothing between them.

Nick's mouth took hers again, his tongue diving in and exploring her, tasting. Lighting fires in her with every tempting brush. She rubbed herself against his front, dying to have him inside her. Her hand went between them, sliding below the elastic of his sweats and wrapping around his cock. Noel released a sigh as she stroked him, catching his moan in her mouth.

Suddenly, he wrenched away from her, hovering on his hands above her. Her legs still locking him to her, Noel's hand clasped around his dick, staring up into his dark gaze. His rapid breathing didn't slow and when she slipped her thumb over the head of him, he shuddered, catching her hand.

"You can stop. I think he's gone."

Ice water rushed over her as his words sank in. "You want to stop?"

Nick hesitated, studying her intently.

"Of course I don't want to fucking stop."

Noel's body relaxed at his guttural response, until she realized he was removing her hand from his cock and sitting back. She ended up straddling his lap, her knees framing either side of his thighs. His hands rested on the small of her back, the position making them nearly the same height and she stared down into his face, features she knew by heart and she hated the strain at the corners of his mouth and eyes.

"I don't want to stop, but I can't have you telling me afterwards that you regret it. That we shouldn't have done it."

Her hands splayed on the tops of her legs, afraid to touch Nick even as they longed to explore every part of him. "And I'm afraid you'll realize I'm not right for you. That Amber will somehow convince you that you should be together again."

Nick threw back his head and laughed. "You actually think I want to get back with Amber?"

She lifted her chin. "You told her about your birthday dinner. Where you were moving. Maybe, subconsciously, you wanted her to be able to track you down because you aren't as over her as you thought."

"Noel, you know me. I'm the guy who shook hands with Grant Lassiter at graduation, and that guy spent all of middle school duct-taping my ass cheeks together. Do I invite him out with the guys? Hell no. But I don't bear ill will towards him. Life is too short to hold grudges. Even if my entire family didn't hate Amber's guts, I still wouldn't have any desire to be with her. I started dating her when I was a kid, but I'm a man now. I know what I want." His hands came up and tangled in her hair. "I don't want Amber. I don't want to go out clubbing with Pike and Anthony. I want this, right here. In my arms. You. All of you. The last thing I want to do is hold back when all I can think about is diving into you. Taking you in my arms and tasting every part of your body. What don't you get about that?"

His speech left her quaking, breathing harshly as he pulled her mouth to his, fingers tightening in her hair.

"Talk to me," he whispered.

Her breathing came out in a trembling rush, the words tumbling from her lips like a land slide. "I've grown up too, but I'm afraid you don't see all of me. I'm messed up, Nick." Her voice broke a little at the admission, and he ran his thumb along her cheek, catching a tear on the end.

"I am twenty-six and I have never had a boyfriend. If a guy starts to show any sign of wanting more, I drop him. Like that." She snapped her fingers. "I avoid spending time with your family because being in the room and watching so much love and joy rips into my soul. I hate feeling that way because I love your family, Nick. I love your dad, with his goofiness and warm heart. Merry, who is always stirring shit and has absolutely no filter, like me. Holly's sweetness and the way she bawls during *Prancer* even though we watch it every year and she know how it ends. And your mom, Nick...your mom lets me pull away. She knows exactly what I'm doing, I know she does, and she never stops reaching out and inviting me and I love them all so much. I love them and I don't know if they know how much—"

"Hey, hey, they know." His voice was a rough whisper, warm against the skin of her neck. His hands dropped out of her hair and circled her waist, squeezing her against him. "They know you love them and that is why we'll never give up on you. They're your family, Noel. I'm your family. Even if we didn't work out, none of us will shut you out, no matter how much distance you try to put between us."

Noel's forehead rested on his shoulder, tears slipping below her eyelids to fall against his bare skin. "But why? You just said it, I push people away. I'm stubborn. I can be such a bitch sometimes, I don't know how you stand me."

"Noel, you can frustrate the hell out of me. When you told me earlier you were going out with Trip, I wanted to ask you not to. To beg you to stay with me and tell him to fuck off." He chuckled sheepishly. "I took my frustrations out on my stuff and now I need to buy new dishes."

Noel choked on a laugh, and she sat up straight, her hands gripping his waist. Their lips so close their breathing mingled.

"If I ever needed you, though, I know you'd be there because you've done it before. I mean, it doesn't happen often because I'm awesome"—she smacked his arm—"but you are the person I call when I have something to say. Good or bad, I want to share it with you. You make me smile when I want to scream and laugh when I want to cry. Like right now, if I walked out there and threw Trip off the balcony, I know you'd ask me which car are we taking and help me hide the body."

Tears streamed down her face at his speech. She didn't see herself as his happy place, not the way he was for her, but here he was, putting to bed so many reasons why she couldn't risk falling for him.

Nick's forehead rested on hers as he choked out, "Tell me

you meant every word you said earlier. That you don't want anything more with me but my friendship. Say no right now and I'll let you go."

In this moment, locked against Nick, anticipating his kiss, she couldn't come up with a single reason why they wouldn't work.

"Say it."

"I can't."

CHAPTER 20

NICK

NICK'S GRIP SLACKENED, DISAPPOINTMENT COURSING through his veins as her words hit him like a punch to the chest. Even after everything, being so close to carrying her down to his bedroom and making love to her, she still pulled away.

"I get it. We've been over all the reasons why we shouldn't and I respect your decision."

Nick tried to get up, but her arms held firm around his waist, pulling him closer as her lips pressed against his. He almost fell back in surprise.

She broke the kiss long enough to mumble, "I meant that I can't give you a reason to stop. Not that I can't be with you. I want you, Nick. Badly."

The first glimpse of his family tree on Christmas morning. The exhilaration of winning a tough snowball fight. The sheer joy of stepping off that plane in Boise and knowing he was home for good.

All of them paled in comparison to this moment.

Nick groaned, his hands gripping her waist, his mouth open, devouring her passionately. Sucking her tongue and grinding against her. As awkward as a teenager, Nick's hand roamed everywhere, eager, memorizing every curve. Their bodies rolled together, the friction driving him insane. He was drowning in Noel and he never wanted to come up for air.

He grabbed the bottom of her blouse and pulled it up over her head, their kiss breaking long enough for him to throw it across the room. The simple white cotton bra she wore and full breasts spilling over it made his mouth water. He'd seen her in a swimsuit, but never dwelled on what Noel might have going on under there. At least, he'd never told anyone, but he hadn't been oblivious. She was his best friend, but he knew she was sexy. He'd had enough of his friends telling him how much over the years, he'd be an idiot not to notice.

There had been a few times growing up when Nick wondered about what Noel was like in bed. They'd never talked about their sexual conquests, but he knew she'd lost her virginity their junior year because the jerk bragged about her during gym class. He'd learned his lesson when Nick, Pike, and Anthony jumped him after school. He'd never told Noel and she'd never asked any of them about it, even when the guy apologized the next day sporting a black eye and fat lip.

When Nick imagined her like this, he'd always assumed Noel would be passionate. That she'd enjoy being in control. Just the way she was in life.

Being intimate with Noel was a dance, but not in the traditional partnership. Both of them took the lead, alternating who was in charge. Nick didn't want to battle though; he wanted to love her. He wanted them to be real, not just have sex to get off. Nick wanted what they had to be different, more than what she'd experienced with any of the other guys who came before. They meant nothing. Not compared to what the two of them had.

He lifted her off his lap to her feet, kneeling on the carpet in front of her. Noel's eyes fluttered closed as his lips covered the spot just above her jeans, sucking sharply. His fingers worked the snap of her jeans and when the *rfft* of her zipper echoed through the apartment, he felt her tremble beneath his hands and mouth. She didn't try to push him away or hurry him along. She let him take his time, trusting him.

She kicked off her shoes and helped him peel her skinny jeans down her legs. Clad in her white bra and…

Nick blinked. *Were those…the Golden Girls?*

He stared at the elderly women's faces on her underwear, grinning at him with unabashed humor, and a bewildered smile spread across his face.

"These were not what I expected to find under those tight jeans."

Noel bit her lip. "I wasn't anticipating getting laid tonight, so I didn't dress for the occasion."

Nick dipped forward, kissing her through the thin cotton. "I'm glad to hear you weren't expecting anyone else to see them, but I need to make something clear." His mouth trailed along to her inner thigh, sucking the skin into his mouth. "You…" He kissed the spot gently. "Are not." Nick sucked the other side, growling when she moaned. "Getting laid." His face buried in between her legs, fingers moving aside the cotton so his tongue could find purpose. He licked along her seam until he reached the top of her mound.

"I am going to make you mine."

He expected her to bolt when he uttered those words, but when she shivered, her fingers kneading his head, Nick nearly shouted with victory.

Instead, Nick hooked his fingers into the top of her panties and dragged them down her hips. They stopped around her knees and he pushed them the rest of the way down, running his hand back up between her legs, parting them. More than anything, he wanted to please Noel. To hear her moan his name. To taste her on his lips once more, this time as she let go.

Grabbing her ass, he maneuvered her to the end of the couch, sitting her on the edge.

"Put your legs over my shoulders."

Noel did as he asked and with his head buried between her legs, staring down at her neatly trimmed pussy, he tasted her again. Running his tongue along the seam until he found the delicate nub of her clit hidden in the folds. Noel cried out, bucking against his mouth as he gripped her cheeks and enjoyed her. He hadn't had a lot of practice at it, but what he lacked in skill, he hoped he made up for in enthusiasm.

Listening to Noel's wild cries and the way she pulled his hair...

"Ow," he grunted when she yanked too hard.

"Sorry, it's just...it's good."

"Yeah?" Nick spread her with his fingers and flicked his tongue over her swiftly, each pass making her cries higher and louder. "How good is this?"

"So good. Great. Superb. Fucking awesome," she gasped as he took the nub in his mouth and sucked. Harder. He slid two fingers into her, working her from the inside out.

Nick knew she was coming before her body shook against him and he kept the pressure on. Listening to her enthusiastic screams was music to his ears. God, she tasted amazing, felt even better, and he couldn't wait for her pussy to convulse around his cock. Their lovemaking would be the stuff of legends. Poetry.

All right, maybe he was overreaching, but damn, being with her was damn close.

Nick kissed his way up her body, stopping to push the cups of her bra down and expose her hard, rosy nipples. He bestowed a kiss on both of them, smiling against her skin when she hummed.

"That was insane," she murmured.

Nick trailed his tongue around her nipple in a wet circle. "Should we stop there?"

"If you stop now, I'll murder you."

He chuckled and helped her to her feet, dipping his head to kiss her. When her hands went to the waist of his sweats, he didn't stop her as she pushed them to the floor.

"Hmmm, easy access. I like it," she teased.

Nick moaned, deepening the kiss as her hand stroked him, rubbing a thumb along the head of his dick. It had been almost two years since he'd been with a woman and he was too impatient to wait another moment.

He picked her up and lifted her against him, walking her back to the wall by the front door. When she wrapped her legs around him, it brought her wet, hot center against him and his dick flexed to get closer.

Nick broke the kiss, taking his length in his hands and running it over her center.

"Are you sure?"

"Mmmm, yes."

Nick rubbed against Noel, groaning, "Shit, condoms. I don't have any."

"I'm clean. Safe. On the pill. I'm comfortable not using one if you are."

"I'm good. And I'm also, ahem..." The last thing Nick wanted to talk about was Amber, but he cleared his throat, praying Noel would understand. "When I found out Amber may have been... unfaithful, I got tested. I'm clean. I haven't been with anyone since. You're the only one I want."

Noel cupped his cheek in her hand and kissed him. "I only want you, too. Please, Nick. I need you inside me."

Nick almost shouted hallelujah as he slipped the head in, his mouth finding hers again, slowly sinking into—

Sharp, rhythmic knocking sounded on Nick's front door.

They froze, Noel staring down into his startled expression.

"Are you expecting someone?" she hissed.

"No!"

Another round of knocking followed by the voice of Chris Winters hollering through the door. "Nick! You asleep, kid?"

"Oh my God. It's your dad!" Noel pushed him away and he almost fell to his knees, weeping at the loss. Noel skidded across the floor and grabbed her jeans, hopping from foot to foot as she tried to pull them back into place.

"Just a second, Dad!" Nick picked up her shirt from the corner, handing it to her. "Get dressed in the bedroom. I'll stall him."

"No, I was going to just stand here naked and say hey."

Nick kissed her hard and fast. "Normally I find your sass charming, but right now my dad is standing in twenty-degree weather wondering what the hell is going on." *And my dick feels like it's about to fall off*, Nick thought to himself.

"You're right." Noel righted her bra over her glorious breasts and took off down the hall, skidding into the bedroom.

Nick managed to get his sweats on but hiding the semi beneath the loose fabric would be tricky. Hopefully, they wouldn't notice. He threw open the door with a smile.

"Hi Dad." Standing next to his dad was his mom, watching him suspiciously. "Mom! What are you guys doing here?"

Nick's mom kissed his cheek as she passed into the apartment, glancing around the living room. "We went out to dinner after the farm closed and thought we'd bring you some food."

"Here you go," his dad said, handing him a takeout bag as he passed by.

Nick closed the door behind them, his heart thundering in his chest. He felt like a sixteen-year-old kid sneaking a girl out of his room before his parents caught him.

"I appreciate the gesture, but you should have called."

"We tried but you didn't pick up."

"That usually means I'm busy, Mom."

His mom's gaze narrowed. "Whose shoes are those?"

Nick looked down to find Noel's white sneakers discarded by a few of his boxes. "Those are Noel's."

His mother's face brightened. "Noel's here? Where?"

"She's in the bathroom."

"Oh, did the two of you already eat?" His dad asked, picking up Noel's discarded bag of food.

"No, that's hers. She stopped by to see the place and help me out if I needed her. She couldn't come earlier because she was shopping with Gabby."

His mom picked up Noel's shoes and put them by the door. "Noel has such a big heart. A sense of humor and kindness are the best qualities a woman can have."

"Doesn't hurt that she is pretty as a picture." His dad winked.

They headed into the kitchen; Nick ready to bang his head against something. If his parents knew Noel and him were starting something, they'd be all up in his business. His sisters were meddling enough, but add his mother into the mix? Pure chaos.

Noel finally exited the bedroom and when she walked into the room, Nick smiled reassuringly. "Here she is."

Noel tucked a piece of hair behind her ear, her appearance giving nothing away. She was so put together, no one would be able to guess that ten minutes ago he'd had her bent backwards over the couch, naked under his mouth.

"Hi!"

"Hello," Victoria said, smiling slyly. "We brought Nick's some food, but I see you beat us to it."

"Oh, well, Nick eats a lot so I am sure we could use the extra."

Nick snorted. "I am a man with a normal, healthy appetite."

"Indeed," Chris said.

Noel's cheeks flushed scarlet and Nick coughed, covering a laugh.

Victoria put her arm through Chris's. "Why don't we check out the bedroom and bathroom since Noel is out of them? We're both excited to see your new place."

"They're pretty thrashed, Mom," Nick said.

"It's all right, sweetheart. I raised you. There is nothing back there that could shock me. Why don't you two get started on dinner while we explore?"

They didn't wait for his consent, but took off down the hallway. Once his parents disappeared, Noel heaved a sigh. "Your mom knows."

"No she doesn't."

"Yes she does. Your dad may be oblivious, but your mom knows I was about to let her only son have his way with me against the wall of his living room."

"She definitely doesn't know that!" Nick came around the side of the counter and kissed her temple. "Relax, okay? My mom doesn't know anything and even if she did, she'd be thrilled."

She worried at her bottom lip. "You don't know that. Victoria may love me, but that doesn't mean she wants me dating you."

Nick pressed his lips against the tip of her nose. "Is that what we're doing? Dating? Because I think if we're going to call it that, then we should go on an actual date."

Noel's eyes widened. "Really? This is when you want to discuss this?"

"Absolutely. What do you say? Go to the Festival of Trees

with me next weekend?" He ran his hand over her shoulder and down her arm, his fingers skimming along her soft skin. "Food, fun, and festivities. It will be a hoot."

"How is someone so hot such a dork?" she said breathlessly, her eyes glued to his mouth.

Nick circled her waist with his arms. "Hot, huh?"

"Don't lose your head."

They heard his mother's voice and separated before she came back into the room. Nick went to the sink to wash his hands.

"It's great for a first apartment," his mother said behind him. "Plenty of room and I like that you have your own washer and dryer."

"Me too." Nick turned around, drying his hands on a paper towel. "That's why I rented it."

"Don't get cute." His mom turned to Noel, adding, "You missed rehearsal for the Christmas concert today."

"Yes, I am sorry, Victoria. Things ran late with Gabby and then I had a dinner meeting I couldn't skip."

"I am only teasing, honey. Nick didn't show up either, but Merry and Holly both said you two didn't need any practice singing together. Natural chemistry is how they described it."

Nick caught the gleam in his mother's eye and sighed. She *did* know there was something going on with him and Noel.

"We hope to do you proud, Mom."

"I know you will." She patted Nick's cheek and cocked her head. "Come on, Chris. Let's leave these kids to eat and hang. Or whatever they say nowadays."

Chris snapped his fingers. "Excellent idea. I can't wait to get home and watch a Christmas movie."

Nick followed behind them. "I'll walk you out."

His parents hugged Noel in turn and headed for the door. As he stood there, holding it open in the bitter cold, his dad shot him a grin.

"Good luck with that one, son. She's going to fight her feelings for as long as she can."

Nick blinked at his dad. "How do you know that?"

"Because your mother was the same way."

His mom smacked his dad in the gut. "I was not. I wanted to be caught. You just took your sweet time doing it."

"We remember our youth differently, my dear."

She hugged Nick, whispering in his ear. "You might want to let Noel know her panties are bunched up under the couch. I pushed them further back with my foot so your father wouldn't see them. I didn't want to embarrass her."

Nick's mouth dropped open, but his mom turned away, returning to her argument with her husband on the way to the stairs. "I remember pretending to break my ankle at our first dance senior year and you sat me in the corner with a bag of ice and left me."

"I went to go get you an Advil!"

Nick chuckled as he shut the door. The bickering and sarcasm were just puzzle pieces in his parents' relationship. Every little part went together, proving their love and creating a stronger structure for their marriage. Perfect relationships didn't exist, but strong bonds did. Nick wanted that. An impenetrable, emotional bond with unconditional love and passion.

That wasn't too much to ask, right?

Nick walked over to the couch and bent down to retrieve

NICK AND NOEL'S CHRISTMAS PLAYLIST **249**

Noel's underwear, shoving them into his back pocket. If he told Noel about his mother's assist, it would only embarrass her further and his mother would never mention the incident to Noel for the same reason. Might as well keep it under wraps.

When he reentered the kitchen, he found Noel taking a huge bite out of a fajita.

"Sorry, stress makes me hungry," she mumbled over the food in her mouth. "I washed my hands, I promise."

Nick laughed. "I believe you. And there's nothing to be stressed about. My parents adore you and didn't suspect a thing."

"Really?" she said, doubtfully.

"Yes. Oh, and I wanted to return these." He dangled the underwear from the ends of his fingers with a smirk. "Although, I have to admit, I kind of want to keep them. Put them in a frame to commemorate this amazing night."

"Give 'em. Those were expensive and my favorite pair."

"Fine." Nick handed them to her and watched her stuff them in her pocket. "Now, the two of us were discussing a date a few moments ago. I would like to solidify this idea."

Noel chuckled, leaning against Nick, her arms wrapping around his shoulders. "I'll go out with you."

"That was easier than I thought it would be."

"I'm still freaking out."

Nick tucked a strand of hair behind her ear gently. "Why don't we make this our trial date?"

"Trial date?"

"Yeah. Eat some food. Talk. I'll walk you to your door after and kiss you goodnight?"

"Oh, so we aren't going to…pick up where we left off?"

He noted the clear disappointment on her face and his chest puffed up. "I'm not going to say no, but I think we should dial it back." Even as he said the words, his dick flexed angrily. But if he was going to go there with Noel, he wanted it to be more than a passionate fuck against the wall. He wanted to take things slow. Make love to her. Show her what they have could be so much more than friendship.

"Fine," she pouted.

"Grab your food and we'll go to my bedroom." Her face perked up and he groaned. "Not for that! It's the only surface not covered in boxes and crap."

Noel huffed as she picked up her bag, although the hint of a smile told him she wasn't really mad. Maybe disappointed, but hey, he felt the same way.

Nick grabbed two cokes from his ice chest, slipped his bag of food over one arm and followed her down the hall. He set the cans on the nightstands on either side of his bed. He hopped on one side, while she climbed up and sat cross legged on the other.

"Now what?"

"I'd say we could watch a movie, but I haven't hooked up my TV yet. Why don't we play a game?"

Noel popped the top of her soda, watching him dubiously. "A game?"

"Yeah, like when we were kids. Let's play two truths and a lie, but it can only be things that have happened in the last eight years. That way, there will be a little mystery."

"All right."

Nick opened his container of food, salivating over the rice, beans, and carne asada burrito his parents snagged him. "Mmmmm."

"Hey hey, eyes up here. This was your idea so you go first."

He took the utensils from the bag and cut a bite off. He could tell she was ready to throttle him. When he finally swallowed, he said, "I hated writing letters to everyone while I was deployed. One of the guys in my squad had three girlfriends. And I got a tattoo nobody knows about."

Nick ate his burrito in silence, checking on her thoughtful expression. After several beats, she finally set her taco down and pointed, "You didn't get a tat."

"Ehhh. I did."

"Wait, where?"

Nick grinned. "Maybe I'll show it to you sometime."

"Tease."

"Yup." He took a massive bite, chewed, and finally swallowed. "Your turn."

"Wait, what was the lie, then?"

"The guy in my squad had four girlfriends. Not three."

"Ugh fine." She took a long sip and covered her mouth to burp discreetly. "Excuse me."

"So hot."

"I know. Now, let's see." She tapped a finger against her bottom lip, her eyes directed at the ceiling, deep in thought. "I started doing yoga. I went on a double date with your sister. And I have a secret TikTok account where I sing."

Nick pointed at her. "There is no way you'd be on TikTok."

"You really think I do yoga?" she huffed.

Nick's eyes widened. "I wanna see!"

"No!"

His brow furrowed in disappointment. "What? Why? You let strangers watch you and not me? Why even tell me about it?"

"It's set to private. No one sees."

"I wanna see it. Please."

"No, let's move on. Your turn."

Nick reached across the bed and took her hand. "Do you think I'll make fun of you? I won't. You are amazing, Noel. I forgot how good you were until we sang together."

Noel hesitated, but finally pulled out her phone and handed it to him with a resigned sigh. "Just tap on the app."

Nick did and watched the first video. She sang a cover of his favorite song and the significance of that was not lost on him. The next song, "Hanging by a Moment" by Lifehouse, was her favorite. Her soulful rendition tugged at him, creating a warmth in his stomach. She closed her eyes, passion and joy etched in her features for the sixty-second-long video and Nick's eyes stung with emotion.

Noel tried to take her phone back but he held it away from her.

"Okay, you saw it. You happy?"

"I want to see them all, but I'll wait for another time." He gave her back her phone, squeezing her hand. "Thanks for letting me see it."

"You're welcome," she mumbled, her cheeks still red.

"Now, about the double date with my sister..."

Noel groaned. "In my defense, you Winterses are a persistent lot."

"Come on. Who did you two go out with?"

"She met a guy on Tinder who had a friend. Worst. Date. Ever."

"I'm surprised you got that far. Isn't Tinder mostly dick pics and hookups?"

"Well we managed to find the only two guys looking for something more meaningful, but as a collective."

"What does that mean?"

"They were together, looking for girlfriends."

"If they were together...why did they want you?"

"They were pansexual looking for a third and fourth member of their duo. Nice guys, but I don't share well. Which is funny, considering my lack of committed relationships thus far."

Nick chuckled. "For the record, I don't share well either."

"I never took you for the jealous type."

"Doesn't happen often." *Only with you*, Nick thought.

"I've been jealous of Amber," Noel admitted. "Of the two of you."

Nick brought her hand to his mouth and kissed the back of it. "You have nothing to be jealous of."

Noel released a nervous laugh and took her hand back. "I need this to eat, Romeo."

"Whelp, I guess it's me again, then. Hmmm... I learned how to speak Arabic. I can crotchet." Nick watched her take another bite and grinned broadly. "And I can't wait for you to finish your dinner so I can kiss you again."

Noel smirked, her mouth still full. It took her a minute to chew and swallow, after which she said, "Oh, that kissing part is definitely a lie. There are so many onions in these fajitas, you do not want to go here."

Nick leaned over their makeshift picnic and ran a finger over her bottom lip. "You know I hate onions, but I still want to kiss you."

"Just kiss?"

"For now."

"I guess I better hurry then."

"I would."

CHAPTER 21

NOEL

"HOW MANY PEOPLE ARE COMING?"

Gabby looked up from pouring M&M's into a little white drawstring bag, the late morning sun spilling across the table, highlighting her hands. They'd agreed to all come over Sunday and make the favors for the wedding reception, but Noel was surprised by the bags of supplies lined up against the wall.

"One hundred people."

Noel blinked. "I thought this was supposed to be small?"

"It was, but with my mom's side, then my dad's side, and Drew's family and friends…it just exploded. I've already called the church and the reception location, so we're good there. My mom is talking about getting my aunts together and making the food if I can't find a caterer." Gabby smiled brightly, popping a stray M&M in her mouth. "It's going to be great though. I have faith."

Noel laughed. "I'm sure it will be, but we are going to need more hands on deck to get these favors done."

"Hmmm." Gabby popped a few M&M's into her mouth.

"No worries, the rest of the girls should be here in a little bit. My cousins went Christmas shopping in the city yesterday, so they are driving back this morning. Amber said she'd be by a little later because she wanted to sleep in. I can't blame her for that. I think after this wedding is over, I might sleep for a year."

Noel almost told Gabby about Saturday with Amber in the bathroom and what a jackass friend Amber really was, but she didn't want to ruin Gabby's wedding. As long as Amber kept her mouth shut and gave Noel a wide berth, she could keep it together.

I hope I can, at least.

They went back to filling their little baggies with M&M's, Gabby's Alexa playing Christmas music for background noise. Noel was glad she got to spend a little alone time with Gabby before everyone else arrived. In high school, she'd spent many Sunday mornings sitting in this breakfast nook with Gabby and her family, having brunch and talking about their upcoming weeks. Since Gabby lived with Drew, and Noel had her own place, she didn't make it over to the Montoyas' often.

Actually, before Nick got home, she hadn't visited the Winterses much either. The last few years she'd made excuses for not spending time with the people she loved, like being busy in school and then work, but the truth was, maybe she'd been distancing herself as a defense mechanism. The less time she spent with people, the less she'd miss them when and if they finally...

Noel swallowed the lump in her throat and pushed away those thoughts. Things were looking up. She was opening herself up to possibilities. Trying things with Nick.

When "My Only Wish" came on, Noel smiled, humming along.

"What was that?" Gabby asked.

"What?"

Gabby sat forward, her chin resting in the palm of her hand. She drummed her fingers along her skin as she smirked at Noel. "That little smile. The humming. The suddenly sunny personality shining through all that sarcastic sass."

"I just like this song is all."

"Bullshit." Suddenly, Gabby's lip curled in distaste and she sat back. "Ew, you didn't get back with Trip, did you? I know you two had that dinner last night, but come on. He is a narcissist."

"No! Absolutely not. You are completely right about him being self-involved. He invited me to dinner because he wanted money for his new microbrewery."

Gabby's jaw dropped. "Trip asked you for money? What a fucking tool!"

"Gabriella Ester Montoya!" Eleanor came into the room from the kitchen, glaring at her daughter. "I don't ever want to hear you use that language again."

"Mom, I'm an adult. I can say curse words."

"Not in my house, you can't!" Eleanor winked at Noel. "You hear her use it again, you smack her for me."

"Will do."

Eleanor walked back into the kitchen and missed Gabby rolling her eyes. "I swear, I feel like a kid being here. She is such a pain in my a..." Gabby glanced toward the door and sighed. "Butt."

Noel's chest tightened. "Yeah, but when she isn't around anymore, you'll miss her like crazy."

Gabby's face fell. "I'm sorry. I didn't mean it that way."

Noel immediately regretted her soft reprimand. "It's all right, Gabs. You should be able to vent to me about your frustrations with your parents. What are friends for? I'm just a little sensitive right now."

An awkward silence stretched between them before Gabby got her pep back. "Back to Trip...what did you do when he asked you for money?"

"I took my food to go, ditched him at the restaurant with the bill, and then hid out in Nick's apartment when Trip showed up at mine all pissed off. It was glorious."

"Oh..." Gabby nodded, a sly smile on her face. "I get it. So is Nick the reason you're all twitterpated?"

"Maybe," Noel said, coyly.

Gabby set her baggy down with a squeal. "Seriously? Something else happened and you were holding out on me?"

"I am still digesting our..." Noel glanced toward the door and whispered, "Near sex experience."

"Oh my God!" Gabby's voice rose two octaves. "You have been here for over an hour and you are just bringing this up? I could kill you!"

Noel leaned across the table. "Then I won't tell you how it was interrupted when his parents showed up."

"No! Cockblocked by his parents?"

"Gabriella!" Her mother hollered from the kitchen.

"Sorry, Mom!" Gabby resorted to hushed tones. "Was it hot?"

"So hot. I get goosebumps when I think about it."

"Oh, those are the best! Every time Drew kisses me, I feel like

I'm going to explode." Gabby cocked her head. "When you say near sex…"

"Rounding home when they came a knocking."

Gabby groaned. "Girl, I would have died! What happened after his parents left? You didn't go in for the big finish?"

"Nope. We ate dinner, played two truths and a lie and then…"

"Yes?" Gabby urged, eagerly hanging on Noel's every word.

"Then he walked me home. It's only a few doors down but it was sweet." So sweet when he'd pushed her up against the door and deepened the kiss, she'd nearly dragged him inside with her. Unfortunately, she hadn't been fast enough, too dazed to catch him before he'd pulled away and told her good night.

"That's it?" Gabby's full lips pursed in disappointment.

"Yes, but it's good. We're taking it slow. We're getting to know each other as a potential couple."

"Couple huh?"

"Yes. We're going to have a trial date and see how it goes. He asked me to go with him to the Festival of Trees for our first official date."

"Not the sexiest venture, but I'll take it. Crowded, so he can't whisk you off into a corner and have his way with you."

"Honestly, although I was extremely not okay tapping the brakes last night, I'm glad we didn't jump into bed. I'm still not sure we're doing the right thing."

"Why?" Gabby grabbed her by the shoulders and shook her. "You are gonna drive me insane. Say it with me. You and Nick are perfect together."

Noel placed her hands on Gabby's shoulders and shook her

back. "Nick wants marriage and kids and I don't. Doesn't sound too perfect."

"Yeah, but...do you actually not want the apple pie, white picket fence life? Or are you scared of wanting it and losing it?"

Noel bit her lip. "If you'd asked me six months ago, I would have lied and told you I never wanted that life, but lately, watching you with your mom, planning your wedding...it's brought back memories of my parents. The life they wanted for me." The life Noel once wanted for herself, if she was being honest. "I think the hardest part about finding someone special is that they won't be with me. All these major events and I'll have no one in my corner to celebrate with."

"Baby, that's just not true." Gabby took both her hands and squeezed. "If you decide you want to marry Nick, I will be right where you're sitting, helping you plan for your special day. And the Winterses adore you. You can't tell me they wouldn't jump into the fray. And the whole time, your parents will be watching over you and thinking how happy they are you found your person."

"And if you decide to have kids, you'll have the very best godmother in me. I'll spoil 'em rotten and give 'em back to you hyped up on Pixie sticks."

Noel wiped the back of one hand over her wet eyes, sniffling. What Gabby was describing sounded pretty great to Noel actually. Especially the kids part. Imagining a little boy who looked like Nick? A baby girl with her daddy's brown eyes and kind soul? Victoria and Chris would make amazing grandparents and Nick's sisters would be the best aunts ever.

The question was, could Noel open herself up after denying

the desire for so long? Could she still be a good mom? Or was she too stifled to give Nick what he needed? What she'd always wanted, once upon a time?

Noel got up and grabbed a tissue from the box on the armoire, blowing her nose loudly. "Stop making me cry. This is supposed to be about you, not me."

"I know, but before we make me the center of the universe, back to, um, you know...third base. Would that be you on him or him on you?"

Noel bit her lip as she sat back down. "Him on me."

"And..." Noel cried out when Gabby slapped her knee. "Woman, it's like pulling teeth with you! Details!"

"I'm sorry I'm not used to giving a play-by-play of my orgasms."

"So you're saying climax was achieved." Gabby filled another drawstring bag, nodding in approval. "Hmmm, this is good. This is promising."

"You're being a creeper. Stop."

The front door shut and they both quieted. Amber breezed through the doorway, slipping off her pink, puffy coat with a sly smile. "Hi, guys. I guess you didn't hear me knock with all this riveting conversation."

Noel wiped any emotional evidence away. The last thing she wanted was Amber seeing her in a weak moment. How long had she been standing inside the house listening and neither one of them had heard her?

"Pull up a chair, Amber," Gabby said cheerfully. "We're working on favors."

"And talking about boys." Amber hung her jacket over the

back of her chair and sat down. "You know, Noel, if you need any advice about Nick, just ask. I know all the little tricks he likes."

"Amber..." Gabby growled.

Noel nearly crushed the bag of candies in her hand. "Thanks. I think we'll be okay."

"Oh, I'm sure you will." Amber picked up a bag and poured in some candies. "It's hard being in a relationship, though. So many things to consider, especially with the state of marriage and how easily romances fall apart. You have to possess that certain something to be the marrying kind. Some women have it." Amber glanced pointedly at Noel. "Others don't."

"Let's talk about something else," Gabby said, always the peacemaker.

"Hey, Amber, I meant to ask you. That white halter top you have. Can I borrow it?" Amber's eyes narrowed when Noel smirked. "It's just so cute."

"I'd say yes, but I had a little accident with a tube of red lipstick. Can't get the stain out."

"Oh, that sucks."

"Yeah. It's a *bitch*!" Amber hissed.

"Language!" Eleanor yelled.

Noel scooted back from the table and stood. "I'm going to head into the kitchen and check in with your mom. See if she needs some help."

"You're so sweet, Noel," Amber cooed.

"I know, *Amber*."

Noel kissed the top of Gabby's head and heard her friend hiss as she left the room.

"What was that all about? I told you to be nice!"

Amber scoffed. "Believe me, that *was* nice."

Noel's hackles spiked as she went into the kitchen, eyeballing every sharp object she passed. She needed to stop letting Amber get to her. Every time they ended up in the same room together, they were sixteen again. Passive aggressive. Nasty.

Even Noel knew her behavior was far from perfect, but she had the hardest time not rising to the bait.

"Noel, hey. You need something?"

Noel met Eleanor's concerned gaze and smiled. "Nope, I was just coming in to check on you."

Eleanor ate a mozzarella stick from the tray she was preparing, watching her thoughtfully. "Is Amber here?"

"She just walked through the door."

"I assumed as much."

She cocked her head to the side, puzzled. "What do you mean?"

"Gabby's mentioned a time or two you don't care for Amber."

Noel released a shaky breath. "I don't. At all. But I am trying for Gabby's sake."

"Me too," Eleanor whispered with a wink.

Noel smothered a laugh. "Really?"

Eleanor shrugged. "Gabby adores her, so I don't say much, but there have been a few times she's hurt my baby's feelings and you know me. Mama bear."

"I know. Gabby says she's got a good heart, but I'm having a hard time seeing it."

Eleanor wiped her hands off on her apron, smiling warmly.

"Well, you can hang in here for as long as you need. I noticed some tension yesterday while we were dress shopping. I can't imagine she's too happy about you dating her ex-boyfriend."

"No, but to be fair, she dumped him."

"Gabby mentioned that too. I was actually surprised when those two got together. Nick is so down to Earth. And cute."

"Yes, he is."

"Anyway, I'm glad to see you two working it out. I always thought you would be good together."

Noel blushed. "I have...issues with relationships. So, we're taking it slow."

"I think that's very smart." Eleanor came around the island and hugged Noel. "If you ever want to talk about these *issues*, I'm here. I know you have Victoria, but Gabby likes to refer to you as her sister from another mister." Eleanor grinned. "Since I'm married to the mister, I guess that makes you my daughter too."

Noel's chest squeezed. "Thank you, Mrs. Montoya."

"Anytime, kiddo."

"I'll get back out there."

"Hang tough."

"I don't know what that means."

"New Kids on the Block!"

"Oh, I forgot. Sorry."

"Now that you've made me feel old..." Eleanor trailed off with a laugh. "I'm kidding. Go."

Noel came back into the room and sat down next to Gabby. "Your mom's snack tray looks excellent."

"Thank God, I'm starving. If I sneak anymore M&M's, we won't have enough for favors."

"Speaking of favors." Amber closed her pouch with a snap. "Do you have the location yet, Noel?"

Noel shifted in her seat. She'd known this was coming, but even the expensive rentals were booked up. There was nothing left in Mistletoe for the holiday season, but she didn't want to tell Amber that.

"No, but I contacted the mobile spa and they're available and Sweetie Pies has agreed to provide breakfast for us. I'm going to grab the champagne and orange juice—"

"And what? We'll enjoy getting facials in our cars?" Amber broke in.

"No…" Noel gritted. "I have a call in to a couple of places. I am sure something will become available."

"Of course it will for Little Miss Perfect."

"What is your problem?" Noel exploded.

"What's going on in here?" Eleanor came out of the kitchen and set a plate of finger foods in the center of the table. Gabby's mother glanced between them, as though sensing the tension. "Is everything okay?"

"Yeah, Mom. We were talking."

Eleanor looked to Noel for reassurance and Noel smiled faintly. "I'm fine, Mrs. Montoya. Just a little disagreement."

"All right. You think you girls can fend for yourselves? I'm going to my book club."

"Code for margaritas and man bashing?" Gabby teased.

"I do not bash your father," Eleanor muttered.

Noel snagged a mozzarella stick from the tray, grinning. "Notice she didn't argue with you about the margaritas."

Eleanor wagged her finger at them. "Mind your own business and clean up after yourselves."

"Yes, Mom," Gabby said.

When Eleanor walked out the door, Amber leaned her forearms on the table. "My problem is you have a free location and you don't want to use it."

"We could just go back to my place, since Drew won't be there."

Amber shot Gabby a withering look. "You know I'm allergic to cats, Gabby."

"What about my apartment?" Noel said.

"It's what, one bedroom? So two in the bed and the rest in sleeping bags on the floor. Sounds uber fun."

"If it means that much to you, Amber, you can take my bed."

"Ew, no thank you. I know where you've been."

Gabby put her hands up and pushed back from the table. "All right, that is enough."

But Amber kept on rolling. "This is your best friend's bachelorette party and instead of helping her out, you are making things more difficult."

"You're the one making it difficult. Every place we suggest you shut down. You're rude and uppity with no compassion for others."

Amber crossed her arms over her chest and sat back in the chair. "Really? Because you are sitting here with the perfect venue and acting like a bitch because you're, what, afraid?"

"I already told you. It's not a party pad. It's special."

"We are all adults. I'm sure we can handle a little alcohol and not mess up your *special* place." Amber threw up air quotes belligerently and Noel lost it.

She slammed her hand down on the table.

Gabby muttered, "Oh fuck."

"It's my place and if I don't want to use it as a party location, it's my prerogative."

"A selfish one. Just like you stringing Nick along when you have no intention of giving him what he needs."

"Me stringing Nick along?" Noel cackled. "You stayed with him for eight years while you partied and hooked up! He thought you were this sweet, loyal girlfriend and no one had the heart to tell him what a horrible person you actually were!"

Amber pelted a handful of M&M's at her, the tiny colorful disks flying across the table and hitting her in the face and neck. Noel barely had time to hold her hands up to block the missiles before one hit her in the eye. Noel cried out, cupping her hand over her eye, blinking back tears.

"Noel!" Gabby cried.

Gabby's voice sounded faint and far away while Noel's one good eye trained on Amber. A red fog swirled across her vision and everything else faded away.

The room stilled for half a second as Noel's blood boiled to the breaking point and without consideration, she scooped up M&M's and chucked them back at Amber.

"You guys, stop!" Gabby cried out, but it escalated too quickly.

"You're such a self-righteous little shit, Noel!" Amber yelled, hitting Noel in the cheek with a pizza roll.

"Better than an egotistical bitch who talks shit about her friends, boyfriends, pretty much everyone she knows!"

Noel got up close and personal with the jalapeño poppers, smashing several against the side of Amber's head and smearing them into her blond hair. Amber retaliated with a palm of ranch sauce across Noel's face, the slap wet, cold, and stinging her cheek.

"You'll always be an unlovable loser, Noel. Forever alone. Forever pathetic!" Amber screamed.

Noel reeled back her arm and punched Amber so hard she flew across the table, taking the favors with her as she fell ass over tea kettle. Amber's arms flapped wildly, reaching out to catch herself. When she accidentally hit Gabby square in the face with the back of her hand, there was a sickening crack before Amber finally hit the floor.

Noel gaped in horror as Gabby leaned against the wall in the corner, holding her nose. Blood gushed between Gabby's fingers, dark red streams oozing trails over her hand and arm.

"Gabs..." Noel took a step toward her bestie, but stopped when Gabby held up a bloody hand.

"No," Gabby whimpered.

Amber moaned as she stood up, her palm covering her cheek. "Gabby? Are you okay?"

"No, I am not okay!" Gabby yelled nasally, blood spraying from her mouth. "You destroyed the favors, the food my mom made, wrecked her dining room..." she moaned as she grabbed a handful of tissues and pressed them against her face. "And I am pretty sure you broke my nose!"

Noel swallowed back a lump in her throat, the vision in her one eye blurred and painful to open. "I am so sorry."

"Fuck your sorry! I warned you several times if you two can't put your shit aside and get along, then I don't want you in my wedding. Hell, I don't even want you *at* my wedding." Gabby headed for the door with her head tilted back. "Clean up the mess you made."

Noel came around the table, following behind her. "Gabby, you can't drive yourself. We'll clean this up and one of us can take you to the ER."

"No." Gabby held up a finger, stopping her pursuit. "I'm so pissed at you right now. I cannot be in a small space with either of you or I may say something I can't take back."

The front door opened and Gabby's cousin Emilia stopped in the doorway, eyes wide. "What happened here?"

"A mishap," Gabby mumbled. "Could you take me to the ER? I need to have my nose looked at."

"Sure, come on." Emilia took Gabby's arm and led her out of the house.

Noel stood for a moment, staring down at the table with her one good eye. The cloth Gabby's mom kept on there to protect the wood was soaked with ranch and water from a knocked over glass. Droplets of blood splattered on the light wood floor and table cloth. Noel silently berated herself. She'd lost control and Gabby paid for it.

Maybe Amber was right about Noel being selfish.

Slowly, she gathered up the plates and carried them into the kitchen. Neither of them said a word as Amber picked M&M's off the floor, setting them into the crystal candy dish with a clack.

Once everything had been removed from the table, Noel gathered up the table cloth, ignoring the throbbing in her eye. "I'm going to put this in the washer."

"Whatever."

Noel stopped in the entryway and faced Amber. Amber's right cheek was swollen and bruised and Noel couldn't help the sliver of satisfaction it caused.

"I don't even know why you are here if you don't like Gabby."

Amber stopped gathering up the favor supplies and stared at her. "I do like Gabby. I can't understand what she sees in you."

"You know what's funny? I wonder the same thing when it comes to you."

"Gabby is my girl. I love her because she doesn't judge people. That's why she's friends with you. It's why she's the only girlfriend you hang with."

That statement was a little too accurate and it stung. "You want to talk about judging? You do nothing but slut shame me, yet how many times have you ditched Gabby drunk at some club so you could hit some after-party?"

"I always asked and she said she'd be fine!"

"How big of you!"

Amber pointed her finger at Noel accusingly. "At least I do fun things with her. You check out for weeks on end, with one-word texts!"

"I do not check out!"

"Really? Where were you when her aunt had cancer and she had to be put on hospice? Did you hold her hand while she waited to say goodbye?"

Noel swallowed hard. Sophomore year. A few months after she'd lost her parents. She'd attended the funeral, but had to leave halfway through. It was too fresh. Too painful.

"I was there for her," Noel whispered.

"Not the way I was. You expected everyone to bend over backwards for you. To feel sorry for you, but you couldn't put anyone's needs above your own. Even your so-called best girlfriend."

"I don't know where you are getting that, but it isn't true."

"Yes it is! You always looked out for yourself, so there was nothing left for anyone else. Always a little bit more than everyone else, including me! A little bit more talented. A little bit funnier. A little bit smarter. I met Gabby first and even she liked you better than me, no matter how hard I tried. You used to look at me so smug every time you beat me at something I wanted. Then your parents died and you stopped competing. You stopped caring about anything and everyone. You weren't just selfish, but you became an empty, worthless shell.

"But people still talked about you. *Poor Noel. Has anyone talked to Noel? Is she doing all right? We sure do miss her.*" Amber's voice grew sharper. "The spring play. Chorus. I played second fiddle to you my whole life but you know what? Not with Nick." Amber smiled, even as tears trailed down her cheeks. "I had him first. He's going to remember me for the rest of his life, no matter who he's with."

Amber's accusations almost made Noel feel sorry for her, if she hadn't played on her insecurities with Nick. Losing the people she loved was her biggest fear, yet she knew at times she pushed them away. She should have been better to Gabby, but she was too caught up in her own grief at the time. Amber had been extracting her revenge for years, all because she was jealous and thought Noel was hurting her on purpose?

"I may be selfish at times and pull away from the people I love. That's on me. But I don't know why you ever thought I was trying to take anything from you. I never gave you a second thought until you started tormenting me in high school. I'm not saying that to be mean, but because it is the truth. We had different friends in middle school. Yeah, we shared choir, but we didn't mesh. I'm sorry, but I wasn't trying to hurt you. I loved singing. Being on stage. Until I didn't.

"You say that I'm not there when Gabby needs me, but she knows she means the world to me. That is the only reason I didn't tell her about you talking shit behind her back."

Noel's words seemed to take some of the steam out of Amber, because her tone hardly had any bite left. "Like you've never said anything that may hurt someone's feelings?"

Amber didn't wait for an answer, just turned away. Noel took the table cloth to the laundry room. She didn't speak to Amber for the rest of the two-hour cleanup, but she did consider her words. Noel hurt people without realizing it. She knew sometimes she could be waspish, but she never set out to intentionally harm anyone who didn't strike first.

She needed to make things right with Gabby. Bury the hatchet with Amber, who'd been holding onto her own resentment of Noel. Amber throwing her relationship with Nick in her face still burned, but maybe Noel should consider Nick's suggestion that she talk to someone. A few appointments to help work through her unresolved anger and hurt. Give her some perspective and teach her to let things go.

Noel thought about the storage unit bill in her purse. She'd planned on stopping by tomorrow and paying another year on the unit to keep her parents' belongings safe. To leave it closed and untouched, but maybe it would help to go through her parents' things. She'd been thinking about them so much lately, that it may be cathartic. Stop keeping her memories in a bubble, away from the world and share them with others.

But first, she needed to go to the ER and get her eye looked at. Amber may be a heinous witch, but she had great aim.

CHAPTER 22

NICK

NICK LOOKED UP FROM HIS guitar when Noel came down the stairs into his parents' basement on Sunday afternoon wearing an eye patch over her left eye, white gauze peeking out beneath the black fabric. His mind immediately went to Trip and his temper tantrum last night.

He stood up, setting his guitar against his amp. His sisters were both running late, so it was just the two of them in the basement.

"What the hell happened to your eye?"

A ghost of a smile flittered across her lips. "A stray M&M. Don't worry, I went to urgent care. The doctor said it should be all right by the weekend."

"Wait, how did a candy end up in your eye?"

Noel hung her coat and purse strap over the end of the banister. "Your ex-girlfriend threw a handful of them at me today and I didn't duck fast enough."

"I have even more questions now."

"Maybe they could wait a while? I've had a pretty emotionally exhausting day."

Without hesitation, Nick went to Noel and pulled her into his arms, holding her against his chest. He ran a hand over her dark hair, stroking her, and he loved the way she melted into him.

"Does this help at all?"

Her arms looped around his waist and she squeezed. "A lot. Don't stop."

Nick chuckled, rocking her back and forth in his arms, humming under his breath. Noel lifted her face to watch him, grinning.

"Are you singing 'Must Be Santa'?"

"Good ear."

"It used to be our favorite. Remember in second grade, before the Christmas recital, our moms banned us from singing it at home because we wouldn't stop?"

Nick chuckled. "Yeah. I don't know what their problem was. It's a very catchy tune."

"Right." Her smile slipped a bit. "During the holidays, when she'd put me to bed, my mom would turn on this Christmas CD before she shut off my light. That song was always first."

He held her a little tighter, noting the sadness in her tone. "She was a great woman. I know she loved you very much."

"Do you think I'm selfish?"

Nick pulled away, holding her by the shoulders. "Where did that come from?"

"Amber said I was being selfish because I didn't want to use my parents' cabin for the bachelorette party."

Nick scoffed. "Please, Amber has no right calling you anything. She once told me she couldn't pick me up from the airport because she had a mani-pedi appointment and," he said in a high falsetto voice, "didn't I want her to look good?"

He fluttered his eyelashes, but she barely cracked a smile.

"But do you think I should let Gabby use it? I can't find anything else available."

"Not if you don't want her to. That is your parents' place. It's special. If Gabby doesn't get that, she isn't a real friend."

"She did," Noel insisted, defensively. "She understood. But Amber got me thinking and then we fought and ruined all Gabby's favors."

"Is that how the M&M pegged you in the eye? Her favors?"

"It only started with M&M's. We moved onto fried food, dip, and finally I just punched her in the face."

Nick coughed to cover a laugh. "Damn. Sounds like I missed one hell of a show."

"Unfortunately, when I hit her, Amber fell back and smacked Gabby in the face by accident. I'm pretty sure we broke her nose, so Gabby didn't think it was very funny."

"Ouch. That sounds bad."

"Yeah. I had to stay behind with Amber and clean up our mess. Amber also informed me that I actually made her life miserable by competing with her in choir and drama and taking everyone away from her."

"Whhhhaaaaat?" He dragged out the *ah* to make her smile. "I thought she used to torment you in high school? That's what you told me."

"Apparently, I started it without realizing, but it made me think... I never understood her insane dislike for me. I mean, I'm not the easiest person to get close to, but I don't think I'm completely unlovable."

Nick tilted his head back and forth, waving his hands like he was weighing the air. "Eh. Not completely."

She pushed him gently, but he caught her by the shoulders, bringing her back to him. "Gee, thanks."

"I'm only teasing. I keep telling you people like you. It sounds like a misunderstanding that festered between two adolescent females brought on by lack of communication. The resentment festered and instead of having a heart to heart and clearing up the infection, it turned putrid."

"Thank you, Dr. Phil."

"I am just saying, it was a long time ago. Maybe we should just sit you in a room with someone to referee."

"Yeah, the last person to try to help us got her nose broken." Noel buried her face in his chest. "She is never going to forgive me."

"Of course Gabby will."

"Amber said I don't have any female friends because I'm a slut and no one likes me. That's why I only hang with guys."

"No, you have other female friends."

"Like who?"

"Merry, Holly."

"We don't hang that much."

"All right, fine, but you talk about other women at work."

"Those are work friends. So far, you have given me family

friends and work friends, but no super close, head to the bar and discuss life's problems, friends."

"Then I'd say Gabby fits all the bills, so you don't need any other close female friends. It's like having a five-course meal, when all you really need is the steak and potatoes to satisfy you."

Noel looked up at him, smiling through her tears. "Are you saying I need Pike and Anthony because you don't emotionally satisfy my need for male friends?"

"No, see, I am boyfriend material, so I am in a class all on my own. Those two can duke it out for the top guy-friend spot. I'm seeking a new position entirely."

Noel leaned up on her tiptoes and kissed him, the salt of her tears on her lips. It was the only thing that kept him from taking the kiss just a little further. Right now, she needed him to listen, not try to get in her pants.

She dropped back onto her heels and wiped at her cheeks. "Ugh, why do I keep crying every time I see you?"

"I don't know, but stop it. I'm starting to get a complex."

"Funny." Noel made a face that said she did not in fact think it was funny. "When I left Gabby's parents' house, I took the favor supplies with me so I could finish them and bring them back as an apology. The issue is, she's expecting a hundred guests and I have to work tonight. It's going to take me days to finish and as far as grand apologies go, they should really be made sooner rather than later."

"What is she doing with the M&M's?"

"Putting them in drawstring bags with a little tag attached that has their initials. Cute but simple."

"You got the stuff with you?"

"Yeah."

"Why don't I rope my sisters into helping us make the favors?"

Noel already shook her head. "We skipped practice yesterday and I have to be at work at six."

"Don't worry about practice. We got this playlist down. Besides, four sets of hands are better than one."

After a heartbeat of silence, Noel cradled his face in her hands and kissed him again.

"Thank you."

Nick pressed his forehead to hers, his arms secured around her waist. "That's what friends with an interest in becoming more do for each other."

She chuckled. "It definitely scores you brownie points."

"Whoo-hoo. How many extra points do I get if I can also help on the location front?"

"A hundred zillion thousand."

"Not an actual number, but I'll take it. It's not a cabin, but I bet if it's available, we could get Charlie at The Rustic to rent you the presidential suite for cheap. I don't think anyone has ever stayed in it since he always insists on keeping it open on the slim chance that some government official is going to stop in Mistletoe. I don't know what you all have planned, but it sleeps ten, so I think it could work for you."

Noel threw her arms around his neck and he sank into her, pulling her tight against his body, their mouths meeting over and over.

"Is that a 'gee thanks'?" he asked between kisses.

"And a big-time thank you." She nibbled his bottom lip, running her hands over his arms. "Maybe tomorrow I could sneak over after work and thank you properly."

"Hmmm, what did you have in mind?"

"A little quid pro quo, Clarice," she hissed, making the sucking noise from *Silence of the Lambs*.

Nick leaned back, frowning in disgust. "Can you not talk like Hannibal Lecter in reference to going down on me?"

Noel laughed, burying her face in his chest. "I'm sorry. I'm still adjusting to being not just friends. Trying to be sexy is rough."

"Hey, you are sexy without trying, except when you're quoting a psychopathic cannibal."

"Noted."

"Now if you were into other role playing, I could be down with that. I've always fantasized about making out with a dirty pirate."

Noel's hands slid into his hair and responded in a husky, pirate voice. "Guess today be your lucky day, argh."

"Mmmm." His hands cupped her butt, bringing her harder against him. "Better."

"Ahem. Seems we're interrupting."

Nick and Noel broke apart at the sound of Merry clearing her throat. Both Winters sisters stood at the bottom of the stairs, watching them with identical grins. Nick shook his head at his meddling siblings but didn't call them out on their lightness of foot.

"Ah, good. You're here."

"Weren't we supposed to be?" Holly asked.

"Apparently, they weren't expecting us anytime soon." Merry wiggled her eyebrows as she thrust her hips.

Noel groaned, hiding her face in her hands.

Nick scowled at the girls and barked, "All right, chuckles, listen up. We are skipping practice tonight."

Merry and Holly looked at each other, before Merry planted her hands on her hips.

"Does Mom know that?"

"She will, don't worry. This is more important." Nick turned to Noel. "Are your keys in your purse?"

"Yes, but the car's not locked. The favors are in the back seat in grocery sacks."

"All right, you two"—Nick pointed to his grinning sisters—"stop gawking. Noel needs us to help her finish the favors for Gabby's wedding, so you two get the supplies and meet us at the kitchen table. Our mission is to finish the favors before Noel goes to work." Nick clapped his hands. "Let's get 'er done!"

Merry shot him a disgruntled expression. "Normally, I'd rebel against you popping off orders, but since it's for Noel, I'll go along with it."

Holly pointed at Noel. "Why are you wearing an eye patch?"

Nick snapped his fingers rapidly. "All will be explained. Now shoo!"

"Nobody likes a tyrant, big brother," Merry muttered as the two of them trekked back upstairs.

Alone again, Nick kissed her, falling into the taste of chocolate and warmth. When they finally pulled apart, Noel's face radiated happiness.

"A girl could get used to this."

I hope you do.

"We better get up there before they start catcalling."

Nick laced his fingers through hers and led her up the stairs. They broke apart just before they crested the main floor, mostly to avoid any more teasing from his annoying sisters.

He was surprised to find his parents sitting down at the table with Holly and Merry, getting organized with all the favor supplies.

The moment Butch spotted them, he made a beeline for Noel, who ducked behind Nick.

"Uh-uh, you got me on the way in, you turkey!"

Suddenly, Noel fell into his back face first, propelling him forward until he caught himself on the counter.

"Really dude?" Noel's voice was muffled between his shoulder blades. "You can't get to my front, so you hit me in the back?"

"It's a sign of affection," Chris called. "Dogs sniff each other's rears to say hello."

"I wish he'd get it through his head I am not a dog," Noel mumbled. "I don't need either my front or my back inspected."

Chris chuckled, whistling at his dog. "Butch. Get over here. Noel doesn't like you."

"I like him!" she protested. "I just don't appreciate him getting so personal."

"You two joining in?" Nick asked.

"The girls said Noel needed us." Victoria grabbed a drawstring bag and poured a handful of M&M's inside. "We're family. This is what we do. We band together in a crisis."

Nick caught the sheen of tears in Noel's good eye and squeezed her hand. "See. Nothing we can't do."

"How did you hurt your eye?" his dad asked.

"Food fight with Nick's ex."

"Ohhhweee, they fighting over you, Nicky Boy?"

Noel shook her head, taking the seat next to his sister, Holly. "Nah, we've never gotten along. She used to pick on me in high school."

"Me too," Merry said.

Holly laughed. "Now I feel left out. I was too beneath her to be tortured."

Nick stood behind Noel, his hands on her shoulders. "How did I not know this?"

"Because you're a guy and she has big—" Holly held her hands two feet out from her chest.

"Holly!" his mother warned.

"What, I'm just saying. Even my perfect brother isn't immune to being a *guy*."

Nick sat down next to Noel. "You might not be wrong about my powers of observation. Seems I missed quite a few red flags."

Noel snickered and he squeezed her above her knee. She burst out laughing, her leg flying up and pain shot up his arm when it slammed into the top of the table.

"Ow!"

Noel reached for his hand, her brown eyes filled with remorse. "Oh my God, I'm so sorry."

"Were you trying to cop a feel?" Merry teased.

"No!" Nick and Noel shouted together.

The Winters family laughed, and pretty soon, Nick chuckled right along with them, while Noel's face stayed tomato red.

"Noel has a habit of reminding me how obtuse I can be. I only squeezed her knee so she wouldn't tell me she told me so. I forgot how ticklish she is."

"We all make mistakes, my love," his mom said, stacking the bags neatly in the center of the table. "We want to see the best in people, even when they show us their true nature time and again."

Merry nodded. "Yep. I dropped most of my high school friends because they were toxic as hell. You're lucky to have Noel and your boys, big brother. Not everyone is blessed with healthy relationships from our childhood."

"Oh, I wouldn't call Nick and Noel just friends, would you?" Holly quipped.

"Not with his hands all over her—"

"Girls. Enough," his mother snapped and the two of them buttoned their lips. "Nick, why don't you help me make dinner? I'm sure Noel wants to eat before she leaves for work and I think the four of them can handle these favors without us."

"Sure." Noel squeezed his hand as he got up, and he kissed her knuckle. "Be right back."

Nick followed his mom into the kitchen, knowing it was code for wanting to talk. He'd been waiting for her to pull him aside since she'd discovered them last night, but he hadn't expected her to act almost grim. He knew she loved Noel, so why the long face?

He stood off to the side while she pulled items out of the fridge, waiting for her to kick off the conversation.

"Nick, I need to ask you...are you two serious?"

"We are just getting started, Mom."

His mom put a pot of water on the stove before facing him again. "You're not even dating yet and already sleeping together?" His mother cleared her throat, lowering her voice. "I didn't mean to sound so judgmental. I just worry that the two of you are jumping into this too fast without really considering what's at stake."

"I'm an adult, so this really isn't your business, but we haven't slept together yet."

"That's good, I suppose. Will you start making the salad?"

"Of course," he muttered, grabbing the bag of lettuce from the counter and tossing it into a large bowl. They worked silently for a few minutes, her breading defrosted chicken breasts while he cut up carrots, colored peppers, and tomatoes for the salad.

"I know you're an adult, but you're also my child. Noel's mentioned to me a few times she doesn't want to get married or have kids. You've talked about a big family since you were seven. You can see my confusion and...concern."

"I know how Noel feels and yes, I do want a marriage and kids. I am not giving up on that. But..." his voice trailed off as he smiled, thinking about Noel's smell, the feel of her skin under his fingertips. It was hardly something he felt comfortable talking to his mother about but he understood she was looking out for him and Noel and he wanted to reassure her. "Every time I'm with her, it's like the world shines a little brighter. Being together feels right and it took some convincing for her to take that leap with me. We have plenty of time to figure out what having a future together means for both of us."

His mom set the tray of breaded chicken breasts off to the side and washed her hands.

"Also, Noel loves kids. I've seen it. She took a job in Labor and Delivery. I know a lot of things changed for her after her parents, but it all stems from fear."

His mother didn't respond right away and these long pauses made him nervous, especially because he never expected his mother to have any qualms about him and Noel.

"Baby," she said, placing a hand on his shoulder. "You are an optimist and I love that about you, but relationships don't work that way. Yes, Noel loves children, but that doesn't mean she'll change her mind about wanting her *own*. If the two of you start out with different future goals, you're going to wake up one day and realize that as much as you care for her, you can't force her to want the same things you do and vice versa. I just don't want you two to start something that may not evolve and then you're both left broken hearted and resenting each other."

Nick covered her hand with his and squeezed. "People change, Mom. Dreams evolve. I can tell you with a hundred percent confidence, I never had such strong feelings for any woman the way I do with Noel."

His mother kissed his cheek, patting his arm as she went back to cooking. "That's all a mother can ask for her son. A good woman and mutual love and respect for each other."

"We have that, without a doubt."

"You sound like you know what you're doing, so I'll just mind my business." Suddenly, she turned around and shook her spoon at him. "But just to be clear, you are giving me grandbabies. Lots of them."

Nick laughed, knowing his mother would respect her children's decisions on whether or not they wanted to reproduce. As far as he knew, both Holly and Merry wanted kids in the distant future. He did too, so his mother's concerns gave him a lot to think about.

If he and Noel worked, if they were head over heels in love, could he forget about kids and marriage if she truly didn't want those things? Would being with the right person mean sacrificing things he'd always expected to have one day in order to hold onto the person he needed?

Nick shook his head, berating himself for jumping three steps ahead. Heavy subjects could wait, at least until after their first date.

His mother was right, he was an optimist. And he wasn't ready to give up on what Noel and he could have before they even got started.

CHAPTER 23

NOEL

ON MONDAY MORNING, NOEL WENT straight from work to Drew and Gabby's place, her back seat covered in grocery sacks full of favors. Nick came by the hospital around midnight and asked for her keys. She'd followed him outside and helped him unload the bags from the back of his truck, still overwhelmed that even after she'd left for work, his family stuck around and finished them for her.

Her family.

The Winterses were her family, even if Nick and she didn't work out. Noel kept telling herself that, because the thought of losing five people, possibly seven if Anthony and Pike couldn't forgive her for breaking Nick's heart, was a crippling thought. And that would be how it ended; she already knew. If things went south between her and Nick, it would be her fault.

She hoped if it did come to pass, it was something forgivable.

Nick didn't seem to have a worried bone in his body, which should have made her feel better. An eternal optimist, he'd wrapped her up in his arms and kissed her, quieting her concerns with playful abandon until she was too caught up returning his kisses to think. He'd left her at the front door of the hospital, smiling like a lunatic, and humming the rest of her shift.

That's what Nick did to her. He made her forget reality.

Still sporting the eye patch, Noel parked the car in the driveway of the house, taking a deep, nervous breath. Drew's parents were real estate agents and owned quite a few properties throughout the area. They'd let Drew and Gabby rent the house on the cheap, as long as they continued to make repairs and upgrades.

Noel slipped the bag handles over one arm, as many as she could and then the rest over the other. Noel's arms ached as she headed up the walkway and stopped in front of the blue door. Her heart hammered as she pressed the doorbell, murmuring a silent prayer that Gabby would answer, ready to forgive and forget.

Instead, Drew pulled the door open, looking rumpled, with a coffee mug in one hand. Drew resembled a young Jason Statham, down to the shaved head and muscles. Only his eyes were a brilliant cobalt blue and he wasn't big on fighting or racing cars. He was bookish, quiet, and had a dry wit Noel adored. The polar opposite of Gabby, but Noel suspected their differences benefited their relationship.

"Hey, Noel. What you got there? And so early?"

"Sorry if I woke you. I just got off work. Last week on the graveyard shift." She lifted her arms like she was about to take flight. "And these are your favors."

"Wow, all of them? Gabby said you guys didn't finish because of the…" Drew tapped the bridge of his nose, lowering his voice. "Nose thing."

Noel's face flushed at the reminder of her terrible behavior. "No, we didn't, but I wanted to make it up to Gabby, so I worked on them yesterday. With the help of the Winterses." Noel cleared her throat. "Could I set these down? They're heavy."

"Oh yeah, sorry, my manners are nonexistent before my first cup of coffee." Drew took some off her hands, leading her into the house and through the dining room. "We can put them on the kitchen counter." Drew dropped them on the white tile surface and tapped under his eye. "How's your wound, by the way? Digging the eye patch."

"Still hurts, but the doctor said it should heal in a week. Just need to keep using my drops and changing the bandage."

"That's good. Glad it wasn't worse."

Noel set the bags down where he said, trying to massage feeling back into her hands. "So, is Gabby still asleep?"

"Let me go see. Just hang tight."

"Drew…"

"Yeah?"

"Her nose. Was it broken?"

"Yeah, but it was a clean break, so the doctor was able to set it. Said it should heal really fast." Drew walked over and squeezed her shoulder. "I know Amber started it and that you didn't mean for her to get hurt. Believe me, I wonder what in the heck Gabby sees in that girl, but you are her best friend. She'll forgive you."

"Thanks, Drew. Gabby really got lucky in the fiancé department."

Drew grinned. "I think so too, but if I'm being honest, I'm pretty lucky myself." He set his coffee down next to the sink. "I'll be right back."

Noel paced the kitchen, waiting for Gabby to come through the doorway with her arms open. Ready to forgive her.

A few moments later, Drew came back, looking grim. "She's still sleeping, Noel. Can she text you later?"

Noel bit her lip, knowing Drew was lying. Her bestie refused to see her. She'd messed up big time.

Noel coughed, trying to remove the emotional lump in her throat. "Sure, she can text me whenever. Could you...could you please tell her I'm sorry and I love her."

"I will. I wouldn't worry too much, okay? In a few days, you two will be laughing about this."

"Sure," Noel mumbled. "I'll show myself out."

She climbed into her car, tears rolling down one side while the other eye's gauze covering caught the liquid from her tears. She'd have to change it when she got home.

This wasn't the first fight she'd experienced with Gabby, but it was the biggest. She knew a lot of childhood friendships didn't survive adulthood, but she couldn't lose Gabby. She needed her.

What about Nick? Can you lose him?

Her chest squeezed at the thought. She knew what it meant to love so much and lose everything. But if Amber hadn't dumped him and they got married, would Noel have lost him anyway? If she kept running scared, afraid to let herself love Nick for real, and to live her life free of fear, would he give up on her and find someone else?

Look at Gabby and Drew. Drew chased Gabby through high school and into college and she'd finally given him a shot. Now, she was head over heels in love and about to get married. Gabby told her life and pain go hand in hand...but if she kept shutting out the good things because she didn't want to get hurt, then she was exactly what Amber called her.

Empty.

Nick made her happy. His smile. His laugh. His caring nature. His dorky side.

Noel needed Nick. Right now.

That's how she found herself an hour later, standing in front of Nick's apartment holding a bag of pastries and two coffees. She just hoped he was up and not still sleeping.

Noel knocked gently, listening for him. After the third time, Nick pulled open the door in a towel, his wet hair dripping water down his torso.

"You always show up at guys' apartments at the butt crack of dawn?"

"Only when I'm bearing crullers and coffee." She held out the goodies, her gaze flicking over him. "Do you always open the door half naked and wet?"

"When I know the girl I'm into is on the other side, then yes I do." Nick stepped back, nodding her in. "Come on, you're letting all the cold air in."

"Oh, I'm so sorry sir." Noel stepped inside, shutting the door behind her. After hanging up her coat and kicking off her boots, she followed Nick into the kitchen. He caught her off guard when he set down the drinks and pastries to sweep her up onto the counter. He stood between her legs, his arms secured around her waist, dropping fast, firm kisses all over her face and neck.

"Hmmm, I missed you."

Noel giggled as he found the sensitive spot below her chin. "You just saw me a few hours ago."

"More like six and it felt longer." He gave her a hard, hot kiss, his hand coming up to cradle the back of her head. She'd changed into a pair of fleece leggings and a long-sleeved T-shirt, and with her nipples pebbled against the thin cotton, it was obvious she wasn't wearing a bra.

Noel looped her arms around his neck, enjoying the attention. The distraction of his touch as he slipped his hand up under her shirt, smoothing against the small of her back. When his fingers kneaded there, she moaned.

"Mmm, you sore?"

"Very. I'm usually on my feet most of the night and even with comfortable shoes, my back aches."

"Wanna come to the bedroom and we'll see what I can do about relieving the tension?"

Noel smiled. "Lead the way."

Nick took her by the hand and helped her down off the counter. The closer they got to the bedroom, the faster Noel's heart galloped. Some of the boxes from Saturday had disappeared, leaving just a handful stacked against the wall.

"You've been busy."

"Trying, but for some reason it's easier to pack up for moving than it is to unpack."

"I believe it," Noel said.

"Why don't you take your shirt off and lie down on your stomach?"

Noel's cheeks burned and she turned her back to him, lifting the blue cotton shirt over her head. She climbed up on the bed, aware that from just the right angle, Nick would be able to see her naked breasts.

"Lie flat, however you're comfortable."

Noel tilted her head to the side, watching Nick as he disappeared behind her. She was very much aware that he was naked but for that scrap of terry cloth around his waist.

Nick straddled the backs of her thighs, keeping most of his weight off her. His hands smoothed over her lower back muscles, his fingers working her with firm pressure. She turned to mush as he rubbed his way up her back, squeezing her shoulders and even her arms. She closed her eyes with a moan, on the verge of drooling.

Noel had no idea when she passed out, but she came to a few hours later, curled up under a soft sherpa blanket on Nick's bed. Still topless. Her leggings untouched.

She checked the clock on Nick's nightstand. A quarter after one. He'd let her sleep for almost six-and-a-half hours.

Noel stretched as she sat up, looking around the room for her shirt. She found it folded neatly on his dresser. She pulled it on before opening his bedroom door, and padding down the hall to the kitchen.

Nick sat at his computer, headphones in place. She came up alongside him and he glanced up, a wide smile on his face. He pushed back from the table and pulled her against him, his face level with her breasts.

"Hey, you're awake," he said, setting his headphones off to the side.

"I am." Noel straddled his lap, her arms resting around his shoulders. "Your massage totally knocked me out."

"Good. You seemed tense when you got here this morning. I wanted to make you feel better."

"You did. I went by Gabby's after work to drop off the favors." Noel's voice weakened, filled with grief. "She wouldn't even see me."

Nick cupped her cheek sweetly. "I'm so sorry, Noel. She'll come around."

"Yeah I know. I don't really want to think about it." She kissed the side of his neck. "Feel like taking a break?"

"Sure, what did you have in mind?"

"A little of this," Noel said, kissing his lips.

"Uh-huh."

Noel reached between them and ran her hand over the front of his boxers. "A little of that."

"I'm listening," he moaned.

Noel whipped her shirt off over her head and flung it across the room, losing every ounce of shyness from earlier. She was rested, rejuvenated, and ready to finish what they'd started Saturday.

A loud ringing exploded from his computer and he cursed. "Shit, hang on. It's my boss, video chatting me."

Noel climbed off his lap, smirking. "Now the shirt and tie with the boxers makes sense."

"Business up top, casual below. Just stand on the other side and I'll be with you shortly."

Noel walked into the kitchen topless, sensing Nick's gaze still glued to her as he answered the video call.

"Hey Dave, how's it going?"

"Really good Nick. The creative team is loving your suggestions."

Noel listened with half an ear as he chit-chatted about graphics and strategies, pulling her pastry from earlier out of the bag. She leaned over the counter, tearing off little bits and sliding them into her mouth, watching Nick try to concentrate. She'd never done anything like this before, seducing a guy while he was busy working. She swirled her tongue around the last piece and his eyes nearly crossed.

She finished her breakfast with a smirk and washed her hands.

"That sounds great, Dave. I really think players will enjoy this more."

Noel slid her hands into the top of her leggings and pushed them down. The counter blocked Nick's line of sight, and she giggled as she watched him strain to see what she was doing.

"Nick, is everything okay?"

"Yes, sir, it's fine. My cat is just trying to get up onto the counter and eat my food." Noel stepped into his line of vision wearing only her black cheeky panties. Nick's growled, "Bad kitty."

The gravelly tone caused a shiver to race up her spine and she turned her back to him, running her hand over her butt. Squeezing it.

Nick choked, producing a coughing fit. He grabbed a bottle of water next to his computer and took a long drink. When he finally came up for air, he apologized. "Sorry, got a tickle in my throat."

"Probably allergies. All the pet dander cats have. Well, to each their own. Never could stand cats myself. I just wanted to let you know we are loving everything you're doing and keep up the good work."

"Absolutely, sir. I appreciate it. We will talk soon."

"Bye now."

The call ended and Nick stood up, facing her from across the table. Noel took a step around the counter, backing away as he advanced.

"Have I mentioned I've been wanting a cat?"

"I don't remember. I can't think with your tits bouncing every time you move."

Noel's breath caught as he almost caught her, but she managed to get to the other side of his kitchen table with a soft laugh. Still, he kept coming.

"You enjoyed that, did you?"

Her heart galloped, loving the chase. "I did. Didn't you?"

Nick grinned wickedly. "Not as much as I'll enjoy what comes next."

"And what do you think— Ahh!" Noel squealed when Nick came around the table and lunged for her. She took off running, but only made it halfway down the hall before he caught her around the waist, pulling her back against him. Her butt fit snug against the front of his boxers and she could feel his firm length nestled there, fully at attention.

"You like teasing me," he whispered against the side of her neck. His hands cupped her naked breasts, squeezing them, caressing them.

"Yes." The word came out breathless and harsh.

"Hmm...I liked watching you tease me. It was all I could do not to jump up, bend you over the table and make you squirm."

Noel never would have guessed that kind, patient Nick would be assertive in the bedroom. When she did imagine it, it was always sweet. Lots of reassurances and gentleness. Not this dirty talking stranger whose hand slid down her body and into the top of her panties to...

She gasped, pressing her hand flat against the wall to steady her as Nick circled her clit with his finger. Noel arched into his hand, frustrated by the slow, even strokes he administered.

"Faster," she whimpered.

"No teasing then?"

She shook her head vehemently.

"As you wish."

Noel didn't have time to catch her breath before he did exactly as she asked, his hand moving at the speed of light. Her nails dug into the wall plaster as she closed her good eye, her body shaking with every swift circle of her clit. Noel couldn't stop her hips from bucking of their own volition, needing, wanting, craving his touch. Her release. God, so close. Coming.

Her body convulsed, her pussy pulsating as she came down from each delicious wave. Nick's lips trailed across her shoulders, the back of her neck.

Noel slowly turned, her back against the wall. "Nick..."

She was delighted to find him breathing as hard as she was, his dick causing a massive tent in his boxers. "Yeah."

"My turn."

"Oh yeah?"

Noel took him by the tie and led him gently the rest of the way down the hallway to his bedroom. "Absolutely."

When she backed him up to the bed and pushed him down onto his back, he grinned up at her, sliding his hands behind his head. "Do your worst."

"Oh, I plan too." People took for granted the difference two good eyes made versus one, but Noel managed to slip off his tie in record time, tossing it away.

Nick watched her intensely, his lips cocked up in the corners, a bemused smile on his face. She unbuttoned his shirt, sliding it open to expose his hard pecs and the ridges of his taut abs. Noel's gaze caught his and she stilled for a moment, memorizing the wildness in his eyes and the soft parting of his mouth. How his breath came in swift bursts, his body tight with anticipation.

Mine. His reaction. His heart pounding against my palm. All of that is for me.

Her fingers traced all the planes and ridges, followed by her mouth, power and wonder coursing through her like electromagnetic pulses. Trailing her tongue. Pressing light kisses along his skin. He whispered her name when she nipped at the spot just above his boxer band.

Noel pulled down the top of his boxers and smiled.

"You ready?"

"Fuck yeah I—"

He never finished the sentence.

CHAPTER 24

NOEL

TUESDAY AFTERNOON, NOEL PARKED IN front of Gabby's house just after four, carrying two coffee cups in her hands. She wasn't above ambushing and bribing Gabby with tasty beverages if it meant she'd hear her out.

She set one coffee down on the porch and rang the doorbell. Noel was just standing back up when Gabby answered the door clad in black slacks and a white blouse, with her hair up in a bun. White gauze was taped across her nose and under both her eyes was a nasty purple bruise.

"Hey," she said.

"Hi, Gabs. Can we talk?"

"Sure, come on in." Gabby stepped back, letting Noel walk past her into the foyer. Noel noticed a basket on the decorative bench in the entryway and pointed.

"What's that?"

"Amber brought me a Boozy Basket as a means of apologizing."

"Well, that was nice."

"Yes, everyone is leaving gifts for the forgiveness gods. Boozy Baskets. Finished wedding favors. Coffee." She pointed from cup to cup. "I assume one of these is for me?"

"The one on the left."

Gabby accepted the cup from her and took a small sip. "Thank you. For finishing the favors. It meant a lot."

"I had help. Gabby, I am so very sorry about Sunday. I should have never lost my temper like that, especially in your mother's house. Did she say anything?"

"She mentioned how hungry we must have been since all the food was gone. I didn't have the heart to tell her most of it ended up in Amber's hair."

Noel shuffled her feet. "I really am sorry."

"I know. I was going to call you today to talk, but a lot's been going on. Besides, I know Amber pushed you really hard. I don't know if I could have taken all the crap she was dishing if our roles were reversed." Gabby smiled and held her arms open. "Come here."

Noel fell into them gratefully, returning her hug. "God, I was so afraid you wouldn't forgive me."

"You cleaned up the mess and the favors got done. No harm, no foul." Her hand flew up to cover her nose. "Well, maybe a little harm, but it wasn't entirely your fault. Plus, when I described the fight to Drew, he thought it was hysterical."

"Oh, God." Noel covered her face with her hands, hiding a smile. "The ranch slap."

Gabby giggled. "What about the cream cheese in Amber's hair from the jalapeño poppers? She looked like she forgot to wash all the conditioner out of her hair and it curdled."

Noel joined in Gabby's laughter, following her as she moved into the kitchen. "I'm just glad no one else was there filming it. Angry Bridesmaid Food Fight. That would definitely go viral."

"Believe me, I am going to be ready with my camera phone next time. No way am I going to miss another opportunity like that."

They sat at the oval dining room table next to each other, Noel cradling her coffee cup in her hands. "I have some more good news. I booked us the Presidential suite at The Rustic Inn. It sleeps up to ten people and he'll let us have an afternoon checkout so we can sleep in."

Gabby cried out happily. "How did you convince Charlie Sloan to let you have it? I think he's had that room locked up since the eighties."

"Actually, Nick talked to him. I owe him big."

"Yeah you do. So, did you pay up?"

Noel grinned. "Somewhat?"

"We talking full coitus?"

Noel spit out her coffee, wiping at her chin. "What the hell?"

"Sorry, Drew's been on a whole *Big Bang Theory* kick. We are binge watching it from the beginning and the lingo gets stuck in my head."

"Well, to answer your question, no. Just oral coitus."

"Tell me when to stop." Gabby held her hands a few inches apart and started moving them further away from each other.

"My God, stop it. I don't ask you about Drew's mini me."

"Oh, Drew is stacked. Let me tell you, there is no mini about that man. I have no complaints."

"Neither do I."

"I'm happy for you. You deserve happiness."

"I do need to talk to you about Amber."

Gabby sighed. "Am I going to need to have separate bachelorette and bridal showers for you two?"

"No, I don't think so. She did bring up something interesting though. She told me this whole animosity started long before high school. Has she said anything about it?"

Gabby hesitated. "Only that you quitting choir was the best thing that ever happened to her."

"She said I used to compete with her, but I swear, I didn't do it consciously."

"I wouldn't stress about it. I doubt you did anything. Amber tends to see criticism and slights everywhere. There was a bartender who used to flirt with her incessantly at a club we hit in college. Amber dropped by to see him and found out he had a girlfriend. That he only flirted with her to get tips. She stabbed all four of his tires. Had to pay for damages."

"Jesus."

Gabby shrugged. "I love her, but she needs constant validation. If she doesn't get the attention she craves, then any will do. Pretty sure that's why the two of you could never get along. You don't give any fucks about what people think of you."

"That's not entirely true. I care what you think."

"We're fine, Noel. I already said—"

"Do you feel like I bailed on you when your aunt died?"

Gabby's eyes widened. "What? No. You'd just lost your parents. I knew it was hard for you. I appreciated you even showing up for the funeral. What made you even think of that?"

"Amber. She said I wasn't a very good friend when you needed me."

"Listen, when my aunt was on hospice, it was hard. We were really close and it was a rough death. But never did I question our friendship. You were there for me as much as you could be for a kid who had just lost everything. I had my whole extended family to grieve with. Believe me, I have never held any resentment toward you for that."

"What about for something else?"

Gabby looked up at the ceiling, as though she was straining to think. Suddenly, she snapped her fingers. "You know what! I do have beef."

"Uh-oh." Noel held her coffee cup in front of her for protection. "I'm skerred."

"You should be. How could you bring me coffee when I've already had my allotted amount for the day."

"Allotted amount? What are you talking about?"

Gabby got up and grabbed her phone from the counter. She tapped the screen silently and slid it over.

Noel stared at the picture of a positive pregnancy test. Her gaze jerked up and she caught the sly smile on Gabby's face.

"What? WHAT?!"

"Yep!"

Noel jumped up and hugged her, squealing. Noel didn't make the noise often, but she was so surprised, it escaped on its own.

"When did you find out?"

"Sunday, at the hospital when they checked me out. I took a home pregnancy test yesterday just for the picture. I felt like absolute crap yesterday, which is why I didn't come to the door."

"What did Drew say? Were you trying?"

"He's excited to be a dad. We talked about it a few weeks before he proposed. We thought it would take a while, so I stopped my birth control right after Halloween."

"Are you happy about it?"

"Yes, I'm so happy. We are going to wait until after the wedding to tell our families. But that's why we wanted the wedding this year. We knew there was a chance it could happen and I didn't want to be walking down the aisle with a huge belly if we waited."

"Awww, I am so excited for you." Noel bent down, talking to Gabby's tummy. "Hi pumpkin! It's Auntie Noel! I can't wait to meet you!"

"Stop talking to my uterus, weirdo. They can't hear you."

"Get used to it, because that baby is going to know my voice." They sat back at the table, and Noel shook her head. "Did you tell Amber?"

"No, I was going to wait. I wasn't sure how you were going to react, but I know she will have something to say."

"What, you didn't think I would be happy for you?"

"I know you have your hang-ups on kids and marriage."

"Whoa, time out, those have to do with me and whether I want those things. My own uncertainty doesn't stop me from being happy for others and I am so elated that you're getting everything you ever wanted." Tucking a stray hair behind her ear, she added, "Besides, I have to admit, lately I've been thinking that maybe I was too hasty, writing off love, marriage, and kids."

Gabby took her hands with a squeal. "Really?"

"Don't get too excited! It's got me thinking is all. We will see what the future holds. What I *do* know is I love you and I'm going to be the best auntie to all your babies!"

"Whoa now, let's just start with one. Don't throw that out into the universe or I'll end up with triplets."

Noel took Gabby's hand and squeezed. "I think you should tell Amber. I truly believe she loves you and would be happy for you?"

"Wait, did you just say something nice about Amber? Who are you?"

"Someone who is really trying to grow up."

_____

NICK

Nick knocked on Pike's front door, Anthony at his back. The duplex needed a new coat of paint, but Pike only bought it a few months ago. They'd made plans to have a guy's game night, complete with beer, nacho fixings, and Nick brought his PS4 since Pike had an Xbox One.

Several moments ticked by with no answer.

Nick knocked again. "You think he forgot?"

"How could he forget about us? We are his broskis."

"I'll call him." Nick put the box he carried down and slipped his phone out of his pocket. He found Pike in his contacts, but it just rang. "Weird. No answer."

Anthony set the grocery sacks down. "I've got him on my GPS app. Let's see where he's at." Anthony pulled his phone out of his pocket and tapped away. Anthony's brow furrowed.

"What's up?"

"Where does this look like to you?"

Nick squinted at the screen. "Grey Wolf Lane. Brews and Chews? That's the only thing out there."

"Yeah, but they're closed Sunday, Monday, and Tuesdays."

"So why is he there?"

"Why are you asking me? Let's get in the damn truck and ask *him*," Anthony griped.

"Whoa, you are grumpy." They picked up their stuff and carried it back to Nick's truck.

"Yeah, I'm pissed. He's been dragging ass at work and he changes up when he hits the gym. And now, he isn't even home when we're supposed to be eating nachos and gaming."

"Dude, you sound like a jealous girlfriend."

"I just have respect for my friends, is all. I'm fine with him dressing like a dandy and growing that freaking soup catcher, but bailing on guys' night? That's where I draw the line."

Nick stared at Anthony, who rarely raised his voice above his normal timbre, throwing a fit over a hang.

"Seriously, are you okay?"

Anthony grunted against the seat of Nick's truck. "Yeah. Just hungry and tired."

"Let's go stalk our friend and if he blew us off for something stupid, we'll kick his ass."

"Sounds like a plan."

They pulled into the parking lot behind Pike's Jeep. There were a half a dozen other cars but the doors were shut and the neon signs in the window were off.

"What the fuck?" Anthony said.

"Maybe he joined a cult?"

"Let's find out."

They climbed out of the truck, crunching across the gravel to the entrance of Brews and Chews. They glanced at each other wordlessly before Anthony hammered on the front doors.

A few seconds ticked by before the door swung open and Amber's Thor wannabe leaned out. He wore a blue, shiny robe that fell open to reveal a bald chest.

I say it again, what the fuck?

"Sorry guys, the bar is closed."

Before he shut the door, Anthony put his hand out. "We're actually looking for our friend, Pike. He was supposed to meet us."

"He's on stage right now. I'll send him out when he's done."

Nick looked around Thor's shoulder and caught sight of Pike. He was facing away from them on the stage, throwing it back in a...

IN A THONG!

The door shut in his face and he turned to Anthony.

"What's that look for? What did you see?"

"I have no idea."

"Don't give me that. What did you see?"

Nick stood there, letting everything click into place and he swallowed. Hard. "You know the all-male review they've been advertising? The one Noel is seeing for Gabby's bachelorette?"

"Yeah?"

"I'm pretty sure I just got a sneak peek."

"What do you…" Anthony's eyes widened and he burst out laughing. "No! No fucking way! Pike?"

"Unless there is another reason he'd be dancing around in a thong, I'm thinking Pike."

"Holy shit!" Anthony shook his head, bent over with mirth.

"Why do you think he's doing it?"

"Money? Attention. To have a bunch of women feeling him up? We can ask him when he comes out."

Five minutes ticked by before Pike came outside, carrying a duffle bag. He grinned apologetically, behaving completely normal.

"Hey guys, sorry. Got caught up with something. Ready for guys' night?"

Anthony and Nick looked at each other. Then they started dancing, shaking their hips and singing Rae Sremmurd's "Come Get Her". When Anthony turned his ass towards Nick, he spanked it a couple times until they were laughing so hard, they had to hold each other up.

Pike stared at them, eyes glittering. "You done?"

His fury sobered them up, and Nick straightened. "We were just messing with you, man."

"Yeah, you're always messing with me. My clothes, my hair. I'm just a big joke to you and I'm sick of it."

Taken aback, Nick took a step toward Pike. "Hey man, we didn't mean anything by it. We thought you'd laugh."

Anthony took his Broncos hat off and rubbed his head

nervously. "We're sorry. We were just giving you shit because you blew us off."

"I sent Nick a snap to just go inside. The door was unlocked."

Nick checked his phone and sure enough, there was a message from Pike. "I didn't see it. Sorry, man."

Pike looked between them, still scowling. Then his dark expression dissolved into a shit eating grin. "I got you so good."

He threw his head back and laughed. Nick stared at him for several seconds and then relief rushed through him. "Holy shit. You were fucking with us?"

"Of course. When have I ever given two shits when you two razz me? The stripper song was a good one though."

Anthony grabbed Pike in a headlock. "Little shit, I'mma beat your ass."

Pike broke away from Anthony and ran a hand over his hair. "You mean, this ass?"

Pike grabbed the legs of his pants and they pulled right off, revealing a black G-string.

"Oh, fuck!" Anthony took off running with Pike chasing after him.

"Come here, Tony! I got something for you! Slow down and let me love you!"

Nick whipped out his phone, recording his two friends, laughing so hard the camera shook. Being in the barracks, they'd goofed around and grown close, but none of them could replace these men. They were his brothers. The guys he expected to stand up next to him on his wedding day.

Watching Noel walk toward him.

Nick wouldn't mention any of his fantasies about their future, mainly because he didn't want to freak her out. It didn't mean they weren't there, but if he was going to break through all of Noel's walls, he needed to do it slowly. Carefully.

Texting her how much he missed her would be too much, too fast.

Finally, Pike and Anthony trekked back to the truck where Nick stood.

"What made you decide to do this?" Nick asked.

Pike shrugged as he snapped his pants back together. "Saw the auditions and figured if I got in, strippers make good money. Save up. Have a little fun."

"Aren't you nervous about dancing for women you know?"

"Nah." Pike picked up his bag and slung it over his shoulder. "Now, can we get the hell out of here and get our gaming on?"

Once they were inside the truck, following behind Pike, Nick asked, "Should we tell him about the bachelorette party?"

Anthony shook his head. "Nah, you heard him. He's cool."

CHAPTER 25

NICK

ROWS OF GREEN TREES WITH twinkling lights and festive ornaments filled the large open space of the Mistletoe Community Center. The high ceilings allowed for trees anywhere between six and twelve feet. Different donation bins were placed sporadically around the event for people to donate toys, coats, and hygiene products. All would be donated after the event along with proceeds the event raised to help local charities.

Nick stood off to the side of the pie eating contest, checking out his sister's tree. It was the first time since Holly opened A Shop for All Seasons that she'd entered, always pitching in with his parents to do a joint tree. The independent move put her store on the map, because in Nick's opinion, it was the best-looking tree out there. Even better than his parents'.

Noel grabbed his hand and yanked him towards the pie table. "Come on."

"What are we doing?" He laughed. Since Monday, Noel made it a habit of stopping by his apartment after work to have breakfast

NICK AND NOEL'S CHRISTMAS PLAYLIST 313

with him. Sometimes she brought food or he'd whip something up, but it always ended with them kissing. Touching. Cuddling.

And other more intimate activities.

His favorite meal happened Wednesday when he'd bought Nutella and strawberries for crepes, but they'd never made them. Instead, he'd licked half the jar of Nutella off Noel's body. He'd been sick most of the day from the sweetness, but making her come twice made it worth the bellyache.

They hadn't had sex yet. They'd done almost everything but the whole enchilada and Nick didn't even care. He was having too much fun being with Noel. They were still friends, but better. After they'd fooled around, every day she'd fallen asleep in his arms, in his bed. When she woke up, they'd have lunch and sometimes she'd read or watch TV while he finished working. Other times he'd let her distract him. There was no resisting Noel when she stripped down to nothing, crawled between his legs and made him lose control.

Everything with Noel was amazing and he never wanted it to end.

They stopped next to the pie eating contest, Noel's arms wrapped around his waist as she gazed up at him, that mischievous gleam in her eye. "Let's go next round. Two-to-one odds I beat you by two minutes."

"Please, do you know who you're talking to? I am the pie master."

"We'll just see about that," she said, grinning as she climbed onto the bench.

Nick squeezed in next to her, his hands clasped behind his back like hers, immobilized.

"Eaters take your mark. Get set. Chow!"

Nick dived in, widening his mouth to rake in the soft pudding center and realized too late it was banana cream. He gagged into the pie pan.

Of all the pies in all the world, his had to be that one. Nasty.

He looked at Noel, who took the time to smile, dark brown dessert all over the lower half of her face. It was obviously chocolate, but it didn't make the visual any less disturbing.

Nick closed his eyes, pretending the creamy center was lemons instead of mushy, ripe...

Nope.

Nick got up from the table, wiping his face with the napkin offered to him by one of the high schoolers running around to all the quitters. He watched Noel devour the pie, using her tongue to lick the plate clean.

He probably shouldn't tell her how erotic he found her pie eating skills. She'd think it was weird.

Finally, she whooped, holding her plate in the air for inspection. The fire chief, Brendan Kline, placed a medal around her neck and handed her an envelope. Noel took a napkin on her way back to him, dancing the whole way as flecks of chocolate custard plopped to the cement ground with every move.

"That's sexy, right there."

"Yeah? Wanna clean me up?"

Nick laughed, looping an arm behind her neck and bringing her in for a messy kiss. He smacked his lips. "Mmmm, yum. Why couldn't I get chocolate mousse instead of banana cream."

"You trying to say the only reason you lost is because you can't swallow a little banana?"

Nick took the napkin and wiped it along her cheeks and chin. "I am saying you got mad tongue skills, but so do I. If I'd only gotten a better flavor, I could have showed you."

"Oh, I vaguely remember how good you are with your tongue."

"Vaguely?" He snorted in disbelief.

"Maybe tonight you could demonstrate again. Refresh my memory."

Nick caught the gleam in her good eye and wiped his mouth with the last clean section of the napkin. "Come on, you gorgeous pirate, before I forget where we are and commandeer your vessel."

"Hmmm, keep up with all that and you're gonna shiver my timber."

"What the fuck," he laughed.

She exploded with mirth. "Sorry, I was trying to be all brown chicken brown cow and failed."

"Eh, it kinda works for me."

"Does it?" she whispered, clinging to the front of his shirt as he dipped his head to kiss her.

"Yeah."

"Mmmm."

Nick's hands slid over Noel's back, stopping just short of gripping her ass and pressing her into his hard cock.

"Gross, get a room, you two."

They broke apart to find Gabby and Drew standing in front of them, arms wrapped around each other. The white bandage was still in place over the bridge of Gabby's nose, but the skin under her eyes had faded to blue, yellow, and green swirls.

"Whoa, Gabby," Nick said, at a loss.

"I know, I look badass, right?" Gabby grinned.

The two women hugged and Drew ran a hand over his shaved head with a grin, focused on Nick. "I am just glad they made up. If I had to hear about another reality show crap fest, I was about to run for the hills."

Nick knew Drew was lying through his teeth by the way he watched Gabby, his gaze tender. It was obvious Drew loved his woman and would watch anything she wanted as long as it made her happy.

He could relate. Nick knew if Noel asked him to sit through some ridiculous bullshit, he'd do it with a smile on his face. But he would have done it when they were just friends.

"Thank you by the way," Gabby whispered. "Because of Amber's flying hands, I got a little taken off the top."

"What?" Drew and Noel cried unanimously.

"Oh geez, I was just kidding. My mother would kill me if I altered the body God gave me."

"She still doesn't know about your tat—"

"Shh!" Gabby silenced Noel with a hand over her mouth. "Remember your oath. To the grave."

Nick cocked a brow. "What's this?"

"You aren't the only person to ever get a secret tattoo," Noel said with a wink.

"What, Nick has a tat? Lemme see."

Gabby reached for Nick, but Drew picked her up against his chest. "How about we not try to undress other guys in public."

"In private then?" Gabby smirked.

"Woman, can we get through the honeymoon before you try to bring other men into our bedroom."

"Why's everything gotta be about sex with you?" Gabby sheepishly grinned at Noel. "Such a perv."

"Same with this one." She jerked a thumb in Nick's direction. "Just a few minutes ago, he—"

Nick covered her mouth with his hand. "I think we need to separate them."

"I concur," Drew said, taking off in another direction, Gabby still in his arms.

"I'll text you!" Gabby hollered.

Noel pulled his hand away. "You better!"

Nick slid his arms around her waist, hugging her. "You two are crazy."

"I will take the insanity. You don't know what it was like when she wasn't talking to me. It's only happened a few times since we were fourteen and never for very long, but it's like a hole in my heart." She nudged him with her shoulder. "Kind of like when you were gone."

Nick turned her around and kissed her nose. "The good news is, I'm not going anywhere."

Noel didn't immediately respond and he noted the way her eyes darted to the side. She still didn't believe he really wanted to be with her and that was okay. They had plenty of time for him to prove it.

"What do you want to do next?"

"I think I need to hit the little girl's room before we stray too far from it."

"Gotcha. I'll wait over there."

"Stalker." She waved her hand, disappearing behind the tile partition.

Nick grinned, leaning back against the wall of the community center. Life had a crazy way of taking you right where you needed to go. A month ago he couldn't wait to get home and be with Amber and she'd dumped him. If she hadn't done that and if Trip hadn't moved on with Jillian, he wouldn't be as happy as he was right now. He wanted to believe that even if they hadn't been single at the same time, right when he got back into town, that they still would have found themselves feeling this way, but who knew?

Nick copied the link to "Kiss Me" by Sixpence None the Richer and sent it to her. He could just imagine her expression when she came out of the bathroom, shaking her head, that smile on her lips.

"Hey, Nick."

Nick winced at Amber's high-pitched greeting. "Hi."

His ex wore a fuzzy red off-the-shoulder sweater and blue jeans tucked into black boots. Her glossy red lips wore a broad smile, with just a touch of pleading.

"I know you're probably busy and I hate to ask but, can you help me? My tire's flat and I don't know how to change one."

Nick couldn't imagine why women didn't learn how to change their own tires. Noel could change a tire faster than he could. It was pretty impressive.

"I'm waiting for Noel. Isn't there someone else you can ask?"

Her smile dimmed a bit, and a guilty twinge pinched his

conscious, but he pushed it aside. Any other citizen he'd have already been out the door, but with everything he'd learned about Amber, he knew the chances of her having ulterior motives were high.

"Really? You can't just pop out for a minute to help? Otherwise, I'm going to have to sit outside and wait for AAA."

Then again, Noel had nothing to worry about. No matter what Amber tried, Nick wanted nothing to do with her.

"Fine. I'll help you."

Amber's blue eyes lit up and she beamed. "Oh thank you! You are a life saver."

"Just give me a minute. I want to wait for Noel."

"Oh, sure. I get it."

Noel came out of the bathroom a few seconds later with his sister, Holly. Noel noticed Amber first and her smile faded, her gaze shifting back to Nick.

"Hey, Amber's tire is flat. Do you mind if I step outside and take care of it for her?"

Noel cleared her throat. "Of course not."

"Thanks, Noel. You're a peach," Amber said, sweetly.

Holly glared at her. "There's a hundred tutorials on YouTube that will show her how to change a tire."

"I'll be quick." He leaned over and kissed Noel's forehead. "I'll find you in a bit."

"Sure. Come on, Holly. I want to see your tree again."

His sister kept giving Amber the evil eye until they disappeared into the crowd.

"Shall we?" Amber asked.

Nick nearly told her he'd changed his mind and she needed to find someone else, but Noel said it was fine. He loved her. Noel had to know that. She trusted him at the very least and he'd be quick.

Nick followed behind Amber out the side door to the gravel parking lot. The place was packed but luckily, she'd parked off to the side in the last stall. He grabbed her spare from the trunk of her car along with the jack and tools, wanting to get this done and be back at Noel's side.

Amber leaned up against her car, watching him work.

"I really appreciate this, Nick."

"I understand you didn't want to wait an hour for AAA, but no one else could have done this for you? Aren't you here with someone?"

"You mean Guy? We aren't dating anymore."

"Sorry to hear that."

"Hindsight is twenty-twenty, right." She cleared her throat, taking a step closer to him. "I know I shouldn't be telling you this, but I think I made a mistake, Nick."

He cranked the jack, not even looking at her. "What does that mean?"

"Breaking up with you."

Nick took a deep, even breath. "Let's not go there, okay? I'm doing you a favor. Don't make me regret it."

"Why would you regret helping me?" she asked, angrily.

"I know all about your issues with Noel. Don't try to use me to get to her. It's not going to work."

She opened her mouth and snapped it shut several times,

as though weighing what to say next. Finally, she spoke in an almost regretful tone. "I'm sorry. I didn't ask you to change my tire because I wanted to upset or offend you. I know I do that with people all the time. Even when I care about people, I always mess it up."

He stopped loosening a lug nut and stared up at her. "What are you getting at, Amber?"

"You being home made our relationship realer than it's ever been and you'd been going on about marriage and kids for so long—"

"Amber." She stopped talking when he said her name sternly. "I am with Noel. I love Noel. I think right now you're feeling scared about being on your own and that's normal. But you and me? We're not happening."

"Then why did you help me, if you feel nothing for me?"

"I told you I'd treat you with respect, like everyone else in this town until you gave me a reason not to. And right now, you're being incredibly disrespectful to me and Noel."

"Noel, poor Noel. I am so sick of hearing that! What the hell makes her so damn special?"

God, he was such a fucking idiot. Even his sister thought so. He'd let Amber manipulate him. He'd actually felt guilty for not wanting to help her. And all along it was just a way to get him alone.

"I'm sorry, okay? I didn't mean it. I just...I want you to know that I still care."

Nick finished the tire in silence and stood. "Done. Drive safe."

"That's it?" she cried.

Nick spoke firmly. "Yes, Amber, that's it. You and me, isn't going to happen. Stop seeking me out."

Nick turned away, but before he could take a step, she threw her arms around him, trying to kiss him. He shoved her, surprised by her sudden onslaught and she fell back against her car with a cry.

Nick shook his head, resisting the urge to make sure she was okay. "Stay away from me."

He headed back inside, searching for Noel through the maze of trees. Joyful Christmas music played overhead and he shook with adrenaline. He spotted Holly talking to his parents, but balked when he realized Noel wasn't with them.

"Hey, where's Noel?"

Holly snorted. "She left."

"What do you mean?"

"She looked at my tree, said it was lovely, and told me good night."

His mom frowned. "Honey, what's going on?"

Holly stabbed her finger in Nick's direction. "This moron went outside to change his ex-girlfriend's tire, leaving Noel in here with me. *On their first date*!"

His parents wore identical expressions of puzzlement.

His mom only said, "Oh, dear."

"Why would you do that?" his dad asked, bluntly.

"Because I was trying to be nice."

"She's your ex! You don't have to be anything to her ever again!"

"I really don't want to have this discussion with anyone but

Noel." Nicked leveled his sister with a hard stare. "Do you know where she went?"

Holly hesitated until their mother elbowed her and she grunted, answering reluctantly. "Check by the front entrance. I saw her head that way. Fix it, Nick. All I'm gonna say about it."

Nick took off for the front of the community center and burst through the double doors, searching the parking lot for Noel. He found her off to the side, staring down at her phone.

"Noel."

She looked up briefly, but turned away without fully meeting his gaze. "I don't want to talk right now, Nick."

When she took off running through the parking lot, he chased her. "Noel!"

Noel didn't slow down. "Leave me alone."

"Hold on a second." Nick tried to take her arm in his hand but she jerked away. "I know I messed up going with Amber to help her, but nothing happened. She told me she still had feelings and I shot her down."

Noel spun around, fury brightening her one good eye. "You think I'm pissed because she made a play for you?"

"Um..."

"I am furious with you for leaving me on our first official date. For her! I know you're a good guy and I love that about you, but where she's concerned, can't you just be an asshole and tell her to fuck off?"

Nick opened his mouth to explain, but she kept going.

"I mean, if any of my ex-boyfriends walked up while you were in the toilet and asked me to go outside in the dimly lit parking lot to give them a jump, I'd have told them to go to hell!"

Nick's brow furrowed. "Wait a second, you went out with Trip last weekend."

"That was before we agreed to this." She waved her hand between them, her voice choked up, "To give this a real shot and you blew it."

"I blew it? I asked you and you said it was okay!"

"You never should have put in me in that position! I am not going to make decisions for you, but for someone who is supposed to know me better than anyone, you should have realized there was no way in hell I'd be okay with you leaving me for her." Noel's voice broke as she kept going, "As much as I try to get over my past with Amber, that girl loves to hurt me. She told me that you would never forget her because she was your first time. For weeks she has made digs about you and me, playing on all of my insecurities and you still walked off with her because she needed you! You going outside with her proved everything she'd been saying to me is right."

"Noel, I went out to help her, not hurt you."

"But you did, Nick! You hurt me."

Nick's stomach twisted up and he reached out for her again, but she evaded him. "I am sorry. I wasn't trying to be thoughtless."

"I know. That's what makes it so much worse."

Nick threw up his hands. "Is this really about Amber? Or you were looking for a way out."

"Excuse me?"

Nick shook his head, desperation mixed with frustration

steering the reckless course his mouth took. "Admit it. You've been ready to run since the first time we kissed. Anything close to relationship status and you bolt. You tell me that I didn't think about you tonight, but that isn't true. I knew how you felt about Amber, which is the whole reason I asked. I put the ball in your court and you said it was fine. Now you're punishing me for it. You tested me and I bombed it. I may know you better than anyone, Noel, but I'm not a mind reader."

"You are not naïve enough to think all she wanted from you was help with a fucking tire!"

"I didn't even think about what ulterior motives she could have. I came out here to help, that's it. I don't want her! You are the only person I want. Ever."

"Then why would you put yourself in this position?" she cried, pushing at his chest when he tried to hug her. "No, I just want to get out of here. Alone."

Nick glared at her, his heart breaking even as he whispered, "Fine. Take off. But just so we're clear, I chased you. I did everything in my power to show you how I felt. I'm not running after you anymore. If you want to save what we have, make your move. Otherwise, I'm done trying."

Without looking back, he walked away, his feet dragging the ground like cement blocks, his heart screaming to go back. To beg her not to give up.

But pride won the fight. If she wanted to set him up to fail, they were already doomed.

CHAPTER 26

NOEL

NOEL DASHED AT HER RIGHT cheek, while her tears from her left eye soaked the bandage and eye patch. Frustrated, she yanked it off and stomped it, cursing angrily. At least her eyes had pretty much healed, because salt in an open corneal scratch had been unpleasant Sunday, Monday, and Tuesday.

God, she should have told Nick no when he'd asked about helping Amber, but Noel was trying to take the high road. To show Amber that she wasn't as big a bitch as she thought.

But the longer she waited, the more her imagination ran wild. Amber convincing Nick she'd changed. That Noel wasn't right for him. Nick realizing his first love wasn't as easy to forget.

So she'd excused herself to go looking for them. She'd heard them arguing and then watched Amber throw herself at Nick. She should have been happy that Nick rebuffed her, but instead she was angry. Furious with herself for pitying Amber and giving her the benefit of the doubt. Pissed at Amber for being such a bitch.

And disappointed with Nick for even asking her in the first

place. It was their first date! They should be looking at the ice sculptures right now, laughing over a cup of cider and kissing beneath the random sprigs of mistletoe.

Instead she was standing alone in the dark, wondering if she should go back inside and try to find Holly, but then she'd have to wait until the event was over.

Damn it.

"Noel?"

She groaned at the sound of Trip's voice behind her. "Great. Just what I need."

When she turned, he pushed off the wall of the building, putting a lit cigarette out on the ground. She wrinkled her nose. She'd never let him smoke around her, hated the smell and taste of it. Every once in a while, she'd get a whiff and lose all attraction to him.

Just another reason on the long list of why she was glad they were no longer hooking up.

"I've been trying to get a hold of you."

Noel rolled her eyes. "I thought me ditching you at the restaurant was pretty self-explanatory. It's called ghosting. Take the hint and leave me alone."

Trip marched over, stopping a little over a foot away. In the dim lights of the parking lot, she noticed his eyes were heavy lidded, as if he'd been tying one on for quite a while.

"No. Leaving me was rude, but I'm willing to forgive you."

Noel snorted. "Big of you."

"Why are you giving me attitude?"

"Are you for real? You're a condescending asshat and I want to kick my own ass for letting you in my pants."

"That's a bit harsh, don't you think?" There was a sharp edge to his tone, but Noel ignored it, too fired up to care if she ticked him off. She hurt and she wanted to hurt back.

"Let's see. You take me out behind your girlfriend's back, try to hit me up for money, and *you* forgive *me*? You're right. Douche canoe is more accurate."

"I wouldn't call Jillian my girlfriend."

The man just didn't seem to get the point. "I'll see you around Trip."

He grabbed her arm when she tried to pass. "Now, wait a minute—"

She tried to yank her arm away, but he gripped it tighter. "There is no waiting. I'm not giving you a dime and you can just keep walking the next time you see me. The two of us were barely friends when we were screwing and that hasn't changed. So let. Me. Go."

Trip reached out for her other arm, but Noel evaded him. Still, he didn't ease his grasp on her other bicep. "You're not going anywhere until we come to an understanding."

"Hey!" Pike's angry shout came just before he slammed into Trip, knocking him to the ground. Noel stumbled forward and would have fallen if Anthony hadn't grabbed her, moving her away from the scuffle.

Pike stood over Trip, visibly shaking. "You ever put hands on her again and I will bury you, fucker."

Anthony pulled her into his side, his usually laid-back expression a mask of fury. "You okay, Noel?"

"Yeah, I'm good. Just want to go home."

"No, I need to talk to her," Trip whined, trying to climb to his feet.

Pike pushed Trip with one hand, causing the other man to stumble back. "Then you need to learn how to talk with your mouth and keep your hands to yourself."

"Stop putting your damn hands on me," Trip growled, his left eye twitching.

"Oh, yeah, see, you don't like that huh? Someone putting their hands on you without your permission?"

Trip threw up his hands, yelling, "Fine, fuck it. I'll never come near her again. You can have her." Trip spit on the ground at her feet. "Too much traveled road for me, anyway."

"The fuck did you say?" Anthony started forward but Noel beat him too it. Her palm connected with Trip's cheek with a crack, the sting making her hand throb. She shook it out with a grunt.

"Go home, Trip. Forget you ever knew me."

Trip rubbed his face, his eyes narrowed into slits. When he opened his mouth, Pike took a step toward him. "You don't talk to her, you hear?"

Noel caught his arm with a shake of her head. "I appreciate the assist, but I don't need anyone to fight my battles for me."

"You're just the catalyst. I've been wanting to whoop this dick's ass for years."

Trip put his hands in the air, backing away from them. "No need for that. I'm gone. You won't hear from me again."

"Git then."

Trip didn't hesitate, but took off back into the community center. Noel sighed heavily.

"You know I was handling it, right?"

Anthony put an arm around Noel's shoulders. "We know. I was waiting for you to crack him one, but Pike got impatient."

Noel wasn't the damsel in distress type, but with Trip being drunk and brazen, he might not have backed off so easily if the guys hadn't shown up.

"Thank you."

Anthony squeezed her with a grin. "Come on, let's get out of here."

Pike trailing a foot behind them as they headed toward Anthony's truck.

"What were you doing out here with him, anyway?" Anthony chided. "Where's Nick?"

Noel cleared her throat, trying to get past the lump lodged there. "We didn't work out."

"Fuck," Pike mumbled. "I knew it."

"Shut up." Anthony opened the passenger door, studying her. "Do you wanna get a drink and talk about it?"

Noel paused with her hand on the door, giving him a sad smile. "How about we get drunk and not talk about it?"

"Deal."

Pike got into the back of Anthony's Chevy truck, letting her take the front. He hadn't said a word to her and she cleared her throat before turning around to look at him.

"Thanks for defending my honor."

Pike nodded. "I always got your back. That's what friends do."

The lump in her throat threatened to choke her. "I appreciate you."

"Yeah, sure. I never did like that guy."

Anthony climbed into the driver's seat just in time to weigh in. "Me neither."

Pike leaned back against the seat, watching her warily. "So, how bad was your breakup with Nick and whose fault was it?"

"Pike..." Anthony growled.

"What? I just need to know who is getting me in the split."

"Oh my God, it was barely one date!" Noel cried. "There will be no splitting or choosing. We just need a little time apart and then everything will go back to the way it was."

"Aren't you doing the Christmas concert together?" Pike asked.

Noel clenched her jaw. "Yes."

"So, practices still for another week."

"Uh-huh."

"Geez, yeah, I can see where all that distance is going to come into play."

"Shut up, Fish," she mumbled.

"So much for gratitude."

Anthony's phone rang and the screen of his truck console popped up with Nick's name. He glanced at Noel and sent it to voicemail.

"You didn't have to do that." Noel didn't want the guys to think Nick had done something unforgivable.

"I'll call him back when we get to where we're going." Anthony threw the truck into reverse and slowly drove through the busy parking lot.

"Where are we going?" Noel asked.

Pike's phone blared in the back seat and he answered it, "This is Bad Ass Mother Fucker, how may I direct your call?"

Noel couldn't understand what Nick said until Pike responded, "Why, yes she is. Yeah, she did. Because he was manhandling her. I offered to, but she stopped me. Apparently, she didn't want douche blood on her hands."

Nick's voice carried through the phone for several moments before Pike cut him off. "Look, we will be your boys tomorrow. Tonight, it's tits before dicks. Peace."

Noel scowled at him. "Tits before dicks?"

"What?"

Anthony shook his head. "What did Nick say?"

"Apparently, someone saw what went down and now everyone is talking about the slap heard 'round Mistletoe. Nick wanted to make sure you were all right." Noel's traitorous heart soared. "Then he asked if we wanted to hang. I told him we would be with Noel tonight and we'd see him tomorrow."

Guilt niggled at Noel. "You don't have to do that. He's your best friend."

"So are you. Just because he is a guy doesn't make him any more important."

Pike patted her shoulder and the simple gesture made her blurt out, "I'm the one who called it off."

Silence stretched through the cab, tension so thick you could take an ice cream scoop to it.

"Why?" Anthony asked.

"Because he went out to change Amber's tire." Why did it sound so lame out loud?

Pike spluttered. "So?"

"And she tried to kiss him."

"So?" They repeated in unison.

"He knows Amber and I have a complicated relationship. She's been dogging Nick since she saw us at Brews and Chews. I warned him she wasn't over him and he still asked if he could go outside to change her tire."

"You told him not to change her tire and he did it anyway?" Anthony asked.

"No, I told him he could, but you don't get it. He shouldn't have asked in the first place."

"Hello, we are talking about Nick." Pike leaned over the seat, ticking items off his fingers. "He's a boy scout. He walks grandmas across the road and shit. He went out to change a tire 'cause that is who he is. If it had been me, then yeah, maybe I thought I'd get a little smooch for helping out, but Nick is a great guy. He does shit because he thinks it's the right thing to do."

"That doesn't make it okay. He knows how I feel about Amber and he didn't care."

Anthony held a hand up. "Uh-uh."

"Uh-uh?" she repeated.

"That's right. UH. UH." Anthony pulled the truck to the side of the road and turned in the seat to face her. He flipped on the dome light and she got a really good look at his hard expression. "Girl, you need a reality check. First off, you don't own Nick. He can change a thousand tires for Amber and nothing you do or say controls that. Nor should you want to. Relationships are about trust."

"I trust him, but not her. He set himself up to be alone with her and she threw herself at him."

"Nick is the victim and you're blaming him. If Gabby went out to help some guy change a tire and he'd kissed her, even though she didn't want it, is it her fault?"

Noel's stomach sank. "No, of course not."

"Did he kiss her back?"

"No, he pushed her away."

Pike leaned on the back of the seat, staring at her. "I take it back. We are dropping you off and grabbing Nick. He is clearly the wronged party."

Noel whirled around. "Seriously? You don't understand at all where I'm coming from?"

Anthony shook her shoulder gently. "The place you're coming from is illogical. The man would give his underwear away if he thought someone needed them. The only reason you're freaking out is because you hate Amber. Should Nick have asked you in the first place? No, he should have told her to take a flying leap. But he's not that guy and if he was, you wouldn't care so damn much."

Noel opened and closed her mouth, fighting to form a sound argument, but Pike spoke up before she'd collected herself.

"Plus, I think you might be a wittle skeered," Pike said in a baby voice.

"Scared of what?" she spluttered.

Pike cupped his hands over his heart. "Of opening yourself to love."

Now her stomach churned with guilt, frustration, and

irritation. If she didn't get the heck out of this car, she might puke. "Yeah, you know what? Take me home before I gag."

"I'm not wrong. You kept Nick at arm's length and once you let him in, you couldn't deny your chemistry. You invented this conflict and now, boom! You can pretend that you tried, but you're lying to yourself."

Noel resisted the urge to pop Pike in his smug, self-satisfied face.

"No response because I'm right," Pike sang.

Noel grit her teeth and didn't speak to either of them the rest of the drive. She hadn't overreacted. Being in a relationship meant putting yourself in the other person's shoes. She wouldn't take off with Trip for any reason.

But Nick would. Even if it was someone he didn't like, he'd still help.

Noel's heart sank, deflating her self-righteous anger along with it. Pike and Anthony were right. She'd fucked up because she'd been looking for a reason to run. Instead of putting the blame where it belonged, with Amber, she'd taken all of her bottled up emotions out on Nick.

How did she explain that to Nick, her person? The man she... Loved.

Fuck, what did I do?

Chapter 27

NICK

STRETCHED OUT ALONG HIS COUCH, Nick still couldn't sleep and it was past two in the morning. Pike and Anthony called him back after dropping Noel off, offering to take him out and give him their two cents, but he wasn't feeling it. The last thing he wanted to do was talk about Noel. It's not like he could fully shake her from his mind, living two doors down from her. The fruity scent of her was all over his bed. His house. Everything reminded him of her.

How do you forget about the other half of you? Your person?

Nick couldn't, so instead of sleeping, he'd drunk one too many glasses of whiskey and turned on a movie. Something violent and gory.

No romance whatsoever.

Insistent knocking interrupted his sulking and he climbed to his feet, glaring at the wooden door. He squinted into the peep hole and stilled.

Noel's anxious face stared back at him.

She was standing outside his door at two in the morning in the freezing cold.

His heart thundered as he unlocked it and dragged the door open, staring at her in drunken befuddlement. "You're here."

"Yeah. Can I come in?"

"Sure. Not doing anything."

"Except drinking, I see."

"What? Now a man can't have a spot of whiskey in his own home?" Nick picked up his half-drunk glass from the coffee table and knocked the rest of it down the hatch.

"Oh God, you're drinking whiskey? You always get this weird mix of Scottish and French when you drink whiskey."

"I don't know whatch' talking 'bout." He cleared his throat. "Why you here?"

"I couldn't sleep without talking to you. About earlier. You and Amber. I...I was an ass."

"Aye."

Noel covered her mouth, but he could tell by the crinkling in the corner of her eyes she was smiling. "Maybe I should go and we can have this conversation when you're sober."

Nick sprang for the door, holding it shut with the palm of his hand before she could escape. "I'm sober 'nough to hear whatchu have to say."

"Right." She took a deep breath, fidgeting with her hands. "So, I may have behaved terribly to you earlier and I'm sorry."

"For which part? Calling me stupid or suggesting I wanted to fuck Amber?"

Noel swallowed. "Both. Being a good person, who takes care of others, it's just who you are."

"Yeah, I know. I said this. *You've* told me this."

"But I am not that way," Noel admitted. "I wouldn't piss on Amber if she was on fire."

"Your aim would be terrible and ineffective. You don't have the right equipment."

Noel laughed, covering her face with one hand. "Oh, God."

"What? Tis true. Girls can't aim for shit, unless they have one of those funnel things."

"What are you even...never mind." She sighed. "I just mean that, you are better than me in so many ways. You can put your animosity aside when others are in need. I have always admired that about you, despite recent events that may seem to counter that statement."

Nick raked his hands down his face, wishing he was slightly less drunk so he could follow what she was trying to say easily. All he'd absorbed so far was he was good and she was sorry.

"Noel, as you guessed it, I'm pretty fucked up. You're doing too much talking for me drunk arse to understand, so in the simplest terms, why don't you just be clear about what you're trying to say?"

Noel's hand reached up, cupping his cheek and he leaned into her warmth, thinking how he'd never thought he'd feel her touch again. He lost his balance and nearly toppled over. She grabbed onto his arms to steady him, staring up into his eyes.

"You have been chasing me for weeks, but in all honesty, I should have been the one chasing you. I'm still scared though, so I needed to collect my thoughts and well...I made you a playlist tonight."

She released him and shoved a hand into her pocket, removing an object. She held out a slim, black flash drive and Nick took it from her, their fingers grazing.

"'Sthank you."

"Figured it was about time, since you're always making me mixed CDs. I hope it can give you some insight into what's going on inside my head, because half the time, I'm not sure what I'm trying to do myself."

"Let's give it a listen, shall we?" Nick sat down on the couch, trying to insert the drive into his laptop, but the world tilted on its axis. "Whew, boat ride." He flopped back onto the couch, sliding the flash drive into his pocket. "I'll listen to it later."

"Uh, maybe wait until you've had a cup of coffee or two?"

"Sure. You sure?" The effort to stay awake drained all his strength.

"Yes, I'm sure. Thank you, for hearing me out. I guess we'll talk tomorrow at practice."

"Yeah, we'll talk then."

Noel bent over and kissed his cheek. "I hope you can forgive me."

"Forgive you, always. I love you."

He barely registered the door closing before he passed out. He woke up hours later, his mouth dry and tasting like ass. He grimaced as he blinked his eyes open, the sun streaming in through his open blinds.

"God, what the fuck," he muttered.

He rolled off the couch and hit the floor hard, groaning as his head thundered like a thousand hoofbeats clippity-clopping across his skull. Something wet and sticky covered the front of his shirt and he took it off, dropping it to the floor.

Nick climbed to his feet and clumsily made his way to the bathroom, where he threw up everything fermented in his stomach. Once he'd rinsed the taste of bad choices and regret out of his mouth, he brushed his teeth and took a shower.

He almost felt like a new man, except for the throbbing headache still dogging him.

Nick gathered up the jeans and shirt he'd fallen asleep in and did a load of laundry. After a quick breakfast, he went back to bed. It was Sunday, anyway. Nothing for him to do except...

Nick woke up in a cold sweat and checked his phone. Nick was supposed to help out at the tree farm this morning. His mom would have his head on a pike.

At a little after two, he rolled up to his parents' place and snuck in through the back of the tent, hoping to avoid detection.

"Where have you been all day?" Merry teased.

"Sleeping off a nasty hangover."

"You went drinking last night?" She frowned. "What happened with Noel?"

"She broke up with me."

Merry slapped her hands on her hips. "What did you do?"

"I should have listened to you."

"Oh no...did you kiss Amber?"

"God no, of course not. She tried to kiss me and I shoved her off."

"And Noel saw?"

"No, but I told her. She wasn't even pissed about that."

Merry frowned. "What was she mad about then?"

"Me asking her about helping out Amber in the first place."

"Well, she's not wrong."

"Yeah, but I should be allowed to help someone who needs me. That's being a good neighbor."

Merry's eyebrows jumped in disbelief. "Unless it is your crazy, hot ex-girlfriend who picked on your current girlfriend through her adolescence. Then you tell her to fuck off."

Nick sighed. "Well, I did eventually tell her something along those lines, but it was too late."

"Aw, don't stress, big brother." Merry hugged Nick hard. "Noel will come around. She loves you."

"Like a friend, you mean?"

"No, I mean that she adores your ass and she'll show up at your door soon holding a single red rose and say, '*It's you.*'"

"What?"

"Not your thing? All right, she'll walk up to you in a crowded place and whisper, '*I always believed in you…I just didn't believe in me.*'"

Nick blinked at her.

"Oh for the love of Target, never mind! Pop culture is lost on you, my friend!" Merry shook her head. "All I'm trying to say is she'll show up with some big romantic gesture you won't understand but still love. You'll kiss, fall into each other's arms and live happily ever after."

"You do understand what reality is, right?"

"Reality TV, yeah. For sure."

She walked away from him and he dragged ass the rest of the day, avoiding his mother's watchful eye and managed to get the hell out of there without a lecture. He followed his sisters down to the basement to practice, watching the stairs anxiously for Noel.

Soft footpads sounded on the stairs and his mother popped her head out.

"Hey, Nick. Noel's feeling under the weather and I was hoping you could drop by a container of my healing chicken noodle soup."

"Um, sure." Nick wasn't sure how Noel would feel about him swinging by her place, especially considering he was ass deep in love with her. He should find a way to stay away from her until his broken heart healed, but they were too intertwined in each other's lives for that to happen. The Christmas Concert. The guys. Even family gatherings were unavoidable.

He'd planned on leaving the soup on the mat and texting her it was there, but he knocked instead. She answered it wrapped in a blanket like a burrito, only her face sticking out. Her nose and cheeks were flushed and her eyes watery with fever.

"Man, you really are sick."

"Thank you, Captain Obvious." She sighed. "Sorry, I hate feeling like garbage. It makes me snappy."

"It's fine. Mom made you soup." He held up the bag and her face lit up.

"Bless her. Did she pack crackers?"

"Of course."

Her arm snaked out from between the blanket split, and she tried to take the bag, but he held it away.

She frowned. "What are you doing?"

"Taking care of you. Now go lie down before you fall down."

"You don't have to do that. I don't want to get you sick."

"Believe me, whatever you got, you were contagious long before today, so I'm already contaminated."

NICK AND NOEL'S CHRISTMAS PLAYLIST 343

"That's a lovely thought," she grumbled.

Still, she stepped back and let him in. He couldn't fight a grin as he watched her waddle in her blanket burrito back to the couch and flop down with a moan.

"I hurt everywhere."

"I'm sure you do." Nick walked into the kitchen and poured the contents of the first plastic container into a bowl. He popped it into the microwave, removed a sleeve of crackers from the bag and put the rest of the soup in the fridge. He clicked his tongue at how empty it was.

"Where are all your groceries?"

"I ate them all. I was going to go shopping today and then this happened."

"You got a list somewhere?"

"Corkboard next to the fridge."

Nick grabbed the fifteen-item list on snowman stationery. "Well, if it had been a snake it would have bitten me."

He came back into the room and set her food down on the coffee table with a glass of water. "Have you taken any medicine?"

"Some NyQuil. Should kick in soon."

Nick brushed her hair back from her face, aching to wrap her up and snuggle her against him. Fever, snot, and all.

"Try to eat something. I'm going to the store and I'll be back in a bit."

"My wallet is in my purse by the door."

"You can pay me back later."

"Did you listen to my playlist?" she murmured sleepily.

"What playlist?"

"The one I gave you. Last night."

Nick cocked his head, bewildered. "Noel, I have no idea what you're talking about."

"I am so sorry," she whimpered.

"Shhh." He patted her through the comforter, not sure where but it was meant to be comforting. "You rest. I'll be back soon and we can talk about it."

"Mmmkay."

Nick walked out of her apartment and headed to the store. It didn't take him long to grab the meager things on her list, plus a few more he added. The whole time he kept wracking his brain. What playlist was she talking about? She'd come by last night? What was she sorry about? That she'd ended things before they really began? Or that they'd ever gotten started in the first place?

When he arrived back at her place, she snored heavily under her comforter. He put away the groceries and cleaned up the remnants of her lunch. There was still half a bowl of soup left and most of the crackers. When he finished cleaning up, the playlist still nagged at the back of his mind.

He snuck out to his own apartment, being careful not to wake her. Nick searched around his living room. His kitchen. His bedroom. Not a CD or a thumb drive to be found.

Maybe she'd been hallucinating?

Nick packed up his lap top, figuring he'd get a little work done at her place while he took care of her. Even if they weren't dating, they were still friends. No matter how hurt he was, he couldn't turn his back on her. He needed her. Loved her.

Loved her so much he'd be whatever it took to keep her close.

Even if not being able to tell her how deep his feelings went ate him up inside.

He finished transferring his laundry, and heard the click of something hit the bottom of his dryer. A black rectangular flash drive stood out against the stark white of the dryer.

"Oh shit!"

Nick grabbed the drive, flicking the protective cover off. It didn't look damaged, and he shook it to check for any lingering water.

"Crap crap crap crap." Unpacking his laptop again, he inserted the drive and clicked on the folder. The circle turned, thinking, drawing out the suspense on whether or not he'd ruined Noel's late-night playlist. She'd had to have dropped it off when he was too drunk to remember.

Finally, it opened, revealing a list of songs. He clicked on the first one and "My Only Wish" jingled in his ear. His head bobbed the entire time, clicking onto track two. His favorite song. The next one was the Toby Keith song they'd sung at his birthday and the Mindy McCready they'd danced to at Brews and Chews when they'd had their first, albeit fake, kiss. He clicked onto the next and each one triggered a memory of Noel. When the playlist ended with "Must Be Santa," Nick wiped at the tears in his eyes.

Noel loved him too. She hadn't admitted it out loud, but this playlist proved she did.

And just like that, he was back in the game.

CHAPTER 28

NOEL

ON TUESDAY MORNING, NOEL ROLLED over in bed and stared at the empty space beside her. Nick stayed with her all day yesterday, working at the kitchen table while she slept on the couch. He'd kept her fed, medicated, and hydrated, even when she grumpily told him she could take care of herself. He'd ignored her, of course, and when he'd tucked her into her own bed last night, she'd asked him to stay with her. He hadn't even hesitated. He'd climbed beneath the covers and held her until she'd fallen asleep on his chest.

They hadn't talked about Saturday night or the playlist at all yesterday. They hadn't talked much at all, although his presence was comforting. Yesterday, when he'd sat down on the couch with her feet in his lap, kneading them beneath the blanket, she'd almost blurted out her feelings for him, but part of her didn't feel like she deserved him. He was so sure of himself and who he was, and made no apologies for it. He was kind and understanding and she could be a difficult pain in the ass. In what universe did they work as a couple?

She climbed out of bed, heading for the bathroom to relieve the copious amount of tea, orange juice, and water Nick insisted she ingest before bed. Once she'd finished brushing her teeth and taming the bird's nest on her head, she sniffed at her pits. Noel wrinkled her nose and decided a shower was most definitely in order.

Feeling refreshed, she put some Neosporin on her raw nostrils and came out of the bedroom to find Nick at the kitchen table with his back to her, his headphones in place. Noel rested a hand on his shoulder and he jumped under her touch. He took off the headphones and set them next to his laptop.

"Good morning. You look better?"

"Better than the snot troll I was yesterday?"

"Absolutely. You were a disgusting creature. I didn't want to tell you but every time you turned my way, I quaked with fear."

"Gee thanks," she laughed, warmed that his arm had gone around her waist, pulling her close.

"Wait." Nick squinted at her. "What's the stuff on your nose?"

"It hurt, so I put some Neosporin on it."

Nick blinked. "That's genius."

"My mom always did it for me. Didn't yours?"

"No. Epic failure. I'll have to tell her."

Noel pushed his shoulder gently. "Don't tell your mom she failed!"

Nick chuckled as he stood. "No promises. You hungry? I made bacon and eggs earlier, but saved you some. I can warm it up. Add some toast and orange juice to go along with it."

"I'd love some."

"I'll get right on it."

"I'll help." Noel pulled the orange juice out of the fridge while Nick toasted the bread.

"What were you doing before I walked in?" she asked.

"Shooting an email off to my boss."

"Oh, I saw the headphones on and thought you might be—" she held up her arms like she was carrying a gun, making high pitched *pachoo pachoo* noises.

Nick shook his head. "First of all, the guns in our games do not *pachoo*. They boom. And no, I found a flash drive in my dryer. Turns out it was your playlist."

Noel almost dropped the glass in her hand. "Oh, you remember that? I thought you may have blacked it out."

"Oh, I did completely. I had no idea what it was for, but the song 'I Told You So' and you repeating how sorry you were while doped up on cold meds gave me a small clue that it could be a makeup playlist?"

"Yes."

"The question is…are we making up as friends or more?"

Noel's gaze dropped as she whispered, "I'd like to be more."

She heard the pad of his feet across the linoleum before his bare feet came into view in front of hers. He slid his hand under her chin and raised her gaze to him. His smile sweet. Brown eyes filled with tenderness.

"Me too."

Noel threw her arms around Nick, holding him tight. "I am so sorry. I was such a jerk."

"Yeah, but so was I. You were right. I should have said no."

"I don't want to change anything about you. Just maybe we agree to avoid Amber at all costs?"

"Deal." Nick kissed the side of her neck, cuddling her close. "You want to go back to bed and I'll bring your food into you?"

"Actually, I'm feeling quite a bit better. There was a chore I wanted to tackle this weekend, but since I have the day off anyway, I was thinking of heading over."

"What's the chore?"

"I got a bill for my parents' storage unit. I usually pay a year in advance, but I've been thinking...maybe it's time to face the past. Donate what I don't want. Find a place for the things I do. Maybe we'll find a couple things to hang on these walls and make my apartment look less like a serial killer's lair."

"Hey, you said it not me." Nick rubbed her back as if sensing how much strength it took to suggest doing this. "After breakfast, I'll take you over in my truck."

"Thanks."

Noel tried to mentally prepare herself for seeing all of her parents' things again. The last time she'd been in the storage unit was when she'd been sixteen and thought she may have packed away her favorite book by mistake.

Standing in front of the white roll-up door, she took a breath. Inside this cement building was everything from her life before her parents' death. She'd spent ten years refusing to talk about it, think about it. Avoiding anything that reminded her of them and what she'd lost. In the last few weeks, she'd let memories back in. Realized that by pushing her parents and past away, she hadn't been able to move forward with her life. It left her stunted and closed to all the possibilities life had for her, including love.

Still, standing here, realizing that she was going to find things that would bring the pain rushing to the surface terrified her. The eggs and bacon settled in the pit of her stomach like cement as she waited for Nick to open the locker.

"You ready?"

"Yes," she whispered.

Nick swung the door up and Noel gazed into the dimly lit unit, her heart breaking in her chest.

Heavy-duty black containers stacked to one side, full of photos, mementos, clothes. She took a step forward, swallowing hard as her hand ran over the dusty top of her grandmother's piano.

"I learned how to play all of my mother's favorite songs on this."

Nick's arms circled her waist from behind, unknowingly giving her strength. "I remember. My parents dragged us to every one of your recitals."

"I'm so sorry. I never realized how boring that must have been."

Nick shook his head, turning her in his arms. "Watching you perform never bored me, Noel. Music made you shine. It was the same with your parents." He placed his hand on the left side of her chest, over her heart. "No matter how hard you tried to forget, your parents never left you."

Noel sniffled, emotions already overtaking her. "I think this would look great in the living room. Don't you?"

"Absolutely. Piano goes then?"

"Yes, the piano goes."

"All right. I may need to call in some backup to help me do the heavy lifting." He kissed the bridge of her nose. "You are in no condition to lift a thousand-pound piano."

"You're not wrong." Noel pulled out the first black tote she could reach and lifted it to the ground with a grunt. It wasn't particularly heavy, but she had the strength of a newborn kitten today and the exertion had her huffin' and puffin' like the big bad wolf.

Noel popped the top off, mentally preparing herself. Inside were boxes of pictures, albums, and underneath, a large bridal box.

Noel snapped the lid into place and pushed the tote out of the unit. "This goes too."

Nick picked up the tote and tossed it in the back of his truck. "You doing okay?"

"Yeah, but fair warning," she choked, "I'm probably going to cry a lot today."

"That's all right, I get it. I can't imagine how painful this must be for you. Your parents were amazing people."

"Having you with me helps." She grabbed the next tote, finding stacks of men, women, and children's clothes. "This one will have to be gone through, but I think it can all be donated."

"Can I help with anything? I don't want to step on your toes."

"You're fine. Just help me pull these totes out and I'll look through. Any idea when your backup is gonna show up?"

"It will be an hour or so."

"Pike, Anthony, or both?"

"Both."

"Ah, great. They weren't too happy with me on Saturday night."

Nick pulled the lid off another tote. "They'll get over it. They adore you. This one looks like more clothes."

Noel walked over, lifting the garment and finding a jewelry box on the bottom. "This was my mom's. She had it since she was a little girl."

"So, keep?"

"Yeah, I'll go through it later." Noel watched him pull more totes and boxes from the back, clearing her throat, "I can't believe you aren't still mad at me."

"For?"

"Fighting with you? Blaming you for what happened with Amber."

Nick shook his head. "Being mad at you doesn't get me what I want."

"And what's that?"

"You."

Noel laughed. "A bad-tempered tomboy with a mean right hook? You're right, I totally see the appeal."

"I know you're mocking me and yourself, but..." Nick trailed off, crossing the unit to take her hand and pull her close. "If you look at it from my perspective, I get a fiercely loyal, protective, beautiful, funny woman who..." he waved his hand in a so-so motion, "doesn't have terrible taste in music."

"Whatever, you sent me Sixpence None the Richer."

"So? 'Kiss Me' is a classic."

"A classic, girly piece of crap."

Nick gasped, his hand covering his chest. "How dare you!"

Noel chuckled, extracting herself from his hold after a swift peck. "Come on, goob. We can't sit around here canoodling all day."

"Oh, see, I got you with the canoodling now. Rubbing off on you, I am."

The sound of a vehicle rumbled down the alley way and Anthony backed his truck up next to Nick's.

"Look at that, faster than you thought," Noel said.

"Must have taken a ho bath."

Noel made a face. "Gross. Now they are gonna stink."

"I don't know. A little hard to sweat in this frigid air."

Anthony and Pike climbed out, decked out in heavy coats, beanies, and gloves.

"Heard someone needed a hero," Pike said, holding his phone up. "Holding Out for a Hero" blared from the tiny speaker and Anthony and Pike danced their way over.

"Geez," Noel groaned. "Nerd alert."

"Hey now, no sass out of you, young lady. You're on probation."

"Oh yeah?"

"Yup. You can't make fun of our clothes and you got every round for the next month."

Noel pretended to think about it then snorted. "Nah. That doesn't work for me."

Pike held his arms out. "Fine, I'll settle for a hug."

That she could do. As she stepped into his hug, Nick grumbled, "I'm watching your hands, man."

"I'm behaving. Now, Noel, repeat after me."

"What?"

"Come on. It's part of your probation."

"Fine."

"I, Noel...do solemnly swear...that Pike is amazeballs."

She repeated it in a robotic voice and he gave her a squeeze. "I'll take it."

He let her go and she smiled up at Anthony. "How about you, Ant? You forgive me?"

"As long as you keep your distance with those germs, I'm good."

"Ah, man!" Pike cried. "I forgot she was infected."

Nick pointed the lid of one of the totes at him. "That's what you get for hugging on my girl."

Noel's stomach fluttered.

Pike grabbed another tote and when he opened it, he let out a battle cry. "Oh, oh, this one is all Nick." He pulled out a naked Barbie doll, making her dance. "Didn't you tell us once Nick loved playing Barbies?"

"I never played Barbies," Nick said.

"Oh, he so did. He liked to dress them up and braid their hair."

Anthony nodded. "I believe it."

"All of you, shut up."

"Oh Nick," Pike sang in a high-pitched voice. "Have I introduced you to my boyfriend?"

Pike held a naked Ken in one hand and Barbie in the other.

"Oh, I love you, Ken. Mwah mwah mwah." Pike made the dolls kiss.

Noel shook her head at the immaturity but was also relieved. Doing this was hard, but having them there? She didn't know what she'd do without them.

Pike, the comic relief. Anthony, the voice of reason. And Nick, the shoulder to lean on.

"Thanks for being here, guys. It means a lot."

They all stopped what they were doing and smiled.

"What?" she asked.

"Nothing. You're just so cute when you're sweet."

"Ha-ha. All right, get back to work. We're burning daylight."

CHAPTER 29

NICK

NICK STOOD ON NOEL'S COUCH in his bare feet, slipping the landscape onto the command hooks. "How does it look?"

He glanced over his shoulder at Pike and Anthony, both stuffing their faces with pizza at the kitchen table. Noel's apartment looked like his, chaotic and messy. Between the three of them they'd managed to put the furniture she'd wanted to keep where it belonged, but large black totes made a maze around her place.

Pike licked his thumb and pointed to the left. "Lopsided. Who taught you how to use a level?"

Nick hopped off the couch and eyeballed the painting. "The fuck you talking about. It's perfect."

"I was just messing with you. Looks good."

He shook his head, pretending to lunge at Pike as he passed.

"Oh, bring it on. I'll throw hands, boy, and believe me, you don't want none of this!"

"I'm going to check on Noel. Do not eat all the pizza."

"No promises," Anthony said with a mouthful.

NICK AND NOEL'S CHRISTMAS PLAYLIST **357**

Nick padded down the hall and knocked on her bedroom door.

"Come in."

He poked his head in to find her sitting in the middle of her bed with a giant white box in her hands. Scattered across her comforter were hundreds of photographs in separate piles.

Noel looked up at him, tears streaming down her cheeks and he sat on the edge of the bed.

"What's up?"

"It's just...a lot. Overwhelming."

He put his hand on her knee and squeezed. "I know, babe. You don't have to do this all right now. Why don't we order some photo boxes online and we can go through them a section at a time."

"Probably a good idea," she sniffled.

"What's that box?"

"My mother's wedding dress."

Nick stilled. "Oh."

"Yeah. It's really beautiful." Noel picked up a stack of photos and handed them to him. "And she looked beautiful in it."

Nick thumbed through Noel's parents' wedding pictures, the joy on their faces. The cake cutting. Nick laughed and held up a picture of her dad shoving cake into her mom's face.

"I would have called this before seeing it. Your dad was such a funny guy. Always playing ball with my dad and me when you came over."

"Yeah, they probably would have liked to have a boy."

"Why didn't they?"

"My mom got really sick with me and they didn't try again. I always envied you Merry and Holly."

"Take 'em, they're yours."

Noel laughed.

"I wanted four," Nick said softly.

"Four?"

"Four children."

Nick watched her face, waiting for her to freak out.

"You just want to one-up your parents or something," she said lightly.

"No, I wanted more than two, but with three, there is always the third wheel."

Noel nodded. "Okay."

"The thing is…" he cleared his throat, searching for the right thing to say. The words from his heart that would reassure her that he loved her. That even if she never wanted marriage or kids, she'd be enough for him. Noel was his other half.

"Yes?"

"I don't need to have kids to be happy. I don't even need a piece of paper." Nick took her hand. "You and me? That's all I need. The way I feel for you, Noel, is something I can't control and I don't want to live without you. You are it for me."

Nick didn't want overload the tenuousness of their reunion, but she surprised him when she squeezed his hand, tears in her eyes.

"Thank you for saying that. I really needed to hear it."

Nick brought her hand to his mouth. "I meant every word."

Moments slipped by as they sat there, holding hands, his thumb rubbing over her knuckles.

Finally, she broke the silence, surprising him. "If I had kids, I think I'd like at least two. If I hadn't had you, I would have been lonely. At least with two, they could play together, right?"

Nick stilled, studying her earnest expression. His voice came out hushed, afraid to hope. "Are you being serious? I know you said you never wanted kids or marriage and I respect that. I wasn't lying when I said you were enough for me."

"I know you weren't. I'm still unsure, but I'm opening up to the idea again."

"Again?"

"Before I lost my parents, I dreamed of marriage. I envisioned having a family and my parents being there for all of it. When I lost them, I couldn't face the same future because it meant accepting that they were gone. I know that sounds crazy. I know my parents are dead, but if I didn't make plans or sift through mementos that reminded me, then it didn't hurt so much."

"The way my parents died, so suddenly, I didn't get to say good-bye. And every day, that stays with me, like I forgot to do something. There's something missing and I can't fix it."

Nick picked up stack after stack of pictures, setting them back into the black tote. "They're always with you, Noel. Anything you want to say to them, you just do it."

"You really believe that?"

"I do."

Noel released a wet laugh. "I don't know what I believe."

"Then I'll tell you what I know." Nick slid up next to her on the bed, pushing her hair back from her face. "Your parents loved you, more than anything in this world. They had a fuller life with you in it and you get to carry on the memories of them. And if you do want kids, you get to tell them about their grandparents and how amazing they were. How much they loved you and each other. Carry on the traditions your parents taught you. That is what I know. Kids or no kids, I'm yours."

Noel cupped his cheek and kissed him, the big box poking him in the stomach but he didn't protest. He threaded his fingers into Noel's hair and brought her closer, the box sliding off her lap as they consumed each other, finding comfort in each other.

She broke the kiss and he stared down into her eyes, counting the tiny flecks of black.

"I love you, Nick."

His heart pounded in his chest. "As friends or we talking the big L?"

"Don't joke please. I...I mean it. I love you. I've probably loved you, big love, for years, but was too scared to admit—"

Nick kissed her again, pushing her back onto the bed so they fell over with him on top. He trailed his lips over her cheek, chin, neck. Finally, he held himself up on his elbows, watching as her eyes fluttered open.

"I love you, too. Big L. With six exclamation points."

Noel's eyes twinkled. "Wow. That's a lot."

"I know."

Noel leaned up to meet his kiss and it was the first time he'd felt completely at peace in his whole life. Noel, his opposite in nearly every way, centered him. Brought out the best in him.

Nick sat back, pulling his shirt up and tossing it aside. Noel's hands slid from his stomach to his chest, kneading the muscles of his shoulders and arms.

He lifted her shirt, kissing his way along her stomach until he found the bottom of her sports bra. He helped her sit up and pulled the shirt and bra over her head, exposing her gorgeous, full breasts.

"I love you."

"Are you talking to me or my boobs?" she teased, breathlessly.

"Them. I already told you, greedy."

Noel's giggle ended in a moan as Nick took her rosy nipple in his mouth, tonguing the sweet peak until it hardened. His other hand cupped and kneaded her other tit, and he heard her hum happily.

Nick's hands grabbed the top of her leggings and pulled them down her legs until all she had on were those absurd Golden Girl panties.

"Well hello, ladies. Missed me?"

Noel pushed them down around her ankles with a snort. Her hands went to the button on his jeans and she opened them with a snap. "I don't have the patience for your shenanigans."

Nick let her do what she wanted, groaning as her hands slid inside, gripping his cock as they kissed slowly. Every pump of her hand drove him crazy.

When he couldn't take anymore, he stood up, shimmying out of his pants and boxers, his gaze traveling over her as he realized that this was finally going to happen. The moment he'd been obsessing over, fantasizing about for nearly a month.

Nick lay down over her, slipping his hand between her legs.

Loving Noel, watching her facial expressions, listening to every small sound made everything that much better. She responded to him like she couldn't get enough, which worked because he felt the same way.

Her seam was slick and open, ready for him and he rolled her over him, letting her take control because he already knew making love to Noel would be spectacular for him. He wanted the same for her.

Noel raised herself up and fitted him against her wet entrance, slowly encasing him. Nick threw his head back, eyes closed, groaning as she took him inside, squeezing his cock.

When she moved over him, her eyes stayed on his face as her hips swayed, rolled, rocked.

Oh, god, fuck don't come yet. Not yet. Not yet.

Loud pounding on the door startled them both and Noel caught herself with her hands on his chest, her eyes wide.

"Hey, whatcha doing?" Pike called through the door.

"Oh my God," Noel moaned. "Not again."

Nick cursed. He couldn't believe he'd forgotten Pike and Anthony were still in the apartment.

Clearing his throat, he hollered, "Thanks for the help guys, but we're going to finish these boxes and go to bed."

"You sure you don't need an extra hand?" The doorknob wiggled playfully and Noel flattened herself over him, grabbing for the blanket.

"For fucks sake, get out of here now!"

"Geez, okay okay! Hey we're going to take some money from your wallet and hit the bar, in case you want to meet up after you're done with those...boxes."

NICK AND NOEL'S CHRISTMAS PLAYLIST **363**

Their chortling faded and Nick held onto Noel until the front door slammed shut.

"I am going to kill them."

Her voice came out muffled with her face buried in his neck. "Me too."

Nick buried his fingers through her hair, pulling her face up so he could study her. Her skin was molten, and he shook his head.

"Still love me?"

"Of course I do! I just wish we could finish one time without somebody interrupting!"

Nick rolled her beneath him, lifting her legs up around his hips. "Oh we're gonna finish this tonight. I don't care if the Hulk smashes through that door."

"Almost having those dumbasses walk in on us has kind of put me out of the mood."

Nick slid down the bed on his stomach until his head nestled between her thighs, her legs slung over his shoulders. "I guess I'll have to get you back in the mood then, huh?"

Noel smiled, challenge sparking in her eyes. "Do your worst."

Nick did, loving her with his mouth until she was pleading with him, God, he wasn't really sure, but when he finally pushed her over that ledge, she shuddered against him with complete abandon. Spent.

When he finally pushed into her, balancing his weight on his hands as he rode her body slowly, everything faded around them. All he saw was Noel, eyes half closed, lips parted. Soft breaths escaping as she clung to his arms. Beautiful. Perfect. Home.

Noel quickened under him and he kicked up his speed,

pumping his hips until she screamed his name, arching her back, her breasts pushed forward. Nearly there. Almost.

"Fuck!"

Nick shook as he let go, coming so hard he actually thought he might pass out. He lowered himself to his forearms, trembling as he kissed Noel, sliding his tongue inside to play with hers.

When he could finally move, he rolled to the side, bringing her against him. Arms holding her tight.

"That was..." he whispered.

"Amazeballs."

Nick kissed her temple, chuckling lightly. "Absolutely."

Noel snuggled into him, yawning. "How much you want to bet they ate all the pizza?"

"I wouldn't put it past them. Good thing your man was smart enough to order an extra pie and hide it."

"Mmmm, my man. I like that. Boyfriend. Hunk of sausage."

"Hey now, it's bigger than a sausage."

Noel giggled.

"Seriously, I liked it better when you compared me to a donkey."

She sat up, her tangled falling around them. "Compared you to a what?"

"Remember when all the pregnant women wanted to know what I was like in the sack and you said you'd told them I was hung like a donkey."

"Hmmmm..." she laid her head on his chest without saying anything else and he nudged her.

"Hey! Is that all you're going to say?"

"I already called you amazeballs."

"Gee, so generous with the compliments."

"Honestly, it's all a little hazy. You might have to do it again so I can give you a proper review."

Nick locked his arm around her while he tickled her ribs. "Review? You're gonna give me a play-by-play critique?"

Noel gasped with laughter as she begged, "Okay, okay, stop! Stop!"

Nick frowned ferociously. "Well?"

"Nick, it was so good, I want to do that three times a day every day and five times on Sunday."

Nick blinked down for half a second before his face split into a wide grin. "Challenge accepted."

Chapter 30

NOEL

THE SWELTERING AIR INSIDE BREWS and Chews smelled of floral and fruity perfumes from the dozens of women waiting impatiently for the show to begin. The scent of so many perfumes mixing together gave Noel a migraine, but she smiled brightly as Gabby came back from the bathroom, her white veil covered in neon bright condoms trailing behind her as she shimmied into her VIP chair at the front of the stage. Her nose was still held in place by the white splint, but at least the bruising was better.

"Who is ready to see some nearly naked men?" Amber hollered, setting a tray of brightly colored shots on the table.

Noel smirked, thinking that she already had a man at home she could strip naked whenever she wanted. She hadn't ever seen the appeal of a boyfriend before Nick, but over the last week, she understood Gabby better. Finding a man who got you on every level was a rare find and Noel couldn't help feeling blessed that she'd let go of some of her fears and let Nick love her. Really love her.

Gabby hollered, dancing in her seat. Her two cousins had

NICK AND NOEL'S CHRISTMAS PLAYLIST 367

come down with the stomach flu yesterday and even though they were feeling a little better, Gabby had told them to keep their asses home and away from her. That meant the rockin' bachelorette party consisted of the bride, Noel, and Amber. She'd done a pretty good job of ignoring Amber so far and if she could just get through the next...

Noel checked her phone for the time and found a new message from Nick.

> In case you get tempted by all the other slongs in your
> face, remember you have this cock at home.

Noel burst out laughing at the picture he'd attached. Noel bought him a rooster thong as a gag and shipped it to his house while she was at work. She'd come home that night to find him sprawled across her bed, wearing it. The red head with bright, colorful fabric plumage flopped to the side.

"What's funny?" Gabby asked, reaching for her phone.

"Ah, nothing, nothing!" Noel deleted the picture fast and put her phone away. "So, when is this shindig supposed to kick off?"

"Any minute. You eager for a lap dance, Noel?"

Noel caught Amber's sneer, and chose to take the high road. Amber's unhappiness was her own and Noel wouldn't let it ruin Gabby's party.

"I might. How about you, Amber?"

"As the only single girl in this threesome, absolutely."

"Awesome." Noel passed Gabby a glass of water. "I got you a water while you were in the toilet."

"Bring it on," Gabby hollered, taking a gulp of water.

"Gabby, I bought shots! Why aren't you drinking?"

Gabby took another drink of water, so Noel jumped in. "What if I took hers. I'm ready to get this party started."

Noel picked up two shots and held them up. "Cheers."

She downed one then the other while Amber cheered. "I think I misjudged you, Noel! You drink like a champ."

The lights dimmed and colorful strobe lights lit up the stage. "Ladies, please welcome to the stage Mistletoe's All Male Review."

The crowded bar erupted with screams as a line of shirtless men in Santa hats and pants danced out onto the stage to the tune of Santa Baby. Gabby and Amber jumped out of their seats, waving their hands excitedly, while Noel studied the dancers in horror.

Noel recognized every single one of them, her cheeks burning as they gyrated their hips. But when a bearded Santa slid across the stage almost directly in front of her, lifting his pelvis to the sky, she covered her mouth with both hands.

Pike humped the air three feet in front of her in a black leather thong and Santa hat. The minute he caught her gaze, he froze mid thrust.

Gabby danced up to the stage, waving a handful of ones. "Damn, Pike! I didn't know you were a stripper."

Noel closed her eyes in horror as Gabby started stuffing the ones into her friend's G-string like it was a slot machine.

When she opened her eyes again, Pike had moved to another group of women and she got a good look at his tight butt cheeks.

She was never going to be able to look him in the face again.

"Are you surprised?" Amber hollered over the music, a faster version of "Jingle Bell Rock."

Noel nodded. "Yes! Did you know?"

"Of course. Guy is one of the strippers. See him in back? He's the one who told me about it."

"You could have warned me!"

"I wanted to see the look on your face. Sorry."

Gabby grabbed her hand, pointing at a guy swaggering toward them. His dark curly hair fell to his ears and his light piercing eyes stayed on Gabby the whole time.

"Check him out."

He walked up to Gabby, grinning like a sinner. "I see we have a bachelorette in the house."

"Yes we do," Amber screamed.

"Then we need to celebrate." The guy lifted Gabby out of her chair and led her up onto the stage. Another man slid behind her, holding her hands above her head.

Amber leaned towards Noel, clapping. "I paid them a hundred bucks to do this."

"She looks like she's enjoying it."

Gabby squealed when the curly haired guy threw her legs over his shoulders and buried his face between her legs.

Noel covered her face with her hand, laughing into her palm, horrified and amused all at once.

"She's having fun, right?"

"She is. Thanks for setting this up. I know I wasn't completely on board at first, but she deserves to have an amazing time."

Amber looked at her, as if she couldn't figure her out. "Why are you being so nice to me?"

"Because I don't want to hate you anymore, Amber. Two of the people I love most in the world saw something good in you. I'm choosing to do the same."

"But…a week ago, I was trying to get Nick back."

Noel's lips thinned momentarily and then she breathed out. "I know. I don't like what you did, but I'm hoping that now we can all move on." Noel laughed as a blond stripper brought a chair onto the stage and Curly sat Gabby in it, rubbing his balls in her face.

"Are you going to tell Gabby what I did?"

Noel shook her head. "I'm not going to ruin your relationship with Gabby. What happened is between you and me. Besides, she's got enough going on without getting pulled into our drama."

"So, what? We pretend to like each other?"

"No, I don't think we'll ever be friends. But maybe we don't have to be enemies."

The strippers led a very mushed, happy Gabby down the stairs to her seat. Curly kissed her knuckles.

"Have a wonderful wedding, beautiful!"

Gabby fanned herself. "God, I wish Drew were home. I would wreck him right now."

Noel, feeling the shots she'd shotgunned, laughed. "You gonna be okay, sweetie?"

"Yes, except all the extra blood is rushing to my hoonany and making me horny!"

"Extra blood?" Amber asked.

Gabby cleared her throat and turned in her seat to face Amber. "I'm pregnant."

"What?" Amber screamed, grabbing Gabby's hands.

"I wanted to tell you sooner, but I didn't want to ruin the night."

"Are you kidding? Nothing could ruin this night." She hugged Gabby, catching Noel's eye.

"You knew, huh?"

"She only told me earlier because I caught her puking."

Amber smiled softly and pulled away from Gabby. "Guess we didn't need those mimosas."

"Sure we do," Noel said. "She can have the orange juice and we'll drink the champagne."

Gabby's gaze shifted between them and held her hands up. "I know I asked you two to get along, but this is too creepy."

Noel patted her leg. "I'm going to use the bathroom and I'll get the next round for Amber and me."

"Oh, will you get more ones? There's a cute Santa over there who needs a tip."

Noel rolled her eyes. As much as she hated to admit it, she wasn't having a terrible time. It wouldn't be her choice for a bachelorette party, but tonight was about Gabby, who happened to be having a ball.

For her own last girls' night, she'd love to do something she'd never tried before like roller derby.

Noel almost stumbled, realizing that she'd thought about a bachelorette party for herself without panicking.

It was progress.

A hand touched Noel's arm just before she reached the bathroom and she turned. Pike stood next to her, still in a next to nothing thong. Santa hat askew.

"Anthony said you would be here, but I didn't believe him," he said.

"Why not?"

"I didn't think this was your scene."

"It's not. I came for Gabby." Noel cleared her throat, unsure what to say. "I didn't know you were a stripper. Why didn't you tell me?"

"I figured Nick would. He knew."

"He did?" Noel shook her head. Of course they did. They were probably having themselves quite a laugh at the surprise they'd given her. "I can't believe neither of those bastards warned me."

"I'm sorry. We good?"

Because there was nothing else to do, she laughed. "Of course we are. I was just shocked. But...why?"

"Honestly? It's a rush. Plus, the money isn't bad."

Noel squeezed his arm. "As long as you're happy, then so am I."

"Thanks."

"I really need to use the restroom, but we'll talk later, all right?" Noel turned to walk away but his voice stopped her.

"Noel?"

She stopped outside the bathroom door. "Yeah?"

"I'm glad things worked out for you and Nick. You deserve the best."

Noel blinked back tears at the sincerity in his voice and the tenderness in his expression and it hit her. Pike's flirting. His teasing. His defense of her honor. He'd liked her for real. She'd rebuffed him with little consideration because she'd thought he was only playing.

Just another mistake to add to the list.

"Fish…"

He held up his hand. "I know. We're buds. I love you, but I accepted a long time ago that's all we were ever going to be. No need to feel bad. I'll get over it."

Noel took a step toward him. "I would hug you right now, but you're nearly naked and it would be weird."

"I'll collect one later. Gotta go. Those laps won't dance themselves." Pike walked back towards the stage and she spun around, away from his naked rear end. This had to be the craziest, awkwardest night of her life.

Noel came back with six shots and set them on their little table. Gabby danced in her seat excitedly. "Guess what?"

"What?"

"Amber bought us all lap dances!"

Noel shot Amber a disgruntled look. "You didn't have to do that."

Gabby actually jumped in. "I insisted. I know you and Nick are official, but Drew and I made a pact that we were going to enjoy our parties with a strict no-jealousy rule. So if you need to text Nick to see how he feels, I totally get it."

Noel shook her head. "Nick told me to have a good time, but I don't know if I want some guy's crotch in my face."

To her surprise, Amber was the one to throw her a lifeline.

"I tell you what. If you really don't want one, I'll take yours."

"Screw that," Gabby shouted over the music. "If anyone's getting an extra lap dance it should be me! I'm the bride-to-be!"

Noel arched her eyebrows at Amber. "You'd never guess she wasn't drunk, would you?"

"I guess this is last-night-of-freedom buzz."

Noel caught Pike's eye on stage and he winked at her as a group of women in their forties threw money at him.

She pulled out her phone and snapped a picture. When she forwarded it to Anthony and Nick, she captioned it, Y'all have some explaining to do.

Both sent back laughing emojis and Noel shook her head.

Despite Nick and her being official, nothing had really changed with her friends. Another fear put to rest.

Her phone vibrated again and she opened the message from Nick.

Have fun. I love you.

A month ago, she'd never imagined she'd be in a darkened bar, getting along with Amber and watching Pike gyrate around in a Santa hat. Even more surprising was being able to type back four little words without any hesitation or sweaty palms.

I love you, too.

CHAPTER 31

NICK

"NOEL! HAVE YOU SEEN MY tie?"

Noel stuck her head out of the bathroom, her toothbrush hanging out of the corner of her mouth. "I hung it over the back of the chair in the kitchen."

"Which one?"

"The only one that has a tie on it, goob!"

Nick threw his pillow at her and she closed the door before it connected, her laugher muffled.

In the eleven days since they'd exchanged I love yous, Noel hadn't balked at their relationship once. She'd come home the day after Gabby's bachelorette party seeming lighter, freer. When he'd asked how Amber was, Noel just said they'd had fun.

Which is exactly how Nick felt about his time with her. They teased. Wrestled. Kissed. Cuddled. And loved. Boy, how they loved.

Today was the Christmas concert and Wednesday, Gabby's wedding. If Noel was nervous about either, she hadn't let on. He hoped that he held it together tonight, as he wasn't completely over his stage fright.

Nick found his tie on the floor, underneath the chair he always sat in for work. He stared down at it as he tried to tie it without a mirror, looking up when he heard Noel clear her throat.

She stood at the end of the hallway in a red, shimmering dress. The off-the-shoulder and sweetheart neckline showed just a hint of cleavage. The dress nipped in at the waist and flared out to just above her knees, highlighting her long, smooth legs. Simple black flats adorned her feet and they were in contrast with the fancy, familiar feel of the dress.

She'd pinned her dark hair back from her face, and it fell in dark curls over her shoulders.

"Well?"

Nick crossed the hallway to her, cupping her cheek in his palm. "You look amazing."

"Thank you. It's the dress my mother wore to the concert every year. Is that weird?"

"Considering this concert is about honoring her and your dad, no. I think it's fitting."

Noel took the tongues of his tie, lowering her gaze, but not before he caught the shimmer of tears. "I'm so nervous, I feel like I may be sick."

"Nope, as my sisters will remind you, nausea related to performing is my forte. You stop trying to steal my stuff."

Noel finished his tie and used it to pull him down for a kiss. "So no more borrowing your T-shirts, then?"

"There are some exceptions. Especially when you look so good in them and nothing else on."

Noel moved away from his wandering hands. "Uh-uh. I need to go apply some lipstick and then we need to go. If we're late because we wind up back in bed, your mother will murder us both."

Nick waggled his brow. "I think it may be worth it."

"Not today, Satan!" She backed into the bedroom and he chuckled, heading to the front door to shrug into his suit jacket.

When she came out in her black dress coat and black clutch, he couldn't believe they were here and she was here.

"You're sure you don't want to test my mother's wrath and go back into the bedroom."

"I promise you all kinds of hot, sexy times tonight, but right now, it's about my parents. I will not be late to an event in their honor."

Nick took her hand, leading her out the door and down the stairs to the truck. He'd used the remote start to defrost and warm up the cab, so when she climbed inside, it was toasty warm.

"Hurry up, Nick."

"I'm hurrying!" He shut the door on her and jogged around, keeping his promise as he got them to the community center a half an hour before they were scheduled to go on stage. They took the steps two at a time, pushing through the doors and almost whacking his mother in the face.

"Oh, good! You're here." Victoria's eyes widened as she looked Noel over from head to toe. "Oh honey, is that your mother's dress?"

"Yes. I found it in a garment bag below a bunch of Christmas decorations."

"Well, you look just as lovely in it as she did. What a perfect way to honor her."

"Thank you."

Victoria waved them all the way in. "Go ahead backstage and get set up. I'll find you afterward. I hope you like the memorial."

"I'm sure I will," Noel murmured.

"Come on, Noel. We've got twenty minutes."

Victoria hugged Noel one last time, before letting Nick lead her away to the stage area. Sonia, the event manager, waited with their mics. She put Noel's on first, making sure it sounded clear.

"You're good to go."

Noel formed her hands into a heart and blew him a kiss. "I'm going to go find your sisters really quick and get their approval. Be back in a bit."

"What do you need them for? I already told you how beautiful you are."

"Yes, but you're biased."

Nick shook his head, grinning at Sonia. "You saw her. Am I wrong?"

"No, you are absolutely right. She is breathtaking. Reminds me of her mother." She taped his mic onto his cheek and secured the belt around his waist.

"Sing something for me?"

Nick sang a few bars of "Must Be Santa" and Sonia gave him a thumbs up.

"Break a leg."

"I'll do my best." Nick tried to shake the butterflies in his stomach as he peeked between the curtains into the packed community center. Nearly the whole damn town was there. He knew it would be a packed good turnout, but the reality of it still jarred him a bit.

"Hey, you okay?" Noel asked, coming up beside him.

"Yeah, just picturing the audience in their underwear."

Noel laughed, looping her arms around his neck. "You're gonna be great."

"We're going to be great."

"But I do have a request. It you are going to puke, aim for your sisters. Not me."

Nick chuckled. "Done."

"I love you."

He kissed her hard. "I love you, too."

"Dammit, now I have to reapply my lipstick. Curtain up in five. Don't forget to turn your mic on."

She disappeared back into the dressing room and Nick flipped the switch on his mic. He squatted down to check his amp and guitar, making sure it was plugged in correctly.

"Nick," Amber called off stage.

He groaned. Why couldn't she just leave him alone?

When he didn't go over she walked onto the stage. "Nick, I need to talk to you."

"Amber, I don't have time for any of this."

"I screwed up. Please hear me out. I know I've been terrible and thoughtless, but I really want to change for the better." She took a deep breath, a slight tremble in it that made him pause.

"I should have never tried to get between you and Noel. It was wrong and I'm sorry."

Nick stood up, still leery of her motives. "I appreciate the apology."

"You were right when you said I was scared to be on my own. You are a good guy and you deserve to be happy. I am sorry I couldn't do that, but I am hoping that by taking some time to get to know myself, maybe I'll grow and become a woman that a guy like you could love."

Nick cleared his throat and smiled. "I wish you nothing but happiness."

"Noel, she's...well, I may have misjudged her. Or I just let my jealousy get the best of me. Regardless, I hope she makes you happy."

"She does. She's my love, my family. My person."

"What about...marriage and kids?"

"Amber..." he warned.

"I'm not being an asshole. I am just curious, because with us, you never stopped talking about those things."

"Because I never considered you'd want anything different until you did. With Noel, we've talked. We've discussed our wants, our fears, and our needs. We are on the same page. Maybe we'll get married, but if not, I'm okay with that. God willing, we'll have kids too, but even if we don't, all I need is her. Whatever our future may hold, it's between the two of us and while I appreciate your apology, this is the last time I discuss the woman I love or my relationship, with you."

Amber nodded.

A mix of thunderous applause and cheers exploded from

the audience beyond the curtain. Nick looked around to find his parents, his sisters, and Noel watching them from the other side of the stage. Merry pointed to her mic and clapped.

And it hit him. Everyone in the place had heard this exchange.

Noel, Merry, and Holly walked onto the stage, taking their places as the curtains opened. Nick stared out on the sea of faces, continuing to cheer. Amber stepped off the stage and walked out into the audience, taking an empty seat next to Gabby and Drew.

Noel stepped into the spotlight on center stage and waved. "Welcome to the Mistletoe Christmas Concert! Thank you all for being here, celebrating this wonderful occasion. If you don't mind giving me one second while I kiss my boyfriend. You guys okay with that?"

The town went wild as Noel strutted across the stage and kissed him, his guitar pinned between them.

When she pulled back, Nick was too dazed to say anything until she covered his mic.

"Thank you."

"For what?"

"Loving me."

Nick pressed his forehead to hers. "Forever."

There was no panic in Noel's rich brown eyes, nor tension in her face. Only joy.

"You ready to do this?"

Nick took her hand and squeezed it. "I'm ready when you are."

NOEL

Noel's heart hammered as she returned to center stage, Nick's declaration ringing in her head. As she stared out into a sea of faces, she focused on the people she loved and took a breath. "The Carter Family started the Christmas Concert five generations ago. Traditions were passed down over the years, like the Carter Lemon Shortbread cookie and the concert set list. Things we looked forward to every holiday season."

She took a breath, trying to find the words she'd been practicing all week for this moment.

"When my parents passed away ten years ago on their way to this very concert, the town of Mistletoe grieved their loss. The loss of their talent. Their kindness. And most of all, their love of Christmas."

The crowd clapped, showing their love and support, and Noel's eyes stung with tears.

"For the longest time, I couldn't bring myself to attend this event so beloved by them and the people of this town. I blamed them for wanting so badly to be here with all of you and with me, and I couldn't move past it.

"This year I've learned a little something about perspective. How some events can be viewed differently all due to the circumstances the observer may be in. It took me ten years to put myself in my parents' shoes and realize that I'd failed to honor them when I abandoned the things they loved, like the Mistletoe Christmas Concert.

"Tonight is dedicated to not just my parents, but to all the loved ones we've said goodbye to over the years. May they join us tonight in spirit and in our hearts."

Noel turned her head, wiping at her wet eyes, and nodded at Merry. She caught Nick smiling at her, his face alight with pride and he mouthed *I love you.*

Merry counted them in.

The beat to "All I Want for Christmas Is You" burst through the speakers and Noel sang her heart out. For two full hours, they kept Mistletoe swinging.

When the curtain finally closed Nick shut his mic off and met Noel in the center of the stage.

She slipped her arms around his waist. "Look at that. We cured your stage fright."

"Yeah, nothing like the whole town hearing you bare your soul to get rid of the performance jitters."

"I was thinking, you and me, Gabby's wedding next week? Wanna be my plus one?"

"Sounds good. Maybe we can sneak out early to celebrate the birthday girl?"

"Hmmm, sounds perfect. Like my birthday and Christmas rolled into one."

"Funny. Being with you makes me feel like that every day."

"Goob."

They stepped down the stairs of the stage, and Noel lost track of Nick as people surrounded her, sharing stories about her parents. Victoria finally pushed her way to the front and led her over to the corner, where a green Christmas tree sparkled with white blinking lights.

On every branch hung a picture frame ornament. Inside were photos of her parents at the concert over the years. There were even some photos of when they were children, but the one that really struck a chord with Noel was the picture eye level on the front of the tree. It was the concert the year before her parents died. They stood in front of a tree much like this one, their arms wrapped around Noel's shoulders.

"Do you like it?" Victoria whispered.

"I love it. Thank you."

"You're welcome, baby."

"Hey, Noel?" She turned around to find Henry Garret standing with his Nikon camera. "I'd like to get a picture of you with the tree, if that's okay?"

Noel wiped at her wet cheeks and smiled. "Yeah sure, but can I have my family with me?"

Henry appeared confused. "Well, sure."

"Oh, good. Victoria? Do you see Chris and Nick?"

Victoria's face brightened and she hollered, "All Winters, report to the Christmas tree!"

Noel spotted Gabby and Drew and waved them over.

Nick was the last to join them, flanked by Pike and Anthony.

Noel stood in the middle with Chris, Victoria, Merry, and Holly on her left. Gabby and Drew on her right.

Nick squeezed in next to her and Noel pointed to her right. "You two! Get in here. I need you!"

Henry shook his head. "I'll have to rearrange you to get you all in."

"That's fine, as long as we get everyone."

Henry moved Pike, Anthony, and Nick's sisters to where they were kneeling in the front and by the time they were done, there was a lot of griping about hard wood.

Noel studied the pictures over Henry's shoulder and pointed. "Can I get that one on an eleven-by-fourteen canvas?"

"Sure, but I'll have to charge you for it."

Noel smiled, watching the people she loved most talking and laughing.

"Doesn't matter. Whatever it costs, it will be worth it."

Epilogue

NICK

NICK STOOD BY THE BAR, sipping Crown and Coke as he watched Gabby and Drew share their first dance as man and wife. Blake Shelton's "A Guy with a Girl" played through the speakers, a faster tempo than most couples would have chosen, but Drew was surprisingly nimble as he twirled Gabby in a two-step across the dance floor. He smiled at the end as Drew dipped Gabby back, delivering a long, slow kiss before standing her upright.

Another ballad began and someone tapped Nick on the shoulder.

"Wanna dance with me, hot stuff?" Noel asked, coming around to stand in front of him, her hand held out expectantly.

"Shouldn't you be doing maid of honor duties?"

Noel scoffed. "I have delivered the bride to the church, held the groom's ring, held her bouquet, kept her dress up every time she's had to pee, made sure she ate and is drinking plenty of water, and I gave a very sappy speech that moved everyone in the audience to tears. I'd say I am due for a break."

"If you insist." Nick took her hand and when they stepped out amid the other couples, she slipped his arms around her waist. "Have I told you how beautiful you are?"

"Hmmm, earlier when you saw me for the ceremony. You pulled me into that closet and kissed me."

Nick grinned, pressing his lips next to her ear. "I seem to remember I did more than kiss you."

"Yes, but I do not want to remember how the pastor officiating my friend's wedding found me in a closet with my boyfriend's hand up my skirt."

He chuckled, kissing the side of her neck. "Honestly, I thought it was rude of him to just barge in without knocking."

Noel rolled her eyes. "Or maybe next time you want to have a little tryst, we find a room with a lock on the door."

"Where's the fun in that?"

"I thought you were supposed to be a good boy?"

"I am, most of the time. For some reason, being with you brings out my naughty side."

"Well, I guess we'll have some fun stories to tell the kids one day."

Nick stilled their movements, staring into her eyes earnestly. "What did you say?"

"Which part?"

"I heard the word children."

"I told you. I'm warming up to the idea."

"Oh yeah?"

"Yep." Noel looped her arms around his neck and grinned. "Maybe in a couple years we can revisit the subject?"

"I'd like that," Nick said, afraid to ask too many questions and freak her out. "So, how many more duties do you have before we can get out of here?"

"What's the rush?"

"I have a surprise for the birthday girl."

"Really? What is it?"

"I'm sorry, do you not know what a surprise is?" he asked.

"I was just asking! See if I give you sweetness later."

"Oh, I'm getting all your sweetness. Just you wait!"

"Mmmm, so confident."

"I like my odds."

"Well, I have to stick around at least through the bouquet toss and cake cutting, so, an hour, maybe? Think you can handle it?"

Nick gave her sweet, fleeting kiss. "I guess I'll have to."

"Good." Noel snuggled into Nick and sighed. "To be honest, I can't wait until we can go home. Gabby threw up on my tennis shoes this morning and I haven't had a chance to wash them yet."

"Why did Gabby throw up? Nerves?"

"No, she's pregnant. They haven't officially announced it yet, so not a word."

"I won't, but that's awesome. They must be excited."

"They are, very much."

"Is that the sudden interest in kids? Because of Gabby?"

"In a way, Gabby has been a big help with me coming to terms with my insecurities and fears. She helped me talk out a lot of them, but no. It's not just because Gabby is pregnant that I started thinking about kids. It's the pictures on the Christmas tree the night of the concert. My dad and mom as kids, learning music from their parents, and me learning about music from mine. My parents had dreams for me. I had dreams for me before I lost them. I've been so consumed with them not being here, I forgot that I'd wanted to get married and have kids one day. After they passed, I told myself I didn't want those things because they wouldn't be there to celebrate with me, but that isn't fair to them, me, and most importantly, it isn't fair to the man I love."

Nick kissed her forehead, wanting to shout with joy to the rooftops.

"Just so you know, I have no plans to pressure you about marriage or kids. We'll take our time and when you feel that you're ready for one, the other, or both, I'll be on board."

"Thank you."

"Hey, Noel," Amber said, coming up alongside them. "Sorry, but they're getting ready to do the bouquet toss."

"Thanks, I'll be right there."

"Sure. Hey, Nick."

"Hi." When Amber walked away, Nick shook his head. "I feel like she's becoming a completely different person."

"She's trying. It's all any of us can do. Just try to be better every day." Noel gave him a firm, hot kiss. "I'll see you in a little bit."

Nick's phone vibrated in his pocket and he moved out into the hallway to take it.

"Yeah?"

"Everything is set up and ready for your arrival," Anthony said.

"Great, thanks for doing that. I know it probably isn't how you wanted to spend Christmas Eve."

"Nah, it's cool. Good luck, man. Hope she likes it."

"Merry Christmas," Pike yelled in the background.

"Merry Christmas to you both."

The next hour seemed to go by in slow motion, except for the moment during the bouquet toss, when he watched Noel jump into the air and snag the round mix of red and white roses, her face split into a proud smile.

Noel finally came along the edge of the dance floor and took his hand. "I'm free."

Nick held out his arm and she slipped a hand through his, leading her out to the parking lot and his truck.

Once they were inside his cab, letting the heater blow full blast in their faces, Nick handed her a black velvet jewelry box.

"Happy birthday."

She took it slowly and he knew she was probably worried it was a ring. When she popped the lid and found a key, she held it up, puzzled.

"What's it for?"

"My apartment. The key is so you can just let yourself in whenever you want. It is also an open-ended invitation for you to move in with me. No pressure."

Nick put the truck into drive without gauging her reaction, afraid he'd miscalculated the situation. When they got back to the apartment building, she didn't even turn toward her place but followed him right inside his.

Noel gasped as Nick flipped on the light switch and the place lit up with twinkly lights. The ceiling, around the windows, and strung along the limbs of his Christmas tree.

Underneath the tree was a pet carrier, but Noel was too busy looking at the lights to notice.

"When did you do this?"

"Anthony and Pike did it while we were at the wedding." Nick nudged her with his arm. "Why don't you go see if there's something under the tree."

Noel spotted the carrier and smothered a cry with her hand. "No!"

At first, he thought she meant she didn't want it, but then she practically tripped over her dress in her hurry to get to the tree. She opened the top and Nick flipped on the ceiling light, as she pulled a tiny black-and-white kitten out of the box.

"Oh my God. How did you know I wanted a cat?"

"You talked about it before our first date, when you stripped down during my video chat with my boss."

"I didn't think you were paying attention."

"As distracting as you were, I make it an effort to listen to the things that make you happy. But, if you aren't sure you really want one, I could keep it here and it could be my cat."

Noel snuggled the kitten into her chest, stroking its head. "Are you seriously talking about keeping my birthday present?"

"No, he's yours."

Noel climbed to her feet and kissed him while the kitten purred against her chest.

"Thank you."

"I have one last surprise."

"I don't know how you're going to top this."

"Come into the kitchen with me."

Nick got there first and picked up the plate with tiered lucky treats, complete with twenty-seven candles ready to be lit.

"Happy birthday, Noel."

"Wow, this...thank you. I feel totally spoiled."

Nick set the plate down and pulled her against him, being sure not to squish the kitten. "I love you."

"I love you, too."

"What are you going to name your pet?"

"Lucky. It's the best word I can come up with to describe how I'm feeling."

"I think it's a great name."

"One more thing...about the key."

"Hey, like I told you, no pressure."

"Will you hush and let me finish?"

Nick zipped his lips.

"I have to give thirty days notice before I can move out of my apartment. Do you think you could get some backup to help move my stuff at the end of January?"

Nick dropped his forehead to her and took a deep, shaky breath.

"I think I can swing that."

"Then we're all yours."

Nick and Noel's
Happily Ever After Playlist

1. Joe Diffy—Bigger Than the Beatles
2. Nelly—Hot in Herre
3. Bing Crosby—White Christmas
4. Bing Crosby—I'll Be Home for Christmas
5. Confederate Railroad—Trashy Women
6. Zac Brown Band—Colder Weather
7. Britney Spears—My Only Wish
8. Lizzo—Truth Hurts
9. Puddle of Mudd—She Hates Me
10. Wham!—Last Christmas
11. Mindy McCready—Maybe He'll Notice Her Now
12. Toby Keith—You Shouldn't Kiss Me Like This
13. Eagles—Witchy Woman
14. Walker Hayes—You Broke Up With Me
15. Gwen Stefani—Hollaback Girl
16. Imagine Dragons—Thunder
17. NSYNC—Under My Tree
18. Aretha Franklin—Oh Christmas Tree
19. George Strait—Christmas Cookies
20. Taylor Swift—The Best Day
21. Bing Crosby and Johnny Mathis—Silent Night
22. The Lion King—I Just Can't Wait to Be King
23. Ingrid Andress—More Hearts Than Mine
24. Michael Bublé—Holly Jolly Christmas

25. John Legend—Baby, It's Cold Outside

26. Carolyn Dawn Johnson—Complicated

27. Jason Mraz ft. Colbie Caillat—Lucky

28. Weezer—My Best Friend

29. AC/DC—You Shook Me All Night Long

30. Kiss—Rock and Roll All Nite

31. Daniel Powter—Bad Day

32. Queen—We Will Rock You

33. Justin Timberlake—Cry Me A River

34. Miranda Lambert—Crazy Ex-Girlfriend

35. Monica ft. Twista—Hell No (Leave Home)

36. Selena Gomez—Hands to Myself

37. Fabolous ft. Tamia—So Into You

38. Jordan Davis—Singles You Up

39. Lifehouse—Hanging by a Moment

40. New Kids on the Block—Hangin' Tough

41. Twisted Sister—We're Not Gonna Take It

42. Brooke Valentine—Girlfight

43. Rae Sremmurd—Come Get Her

44. Zac Efron and Zendaya—Rewrite the Stars

45. Sixpence None the Richer—Kiss Me

46. Bob Dylan—Must Be Santa

47. Bonnie Tyler—Holding Out for a Hero

48. Levi Hummon—Wedding Dress

49. Blake Shelton—A Guy with a Girl

50. Anne Murray—Could I Have This Dance

51. Sam Smith—Have Yourself a Merry Little Christmas

ACKNOWLEDGMENTS

So many amazing people went into making the Mistletoe series a reality. Thank you to my lovely editor, Deb, for falling in love with Nick and Noel. Big hugs to Stefani in Marketing! You rock! To Jessica and Jean for scrubbing this baby up once again! And to the rest of the team at Sourcebooks for this opportunity. This book would not have been possible without the fantastic team at Audible, most importantly my amazing editor, Allison! Thank you for helping me bring Nick and Noel and the town of Mistletoe to life!

My agent, Sarah, who asked me if I had any holiday romance ideas. You have been there through my ups and downs, believing in me and the stories I want to tell. Thank you.

To my loving family, Brian, Hunter, and Rylie, who deal with my overly caffeinated self during deadlines and still love me. You are my heart and soul.

My parents and in-laws, who took my kids for two weeks so I could finish my edits. My reader and writer friends, who shared and supported this new and exciting venture. And to the lovely ladies in a very special Facebook group, who made me laugh and lightened my heart during these troubled times. Thank you very much.

ABOUT THE AUTHOR

Codi Hall loves writing small-town romances with big feels. As a Northern California native living in Idaho, she fell in love with the big sky, amazing people, and brisk winters. She enjoys movie marathons with her family, snuggling with her furbabies, creating funny TikToks to share with the world, and snuggling under a blanket with a good book! She also writes contemporary and paranormal romance under the pen name Codi Gary. Readers can get in touch via her website authorcodihall.com.

MOOSE SPRINGS, ALASKA

Welcome to Moose Springs, Alaska, a small town with a big heart, and the only world-class resort where black bears hang out to look at *you*.

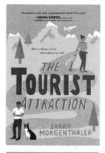

The Tourist Attraction

There's a line carved into the dirt between the tiny town of Moose Springs, Alaska, and the luxury resort up the mountain. Until tourist Zoey Caldwell came to town, Graham Barnett knew better than to cross it. But when Graham and Zoey's worlds collide, not even the neighborhood moose can hold them back...

Mistletoe and Mr. Right

She's Rick Harding's dream girl. Unfortunately, socialite Lana Montgomery has angered locals with her good intentions. When a rare (and spiteful) white moose starts destroying the holiday decorations every night, Lana, Rick, and all of Moose Springs must work together to save Christmas, the town...and each other.

Enjoy the View

Hollywood starlet River Lane is struggling to remake herself as a documentary filmmaker. When mountaineer and staunch Moose Springs local Easton Lockett takes River and her film crew into the wild...what could possibly go wrong?

"A unique voice and a grumptastic hero! I'm sold."

—Sarina Bowen, *USA Today* bestselling author

For more info about Sourcebooks's books and authors, visit:

sourcebooks.com

LOVE, CHAI, AND OTHER FOUR-LETTER WORDS

Kiran needs to fall in line. Instead, she falls in love.

Kiran Mathur was the good daughter. When her sister's defiant marriage to the wrong man brought her family shame, Kiran was there to pick up the pieces. Nash Hawthorne had parents who let him down, so he turns away from love and family. After all, abandonment is in his genes, isn't it?

If she follows the rules, Kiran will marry an Indian man. If he follows his fears, Nash will wind up alone. But what if they follow their hearts?

"A sweet story of finding love where you least expected."
—Sonali Dev, author of *Recipe for Persuasion*

For more info about Sourcebooks's books and authors, visit:
sourcebooks.com